The Return of Lady Brace

Also by Nancy Wilson Ross

Take the Lightning
Farthest Reach
The Left Hand Is the Dreamer
Westward the Women
I, My Ancestor
Time's Corner
Joan of Arc (for children)

The
Return
of
Lady Brace

by Nancy Wilson Ross

Random House   New York

Library of Congress Catalog Card Number: 57–10029

PRINTED IN THE UNITED STATES OF AMERICA BY
KINGSPORT PRESS, INC., KINGSPORT, TENNESSEE

THE RETURN OF LADY BRACE

by Nancy Wilson Ross

REPORT BY JOHN MASON BROWN

Reprinted from the Book-of-the-Month Club News

ALTHOUGH many people have books published, and hence are technically authors, not all of them are writers. Nancy Wilson Ross is a true writer. She can bend the language to her will. Her gifts do not stop with the dexterity and felicity of her style. *The Return of Lady Brace* is a novel which reveals again, as did *The Left Hand Is the Dreamer,* how discerning is Miss Ross's observation of people, how admirable her ability to summon a scene, and how searching and compassionate her mind.

WHEN we speak of wise men, we do not as a rule have novelists in mind. This is sheer ingratitude, because there are novelists who are wise in addition to being skillful. They are historians of the heart who are wise in the ways of daily life. They are men and women who can see through doors closed to most of us, because of their uncommon insights into character, behavior and motive. Miss Ross belongs to this happy breed. *The Return of Lady Brace* makes this clear on one perceptive and delightful page after another.

CHANGE incessant and bewildering, change jet-propelled and on a Gargantuan scale never before known, is the dominant condition of the world in which we find ourselves. And change, in terms of the adjustments it demands in one family, is Miss Ross's concern in *The Return of Lady Brace*. Her central character is an American woman who, after the death of her English second husband, returns to this country and, while here, learns at first hand what has happened to her brother, her two sharply contrasted daughters and their families, and America itself. Lady Brace is a figure from the near past who finds herself in a new world in the great Long Island home that was once hers. Brought up in an environment of elegance, with manners and assumptions no longer valid, she is the more disconcerted because the setting she revisits, though familiar, contradicts her memories and is alien to her standards.

WHERE she was reared on a large estate in a house filled with servants, she comes back to a place victimized by a different economy and staffed by a young couple treated as members of the family. Her grandchildren instead of being taught courtesy are free to follow their impulses. Even her daughters are comparative strangers, leading in her opinion disordered lives. One of them, the divorced and unhappy Lydia, shocks Lady Brace by admitting that she is prepared to go to the Orient as the mistress of a rich married man who is Lady Brace's contemporary.

MISS ROSS enriches her survey of this changed America by approaching it from four angles. The first is the new American society, which "Lady B." appraises in terms of the society she knew. Another is the acquired English attitude that she brings to her judgment. The third is today's younger America, more frenetic, less genteel but still privileged, that has rejected an earlier code. Finally, there is this tangled household seen through the eyes of a serene Oriental priest who has been brought to this country as the guest of Lady Brace's unorthodox brother.

SURELY, there is no need to apologize because Miss Ross is writing about a very special world. All that matters is that she brings no less special gifts to her account of it. Hers is an exceptionally able book, warm in its compassion, brave in its search and beautifully civilized in its subtleties. As a study in manners, *The Return of Lady Brace* is an American counterpart, though in no way an imitation, of Enid Bagnold's *The Chalk Garden*.

Some readers may balk, as I did, at Venerable Sir, her novel's all-knowing priest from Ceylon, and be dissatisfied with his attempts at final answers to eternal questions. Nonetheless, it is hard to see how anyone can fail to admire Miss Ross's telling of her story, the use to which she puts her flashbacks, or her drawing of such characters as Lady Brace's brother (a brilliant portrait of an irresistible eccentric), her two dissimilar daughters and their households, and, above all, Lady Brace. Lady Brace may come to see herself as a failure, but Miss Ross's revelation of her is one of the most successful characterizations of current fiction.

BOOK-OF-THE-MONTH CLUB, INC.

345 Hudson Street, New York 14, N.Y.

The Return of Lady Brace

1

While the noise of the departing taxi died away down the dusty drive, Caroline, Lady Brace stood in the oppressive August heat savoring, almost childishly, a feeling of triumph. She had succeeded in doing what she had made up her mind to weeks ago in England: she had arrived at Fox Meadows before she was expected. The practice of some harmless deceit by letter had made it possible for her to avoid the fuss of being met at the pier, and enabled her to enjoy, without personal distractions, her first journey in many years from New York City to her childhood home on Long Island's North Shore. She would now be able to take by surprise Rosemary and Lydia, her two American daughters.

Since no one was in sight, and no one had apparently so much as noticed the arrival of the taxi, she stood for a moment in the sleepy silence to get her bearings before ringing the bell. She looked across the cobbled courtyard to the two Chinese chimeras who had stood guard, as long as she could remember, over the inner sanctum of Fox Meadows. She smiled at them above the disheveled mock-orange bushes as though greeting old friends, and they laughed back at her, as always, with their great stone tongues lolling down their cleft chins.

"Hello," she whispered, "Para and Dox." This was the last of several names her brother Stephen had given them, and she could see him standing beside the two lionesque creatures in a long-ago twilight, tracing with his bony delicate hand their contradictory forms, half threat, half play: the fierce arrogance of their out-thrust chests denied by tiny cartoon feet. "Para and Dox!" he had said, as if speaking to himself. "From the Land of Paradox." And then to her, solemnly, "We must never again call them Pooh and Bah."

With the return of this memory a sudden melancholy, almost a sense of foreboding, threatened to take hold of Caroline Brace. "Oh, Stephen," she said to herself with a pang of longing, "how I am going to miss you here. You might have come back, just this one last time!"—for a three-generation tenure of the Langdon family on a large stretch of Nassau County acreage, and the ownership of the sprawling semi-Colonial house at whose entrance she stood, was about to end. She turned abruptly and rang the doorbell.

When at her third ring no one appeared and she could hear no signs of life within, she tried the enormous brass knob. It yielded at once and she stepped into the main hall, though not without a slight sense of unease. There seemed to her something intrusive, even ill-mannered, about entering the house now occupied by her daughter Rosemary without having given fair warning.

Inside the large cool hallway she again stood listening. "Hello," she called. There was not a stir, not even a fly or a bee to break the heavy silence. "Hello," she repeated.

Still no one came. Where, then, were the servants? And her grandchildren, or even the dogs? Surely there must be dogs. There had never been a time when the family's famed springer spaniels had failed to lumber forward on splayed feet, barking an unconvincing warning at all visitors while their tails wagged betrayal.

Then on the floor she saw a large square of white paper held flat with a croquet mallet. It had been written on with lipstick. Taking her glasses from her handbag she read: *All gone to beach except S. and Venerable Sir. They've disappeared. If man appears to photograph Pooh and Bah put him off if possible. But he can measure, I suppose.*

The note was unsigned, but the large round hand resembled Rosemary's. Lady Brace returned the paper to the rug and replaced the croquet mallet.

S. and Venerable Sir—dogs, no doubt. *A man to measure and photograph Pooh and Bah.* This sounded ominous. It meant that the dissolution of Fox Meadows was well on its way. Unhappy details, softened by the distance between America and England, would now become vivid and real. Alone in the once familiar hallway with the steel engravings of intricate Chinese palaces, the breakfront displaying the museum collection of blue-and-white

4

Lowestoft, the worn Ming rug, she wondered for a moment why she had given way to all the entreaties and come back to take one final look at her childhood home. How had she been tempted into this morbid indulgence?

She had been married the first time on the lower landing of this very staircase towards which she was now walking. She had stood just here among roses and lilies—and a year later, on the same landing, with giant pots of poinsettia on either side and mistletoe hanging from the enormous chandelier, Ralph had struck her the first of many blows with his riding crop. There had been lilies again, early ones, on that fatal day when her sister-in-law Bertha Reed, in her muddy riding habit, crossed the Ming rug to tell her what Caroline had already guessed: that Ralph was dead. What a spontaneous sensation of release had surged through her then, followed by a rush of guilt and fear. . . .

As she paused in the center of the well-remembered room, with its unfamiliar subtle air of neglect and untidiness—for there were withered flowers in a Canton vase, dust on the woodwork, a sprawl of mail on the table—she was again aware that a shadow had brushed her spirit.

But this was not the kind of feeling Lady Brace permitted herself for any stretch of time. "I must tidy myself before anyone comes," she said aloud, and looked about, trying to recall where the new "powder room"—added since her last visit—had been built. It was off this hall, she believed, and going to a paneled door she opened it. Stepping over a pair of abandoned children's dungarees and some dirty tennis sneakers, she made her way to a marble basin.

She washed her hands, drying them on one of a row of paper towels with an elaborate stamped monogram, J—for Jordan, Rosemary's married name. If *only* they wouldn't monogram the paper ones, she thought, looking about for a way of disposing of the unattractive wad. Next, very quietly and deliberately, she restored her simple make-up, brushing her short gray-blond hair, putting eyedrops in her large, still clear, blue eyes, with their surprising fringe of dark lashes.

"Now," she said, "I shall explore," and she was aware of a small uprush of anticipation.

But because of the dust in the hall and the abandoned children's clothes in the powder room, she decided, on the very threshold of the large drawing room, to turn back. She would not spy further on Rosemary's housekeeping.

T W O

Beyond the main hall was a room always called the sun porch, furnished still with the same old-fashioned wicker furniture, immense fan-back chairs of raffia woven into complicated designs. Lady Brace glanced, in passing, at a half-completed picture puzzle on the center table, a dog's unfinished meal in a dish by the door, several plastic toys and a rubber bone on the frayed matting.

It was quite plain that Rosemary was no housekeeper. Perhaps this was what Lydia had meant by a recent letter which hinted something about the "confusion" at Fox Meadows and offered her mother the alternative of coming to her little house on Gracie Square: "I've air-conditioning in the bedrooms—and the children will be away with Jack and his family."

Recollection of Lydia's letter made Lady Brace sigh. Lydia had divorced her husband a few years back. Caroline had never known the reasons. Lydia had not volunteered any information, and she had not presumed to ask. It was, she thought now, probably quite unnatural for a mother and a daughter to maintain such reserve. Had circumstances brought it about, or was it a part of both their natures to withhold intimate confidences? She considered this question as she sat down for a moment in one of the fan-back chairs and reached for an infrequent cigarette.

The cigarette was quite wilted but she managed to light it and take a puff or two. She then let it go out in her hand as her mind traveled back to Rosemary and Lydia coming to England, to Braceledge, Bishop's Stile, Bishop's Overpass, Somerset.

How they had made fun of that address! Obdurate and hostile, not only towards their stepfather but towards all things British, the two little girls had made life quite unbearable for everyone. Humphrey's awkward but sincere patience with tennis lessons and homemade herbariums, his humorous, knowing information on bird watching, had failed to soften them in any degree. When even the birth of a half brother did not appear to please them,

Caroline Brace had given in to their endless pleading. She had permitted them to return to America and spend their school years with their childless Aunt Bertha.

On the whole this arrangement had seemed to work well enough. At least it had saved her second marriage—so she had often told herself. And with the passing of time the rift—if rift it was—had apparently healed. Even before Bertha died, the girls had spent parts of many holidays at Braceledge; visited on their honeymoons; come later to show off their children. They had seemed then to enjoy Humphrey and their half brother, Rupert, and to be quite adequately affectionate towards her.

The truth was Caroline Brace had never worried very much about them after they left—for they had seemed to adjust so happily to their American life. Lately, however, particularly since Humphrey's death, she had found her thoughts turning more and more to her daughters. Waking in the night, hearing the old owls in the tower of Braceledge, or digging in the rock garden, pausing with trowel in hand, she would find herself thinking: What are Rosemary and Lydia really like? It was the persistence of this thought, she was quite certain, which had brought her back now to Fox Meadows.

She felt suddenly nervous and impatient—impatient to have it all "start," now that she had come. She would walk outside to pass the time while waiting for the household's return.

THREE

Beyond the sun porch lay a bricked terrace, bordered with box, and beyond it a small lawn where the croquet court had once been and probably still was. A brick-walled garden bounded the scruffy turf at the far end.

Lady Brace slowly crossed the lawn to this small garden, entering where gates with spread-tailed golden peacocks had formerly hung. These gates had already been sold, along with the famous ones at the front entrance, to a Mr. Lorenzetti, a successful local contractor whose father had been the head gardener at Fox Meadows. Young Mr. Lorenzetti had been pleased enough with the enormous entwined monogram, dominated by the letter L, to offer a handsome sum, so Rosemary's lawyer husband had written.

Within the brick enclosure there were definite signs of continued care. Someone, then, was keeping up this small part of the once noted grounds. The little pond appeared clear of algae; she caught the dart of bright fish under the green pads of the lilies. Though rather bare of color at the season's end, the flower-beds looked spruce and orderly; so did the bushes of azalea and espaliered japonica, the elaborate, formally placed trellises of wisteria and clematis.

A few of the old Chinese garden figures also remained. The one she remembered best still stood in its corner near a large white-azalea bush famed for its prolific bloom and the size and texture of its flowers. Wearing the secret smile of a Gothic angel, with a broken lotus in her hand and a cracked water jar on her shoulder, the dreamy Oriental lady—or was she a goddess?—remained just where Caroline Brace's father had placed her over half a century ago.

The serene smiling figure roused questions Caroline Brace had often asked herself in the past: What was it in the Far East that had so strongly captured the fancy of that most conventional of men—John Livingston Langdon? And did her father's interest, though essentially only that of the rich amateur collector, somehow account for her brother's far deeper attraction—one might almost say his "commitment"—to this other part of the world? If so, how strange! This tenuous affinity for things Asian had been the only taste they had ever held in common.

From early childhood Stephen Langdon had exhibited a marked unease in his father's presence, an unease not shared by Caroline, always admittedly the favorite. "Ladybug" her widowed father had called her, and "Ladybird"; tender pet names shortened by Stephen in his teens to "Lady B," a name which her two daughters had also adopted—perhaps somewhat in youthful scorn —when she became Lady Brace.

She thought again with longing of her brother, of how much she was going to miss his presence here in a place filled with memories of their childhood. But Stephen was far away. It was years since he had taken that part of the inheritance his annoyed father had permitted him to have "before reaching the age of sixty" and gone off to the Far East. He now made his permanent home on a floating fragment of tropical land off the southern tip of India—the island of Ceylon. There, just once, she had visited him—a disturbing and unresolved experience.

She turned with a nervous movement, unlike her usual calm manner, and began to follow the flagged path that ran along the sides of the enclosed garden. As she walked she came upon a fretwork of green *chinoiserie* tiling, set into the brick wall. The design had a center opening, wide enough for a slim body. After a moment's hesitation Lady Brace stepped through.

F O U R

Beyond the hedge of lilac bushes bounding the brick wall, all order was left behind. To her surprise she found herself in an unrestrained jungle of vine, weed and shrub. At her coming a cloud of white moths staggered off into the green air like guilty and silent participants disturbed at some secret orgy. . . . Her thoughts were beginning to assume the fanciful shapes that Stephen's so often had in the past. This neglected garden, bursting with exuberance, as though some restraint had been lifted from its invisible energies, brought her brother even more strongly into her memory, for he had always been drawn to wastelands, swamps, tangled thickets. He had loved nothing so much as exploring the tattered fields of an abandoned farm within easy riding distance of Fox Meadows.

She could see him now, standing, suddenly transfixed, in the midst of what had once been cultivated land, repeating to himself, as if some special mystery lay under the words, "gloomy and nameless weeds." He managed to weight the phrase with a special intonation of decay and doom, designed, she could not help but feel, to frighten her as well as himself.

These four inconsequential but haunting words—and how odd that she could recall them exactly after such a stretch of time!— were from Aubrey Beardsley. She had subsequently come upon them in a marked copy of *Venus and Tannhäuser*, found in a pocket of one of Stephen's blazers.

The Beardsley volume—"privately printed," she had noted—

had piqued her adolescent curiosity. Although she still remembered her shocked response to certain passages in that hurried scanning, she could recollect only the one Stephen had darkly whispered: ". . . gloomy and nameless weeds." But she could recall, easily, the picture of Beardsley in the frontispiece: the sensitive bony fingers, splayed up along the half-concealed ear; the pushed-forward but thin lower lip, its sensual protrusion denied by its narrow contour; the great, indeed the prodigious, nose; the feminine eyes and the ridiculous bang of light hair.

Why, since there was nothing in the image that physically resembled her brother, had she seemed to catch some disquieting likeness? Was it some shared point of view, some preoccupation with uncommon subjects? Impossible to analyze now, as it had been then.

She had paused in her slow progress through the clinging weeds to recall all this, as though it was somehow important that she do so. And, as she stood, letting her memory slowly open, her eye fell upon a bee extended full length, fiercely at work on the multiple white bosoms of an everlasting-flower.

The sprawled bee appeared in this moment the blind and helpless victim of some vast, insatiable, irresistible appetite. Could this intense urgency, this automatic ecstasy, really be necessary for the pollenizing of plants, the making of honey? The idea was intolerable. She turned away in distaste. Yet, in averting her glance, the half-formed thought occurred that her unusual and extreme response to the feeding bee might well have sprung from those carefully buried adolescent images from *Venus and Tannhäuser*.

She had come again to the tiled panel in the brick wall. As she stepped back into the orderly garden, she shattered against her skirt the white seed-head of a dandelion. Its minute arrowed shafts floated off, out, down—a few tufts landing on her narrow pointed shoes. "Dandelion clocks," she and Stephen had called, in childhood, these airy globes. But why "clock"? The very word applied to the last form of a golden flower brought a sense of time sadly turning, turning, in irrevocable cycles.

She quickened her steps towards the gates that led to the open lawn, where she could see the late sun still falling in strong slanting light. Surely by now someone could be found in the house to welcome her and show her to her room. She hoped so, for she had been alone with the past long enough.

2

When Lady Brace emerged from the empty gate where the iron peacocks no longer unfurled their golden tails, she saw coming towards her, from the direction of the main house, two figures. She could not at first distinguish who they were, but by straining forward she made out vaguely what they were like.

The figure on the left was a tall thin man, lame, wearing a white suit; the other, short, round, bald, appeared wrapped in a garment like a yellow bathrobe. The taller man was walking, supported by a stick, and when he moved forward she saw his right arm held stiffly across his body as though pinned in this singular position, while his right foot, with each step on the uneven grass, swung out in a half arc, like an absurd travesty of the Charleston.

Caroline Brace took refuge behind the trunk of one of the immense copper beeches, waiting for the figures to move within clearer range. After a moment she was able to recognize, to her surprise, that the smaller of the two was an Oriental; some kind of priest, for his head was not bald, as she had first thought, but only close-shaven, and he was wearing, not a bathrobe, but the traditional yellow garment of certain Eastern religious orders.

Then recognition of the taller figure broke upon her. Her heart missed a beat. It was her brother Stephen. And he was terribly crippled!

She raised her hands to her breast and a small sound, half cry, half sob, escaped her. "Oh, no!" she said aloud. Her first impulsive reaction was fear, and a wish to escape. If she turned now, and ran, she could cower unseen in the neglected weedy jungle she had just left. Even if her brother walked near, along the bricked paths of the little garden, he could not possibly see her. From her hiding place she could listen to, and steel herself for, the sound of a dragging foot, the tap of a faltering stick on the garden bricks. Time! She must have time to prepare for this new and shocking Stephen.

She turned back instinctively toward the little enclosed garden, to put a wall between her and the sight of once light-footed, swift-moving Stephen shambling across the grass like a spastic puppet. But the knowing secret smile of the Chinese goddess in the corner above the white-azalea bush halted her flight. "Why?" the smile seemed to ask. "Where will you go?" "The Goddess of Compassion," someone had once told her long ago, some professor, commenting in a dry nasal voice tinged now with scorn, now with envy, as he walked behind her father on the little tour of the gardens which always followed Sunday lunch on a fair day when guests had included "p's and p's"—pundits and panjandrums, a phrase of her father's, borrowed from her dead grandfather, to apply to those knowledgeable people, often more odd than impressive, who chose to live outside the realms of sport and finance . . . *Goddess of Compassion?* What had this inquiring reflective smile to do with the quality of mercy? And what curious design was her shocked mind weaving as she hesitated, trembling, behind the trunk of the beech tree, postponing the moment when she must move across the lawn to her crippled brother and his strange companion?

She had clasped her wrists with her hands and was pressing them convulsively against her abdomen, hoping to still the palpitation that made her heart pound and her breath flutter. After a moment, "Go now!" she commanded, and she pushed her reluctant body from behind the tree and began to propel it across the grass in the direction of the two figures advancing towards her. As she moved she was again acutely conscious of her hands. She could feel them dangling, heavy and awkward, at the end of rigid arms. Inside her head a voice kept repeating, "Oh, no, no, I can't bear it!" but all the time she was hastening in the slanting light across the grass towards the main house.

When she cried out, "Stephen!" both men stopped. She called the name again, "Stephen," and then, "It's me, Caro!"

Her voice quavered. She started to run forward with tottering uneven gait over the neglected turf. But almost immediately she checked this movement. Stephen's critical eyes had never missed the slightest hint of physical gaucherie. She would not risk his teasing scorn.

"Lady B!" she heard him cry. His voice, though pitched high with surprise, sounded somehow thicker than she remembered. "For God's sake!" And as she came nearer, "What are *you* doing here? You're not expected yet. Not for a whole week at least."

"But I *am* here," and she had reached him. She was putting her stiff frightened arms around him, almost unbearably aware of the broken body they encircled. "And *you* weren't to be here at all."

She succeeded somehow in embracing him, kissing him to one side of the twisted mouth. As she did so, she looked into his gray-blue, slightly protuberant eyes. They were soft, moist, heavy with tears. Stephen with tears in his eyes—something she had never seen before!

"But I did come," he was growling. "What's left of me! And this is the Venerable Ananda Thera—my sister, Lady Brace."

Before she could remind herself of the restrained style of Eastern greeting she had put out her hand. There was no withdrawal on the little priest's part. As he lightly but not unwarmly touched her extended hand, his pale-beige face was beaming, his round, brown-velvet eyes sparkling behind rimless glasses.

"Oh, how lovely, what a joy!" He spoke in a childlike voice, piercingly sweet, faintly tinkling. "The meeting of brother and sister after many years. What an encounter! What a marvelous happiness! *Reunion*."

The small beaming man in his shapeless yellow garments gave the word "reunion" a special emphasis, investing it with both poignance and exhilaration. As for the word "encounter," it too seemed lent by him the quality of wonder, as though some rarely observed law of life, mysterious and exciting, had been caught in operation.

Perhaps merely in contrast with the little monk's exuberance,

Stephen, so fond of dramatics over trifles, was able to refer quite simply and quietly to his serious infirmity.

"I didn't want to write you." The turn of his head, the side glance at his right arm, folded like a broken wing, the quick down-look at the lumbering spastic leg, indicated his meaning. "I knew you'd only worry uselessly. I'm so much better anyway, and I'll improve even more, they tell me."

Lady Brace stood now facing her brother, her hands clasped over his on the head of his walking-stick. "Oh, darling," she murmured, not able to say more.

The timbre of his voice had changed, she was certain; there was something thick and blurred in it; but he was going on steadily with his explanation. "I decided to come to New York for treatment. Not that I haven't been given the kindest and best of care out there."

"Oh, I'm sure you have," she agreed with haste, thinking his reference might be not so much to Ceylon as to his companion in the yellow robe. "But when—?" she began, her voice tightening again with concern.

He cut her off. "Let's not talk about it now. Later."

Then, as though sorry to have spoken with impatience, he gave one of his short, sharp laughs, the laugh that she remembered so well: half merriment, half scorn. "If we can ever find a moment to talk in peace. This is a wild household, I warn you, Lady B. No order or discipline *at* all. Venerable Sir adjusts to it better than I, but I've been pretty good on the whole, considering my stinking nature."

"Oh, dear me!" cried the little monk. "Oh, good gracious, just listen to him." He gave an almost childish giggle. " 'Stinking nature,' he says of himself. Oh, what an apt pupil!" He went off into small fits of infectious laughter, ducking his head into the neck folds of his yellow robe.

Stephen cast him an ironic glance but made no comment. Lady Brace had a sense of some significant exchange between the two men, even on this light, amused level—one she was not able to follow. She was, indeed, more aware of a faint dizziness, as though, in a familiar setting, she was suddenly at the mercy of unfathomable elements.

The little monk continued to burble with pleasure, beaming directly at her through his thick glasses with an expression that could only be described as benign.

T W O

The three figures slowly crossed the sun-burned grass to the bricked terrace. Here Stephen dropped, with evident relief, into the first chair. As his sister sat down near him he gave her a long, candid stare.

"Lady B, you are still very beautiful—almost more so."

Caroline Brace, taken by surprise, felt her color rising. "Why, Stephen!" she stammered. "How sweet of you to say so."

Returning to his growling voice, he insisted, "It's the truth. Old age agrees with you."

"Old age agrees with us all," remarked the little monk airily, pulling up a hassock so that Stephen could stretch out his legs. He made a humorous bow in Lady Brace's direction, as if to relieve his remark of any possible rudeness, and added, "If only we let it."

He bowed again. "And now if you will please excuse me, I'll go into the house and leave the brother and sister together to enjoy their so happy reunion," and cupping his yellow robe around him in large loose folds, he walked off, soft and light, in his open sandals.

As the screen door closed, Stephen, looking after him, remarked before his sister could question or comment, "There goes an authentic saint, a completely unsanctimonious but, I believe, fully *realized* saint."

When Lady Brace only murmured, puzzled by his use of the word "realized," her brother added in a crisper tone, almost mocking, "A saint who didn't get there by torturing himself in the desert either, or by resting on beds of spikes, or—aha! and this is quite a point!—by having torture handed out to him by fate."

Lady Brace murmured again. "He seems very nice—so gentle. . . ."

Stephen snorted, "Gentle! Don't fool yourself! He's as tough as nails."

"Have you met your match then?" The words leapt from her

mouth before she was aware of them. It was not at all the kind of question one ever put to Stephen, who was apt to strike back at any remarks or inquiries of a personal nature.

To her relief he only replied, still calm, "You may well ask." He lay back then and closed his eyes. After a moment, "I could use a drink," he said. He conveyed the impression of sudden, complete exhaustion.

In immediate agitation she half-rose from her chair, "A drink? Of course, darling, let me get you one."

But he waved her back with the end of his stick. "Don't stir! It's no use." When, obedient, she sank down, he added in a weary drawl, his eyes still closed, "The liquor is kept locked up. Rosemary has her eye on it. Not because of me, may I say—I'm a reformed character—but because of the summer help. The sitter and her boy friend, I suspect."

"I don't understand." She sounded anxious and confused as she repeated, "The sitter and her boy friend?"

"I refer to a couple of just-as-good-as-you-are-if-not-better kids who are supposed to be taking some of the domestic chores off Rosemary and Todd." Stephen opened one eye and, seeing her puzzled expression, made an effort to be more explicit.

"The girl's a psychology major, or something exalted like that. The boy's studying law in Todd's office. I believe they're *betrothed*." (He gave the old-fashioned word an ironic twist.) "Anyway, the girl is expected to relieve Rosemary with the brats. The boy's supposed to do lawns on weekends, wash up at night, that sort of thing."

"Has Rosemary no other staff in this big place?"

"Oh, yes, there's an intermittent body who cleans by the hour. And an old hag named Clara who cooks when Rosemary doesn't. She must be a hundred and twenty, if she's a day. Proof positive that longevity and grace have no connection—in spite of Venerable Sir's opinion. Clara is the *ultimate* in meat-axes."

It was actually a relief to Lady Brace to hear her brother talking in this remembered mock-critical vein.

"Mercy, what a household!" she said mildly. Stephen's silence was eloquent. "How do you stand it?"

16

He grinned and she noticed that only one side of his twisted mouth moved upwards. Her heart contracted at the sight, but his voice was quite gay as he replied, "I stand it by telling myself it's good for the soul. No worse really than all those monkeys I kept once in Madras."

He shifted his position awkwardly in apparent discomfort, yet his cheerfulness still did not falter. "Or those caste-ridden house-boys I had in Benares. I remember telling Humphrey once that the only time I felt Christian missionaries had done a real world service was when I finally got a houseful of Christian servants out in India. They weren't quite as loving and simple-minded as pure Hindus—mission education had spoiled that side of them—but at least it didn't take three men to do the simplest job, because of caste rules about who handled *what* and *when.*"

Yes, she thought to herself, except for the slight thickening in his voice, he sounds quite natural, quite the same. If she looked away, she could imagine him unchanged. But when she glanced at him cautiously as he talked on, she was startled by the pronounced pallor which now appeared to be seeping through the deep tan on his face.

"Stephen," she began. But she spoke in a voice so tremulous that at once—fearing he would growl at her—she added quickly in an impersonal tone, false even to her own ears, "There's so much to talk about, isn't there?"

For a long moment he said nothing. He lay with his eyes shut and she waited, preparing for his possible question, "*What,* for instance?" Would she dare then inquire more specifically about his physical condition; ask some further questions about the little monk?

Beyond the hedge a catbird began to mew plaintively. She saw Stephen's right hand release the head of his heavy walking-stick. It fell back with a soft thud onto the padded sailcloth upholstery, and slipped on down to the terrace. She leaned forward to pick it up and replace it near his hand. As she did so she saw the design of its head, a meticulously carved serpent with tail in mouth. Through the opening made by the circular snake her brother must clench his half-useless fingers as he walked.

She was about to remark, "What a curious carving," when

Stephen opened his eyes to smile directly at her with a sweetness she had seldom seen in him. As she was returning the stick to his chair he stretched out his good hand to catch at hers. "Darling Lady B! I can't tell you how wonderful it is to see you." His voice broke slightly.

Then once more, to her stupefaction—even to her embarrassment—tears welled up in his eyes. They grew slowly and fell, large, round, separate and firm as beads, down his gaunt cheeks. She wanted to look away but could not. There was an irresistible fascination in the face before her. Its expression had become quite blank and the enormous tears looked unnatural and artificial, like the water drops so carefully placed on the weeping Christ of those cheap machine-made crucifixes sometimes to be seen in the windows of religious-goods stores. These large tears seemed to her wholly unreal, bearing no relationship to any emotion. She was wondering, in acute dismay, if this was only some involuntary weakness of the tear ducts, brought on by his paralysis, when Stephen spoke.

"Wipe them off, will you?" His voice was dead and cold. "I can't seem to help doing things like this since—since the stroke."

Lady Brace fumbled with awkward haste for her handkerchief. When she found it, she rose to stand behind him, passing the soft piece of linen across his cheeks and over his eyelids. She was struggling not to let her own tears fall in his presence. It seemed to her unbearable that such a monstrous trick should have been played on Stephen, always so controlled, the master of any situation, and so fiercely private.

"Oh, Stephen," she whispered. "There has never been anyone like you." And before he could reply with some sardonic remark she bent down and kissed the top of his still thick, light hair. She yielded to an impulse to press her palms over his small, pointed, close-growing ears and to hold them there a long moment. She felt she could not contain her own grief for him if she did not express her love in some actual physical contact.

Her brother lay unmoving under her touch. But when she had gone back to her chair he spoke in a quiet voice. "You couldn't ever have said or done that to me in the past, Caro. Not in that way. You've changed. Or is it just the shock of seeing me like this?

Sometimes I think only severe shocks ever get us to act human. Or maybe it *isn't* acting like a human to be honest or loving. One sometimes wonders."

The same old Stephen, forever perverse and contradictory, giving with one hand and taking away with the other. But she had an inward sense of some crisis having been passed between them.

THREE

She felt no necessity at the moment to reply to his comment on the change in her.

Here in the quiet grounds behind their old home—soon to be theirs no longer—she had an unexpected feeling of opportunity. The idea occurred to her that a whole new range of subjects on which neither of them had ever touched before might now be explored.

Along with this curious, only half-admitted sense of anticipation there came also a wave of something very like fear; once again the uneasy tremors of the moment in the hall, and again in the garden, quivered through her. Emotions were pressing too thickly upon her; the weight of old memories would have been quite enough without adjustment to so much that was new and unexpected. She thought: Now if this scene were taking place in a drama, or a novel, the author would break at this point, offer the reader quick relief, but since this is actually happening and since I still do not know which room I am being given in my father's house I must go on enduring whatever my brother puts me through—even though I am well past sixty, have missed my afternoon nap, my afternoon tea, had a dirty train-ride and sustained a severe shock.

But so deeply ingrained was Lady Brace's habit of consideration for others that, fearing Stephen might become aware of her momentary depression, she forced herself to ask in a perfunctory matter-of-fact voice a question about her younger daughter. "Have you seen Lydia?"

"Yes. Several times. She's due out here again tomorrow or the next day, I believe. Maybe even this evening. I'm not sure."

"There was a note on the hall rug. Perhaps it was for her."

"No, that was for Todd. He was planning to get home early

tonight. Probably detained by the traffic. He commutes every day. Beastly, I'd think. I don't know how he stands it."

She did not want to drop the subject of Lydia. "How did Lydia seem when you saw her?"

"Lots of style," Stephen said. "She's not really beautiful but she's got something very alluring about her—in a cool way. Odd air of mystery. She seems very detached."

"Is she unhappy?"

"Of course."

This reply troubled her, but she felt it unwise to inquire what he meant. She was not sure whether she doubted his being able to tell her what made Lydia unhappy, or whether she simply did not wish, at the moment, to hear about it.

"She's got a charming little house in New York," he went on. "I've gone there to rest after my treatments and she's given me tea."

"How often do you go to New York?"

"I'm supposed to go twice a week."

"Who drives you?"

"Venerable Sir."

"He *drives?*" Caroline Brace's voice expressed extreme astonishment.

Stephen laughed aloud. "Yes," he said, "he prepared himself for America by undertaking certain rigorous training in mechanical techniques. I bought him a Thunderbird. You should see the eyes popping on the highways when we pass," and he laughed again, this time in genuine merriment.

Lady Brace felt she could now venture a personal question. "Is he your nurse, or your guru, or what?"

Stephen grimaced. "Not my nurse, certainly. Guru? Well, maybe —but not a teacher in the way you'd imagine. He helped me in Ceylon, stood by in a dark hour. In return I paid his way to America. He isn't here just to wait on me, you know. Not by a long shot! He's here looking at America—New York in particular— as a possible place to establish a mission."

"Mission?"

"Haven't you heard?" he inquired, mocking. "The East is preparing its revenge. It is planning to evangelize the West."

3

Before she could think of anything to reply she heard a sound of wheels on the front driveway. Car doors slammed, dogs barked, children shouted, screen doors banged, adult voices rose in admonition. Then came cries of surprise, followed by a rush of steps across the sun porch.

"Lady B, for heaven's *sake!*" Rosemary exclaimed, plunging into view. "I knew you were here when I saw your handbag. I can't *believe* it," and she ran down the steps like a young girl, with her dark hair ruffled, her great blue eyes shining, to catch her mother in a boisterous, excessive embrace.

"*Angel*, how good to see you! You look marvelous. What a chic suit! Doesn't she look divine, Uncle Stephen? Oh, *Mum*, there's so much to tell you. I do hope you aren't simply *dead*. Your rooms are ready, I'm glad to say. I must have had a premonition you'd arrive early. You've got Granddaddy's suite. Very grand! Its been closed off for ages, because of the dusting and all that, but I had a woman in to do it up specially for you. You'd probably love a bath right away."

Two children, a sturdy dark boy of five and a thin pale girl of nine, had appeared on the steps. "Come, babes!" Rosemary cried. "Here's Gran, come all the way from England to see you. Remember, Jennifer, when you visited her and Humpy over there; the swans on the lake and the pony cart?"

Neither child moved or spoke. They both stood staring fixedly at Lady Brace out of large blue eyes very much like her own. There was something guarded and wary in their attitude. Was this, Lady Brace wondered, checking the impulse to extend her arms, normal behavior for children brought up the modern way, without parental pressures, nursery disciplines; no curtsies, no bows, no unquestioning obedience?

Rosemary was taking their conduct quite blandly, appearing not in the least concerned by their lack of response. After a moment's wait, "Oh, all right," she said in a light, offhand voice. "Run along if you can't be polite."

But Stephen's cane struck the bricks beside his chair with three loud cracking sounds. "Little monsters!" he cried. "What appalling manners! Come straight down here, Jennifer, and greet your grandmother properly. I'm ashamed of you."

As soon as Stephen spoke Jennifer advanced towards Lady Brace.

"As for you, Elliot, you little beast, *you* don't need to," Stephen went on. "Your paw is far too filthy to offer to anybody."

The little boy, with a half grin, at once took a step after his sister.

Rosemary burst out laughing. "You're really terrible, Uncle Stephen. But your methods *do* seem to work, though they wouldn't for any of the rest of us, I'm sure."

"Children always have a morbid interest in cripples," Stephen remarked sardonically. "That is really the secret of my power over them."

"Hello, my darlings," Lady Brace said. She took the thin little girl with the matchstick arms and pale long hair into a careful embrace. "How you've grown, Jennifer!"

To her surprise and relief—for she dreaded cold children, of whom one seemed to encounter so many lately—her granddaughter returned her kiss with warmth. The little boy pressed forward for his hug too. They both now seemed quite at ease and disposed to be friendly.

"We've got a new dog," Elliot said. "Mr. Tandy at the farm gave him to us."

"He can't walk yet," Jennifer said. She stood abruptly on one leg and pulled at her long blond hair hanging straight as water on either side of her head. She turned in a half circle on the one leg and back again.

"He puddled the rug and Alice hit him." Elliot's earnest blue eyes gazed deep into his grandmother's.

Jennifer showed her teeth in amusement at her brother. They were large, square, rather uneven teeth, out of all proportion to her tiny face and pointed chin. Oh, dear, braces for sure! her grandmother thought sadly.

"And what's more I'll do it again," cried a brisk voice. A barefooted young woman in abbreviated blue-striped shorts and barely adequate red halter, exposing an impressive suntan, appeared in the door.

"Mummy, this is Alice Ford," Rosemary said. "She's helping me with Elliot and Jennifer this summer—and supposedly getting a little direct clinical experience in child psychology on the side."

"And how!" In spite of this curious expression—an Americanism that must have been borrowed from the Red Indians—and in spite of Alice Ford's somewhat breezy air, at least the girl's manners were not remiss. She came forward politely and offered her hand.

"How nice to meet you at last, Lady Brace. I feel as though I know you already from hearing Rosemary talk of you."

That her daughter should have been speaking frequently of her astonished Lady Brace, but there was no chance to remark on this, for again Rosemary in her vivid energetic fashion demanded her attention. "Have you met Venerable Sir yet, Mummy?"

"Yes." So they all addressed him as Venerable Sir.

"Isn't he a *dream?*" Rosemary cried. She had pulled Jennifer towards her and begun to braid the child's pale dangling hair.

At Rosemary's remark the girl in the shorts and halter did a quick side-step on the terrace bricks, a hesitation followed by a long slow slide, a sharp tap of the bare toes. *"Did you ever see a dream walking, well I did, well, I did . . ."* she sang softly. "They've revived that old song," she remarked to no one in particular. "It really is the most!"

"Ouch, Mummy, you're pulling!" Jennifer cried. Standing between her mother's knees she stamped her foot like a fractious colt.

"Come along, kids. Wash up!" Alice Ford ordered, and the children rushed headlong for the steps.

How much movement there is, thought Lady Brace, in dismay. Constant movement. Is this the energy from vitamins and sun lamps? Will I feel old and broken here?

Stephen was beginning to rise from his chair. At once Rosemary stepped towards him. Lady Brace, too, made a movement in his direction. He waved them off. "Don't dart at me like flies to carrion. I can still manipulate my legs. Rosemary, take your mother up and let her have a few quiet moments and a hot tub. She needs them both."

"Right." Rosemary again put her arms around her mother. "Oh, Lady B, imagine you here after all these years! Oh, *dear*, I do hope it's not going to be *too* depressing for you."

"Not at all, darling, I'm sure not." At once Lady Brace feared that she might have spoken a little too crisply in her hope of averting any extravagant expressions of regret from Rosemary about the sale of Fox Meadows. To make amends she added in a gentler voice, "For one thing, it's going to be such heaven to be with all of you again."

Yet as she walked with her child into the sunroom she could not help recalling how Rosemary's outspokenness and lack of social finesse, her constant italicizing of words and phrases—particularly in her intense college years—had always made her very uncomfortable. Even Humphrey, ever kind and gentle, had admitted that Rosemary's eager bounce, her argumentativeness, filled him with a vague unease when she came to Braceledge in the summer holidays. Now she hoped—she told herself she *felt*—that these qualities in her older daughter would prove only refreshing.

T W O

Upstairs in the spacious room overlooking the walled garden and the terrace on which they had just been sitting, Rosemary darted to open windows, turn on lights. "I'd have had flowers for you, Lady B, if only I'd been forewarned. Or do they still give you sneezes?"

"Very rarely. I brought my spray, just in case, but I doubt my needing it." Automatically, however, Lady Brace rapped on the wood of the dressing table. Then she turned to look around the enormous room with its curtained and hooded alcove where the great walnut fourposter stood, its carved spiral posts surmounted by elaborate wooden pineapples. Although the room had a wintry and somewhat theatrical appearance with its dark woods, deep red carpet, and yellow silk curtains, all its details delighted her. "Not changed in the least. I'm so glad!" she exclaimed.

Rosemary paused to cast an appraising glance, as if seeing the room for the first time. She shrugged. "I do think it's a bit overwhelming."

She then continued her darting circuit, pulling shades, turning on lights, plumping up pillows. "But I suppose you're used to it. I mean it's very English in feeling, I think. I remember how our rooms at Braceledge used to depress our spirits; Lydia's and mine."

Lady Brace was aware of an interior twinge at Rosemary's brusque indication of enduring distaste for things British. But she doesn't mean to be tactless and abrupt, she assured herself, for she is really warm-hearted.

She put out an impulsive hand towards her daughter. "Come and let me look at you! You do look so young, darling."

"Pushing forty," Rosemary remarked cheerfully. She crossed the room to the great bed and sat down beside her mother.

"What lovely hair you've got," Lady Brace went on, longing to run her fingers through Rosemary's red-brown mane but checking the impulse from shyness. Instead she softly stroked the hand her daughter had dropped in her lap.

"I'm afraid it's a blow-away mess."

Rosemary spoke with indifference. She had become suddenly remote.

"Tell me about your—life," Lady Brace suggested, feeling a little awkward but forcing herself not to retreat.

"Nothing to tell, Mummy—about me, anyway." She shrugged again. "My life just goes along in the same old groove. One day very like another. Not that I'm not *busy*. I'm very busy, really. No help at all—domestic, I mean—practically none, anyway. Simply can't be found, you know. And everything's *hideously* expensive. The grocery bills—*staggering*. And taxes—*outrageous*. But there—you know all that—and we manage beautifully, really! Todd's doing very well. His father says he's a *natural* lawyer, and I suppose his father should know. He's been one himself for about forty years."

Lady Brace wondered what a "natural" lawyer was, but did not ask. She did not want to be sidetracked onto Todd just now. "Tell me about Lydia."

Rosemary shrugged. "You'll see her tomorrow. She's dropping past, on her way to the city. She's been in Southampton for a week. I'll call her and let her know you're already here. Maybe I can persuade her to stay for lunch, or overnight, when she comes. She's hard to pin down."

"How is she?" Lady Brace quietly persisted.

Rosemary hesitated. "Well, Mummy, you'll see. She's—well, she *seems* all right. I can't tell. You know Lydia, she's hard to *dig* —as Alice would say. Has she been writing you?"

"Yes, quite frequently lately—for Lydia. Just little notes, of course."

"I mean has she written about—about the new—" Rosemary hesitated again "—*romance?*" she finished.

"Romance? No, though she did say she had something to tell me that might surprise me. Who is it?"

Rosemary's open sunny face clouded over at her mother's question. She shook her head. "I don't think I should go into it with you, Mummy. I'll let her tell you. I will say this, only this, just be prepared for a shock. A real shock. Don't exclaim, or cry out *no* or anything like that. I think Lydia is really very sensitive about it somewhere deep inside. And I think she still loves Alex White and I think she's *terribly* sorry she ever divorced Jack. But there! I'm talking too much. I always do, Todd says. I'm going to get right out this moment and let you lie down. It's Clara's day off, so I'm getting the supper. It won't be for another hour at least, though Todd should be here by now. Traffic must have been *terrible*. Just lie down and take a nap if you can."

"Let me come and help you." She did not want to relinquish the topic of Lydia in this abrupt fashion.

"Nonsense!" Rosemary cried. "Never! We'd be humiliated. I'll give you warning in time." And kissing her mother lightly she dashed out the door.

4

Removing only her pumps, Lady Brace lay down flat on the tufted silk counterpane. Oh, what can it be with Lydia? Is she going to marry some South American roué, or some jazz-band musician, or someone of that sort?

Thank heaven for Stephen's being here, she thought. Stephen can reduce anything to insignificance—perhaps now, even pain; and she lay thinking of the new expression she had caught in his eyes when first she looked into them on the lawn: a faint, altogether unlikely reminder of a look she had sometimes seen on Humphrey's face during his long invalidism, as though he had detached himself from his useless body and was observing it, with a rather wry curiosity, from some distant place.

Certainly she had never expected to find any point of comparison between gentle, steady Humphrey and unpredictable, erratic Stephen. Was pain truly the great leveler?

As this question crossed her fatigued mind, it led to a disturbing thought: Four times in her life she had found herself beside broken bodies: both her husbands, her adored only son, and now her brother. Was there, could there possibly be, some special significance in—she groped for a descriptive phrase—in this *recurrent motif* in the pattern of her existence?

With impatience she dismissed this fanciful notion, reminding herself that she had long known that no amount of the cleverest manipulation of the separate pieces of an individual life ever produced a clear picture. No matter how one attempted to fit the scattered parts into a coherent whole—and an image of the unfinished picture puzzle in the shabby sunroom below rose before her—large segments remained formless. One could only guess at the missing sections, decide finally that whoever (whether with large W or small) created the original design had intentionally, or carelessly, omitted certain bits altogether.

She began to doze.

TWO

How long she slept she could not have said, but the next thing of which she became conscious was the sound of a wild clanging. She sat up in the fading light, her heart beating violently, not knowing for a moment where she was or what she had heard. With a trembling hand she reached for the bedlight and her watch. Seven o'clock. Then she caught the distant noise of children and dogs and remembered that she was at Fox Meadows. The clanging must have been a dinner gong.

She rose at once to tidy her hair, and was sitting at the dressing table with its wide three-way mahogany mirror, its old-fashioned silver and crystal fittings, when Rosemary put her head around the door.

"Mummy, I *do* apologize. That *ghastly* gong. I'm sure it startled you."

"Just a little," Lady Brace admitted. "I was dozing. I'm afraid I'll have to appear again in this rumpled suit. I left all my bags in town because I was taking the train out here. I was told there were no redcaps on the Long Island line."

"Oh, *why* didn't you let us know?" Rosemary cried. "You could have come out with Todd. Still, it *is* rather fun to be on your own once in a while. I *love* it when I get a chance to myself. All too seldom! But don't worry about how you look, Lady B. It *couldn't* matter less, and anyway, you look marvelous."

As they left the room Rosemary remarked in an altered voice, "I've been talking to Lydia in Southampton. She's coming to lunch tomorrow." There was a little pause. "Frederick Hollis is going to drive her over." She added, "I thought I *had* to ask him to stay for lunch."

Caroline repeated the name. "Frederick Hollis. Oh, really. How nice! I knew his father. He married a great friend of mine, Belle Stewart." She linked her arm through Rosemary's as they walked down the hall.

"This is *not* Frederick Hollis's son, Mummy," Rosemary said briskly. "It *is* Frederick Hollis." She gave her mother a direct, meaningful look.

"But," Lady Brace began, "You mean . . . ?"

"I haven't said a word," Rosemary said. "Just remember that, Mummy. But at least you're *warned*."

"Tell me," Lady Brace began in some agitation, "I must know, Rosemary. . . ."

But by now they were in sight of the lower hall, where her son-in-law Todd Jordan was waiting. He came up the stairs eagerly to greet her. "Lady B, what a pleasure to see you." Light from the gold and black eagle sconces shone on his cheerful, tired face, his close-cropped boyish head and dark-rimmed glasses. "You're visiting a wild household. I hope your constitution is up to it."

She smiled back at him, warmly. "It's good to have my atoms jolted a bit."

Lady Brace was very fond of Rosemary's husband, with his easygoing, kindly manner and casual sense of humor. He and Humphrey had hit it off very well on the two occasions when the Jordans had come to visit at Braceledge. Both men were ardent bird-watchers and this had happily solved all their conversational problems. "The marsh harrier is in a jolly bad way right now. Worse off than the kite," Humphrey would be saying in a doleful mutter from his wheel chair as she joined them on the terrace. "How about the hen harrier?" Todd would surprisingly counter. "Only in Orkney now. Jove, I'd like to get up to the Outer Hebrides again! How about your bitterns?"

She was recalling this as her son-in-law with a cozy gesture pulled her hand through his arm and walked her into the dining room, speaking of the traffic through which he had just driven. (Was this the third or fourth mention of the subject since she got off the train a few hours before?)

"No time for bird-watching?" she asked.

"Precious little," he replied with a rueful lift of his brows.

In the dining room, portraits of her mother's family, the Virginia Archers, gazed down on a fine Duncan Phyfe table, laid as if for a picnic with paper napkins and straw mats. Four cardboard containers of milk flanked what Lady Brace had reason to believe was a hastily gathered bowl of roses.

"I'm afraid there's more substance than style at our board," Todd said, glancing at the milk containers with a faint air of embarrassment. Lady Brace had the impression, however, that he noticed the table's casual setting only because of her presence.

"How lovely the roses are," she murmured. She could not quite bring herself to say the table's disorganized appearance was not important, for she did not feel so.

"Don't apologize, Toddy," Rosemary cried with a certain hint of defensiveness, entering from the kitchen carrying a large ham on a silver platter that she thumped down unceremoniously at her husband's place. "Mummy knows how life has changed. She hasn't exactly been put away in moth balls. It isn't roses that you're allergic to, is it Lady B?"

"No, no," her mother said quickly. "Please don't worry about my allergies, darling. I'm rarely bothered now. They say they're entirely mental.

"We've all had the word!" was Alice Ford's comment. She had not bothered to change from shorts and halter. Pouring glasses of milk, she added, "It's psychosomatic."

Just then Stephen came limping in with the children, who, barely out of reach of his awkwardly swinging right leg, followed each spastic movement with an air of impersonal fascination. There was a slight tussle for possession of his chair at the table.

Stephen arbitrated. "Jennifer's turn tonight. You can do your grandmother's chair, Elliot. She's a helpless old lady who loves attention."

When she had managed to seat herself with Elliot's hindrance, Lady Brace asked, "Where is Venerable Sir?" She addressed no one in particular, as she unfolded her paper napkin and tried to moor it to her lap by creasing her light silk skirt across her knees.

"He doesn't eat after noontime," Rosemary explained. "And anyway, he cooks for himself. He has the nursery rooms on the third floor. There's a little electric stove up there, if you remember. I moved the children down to lower floors *ages* ago. Those three flights were just *too* much. They've got their practice piano and junk like that in Grandfather's Trophy Room now. I hope you won't faint when you see it. It's a *scream*—Old Miss Hawley giving them *Ave Maria* under the tiger's head. I think the room scares her to death. Oh, here you are, Julius!"

She addressed a young man in faded dungarees, a clean cotton shirt and soiled white tennis sneakers, who had entered from the butler's pantry carrying a large wooden bowl of tossed green salad.

Todd said casually, "I'd like to present Julius Carozzi, Lady B. He's living with us this summer. Just pass that, will you, Julius, like a good fellow? The kids make such a mess of handing it around."

"O. K." Julius responded. He nodded in Lady Brace's direction. "How do you do." He began at once to speak to Rosemary about the salad dressing: something about the vinegar having run out, that he could only find half a lemon. Lady Brace did not listen closely to the words, but she was fascinated by his accent, with its curious overemphasis on the "d's," a sound of elided "g's" between the words. It did not sound American, and certainly not Italian. And how demanding it all is, she thought, the entire household caught in interlocking personal relationships.

Todd was addressing her. "I'm sorry you didn't get your cocktail, Lady B. We debated disturbing you but decided rest was more vital."

"Anyway, we've got some not bad white Bordeaux," Rosemary put in. "Todd got it at a sale. It's on the ice. Hop up, Alice, like an angel, will you, and snatch it out of the icebox before it's frozen solid."

Alice hopped up as bid, disappeared, reappeared to inquire, "What glasses? I can only find three wines."

Rosemary made a face, "Oh, yes. They went, didn't they?—in that fatal crash at Thanksgiving. Never mind. Give one to Lady B, and one to Uncle Stephen and one to Toddy. I'll use a juice glass. I don't mind."

"No wine for me," Stephen said, "I don't share your enthusiasm for California grapes." He added, sourly, "Old John made better wine out of parsnips and dandelions during Prohibition."

"It's not California, you snob," Alice Ford said, displaying the bottle. "It's French."

"We can't afford California wine," Todd remarked, lowering his head to look over his glass rims at Lady Brace, and grinning. "It's too expensive. Imports are cheaper—in our price range."

Alice Ford was holding the bottle under Stephen's disdainful nose as she read aloud from the label. "Bordeaux Supérieur, 1949, Broufant et Cie., Négociants à Bordeaux."

To Lady Brace's surprise the girl's accent was extremely good. How mixed up everything is! she thought again.

"Whatever it is, it's overchilled," Stephen was replying, feeling the wine bottle with his left hand.

"Were you drinking during Prohibition, Uncle Stephen?" Rosemary demanded, snatching up the dinner plates one by one and slapping hot macaroni on them. "You must have begun very early."

"I developed all my vices in early infancy," Stephen replied. "Ask your mother. She is more familiar with them than anyone in the world."

"I remember not a single vice." Lady Brace looked across the table. She wanted to put into her voice and glance the love she felt, but just then Julius, who had come this far with the wooden salad bowl, paused to take up Stephen's knife and fork to cut the meat on his plate into small, easily managed bits.

The sight was so distressing to Lady Brace that she looked quickly away. That Stephen should have come to such a pass! Stephen—always so proud, so independent and free—the freest person she had ever known—now so helpless, so at the mercy of others. Did he manage to dress himself alone? she wondered.

For some reason the word "free" caught her attention, and she began to question it. Did she really mean that Stephen had always been free? No, for freedom must surely hold a connotation of happiness, and she did not believe that Stephen had ever been truly happy, in spite of having apparently done as he pleased all his life.

She glanced again at her brother, now awkwardly feeding himself, and at once the face of John van der Wadel with its unfamiliar dark brooding beauty rose between them. Where was that disturbing young man who had been her brother's companion when she visited him in Ceylon? How was it that Stephen had come back to his childhood home with a little Eastern monk rather than that arrogant young scholar of mixed native and European blood, who had shared his remote island bungalow?

THREE

As she picked absently at her food while the table talk, trivial and light-hearted, whirled about her (even Jennifer and Elliot were permitted the usual egocentric, competitive exchange of children) she saw Humphrey laying aside his binoculars on the terrace at Braceledge in order to look at the tabloid story about Stephen which Bertha Reed had so carefully sent all the way to Somerset.

She had never thrown away that newspaper, with its distressing headline: *Former Society Playboy Studies Evil in Far East.* Only a few months ago, after Humphrey's death, she had come on it in a trunk, yellowed with age but still quite legible. Even the pictures with which the anonymous writer illustrated his vague but scurrilous hints of Stephen's activities were still intact—a whole page of them. There was not only a view of Stephen's bungalow on Ceylon (referred to as "the Pearl of the East") but also of the "mansion" at Fox Meadows; a photograph of her father taken years before at Belmont, receiving a cup; one of her in the long draped gown from Worth, the ostrich plumes and fan of her first presentation at the Court of St. James in the twenties; finally, Stephen in shorts and solar topi standing in a jungle setting with his hand resting on an immense carved serpent of stone.

Humphrey had dismissed the tabloid's sly suggestions that his wife's brother was a decadent crackpot by huffing testily, "Probably not a word of truth in it. These gossipmongering chaps ought to be called to account. Reckless irresponsibility with other people's names and reputations!"

But Humphrey's dismissal had not enabled Lady Brace to put the cheap, printed words from her mind. Not only was there something troubling about the thought of her brother spending his time cross-breeding orchids to produce "obscene monstrosities"— as the paper phrased it—she found even more disturbing the snapshot of Stephen in the jungle with his hand on the sculptured stone serpent. Could he perhaps be indulging in some kind of weird Oriental orgies?

Humphrey had only laughed at her qualms about orchids and serpents. "All orchids are obscene. Never could bear 'em myself. As for stone serpents—the place is teeming with them. Any time you want to be photographed with a stone snake out there you can lay your hand on one—usually right in the back yard. Makes rather an effective pose, I'd say."

Since Humphrey had been born in southern India, the son of an eminent British civil servant, he spoke with authority, yet his light remarks could not dissipate her nagging worry about the younger brother who had always dominated her, even frequently bullied her, yet for whom she continued to feel a quite irrational responsibility.

When Humphrey saw that his reassurances were not putting her mind at rest, he changed his tack and began to urge her to make the trip, to see for herself what was going on. In his careful factual way he got out maps to show her where the island lay off the south-ernmost tip of India, a little to the east of the vast subcontinent. He had been there himself on several occasions for extended stays and had some first-hand knowledge of the place. This he passed on to her in his typical, broken-phrased fashion. "Probably part of In-dia once, or some land mass now under water—the natives tell the usual deluge legend. They say there are signs that human beings lived here at least a hundred thousand years ago . . . inde-scribably beautiful, especially the uplands—not unlike Scotland in places—cool mist and heather with sea and tropical jungles lying just below . . . Alexander the Great is said to have visited the island. Not verified. Marco Polo did. . . ."

She had finally given in to Humphrey's urgings, and her own curiosity, and had made the long journey to Ceylon—though it had meant going alone, for Humphrey's arthritis was already trou-bling him; a prolonged sea voyage was deemed inadvisable by his doctors.

F O U R

Her first glimpse of her brother at the dock in Colombo had been a pleasant surprise. He looked less strung-up and nervous than she ever remembered seeing him. He had even put on weight.

His words of greeting, uttered in a triumphant voice, were, "I never thought you'd do it."

"Do what?"

"Leave Humphrey behind and come." Plainly her journey so far alone afforded Stephen deep inner satisfaction. He had, as yet, no clue to the real motives behind her visit and he made no attempt to hide how excited and happy he was at the prospect of having her to himself. "You're going to love it here," he cried.

How wrong he had been!

Her dislike of the fabulous island began, she had often thought, with the first sight of Stephen's orchids. He could hardly wait to display them. She had been allowed no chance to rest after their rough ride by car to the uplands where his luxurious bungalow lay, before he was crying, "Come view the monstrosities!" She had noted, uneasily, his use of the very word of the tabloid description.

She had to agree that it was the one apt name for these air-fed, nightmarish plants. To her they appeared not in the least like flowers, but more like fantastic artifacts born of some sick, erotically obsessed imagination. Her face must have expressed her dismay and absence of pleasure, for Stephen shouted with laughter when he looked at her.

"Not much like those Uncle Reggie grew at Rhinebeck, are they? Here's a particular pet. Flamboyant Diseased Crow, I've named it. And *that* one"—and he indicated a repellent phallic object erect on the languid air.

He had been quite willing to explain what got him started on orchid growing. He had leased the bungalow from a temporarily exiled Indian prince who had whiled away his period of penance by cultivating uncommon varieties of epiphytes. Stephen's fancy had been caught by these exotic hybrids, and when he leased the bungalow, he kept the old Tamil gardener whom the prince had originally trained.

But her brother's orchid growing was, Lady Brace soon found, incidental to his main activity: an intensive program of research and writing to which he referred only matter-of-factly, offering no enlightening details. She surmised that this might well be the "Studies in Evil" at which the newspaper had so luridly hinted. Long acquaintance with Stephen's dislike of direct inquiries kept her, however, from showing any immediate curiosity. She would wait for just the right mood and moment to question him in the hope that she would not then be accused of "prying."

Stephen had built a library onto the large, comfortable bunga-low. He had even installed, at great expense, a dehumidifying system to keep down the mold on his books. In this library he worked every day until lunch and sometimes after dinner at night, along with his "secretary and assistant," the young man named John van der Wadel, of mixed Sinhalese and Dutch de-scent—a Burgher, as this product of two distinct racial strains was known in Ceylon society.

Lady Brace found her brother's companion both perplexing and unsympathetic. She could discern in him little trace of the Eu-ropean genes that were allegedly present. His delicate, deceptive languor, his cool apathy, seemed far removed from the genial sto-lidity she associated with the Dutch. To her, John van der Wadel appeared as exotic in every way as her brother's hybrid orchids; quite unrelated to any quality implied by the prosaic term "burgher." His immense dark eyes, liquid and pupil-less, were to her the eyes of a recently tamed animal, and he moved, too, with the almost stealthy grace of an animal. His native voice, softly trilling like running water or distant calling bird, made its overlay of British accent sound like a ventriloquist's trick. She discovered he had acquired this accent in England, where he had gone to study law like many members of his family before him. Now, how-ever, he was not a practicing lawyer. He claimed to be rather "an amateur anthropologist"—a designation to which Stephen had added the word "genius."

Lady Brace would have said that she did not normally dislike encounters with the unfamiliar, yet it was not only Stephen's odd activities and his strange companion that put her off. The spec-tacular physical beauty of the landscape itself—though she often caught her breath at its splendor—left her more disturbed than delighted. The fantastic cloud effects, night and morning, the curious blue tinge to the air, the black-green layers of tropical forest relieved only by the dazzling flash of bird wing or the vivid shock of some unfamiliar bright flower—all seemed attempting to lay on her a sensual demand she could not fulfill. The palms waving, whis-pering, stroking the air with sensuous fronds; the very curve of the sails of the catamarans drawn up waiting on the beaches, or belly-ing out with the wind on the chromatic sea; the giant lotus flowers, red and white, opening in languid expectancy on their platforms of floating leaves—all these served as a reminder of forces and appetites once alive in her, and now dead.

"It is all—too much. It overpowers, almost frightens me," she had confessed to Stephen in the first week of her stay.

He had regarded her with genuine amazement. "How odd! When I first came here I felt like a starving man who has found food at last—food for his senses. All the beauty, plus the romantic fables—matchless! I've wanted to see Lanka—Ceylon—ever since I read the *Ramayana* in my teens: The prince's faithful wife, Rita, spirited off from India to this enchanted island by the demon king whom she never permitted to be her demon lover; her final rescue by an invasion of monkeys led by the Monkey God—that fantastic legend that's carved and painted on half the walls of this part of Asia. . . . And then there are all the rest of the glorious local yarns. The great days of the Kandy Kings. The stories from the City of Gems. Buddha's footprint on Adam's Peak—though the Moslems say it's Adam's footprint, made when he landed, hurled from Paradise; and the Catholics attribute it to St. Thomas, who passed this way; and the Hindus worship Siva at this spot. . . . Anyway, they *all* climb the Sacred Mountain, sacred to pilgrims of *all* faiths. That's *something*, isn't it? And it's this that makes it possible for me to believe the theory that if there ever *was* a Garden of Eden, Ceylon was the spot. Certainly geologically it's just about the oldest land mass in the world, so one might expect to find the first man here, mightn't one?"

He was rubbing his hands together, clasping and unclasping his long fingers in a way he had when stirred by a flood of ideas. After a moment he added, "Of course it's full of ghosts. A haunted island."

"Whose ghosts?" Caroline had asked, trying not to sound timid.

"All the murderers and the murdered," he replied, with a sardonic grin for her benefit, "for although Ceylon began as the Garden of Eden, like the rest of the earth it's had a very bloody history —one of the bloodiest, as a matter of fact. Also one of the most remarkable." He broke off and after a moment, as though in necessary amplification, but with the intention of teasing her, he added, "And as you may or may not know, Lady B, ghosts never get off islands. They don't take kindly to water travel. That's why places like Ireland and England have their troubles with the departed, too."

To her relief he had dropped the subject there, and she had not asked him any further questions, for she did not wish to be more disturbed than she already was. . . .

FIVE

The ham was going around again, and the salad. How fast they were all eating, except Stephen—stabs of ham, slabs of bread, gulps of milk.

"I'm afraid I have very dawdling eating habits," Lady Brace apologized. She began on her salad with knife and fork; caught Alice Ford eyeing her. Probably taught this style of eating was bad manners.

"We're bolters," Rosemary said complacently, smiling the length of the table at her mother. "It's perfectly disgusting, but we can't seem to change. I suppose it's the tension we live under."

Lady Brace was silent. Did her daughter take pride in what seemed, to her at least, a most unhappy condition?

Outside the windows in the green twilight she glimpsed a yellow figure crossing the terrace, bound for the gardens: Venerable Sir. Her eyes followed him until he blew lightly from her sight like the dandelion clocks she had disturbed that afternoon, and she thought of them both—the flower and the little monk—as ghosts: ghosts of a golden period.

Once again pictures of Ceylon's fabulous Lost Cities, to which Stephen had taken her before her return to England, traversed her memory. Scattered through the jungle, these vast architectural fragments told, in their ruined beauty, a silent tale of an almost incredible culture: a great "irrigation civilization," neglected by archaeology, even by history. Was it, after all, so far-fetched to see their Eastern visitor—glimmering wraithlike in the dusk of a Long Island garden—as a ghost; a twentieth-century messenger from that ancient Golden Era, the gentle guardian of some curious forgotten wisdom perhaps not really gone to ruin, not "lost" like the old cities, but only for a time gone to seed?

5

The moment they had had their coffee, Stephen excused himself to go to his room. Over Lady Brace's feeble protests he insisted to Rosemary that her mother must also retire at once. "And you're to have a tray in bed in the morning, isn't she, Rosie?"

"Absolutely, Uncle Stephen," Rosemary agreed. She rode down her mother's objection by adding, "It's really much easier for all of us, Mummy. Mornings around here are just *sheer* chaos."

Lady Brace was touched by her brother's concern for her fatigue. She longed to go and put her arms around him once more as she said good night, but he had always disliked having any of his kindly impulses observed and so she did not dare. Besides, there was something stern and bitter, almost angry, in the expression on his face when, having curtly refused all help, he started his painful ascent of the long curving double staircase. She even hesitated before calling across softly, "Sleep well, darling."

"You too." His stiff voice reflected the strain the climb was imposing on him.

Rosemary came up behind her mother to put an arm around her waist. "Mummy, you're so slender I could carry you. Lydia got your figure—darn! I really envy her. I guess I must take after Daddy's side of the family."

Stephen spoke from the upper hallway, where he had paused to rest. His voice sounded almost jeering. "The great football player. All-American." He leaned over the banisters with a mocking grin.

Lady Brace ignored her brother. "You've hardly got a football player's figure, darling," she replied to Rosemary.

Rosemary gave a little self-conscious laugh. "What I mean is, I do have to fight weight like *mad*, and I've always thought Daddy probably did too. I don't remember, of course, but judging from his pictures. Those *shoulders!*" She gave another little laugh.

"Of course Todd claims he likes my type. He calls Lydia skinny. I tell him he must be the audience all those bosomy subway ads are aimed at. Aren't men funny? So *different!"*

Lady Brace imagined that she caught in Rosemary's words a faint hint of jealousy. Had the difference between the girls not diminished with the passing years? She remembered how, as a child, Rosemary had been forever trying by stubborn pressures to engage her younger sister in hearty projects on which Lydia invariably turned a cool rejection.

They had reached her bedroom door. Lady Brace pleaded, "Oh, do come in for just a moment, darling. I'm really not terribly tired, and there's so much to talk about." Rosemary stepped inside the door.

"Tell me truly," Lady Brace continued, "are you finding it difficult to have Uncle Stephen here—and his friend?"

"Not at all, Mummy, honestly. At first, I may as well admit, it was rather a shock. Those costumes of Venerable Sir's, those bare feet, and all that. But the children took to him at once. Toddy suggested it might be partly the Hallowe'en color of his outfit. And then both children simply *adored* Uncle Stephen straight off, which really surprised me. He used to frighten the wits out of me when I saw him years ago—once or twice."

Lady Brace determined to ask a further frank question. "And is Uncle Stephen—" she hesitated "—paying for his friend; I mean, for Venerable Sir?"

Rosemary's reply was immediate and heartening.

"Yes, and *more* than generously. Venerable Sir eats none of our food, after all, and he takes care of his own quarters. He's *terrifically* tidy. No, really, he's a very pleasant influence to have in the house."

"Oh, good!" Lady Brace murmured absently. It was one of the automatic phrases she used to fill conversational gaps while she thought of other matters. She was trying to work her way back to the subject that had come up before dinner. She decided to attack it quite directly. "Do tell me more about Lydia. What you said before dinner worries me. Can't you tell me just a little more?"

Rosemary, who had remained standing near the door up to now, decided to sit down. "Oh, I suppose I *could* perfectly well. It's not exactly a *secret*—only I just do try never to discuss Lydia with anyone. People are always trying to pump me about her. I'd just rather *she*'d do the telling, that's all."

She had chosen a low dark-green velvet chair at the foot of the bed. She kicked off her flat slippers and began to do foot exercises on the red rug. "My transverse arches are getting lazy," she remarked, flexing her toes with faint cracking noises.

Her mother held tenaciously to the subject of Lydia. "But you seemed so troubled too, dear. Is something wrong with Frederick Hollis—other than the age difference, I mean?"

"Isn't that enough?" Rosemary demanded. "Good heavens! He *could* be her grandfather—almost." She shrugged in pretended indifference. "Then, of course his wife's not even dead—yet— though dying, I guess." She separated both large toes from the remaining ones and held them apart for a moment with an air of triumph before concluding, "It's just that—well, Lydia's life does seem a bit on the messy side. Not on the surface. Not a *bit* there. She's always so *controlled* and, well, *expert* about handling situations that would be *ghastly* for other people."

"Do be more explicit, darling," Lady Brace said, making an effort not to reveal any irritation. "It can't make one bit of difference whether I learn today or tomorrow, and I certainly shan't tell Lydia that we talked. Why is her life such a mess? Is it because of the children—or what?"

"Again, Mummy, that may just be me reading something into the situation that isn't there at all." Rosemary's anxiety not to outweigh evidence with conjecture seemed quite sincere to her mother. "About the children—well, Little Bill *is* rather more edgy and nervous than a boy his age should be. And I think Pammy's almost *too* phlegmatic, as though she's repressing a lot—which of course you can do at eight just as well as at eighteen. You know, of course, Little Bill was a frightful problem for a time—gave them a lot of trouble."

"I know nothing," Lady Brace said. Had her voice sounded aggrieved, or relieved?

"Well, Bill was *something*, I know—not from Lydia but from his old nurse. He has always simply *adored* his father, of course."

Lady Brace could not shake off the feeling that much more than

41

she could imagine lay beneath Rosemary's disjointed phrases. "But Jack does see the children, doesn't he?"

"Oh, yes, every summer. He takes them to Maine to his family's place. They're with him now, as a matter of fact."

"Is Jack still living in Texas?"

"Yes, and he *says* he loves it. We always see him when he comes on. He'll probably be down from Maine before you leave. I'm sure he'd love to see you. He's doing very well out West, Toddy heard. Nothing fabulous, no gushers or anything like that, but. . . ."

"Gushers?"

"*Oil*. But I do find him greatly changed. He looks sad and—and sort of dead—when he's off guard."

Rosemary stood up abruptly, put on her bright slippers and walked towards the dressing table. She took one of the large old-fashioned silver-backed brushes and began to run it over her thick hair. "I got these brushes out of the vault," she said. "I know you always liked this old set. Granny's, wasn't it?"

Not waiting for a reply, she dropped the brush and picked up the small leather folder holding the six photographs Lady Brace always carried with her when she traveled: the view from her windows at Braceledge over the old garden with the crumbling wall at the far end—all that remained of a fourteenth-century nunnery; Humphrey, prior to his wheelchair days, leaning from a lower window laughing at some forgotten incident—his son at play, perhaps; then Rupert as a schoolboy; Rupert in his Air Force uniform; Lydia and Rosemary as leggy little girls on a beach with spades and pails; Stephen standing alone near a headless figure of a Buddha in the old Ceylon city of Anuradhapura—one she had taken of him on their trip to the Lost Cities.

Rosemary stood gazing at the photographs one by one.

"Is this Uncle Stephen in Ceylon?" she asked. "What is that headless figure?"

"Yes, Ceylon," Lady Brace murmured. "It's a very old Buddha."

"I remember when you went out there," Rosemary said, still holding the leather folder. "You sent us some pictures. I wonder what became of them! Maybe Lydia kept them. And you had Humpy send on to us, after he and Rupert had read them, what you called your 'descriptive letters'—all full of strange birds and snakes and flowers. Very *scary*, I found them."

"Did you, dear?" Lady Brace said. "I'm so sorry. Perhaps that was because I found some of Ceylon scary too."

Rosemary hardly seemed to hear her mother. She stood very still beside the dressing table as if making a special effort to recall what her mother had written so many years ago. She spoke in a level voice, without her usual italics.

"I remember you said the squirrels flew, that they had a sort of parachute for landing; and the lizards had pneumatic footpads that made it possible for them to walk around on the ceilings upside down eating moths and flies. I had terrible nightmares over those lizards! How well I remember!"

"Oh, dear, I *am* sorry," Lady Brace repeated.

Abruptly Rosemary dropped the subject of Ceylon. She continued to hold the leather folder, only now her gaze shifted from her uncle, standing among the ancient ruins of Ceylon, to Rupert in his Air Force uniform. In a quite different tone she remarked, "How handsome Rupert was!"

There was some quality in her daughter's tone that Lady Brace could not analyze; something cold and distant. Yet when she spoke next her voice was astonishingly full of feeling, even passionate.

Turning from the dressing table to face her mother, she exclaimed, "Oh, Mummy, you simply can't imagine how glad I am that I was never put through this divorce horror as a child. I've seen so much of it, and almost all of it is disastrous for the children. *Fatally*, I think."

Now how, Lady Brace asked herself, has Rosemary made this extraordinary leap from my Ceylon letters, through her dead half-brother's good looks, to the subject of divorce? Was the word "nightmare" the clue to it; some memory of shapeless childhood terrors clustered around upside-down lizards snapping at moths on a tropical ceiling?

She found herself murmuring, "But you lost your father, anyway."

Rosemary nodded, her face still tense and distant.

"Yes, and that was bad enough, but I think divorce is far, *far* worse—for a child. Oh, believe me, I think it's really a very different thing altogether. It sounds awful to say, but death is *really* easier for a child to accept."

"I don't entirely understand why."

Lady Brace had become aware of a quickened beating of her heart, as though in the presence of concealed danger. Why should she feel that Rosemary intended some indirect, one might even say circuitous, but nonetheless intentional, criticism of her? Immediately she dismissed this idea as unjustified. It was merely Rosemary's overemphasis and fervor that put her off, the suggestion of an unshakable complacency that lurked under even her obvious concern for her sister.

Yet Lady Brace had to check a momentary impulse to shake her older daughter's smugness. She almost gave way to a never-uttered confession; one she would surely have regretted: *The truth is, Rosemary, if it hadn't been for a horse that fell jumping a ditch—a fall that killed your father—I would surely have had to get a divorce at no matter what cost to you and Lydia.*

Could it be that Rosemary remembered nothing of the tension of those early years; had caught no hint of the scenes that did not always take place behind closed doors? Had it really all been successfully concealed from the children, so that their father remained to them only a vaguely romantic memory embodied in photograph albums and the portrait of him, mounted for polo, that hung in the Trophy Room? Yes, this was quite probably true, for domestic life among people on their social level had been far more stratified in the past, making easier the separation of child from parent after a fashion no longer possible in the loosening structure of present-day society.

It seemed to Caroline Brace that too many moments had passed since either she or Rosemary had spoken. She summoned her flagging energies to utter affectionate appreciative phrases, good-night wishes, plans for the morrow. But before she could speak she saw, across her daughter's shoulder, the reflection of her own face in the mirror, pinched, gray, its contours sagging.

Rosemary must have caught the image at the same moment, for she turned quickly, saying, "Lady B, forgive me. I shouldn't have stayed so long talking. I can see you're utterly *pooped.* I'm going this very sec. Are you sure you've got everything you want and need?"

"I'm sure," Lady Brace said. "Thank you so much for everything, darling. It's heaven to be here. Good night."

Rosemary's embrace was warm, generous with feeling. It seemed to hold nothing back, no lingering tendrils of longing or need; arms, hands, cheek and lips were given fully.

"You and Todd are happy together, aren't you, darling?" It came out less as a question than an observation.

"*Perfectly*, Mummy! Isn't it wonderful? Such good luck!"

"I'm so glad," Lady Brace murmured.

But when she had undressed and lay in the center of the wide bed she asked herself why Rosemary's enthusiastic reply gave her so little inner satisfaction. It was almost as though Rosemary's quick over-easy emphasis robbed the Jordans' relationship of some vital quality.

She rebuked herself. Was it perhaps some tenuous values of her own that were, as the saying went, "warped," rather than something really lacking in Rosemary? But, granted a lack—what then was it?

The word "reality" presented itself, and she considered it with care. Perhaps that was what she meant, though the significance she attached to this word and its dictionary definition had never agreed. Reality, to Caroline Brace, had something to do with "feeling" shorn of all thought, some immediate connection of herself with another, indeed, a dissolving of the very sense of self—as when she had melted into the burning embrace of Ralph Parton, summoning her to pain and ecstasy on the shore of a deserted lake over forty years ago; or when she had moaned in silent anguish over her mutilated son dying in coma; or when her palms had folded around her brother's pointed ears a few hours ago on the terrace.

Tears as sharp as bits of glass pricked her lids for a moment before there rose to the surface of her tired and confused mind a lesser memory—another "reality"?—the bee's blind urgency on the bosom of the everlasting-flower that afternoon in the garden. It was her last conscious image before sleep overtook her.

6

Lady Brace woke early, a habit that had been growing on her since she turned sixty. Some years back she had yielded to the imposition of this new pattern in sleeping and waking. During summers at Braceledge she rose with the first light and went out to work in the gardens before the one remaining gardener, and his part-time assistant, appeared. After an hour or two she would return to bed for tea and a book, remaining there until ten o'clock, when she had regularly gone to Humphrey's room to see what kind of night he had spent.

As she lay now watching the light push slowly into the big room, reaching towards the ponderous forms of the furniture Rosemary so deplored, she was thinking how her late husband's prolonged invalidism had laid an almost ritualistic form on her life. Would she now, as a widow, continue to maintain a semblance of this ritual, or would her trip to America, her return to Fox Meadows as a witness of its final dissolution, propel her out of the familiar orbit of her existence?

Aware of a definite withdrawal somewhere in her interior at the thought of any new and unaccustomed demands being laid upon her, she got out of bed to pull apart the curtains and see what sort of day was promised.

As the curtains folded back she saw first the suffusion of a rosy dawn and then, to her surprise, the yellow-robed figure of the little monk emerging from the gate of the walled garden. Venerable Sir was walking with his full garments caught up from his bare ankles and cupped in loose folds around him; his head down, his step slow but light.

The incongruity of a Buddhist monk's presence here in her grandfather's traditional Long Island house struck Caroline Brace more forcibly than it had the night before. She thought of Stephen's half-mocking speech on the terrace about "missionizing" the West. "The East is preparing its revenge," he had said. Surely such ominous words could never be applied to the peaceful figure passing so quietly now across her view.

She slipped behind the curtain to watch him—though it was not likely that he would glance up at her windows, for he was deep in reverie. Something in the way he moved—unaware, concentrated—seemed to her of special significance; and once her attention became fully arrested, it appeared of the utmost importance that she try to analyze her impressions of this startling figure wandering in the dawn at Fox Meadows.

It is, she thought, as though he carries about with him his own distinct and private space. Yet it was not a sense of actual separateness which he conveyed. He seemed, indeed, very much *in* the scene through which he was now passing: the spreading light on the wet grass, the bird that rocked for a moment on a branch near her window. He appeared related to it all and at the same time subtly, infinitely removed, not only from her, spying on him unseen, but also separated by an incalculable span from the flash of young crows jerking disdainfully at tidbits under the hedge, and even from the last of the pink and purple petunias fading in tubs on the terrace.

Could it be that he was enclosed in the invisible frame known as an "aura"?—for she supposed he had been meditating in the dawn. How did one go about it—meditation—that singular activity, at once quiescent and dynamic, on which the Far East laid such stress? Perhaps this was something, too, about which she might feel bold enough to question Stephen in the next days, for surely her brother could not associate on such intimate terms with the little monk without understanding some of his practices.

What, she asked herself, still standing at the window bemused with the rosy light and her half-awake thoughts, did this stranger, from a world so distant and so unfamiliar, make of the maelstrom of America into which he had so boldly plunged, wearing saffron robes, driving her brother's Thunderbird?—and she smiled at the thought of his bare feet on the pedals.

Fragments of last night's table talk, half-heard, drifted into her mind. . . . Stephen saying, "He doesn't criticize America, he pities it."

"If he weren't such a sweetie pie I'd think that was a little cheeky," Alice Ford put in, but Stephen had ignored her.

"Just the other day," he said, "as we came onto the East River Drive—he hesitated a second too long at a green light and someone yelled, 'Hey, yah jerk, watch what you're doin'!' He managed to bow, to smile sweetly, to say, 'I'm so sorry,' and to get his foot on the pedal all in one motion, and off we shot! Later, when I said what I thought of the fellow who'd yelled at him, he replied mildly, 'It just shows the great strain people are placing on themselves. Poor, poor chap,' he said, 'think of his arteries.' "

Stephen's mimicry of the contrasted voices of Venerable Sir and the irate commuter had made everyone at the table laugh.

"What does he think the strain is?" the Carozzi boy had inquired, his mouth full of hot macaroni.

"Too much activity on the outside, not enough on the inside," Stephen answered promptly, his tone a little acid.

"The plain facts are that we're all running like hell just to continue standing in the same place," Todd had commented.

Then Rosemary, instantly defensive, "But that's hardly *our* fault!"

And Stephen again, "*Whose*, then? All this high-pressure living everybody talks about in America simply comes from *wanting*, doesn't it? If you didn't have such complicated desires, you wouldn't have such complicated lives."

Several voices had spoken up at this point and Lady Brace had not followed the discussion further.

Now with a sigh she looked after the retreating figure in the half-comic yellow garment, the strange little visitor living in the abandoned nursery, cooking his own meals on a two-burner nursery stove.

Her thoughts moved up a flight from the nursery to the waiting attic, to the long-unopened trunks for which she had brought, from England, a collection of miscellaneous keys. For a moment she dwelt unhappily on all the divisions, the parceling out of possessions, in which she must participate during the coming days and weeks. She sighed again. Visions crossed her mind of nuns in bare cells with a small list of fixed possessions, none of them personal; of Thoreau, alone on Walden Pond, almost, but not quite, using a pumpkin for a chair. It was Humphrey, oddly enough, who had told her this about Thoreau, on the day the news came of the bombing of their London house. He had spoken of Walden Pond on the one hand, and, on the other—surprising her with his information—had reminded her of older and nobler works of man that had perished in recent bombardments: the great murals in Pisa, the castle square in Warsaw, Gothic monuments, medieval landmarks. . . .

T W O

Lady Brace drew the curtains once more against the growing light and returned to her bed. She began again to think of the little monk, to wonder how Stephen had come to know a spirit so seemingly detached and pure. Could research in the realm of Evil have brought her complex brother to this association, following one of those ever-turning spiral paths that link together unrelated parts of life? The head of Stephen's walking stick rose before her; the coiled serpent swallowing its own tail. She found the image of the closed circle disturbing. It seemed to imply some oppressive intimation of the fixed and unalterable, to suggest, by association, the destined, even the *pre*-destined. She was waking, she feared, to the very type of thought to which she had so unwillingly yielded the night before.

Perhaps if she lay flat on her back and counted her breathing, she might drift off to sleep once again. But the moment she turned and began to watch the rise and fall of her breath, every nerve in her body sprang to attention; all her senses suddenly seemed sharpened. She caught the noise of trucks on a nearby road; she heard a distant whistle, a blare of harsh ugly sound repeated in convulsive blasts like an expiring mechanical monster.

Nowhere, she thought, could it be escaped any more—noise! Everywhere one encountered the intrusive, insistent whirr, whiz, buzz, grind, chug, churr, clatter, bang, whine, scream, blast. . . . The very sound barrier of the upper atmosphere itself protested when ripped apart—with a clap that could stun thunder. She had heard it once—the sound that announced a new era—on the

English downs; reducing to fossil forms the mouse that quivered beady-eyed in the rusty furze, the wild pony that galloped, fear-maddened, from her sight. Over the old stone house at Braceledge the training jets had plummeted and plunged, soared and swooped. They would be rending the air here too, no doubt, since there must be bases nearby. Humphrey had once suggested a device to slow the pulse and still the mind when the jets shrieked as they dropped through space: the murmuring, in groups-of-three, of old odd words from a dying language: lea, brae, heath; loch, fen, bog; gorse. . . . She had forgotten the rest.

Perhaps these thoughts of Humphrey made her aware of the crows busy now at their morning exchange: gossip, advice, signals of warning and admonition. A real language, Humphrey had told her: "Watch out! Strangers. . . . All clear. Safe! Not a gun barrel, only a walking-stick! . . . Here's a choice morsel!" Yet how raucous, how rude their voices! She could not feel tender about these brash creatures no matter how solid their family relations, how surprising their intelligence. A moth fluttered up beside the bed; it fluttered in silence, in its own silence. Like Venerable Sir, she thought.

She turned on her right side to plug her keener ear with a fold of the sheet, hoping to shut out the waking world. At once she became aware of her heart. As she turned it had leapt deftly from her chest to her ear and was tub-thumping there in frenetic rhythm. What could account for this perversity of the body in the face of the wish to relax? There was no going against it. She got up to search in her bag for a small yellow pill recommended by her doctor for sleeplessness.

She crossed the room to the dressing table where she had placed her small medicine kit the night before. As she reached for it, her eye fell on the leather folder of photographs. Again she saw Rosemary picking it up, examining it, heard her voice, with the undertone she had not been able to analyze, "How handsome Rupert was!"

Lady Brace took the folder in her hands and stood holding it for a moment looking at the face of her dead son. The familiar pain seized her. *Why, why, why?* The old question. Why did it have to be Rupert?

This was a question no one had ever been able to answer in all the weeks the surgeons were removing skin from one part of her son's body surface to graft on another; while they purchased blood at so much a pint for transfusion into his parched veins; while they hideously and artfully applied their skills to hold back the mounting septicemia, removing parts of him slowly, piece by piece, until at last Rupert gave up and died, worn out with the struggle. Now, almost a decade later, she still did not understand any of it: neither his going from her in such agony and mutilation, nor the meaning of bearing him in the first place—the one child who had claimed the very depths of her maternal instinct; born of a gentle, undemanding union that had lacked all the fires, the joys and frenzies, of her first marriage.

Lady Brace closed the folder and put it face down on the dressing table, then fumbled in her kit until she found the little yellow pill. Pouring water from a carafe, she swallowed the pill and returned to bed.

No, the years had not answered her questions, rather they had, mercifully, blunted the nerve ends, dimmed the agonies; as now the little pill would slowly, surely, enfold her in the protective pause of a deep sleep. Perhaps a pause was all one could ever expect, or even hope for. Perhaps Stephen, now never free of physical pain himself, would tell her that this—a brief respite— was all for which one might ever dare petition the inscrutable and invisible Powers one blindly turned to in the darkest hours of life.

7

When Lady Brace awoke again, several hours had passed; the sun was high, the sky a cloudless blue. Because she had promised to remain in her room, she rang the bell for her breakfast.

After some time a wheezy old woman with hair dyed red and apron askew came bringing a tray and the message that Mrs. Jordan had gone to the beach with the children and wouldn't be back until afternoon. Also, Mr. Langdon was about to join her.

She was pouring her second cup of tea when Stephen rapped and put his head in. "Are you viewable?"

"Yes, though not very glamorous, I'm afraid."

"Remember, I said you were beautiful," he replied, making his way across the room, his pinioned arm fixed across his body, his left leg swinging wide. "Don't forget it."

Again she turned her eyes from the painful sight of his lameness. "I'll try not to. Have you breakfasted?"

"Long since. I rise with the dawn."

"Is this a part of some—new regimen?"

"I've been a dawn-waker for years." He was lowering himself onto the chaise longue, all the while making brisk small talk as though unwilling to permit any concessions to his infirmity. "In the East, you may remember, everybody gets up at dawn. In India, particularly. At sunrise they're all out bathing themselves and their cows in any handy pool of scummy water, taking knee bends, chanting prayers."

The sentences issued from him in jerking spasms while he pulled, slid, his stubborn body onto the couch.

Caroline poured more tea, her hands shaking. "Then you aren't —I mean—you don't do morning meditations or anything like that?"

He said shortly, "I try." The tone of his voice informed her that he did not wish to discuss it. "I've persuaded everyone to go along to the beach and give you a free hand with the lovebirds at lunch."

For a moment she did not understand; she had forgotten Lydia and Frederick Hollis. Then she protested. "Oh, Stephen, you shouldn't have done that. I do *so* want not to disturb the household in any way while I'm here."

"Don't be absurd," he rapped. "No one's upset. Much easier all the way around. Rosemary thought it a marvelous idea." He gave her a sharp glance. "And anyway, what are you being so careful about? This place is still yours, technically, isn't it?"

"You know that's not the point."

"Of course I do, but I really can't see why you have to act like an intruder." He put an abrupt question to her. "Are you really sad about seeing this place go?"

She temporized. "I'm not quite sure. Are you?"

"Hardly!" The single word was uttered with a flat finality. After a moment, when she remained silent, he added, "I always hated it—the very name, Fox Meadows. It conjures up a whole era."

"I never loved it as much as the camp in the woods. But of course that's been gone so long." Her voice trailed away on a note of deep personal nostalgia.

Stephen's response to the mention of their father's mountain camp was almost harsh. "The Adirondacks place? I hated that even more."

"I know," she murmured, but in spite of his tone of dismissal, she continued for a moment to enjoy her own memory of the moon rising over the smooth crown of Black Bear Mountain, opposite the sprawling lodge of dark-stained logs; the shuddering cry of an owl; the sound of a lovesick bullfrog thudding desperately under the dock as, in the eerie light, hunting bats skimmed the milky surface of the lake. . . . Bat! What was that about a bat? She creased her brow. Some unpleasant recollection hovering just out of reach . . .

"Anyway, I'm through with wanting any complicated possessions," Stephen was saying. "The lighter the load the easier the climb."

For a moment she thought of inquiring: "Climb to *where*; what climb?" Instead she said, "You'll be at lunch with Lydia and Frederick, won't you? I'll need you." She did indeed feel slightly panicky about seeing her daughter and her old friend's husband, alone.

Stephen replied, "I don't eat lunch." He glanced at her disappointed face; relented a little. "But I'll join you for coffee if you like."

"I would like."

Stephen painstakingly fitted a pillow behind his head. Again Caroline looked away in distress.

"You've seen Lydia and Frederick Hollis together—what did you think of it—of them?" she asked.

"What is there to think about? It's all perfectly plain and obvious."

She winced, preparing herself for the needle.

He went on, "Lydia missed out in one area, so she's going to make up for it in another. If she can't have sex, she'll take money. Both forms of energy. Equally abstract."

She murmured a protest. "Oh, Stephen, *don't* talk like that."

He paid no attention. "How our generation still shies away from that word sex," he said. "Maybe the young do too, for all I know, and in spite of all their cool talk. It's probably sensible at that—to flinch from the very word itself. Once you get into any close association with sex you have to immerse yourself totally or give it up altogether. There's no middle ground. That's something only the East has ever really understood. Kinsey and all his so-called findings—bah! That pseudoscientific approach so many Americans fall for!"

This fresh flurry of disjointed talk seemed intended to distract her attention from his further awkward physical maneuvers. He was now attempting to lift his inert leg onto the chaise. She could bear it no longer, "Darling, can't I help?"

"No." He spoke gruffly, then at once, as though in apology, "I'm supposed to make myself do things. It's a form of therapy."

In position at last, he lay back, appeared to make a conscious effort to erase the look of strain from his face before continuing on the subject of Lydia and Frederick Hollis, without, however, altering his former supercilious tone.

"As to Lydia—well, she's your daughter. Suppose you tell me what she's really like. As to Frederick Hollis, you know him quite as well as I do, if not better."

"But I haven't seen him in years and years. I haven't even given him a thought. He will be a total stranger to me." She waited.

"Well," Stephen began slowly, "he's immensely rich—that you certainly know. He spends a good deal of his time keeping fit. Todd tells me he has a body-servant who has traveled with him all over the globe learning to give the massages of every country —and God knows what other fancy manipulations. As a result he has the body of a man of forty—thirty-five, even. He's a great health faddist; smokes not at all; drinks what he likes but only after daily shots of soybean juice, vitamin B, liquid calves' feet. . . . I suspect him of perfectly hideous secret vices."

He broke off at sight of her shocked and apprehensive face, then laughed. "Don't take me so seriously, Caro. You know how I babble. I'm only joking. The health regime is the truth, however. Todd tells me he even invested in a chain of health-food stores as a sort of hobby, and they were a huge success, of course— since he didn't need the money. Todd insists he made another million by bottling algae off old ponds and dehydrating sea kelp —*that* sort of thing . . . And what else? Let's see! Ah yes, his wife—bedridden, a hopeless invalid."

"Yes, I know." Lady Brace hesitated, decided to tell him. "You probably don't remember, but—I was a bridesmaid at their wedding." She added with an irony that she did not intend, "We thought then that Belle was marrying an older man. I think he was five or six years our senior."

Stephen whistled. "That's a touch. Does he remember?"

"I should think he must—but perhaps not."

"Well, I doubt his having mentioned it to Lydia. Oh, one other thing, be prepared for his fancy get-ups. I've seen him twice and both times he was dressed like my idea of a gangster. You know, hand-painted hula-maiden ties and palm-frond shirts, tails out. It's a new style. Hollywood influence, maybe; part of Down-with-Dull-Gentility."

"That does surprise me," she said. "I remember him as rather conservative." She sighed. "Oh, what *can* be going on in Lydia! He does sound rather awful."

"Perfectly familiar species," Stephen said blandly. "Pure power-elite type."

She widened her gaze in astonishment. "Power elite?" she repeated.

Stephen did not amplify the term, and in the silence that followed she thought again of how her quiet years at Braceledge— in spite of the war with its losses and tragedies—had been essentially removed from what one thought of as "the world." The vocabulary employed by Humphrey, and such old friends as infrequently visited him in Somerset, was not really modern in any sense; and its only claim to intellectuality had lain in rather fuzzy discussions about the decline of the British Empire, or, on rare occasions, the status of traditional religion, for Humphrey had always indulged himself in a sort of gentlemanly agnosticism that, to all appearances, flourished perfectly comfortably in the very bosom of the Church of England. She recalled once that Rosemary, in her teens, had been shocked at her stepfather's quoting something from the Bible with mild irreverence.

Her thoughts wandered back to Lydia. "Oh, dear! Sometimes I can't but wonder," she began, and broke off without completing the sentence.

After a moment, Stephen inquired, "Wonder what?"

"If I did right to give in to the girls; let them come back to New York to be with Bertha during their school years, instead of insisting they stay with me. But they were so stubborn about it, so unyielding, and I couldn't see much reason at the time for making all of us miserable. They did so hate their English school. It seemed to have something to do with those long black cotton stockings and no central heating. And they simply refused to be taught at home."

"You've always been too easygoing, Lady B," Stephen said, though not unkindly.

"Yes," she admitted in a regretful voice. "I'm weak-willed."

"I don't know that I'd say that," he replied with a slight note of asperity. "But anyway, isn't it a little late to be worrying your head about what you did or didn't do with your daughters, so many years ago?"

"I suppose so." Yet as she spoke she realized that it did not seem late, or even "past." It seemed a current problem, suddenly become vital and present after lurking for years in the background —"out of mind" as one said.

"Oh, how difficult it is to know right from wrong," she exclaimed. "If one has a choice," she added.

Stephen gave her a penetrating glance. "Ah, that's the point— yes. The terrible luxury of choice. How it complicates one's existence—like all responsibilities."

The idea seemed new to her: choice as a responsibility. She considered it while Stephen, lifting his stick, thrust the middle fingers of his good hand through the circle made by the carved serpent and stabbed lightly at the red carpet.

"That's what we had—choice. We didn't understand what a responsibility it was. We didn't know how to handle it—weren't really taught. Perhaps the chance to use it, understand it—this opportunity, this responsibility—passed too fast. No one was to blame. Not us. Not even our parents, or our grandparents, really."

Ah, she thought, this is something new in Stephen. This is tolerance, almost compassion; he is extending it even to Papa. So he has really changed. She saw the figure of Venerable Sir coming from the garden in the dawn light.

Stephen was continuing his remarks, the metal tip of his stick making a series of dents in a circle on the rug. "Almost before we realized—people of our sort, people with inherited privileges—what it meant to be what we were—" he shrugged "—we were gone. Yes, we may seem only to be *going* in this country, but the truth is we're already *gone!* And it's plain we didn't make much of a record with all we had, did we?"

He was demanding an answer of her. Unprepared for his sudden change of tone, "No, I suppose we didn't," she murmured, hardly knowing what she said.

But because he had created for her threatening images of social earthquake, landslide, avalanche, and she wanted rather to think in terms of erosion, slow mutation, she added on a tentative note, "But surely . . . you can't mean . . . that is, isn't one privileged group going down as another comes up—always?"

He croaked, "Of course. There are always the new barbarians."

There was small comfort in this remark. She wavered between challenging it and plunging boldly into a subject which interested her more—his friend the little monk.

While she hesitated Stephen struck from a new direction. "Tell me, Caro, do you think you ever really deeply loved anyone?"

The startling question, which in the past would have thrown her quite off balance, or inclined her to put up her guard in anticipation of unpleasant probing, for some reason did not disturb her. Instead of parrying as she had learned to do years before whenever Stephen threatened to assault secret feelings, she considered the question gravely. After a moment, her head bent, she answered in a low voice, "I have deeply loved three people. Rupert, Ralph and you." She added, "And Humphrey, too, of course."

"Humphrey—an obvious afterthought," he accused her.

"No, not really. It's only that, well, somehow Humphrey seemed different." It was, she realized, a very lame reply, one not likely to pass unchallenged.

"How different?" Stephen pressed.

She found herself still not resisting this blunt interrogation; she even found something stimulating in it. Many years had passed since she had indulged herself in any frank or intimate exchange. Indeed, Stephen was the one person in the world with whom she had ever approached this sort of talk, though had Rupert lived she believed they might have finally been able to establish an unusual degree of conversational candor.

"Humphrey never seemed—mysterious to me. With you, with Rupert, with Ralph, there *was* something mysterious, something —deep, subterranean, that I couldn't fathom. It went way down somewhere, far below my mind—or even my heart." She broke off, impatient with herself and already a little regretful at having lent herself so fully to Stephen's morning mood.

"Yes," he said in a low tone, "Maybe links from other lives. I've always thought I'd known you somewhere before." And then, with an immediate, almost rough dismissal of his own words, "Which is probably sheer Rosicrucian rubbish. The mystery is probably all to be found in that one word *sex*. Sex pure and simple—which means neither pure *nor* simple, of course."

Lady Brace was tempted to remark that he could hardly believe the application of this abused word simplified a matter as complex as human relationships. But she did not speak, for she had an uncomfortable conviction that Stephen was now preparing one of his shock treatments. She stiffened in preparation for it.

He was looking out the windows at the sky above the garden, his fingers still curled hard on the circular wooden snake. "Had it been real love you felt for Ralph Parton," he said, "you would never have been so relieved to hear he was dead."

Her heart gave a jump. "Please don't talk like that, Stephen."

But he was not to be stopped now. "Oh, I know how you felt about your first husband, my dear—from the beginning, right through to the end. I know what you endured after you married him—even though you never told me, or anybody else. I knew because I had always adored you, Caro, and no one else. And not innocently, believe me, but violently, possessively. I could have killed Ralph Parton the day you married him."

She heard the heavy beating of her heart. Almost in anger she thought to herself: As usual, Stephen has overdone it. Our honest exchange has become an assault on his part. There is a great streak of cruelty in him, always has been. She decided to pull him up short, if possible, with a cold remark.

"I never thought you would commit murder, but I used to be afraid you would kill yourself sometime, in one of your black moods."

He was still looking away, out the window, his hand clenched on his stick. "You were right. I often wished to; even tried to once —years ago. But that's all over now. That's what Venerable Sir has done for me; shown me that I *was* half-dead and that's what made *complete* death seem attractive to me. Now my body may be half-dead but not the rest of me. I'm just beginning to come alive."

There was an almost triumphant quality in his last words. She ventured a question. "Why did you consider yourself half-dead?"

His reply astonished her. "Because I'd repressed so much—to borrow a psychological term."

She wanted to exclaim, "But you never repressed anything! You were forever talking about what you felt, saw, imagined, believed." Ah, yes, she corrected herself, but always with the most intimate kernel withheld. What actually had she ever known of her brother's secret life, from the days of the muttered lines from Aubrey Beardsley, right through the years of association in Ceylon with John van der Wadel, down to the present and his undefined bond with Venerable Sir?

They had been silent for some minutes. Now, as she wondered what she could possibly say to him next, he began to push his body into an upright position, preparing to leave.

"Don't go!" she said. She did not wish to be alone just now.

"I'll see you after lunch." His intonation was final; it permitted no pleading. Without another word he made his fumbling way from the room.

She lay back on the pillow, the breakfast tray pushed to one side of the wide bed. Oh, why did he have to say all this to me now? What purpose was served by any of it, in particular, by his admission of possessive love for me? She felt a dull ache of old resentment; Stephen once more, with his pointed questions, his dramatic statements, his shocking hints, forcing her thoughts, her remembrance, into areas she had no desire to penetrate. . . .

The door was opening, Stephen was thrusting his head in once more. "Lady B, forgive me. I probably said too much. I'm sorry."

He seemed to her like a little boy standing there trying to apologize, his twisted mouth caught in a half-rueful, half-ashamed smile.

"Of course, dear," she said, at once. "I didn't really mind."

"It's just," Stephen continued, obviously forcing himself to explain, "just that I feel—increasingly—that I must get rid of the past. Let go of it. All of it. Not that I ever totally can, of course. But at least I—well, I must at least try to sink a shaft down into it, let in some light . . ." He spoke with difficulty and she saw the pallor again seeping through his suntanned skin.

She could not keep from crying, "But why must you make such an effort—you, or anyone? Why not leave the past alone?"

"Let the dead past bury its dead? Yes, I know. That's one way. But not for me any more. I've got to accept the past—all of it—to be rid of it. And I can't do that if I don't understand it."

She waited for him to continue. He stood quietly in the doorway, not looking at her at all but across the room again, at the sky outside. The silence endured until at last she felt compelled to break it. "Is this a part of Venerable Sir's teaching—what you've just said?"

With the same apparent hesitation he answered, "No, not his teaching exactly. But his influence, certainly." He stopped again. "It's not simple to explain, Caro, but I'll try sometime, while you're here. Or maybe Venerable Sir will talk to you about his beliefs—if you wish."

"Yes," she murmured, but the idea was not appealing. She had last sought answers for disturbing questions when Rupert died. She had found no solace then and had come to believe it was not to be found anywhere. And if solace was not to be had by digging in the depths, why dig?

"And if you accept the past what does that do for the present?" she asked with more pertinacity than she had intended.

Then he did look at her. "Makes accepting it easier too," he replied. He turned and once more went out the door.

For a moment she listened to his stumbling steps echoing down the hall, before again lying back on the pillows. Would it be better if one did remember more? Isn't it really wiser to forget as much as possible? Or does this backward probing really affect the present moment in some specific and important way?

T W O

Deliberately she tried sending her mind back to the summer in the north woods when she had met Ralph Parton. Broken bits of memory, insignificant at first glance, floated to the surface of her consciousness and beckoned her on: slide of canoes in dark water, languorous summer murmur, lap and stir, whisper and stroke—water, leaf, paddle, bird's wing. . . .

The scene widened. A great white moon rose above the lake.

It was the summer always known in family chronicles as the summer Stephen had all his accidents: a fish hook caught in his cheek; a ligament was torn in his knee when he fell on the tennis court; he had tipped over in a squall in the sailboat, the boom knocking him unconscious. It had been Ralph Parton who saved him. Nowadays, she supposed, people would say none of this series of mishaps was accidental—didn't noted psychiatrists declare, "There are no accidents"? And so, she supposed, Stephen's ill-fated summer could be explained as coming only from an upset state of mind.

She felt no opposition to this particular theory, was, indeed, even prepared to lump her various allergies, including her intermittent asthma, under the term Alice Ford had applied to such afflictions at the dinner table the night before: "psychosomatic." Still, the new vocabulary did not seem to make the matter any clearer, or any easier to deal with.

She realized that she was luring her memory away from that special summer in the north woods, tempting her mind to drift into shapeless generalizations, into a field of speculation in which she was, admittedly, not very well informed.

Sternly she forced her memory back. Take the moon you were just remembering—why that particular moon?

It obligingly rose again, over the spires of the spruce, a child's drawing—chalk-white surface, jack-o'-lantern grimace. What was there about this ghostly kindergarten image that could return itself to her, after almost half a century, with more clarity than a moon seen a week ago? Was it perhaps the way it had hung over the trees, like a paper cutout, a little lopsided, magical and laughable, at once implausible and very real?

That late-summer moon had marked the end of a phase of her life. Childhood—was that it? Farewell to naïveté, to innocent imagery? With the rising of this particular moon, nursery shadows—half-delicious terrors—became exchanged for other fears born of knowledge. There followed on this moon's appearance in the August sky, the *necessity*—no longer the *game*—of masquerade.

Just out of reach, in some deeper recess of her mind, a shapeless recollection now hovered, a disquieting episode, not remembered, yet not entirely forgotten either; something involving Stephen, or so it seemed. She waited, thought hard, but could not capture it.

Finally she turned from this apparently inaccessible recollection back to the picture of the milky lake, to the canoe and the young man paddling it. She saw Ralph Parton's striped blazer, his dark slicked-down pompadour glistening under the white sky. Once again she heard the moon-stirred bird calling from some hidden place on the shore. "Listen," she said, "the *weltschmerz* bird."

"The what?" Ralph demanded, half-amused, half-scornful, his paddle held suspended.

"Just a bird," she answered, a shade too quickly.

"What did you call it?"

"Oh, just a silly name Stephen gave it."

"Don't you know its real name?"

She did, but checked the immediate "Of course," and said instead, with a guile that astounded her, "No, and I'd like to."

"Why?"

"Well, to know the name of anything gives you power over it, doesn't it?" Again she was quoting Stephen.

Ralph Parton still held his paddle suspended, looking at her intently. She gazed back into the dark enchantment of the face which had already claimed her, which she was never to understand, was, indeed, to learn to hate and desire in alternate rhythms of fear and rapture, until fear at last triumphed. The extraordinary intensity of the dark-brown eyes, the full mouth, sullen, sensual, cruelly and beautifully formed.

"You're a queer girl," he said, and it was in that instant she knew for sure he was in love with her. "If you really want to know," he went on in his husky voice, "it's a whitethroat—that's half its song only, because it's getting late in the season."

"And I suppose the moon has maddened it," she dared.

But there was no place in Ralph Parton's imagination for this kind of idea. "Just too bright to sleep," he said flatly.

His fumbling statement about the relation between song and love in the whitethroat was, she had sensed even then, as near to poetry as Ralph Parton could ever come. Yet her awareness of this lack in him had served a fateful purpose, had been, in fact, just what was needed to dispel her first instinctive misgivings about a young man so unlike any other she had yet known. It had, above all, stirred her to a deeper pity—a pity already aroused by her knowledge of the many unhappy circumstances surrounding his adolescence and young manhood.

His mother—everyone knew she had taken to drink and been put away in a sanitarium. And hadn't he been raised only by an indifferent father, a grim Scotch tutor and a houseful of careless servants? True, he had a sister, fat, athletic and bossy—"Bustling Busty Bertha," as Stephen called her. But it was generally agreed on all sides that young Parton's home life could well account for his wildness, his aggressive nature, his overweening anxiety to win at games, to assert his physical prowess. What he needed, "they" all said—from old Annie to Mademoiselle Fleury—was a little quiet love, devotion, gentle attachment.

But pity for Ralph had not been the decisive factor in her decision to marry him. The force of his sexual magnetism had been persuasion enough. The evening of the whitethroat and the lopsided moon—that was the first night he had kissed her. It had not been the embrace, furtive and cautious, other young men had tried. It had come with the force—alarming and compelling—of a grown man, an already experienced lover, accustomed to riding with the torrent of his feeling, no checkrein used or wanted. She had known at once that there could be no turning back for her.

In spite of her secret guilt about her wholehearted response to his love-making, she had not feared to tell her father of her wish to marry Ralph, nor felt the slightest apprehension when Ralph, spurred by his delighted parent, came to speak with her father formally. She was certain her father would be pleased, and pleased for a reason beyond the fact that the Langdons and the Partons belonged to the same world, that at her marriage his only daughter would not be moved out of his orbit.

. . . She saw her father making his way along the waterline of a lonely northern lake. He wore only British walking shorts, socks to the knee and a sun helmet; garments considered at that time—locally at least—the ultimate in outlandish apparel. Her father, supremely indifferent to any criticism of his costume, advanced with an air at once guarded and alert, like a hunter stalking a nameless quarry, though he carried no gun.

Just a little behind him walked Ralph Parton, a young man whom she then hardly knew. He was moving straight ahead in the same concentrated, forceful manner as her father.

And here she was behind the two men, feeling strangely cut off and alone, almost fearful. Something in their similar way of moving, in the very sight of the muscles of their wide and powerful backs, the stiff and unnatural angle at which their heads were held, filled her with an uneasy dread.

Then she saw Stephen, a little to one side—as always, a little to one side. Delicate and thin, "spindly," Annie said; she noted how his shoulder blades protruded through the protection of his cotton shirt. His whole body seemed to droop, not from fatigue but from boredom. He was evincing none of the interest he showed on trips with their old guide, tobacco-chewing, grammar-fracturing Ed Mosely, when, together, they freshened blazes, looked for deer beds, otter slides, beaver sign. Stephen had today even been walking in the shallows making annoying splashing sounds on the rocks—certain to frighten off all the wild life they hoped to see on these expeditions—and twice his father had had to ask him, in an exasperated voice, to be good enough not to whistle.

The moment Stephen caught her eye he began to create pantomimes to relieve the tedium of the journey—as if suggesting that she too must feel as he did. He took off his battered fishing hat and, making it into a shapeless puppet, toyed with it on the end of a stick, tossed it dangerously into the air, rescued it ludicrously in the nick of time, flicked it on and off huckleberry bushes and the peaks of low-growing conifers until, "Put on your hat," his father said, without seeming to look around. "And keep it on!" It was not an arbitrary command, for Stephen had fallen asleep on the dock a few days past and come near to sunstroke.

Stephen obeyed without spoken protest, only pausing long enough, before returning the hat to his head, to thrust three large green plumes of fern through its stained band.

At last they had arrived at their fixed destination, a favorite picnic place near a spring, long ago named by Stephen, "The Little Lonely." Here Stephen dutifully opened his packet of sandwiches with the others, but he took only a few bites. He lay sprawled against a mossy log, not joining in the conversation in any way, playing now with the three ferns in his hat band, curling them first one way, then another, saying softly, for her ear alone, "Bersagliere," then "D'Artagnan," then, deftly exchanging the ferns for a tuft of balsam, "Spiessburgher."

"Stop fooling with that hat," her father said, "and eat your lunch! You too, Caroline." He barked it out; a command. They were both too old to be spoken to like children. She grew red; Stephen pale. Ralph looked at them both just once, quickly, and as quickly away.

It was as though the blade of an invisible knife had divided the cool green space between the four of them.

8

Frederick Hollis and Lydia were, it was by now quite plain, going to be very late for lunch. Lady Brace only hoped that Rosemary, before she left, had not planned a menu with possibilities of congealing, slumping, melting, for this meeting with her daughter and Frederick Hollis would surely be difficult enough without the addition of minor kitchen disasters.

She was waiting alone in the sunroom, towards which the entire household at Fox Meadows seemed to gravitate, though the room possessed no real charm—less now than ever, with its shabby jumble of unrelated objects. Was it a special favorite because it offered a ready exit in two possible directions; either towards a hidden back stairway, or the garden?

She rebuked herself for this thought. So far no one in the Jordan household appeared to wish to avoid anyone else. Perhaps her own attraction to the sunroom sprang from her childhood shyness; or from her years of residence here with Ralph, when it had represented the welcome possibility of quick escape from his sudden, towering rages.

Again a shadow of unease fell across her spirit. She rose to walk through the wide hallway, hoping to recapture yesterday's pleasure in the formal arrangement of furniture, in the rich soothing blues of the old rugs and the Lowestoft.

Stephen had asked her how she felt about Fox Meadows going to strangers. Had she temporized with her real feelings in replying, "I'm not sure"? Might she not at any moment begin to suffer at the thought of the Langdon stronghold, and Langdon possessions, passing to strangers?

The question of who would eventually buy the big sprawling place was one not easily answered. "Old estates like this one are a drug on the market," Todd had said. "Even the new millionaires

—and I'm told there are a lot of them—can't recruit the staffs they need. In the firm's opinion," he continued, in what Lady Brace took to be his legal consultant's voice, "our best chance is to sell it for use as a sanitarium. They say there aren't enough around to house all the growing army of addicts—of one sort or another."

Lady Brace's low exclamation of amazement at this piece of news was lost in Rosemary's eager rush of words.

"It *could* make a *lovely* house of retreat. I think our best chance is the Roman Catholic Church. They've bought several old places down here."

"And if neither of these two things occurs?" Lady Brace had inquired.

Her son-in-law had looked at her with an expression of kindness and regret, as though he feared his answer would be painful. "Then," he said, "it will simply have to be torn down and sold for the paneling and the fixtures and the old bricks—that sort of thing."

This brief conversation had taken place just after dinner the night before. Had Stephen not been hovering about, waiting for her to follow his dictum of an immediate bedtime, Lady Brace would have ventured to put to her daughter and son-in-law the question of their honest feelings about leaving Fox Meadows, where they had lived since their marriage. She worried that they might find it difficult to adjust to a less expansive setting, though running this great place with an inadequate staff must certainly have had its drawbacks.

From the entrance hall she now walked slowly into the large drawing room and was relieved, at first glance, to have her trained eye inform her that someone had put the room in order. There were no flowers, but branches of pine and rhododendron had been placed in tall crackleware vases. Their unusual arrangement suggested Stephen. He had probably done it for her, she thought with pleasure.

After her first quick appraisal she glanced about a little warily, as if hoping to avoid any poignant reminders of the past. Her eye was caught by the two Chelsea sporting figures on the mantelpiece. At once there rose her long-forgotten but still lively distaste for these absurd kilted figures with their set poses and loot of dangling birds in listless grasp. Yet it was characteristic that even in the years after her first marriage, when, following her father's heart attack, she and Ralph had come to share Fox Meadows with him, she had not removed these valuable china horrors—or, for that matter, anything else she disliked.

Stephen had accused her at breakfast of being too easygoing. She had countered that she was weak-willed, and this he had denied. What word, she wondered, would most accurately describe that trait—inherent, or early acquired—that made her flinch from imposing her tastes, her opinions, her point of view, on others?

Since she did not feel in any mood for self-analysis, she dropped the question as she walked through the cool, shaded room, noting the old oils: English hunting scenes, Dutch still lifes— valuable, she was sure. There was even a group of family portraits. Stiff and quaint, almost classifiable as "primitives," they had come from a collateral Massachusetts branch of the family. What was to become of such heirlooms? She wanted none of them for herself, and if they made no appeal to Rosemary or Lydia, they might well come to rest in the houses of strangers who, unhampered by genealogical accretions of their own, would gladly bid high for possession of Uncle Caleb Ladd's stern brow, Aunt Hetebel's imposing chignon and furtive simper.

Lady Brace moved on into the adjoining library, where she found the shades drawn tight, perhaps to hide the dust that blurred the long rows of leather-bound classics and lay in a thick film on the worn but handsome eighteenth-century furniture and on the two mammoth, time-yellowed, celestial and terrestrial globes beside the fireplace. Was this neglected room a proof of what she had heard—that Americans were ceasing to read books? She might have lingered to consider the question had her sensitive nostrils not warned her of hidden mold and forced her to leave in haste, glancing back only at the Canaletto hanging over the mantelpiece. The magic golden ambience of long-ago Venice seemed to her more living than anything else in the room.

It was obvious that the formal salon, used in the past for receptions and small balls, was not deserted. Although the cut-glass- and-ormolu chandeliers and side lights hung swathed in veiling, like aging beauties, and all the painted and gilded Louis XV chairs, the little intimate sofas, had been moved against the wall and covered with plastic shirts, this interior was plainly enjoying a new lease of hearty life. A space had been cleared to make room for a ping-pong table, and, at one end, a large television set blocked off the lower part of a floor-to-ceiling mirror. In front of the television box, like a small impromptu theatre, a disarray of miscellaneous chairs and hassocks had been placed. Theatre, thought Lady Brace, has returned to the private residence. The idea amused her.

As she turned to leave she looked at a large bronze clock, designed with sprays of roses and cupids rioting around a flute-playing gentleman and a lady with a fan in Watteau pose. On impulse she approached closer to read the feathery hands. The clock had stopped at two-thirty. How fitting, she said to herself, if it had been midnight: the only proper hour for the private ballroom of a dead era to come to an end.

T W O

There remained to her now only the Trophy Room, perhaps, in a way, the very heart of Fox Meadows, and thus to be approached, after long absence, with a certain stiffening of the spirit. Begun by her grandfather, maintained and added to by her father, it served as a sort of private museum of mementoes attesting to the family's prowess at sports and games, their extended travels in out-of-the-way places, their many intimate associations with celebrities.

At her first glimpse in years of this highly organized clutter Lady Brace burst out laughing. Directly inside the door, Rosemary's solution to the problem of turning the Trophy Room into a nursery adjunct became all too evident. There was a battered upright piano with beginners' pieces on the music rack, and beyond the piano, on an immense center table—a slab of teakwood supported by the lifted trunks of a file of elephants—were scattered schoolbooks, pencils, pens, and a red portable typewriter.

Because of the thick shade cast by the chestnut trees outside, Lady Brace turned to a row of electric wall switches. She succeeded in lighting the graciously curved vitrines built into the four corners to hold the many gold and silver cups, urns, and plaques won by male and female Langdons and their highly bred animals.

The tarnished condition of these objects led her to wonder why Rosemary had not stored them in the vault. Had she left them out hoping perhaps to impress her children, to give them some sense of adventurous ancestry while they sat studying geography and arithmetic under crossed Saracen daggers, ancient Chinese battleaxes and racks of antique guns, in the company of mounted heads of grizzly bear, tiger and rare mountain goat?

So far as she knew neither of her own daughters went in for games or sports of any kind. Had the sporting blood of the Langdons died out?

She picked up a cup or two at random, reading the inscriptions: won by horses for speed and stamina; won by dogs at field trials; won by humans at fly-casting, court tennis, sailboat racing, polo. . . . If she looked carefully she would surely come on one or two modest but tangible proofs of her own prowess, for, since her father had expected it of her, she had learned to ride, play tennis, shoot, sail, and swim—all in better than average style. Yet, she thought now, this entire activity had been the performance of an unknown automaton. Where had the real—or, if not the real, then the present—Caroline Brace been while, as Caroline Langdon, she took fences on Starlight, aimed at clay pigeons, tacked so expertly into the wind on the Sound?

Again, impatient, she was aware of the direction her thoughts insisted on taking these last days. She turned away from the vitrines, from these forever memorialized moments of triumph, exhaustion, elation, pride, towards a wall space given over to photographs, framed alike in white and black, each carefully labeled. There was her father on horseback holding the lead rein of a pony on which she was sitting: *J.L.L. on Fidelity: Ladybug on Mouse*. Next to it, mounted, dressed for a hunt: *Carol and Stephen on Starlight and Corsair*.

Her brother's glum looks registered down all the years. She heard her spontaneous laughter again ringing out in the musty room. Stephen, who loathed to hunt and cared little for horses, had ridden Corsair so hard he had broken his wind. After that no one had bothered to bully him into his riding clothes.

She heard her father saying, "Lady B, I don't know why you won't work a little harder at sports. You could be very good, you know. I'm afraid Stephen's a bad influence."

But had it been Stephen? Had he been the one who made her feel it did not matter to improve her backhand or be in at the kill? Was it not perhaps some strain from those "crazy Southern Archers," as her father had upon occasion declared when his impatience at Stephen's inattentiveness and indifference got out of bounds? (One Archer uncle had translated from the French; an aunt had composed music.) Still, one could as well lay it at the door of the Northern Langdons, she thought now, glancing towards a large glass case backed with green baize that held an odd collection of curiously incised stones.

She walked over to read the inscription. *Churinga: Stones from aboriginal Australia; believed to represent the souls of the dead, dropped at sacred spots by the god of their totem.* She had never entirely understood the inscription, did not to this day, but the words "aboriginal," "god," "totem," still sent little shivers up her spine, as they had in childhood.

Grandfather Langdon—family legend and even her father's cautiously censored anecdotes made plain—had definitely possessed a bizarre streak. He had, for instance, refused to permit any departed members of his family (and he had lost all his children but one, and two wives) to have tombstones. In his opinion, tombstones were only relics of an ancient superstition, primitive man's belief that the souls of the dead had to be bound down to keep them from doing harm to the living; a bit of anthropological information picked up, along with the collection of *churinga*, on a fishing trip to Australia during his young manhood.

Of the burial of family pets, however, Grandfather Langdon had made a notable exception. Lady Brace recalled the day Humphrey had paid his first visit to Fox Meadows—a lazy spring Sunday when she had taken him over the entire estate, as far as the remote plot where the family pets lay in impressive rows, under portrait headstones designed by the leading animal sculptors of her grandfather's day: Greylock, the chestnut gelding; Stickleburr, the great three-year-old who had broken his leg and been shot at the height of his career; and the dogs, Robin Goodfellow, a British bull; Lady Guinevere, a collie, "best of breed, best in show.". . .

"Only celebrities?" Humphrey had inquired.

"Oh, no," she had denied, "not at all. I remember Papa making that point with us once, right at this spot. Somewhere there's a headstone to Champion, who was definitely backstairs. It reads, 'Champion, a noble and lion-hearted mutt.' "

She hadn't been sure that she entirely understood Humphrey's laughter or his remark, "If your family should ever get really hard up, you might charge admission to this graveyard. One of my great-aunts in Somerset did that with a private burial ground. She got it listed in tourists' sights. Pays for its upkeep that way."

What, Lady Brace wondered now, *had* been done about the unique animal graveyard at Fox Meadows? For a moment it seemed important to her, this small spot of earth which significantly and permanently revealed the streak of eccentricity underneath all the conventional outer surface of her grandfather Langdon's successful career; the career in which, as set down in American financial history, mergers, coups, even crashes involving economic hierarchies and millions in funds, had represented—for the men who participated—a highly personal drama of adventure, not too different from big-game hunting, or the competition for possession of any valuable object that caught their fickle fancies. Yet it had been an adventure of some dimension, she could not but think; an assault, a brigand's attack on life that made the lives of the next generations—hers and her children's—seem dull and anaemic, by contrast.

9

She became aware of wheels on the gravel drive. Crossing to the window, she was just in time to see a dark-green Rolls-Royce pull up under the chestnut tree. Hidden from sight, she stood and deliberately watched the small tableau of the chauffeur, her daughter Lydia, and Frederick Hollis.

The chauffeur, whose livery was the same color as the Rolls-Royce, leapt out and opened the door with the speed, precision, and impassivity of a servant held to a high standard of performance. Lady Brace could not help admiring his demeanor.

Lydia descended from the open car door into the dappled light under the pierced umbrella of the chestnut tree. She wore a tight sheath of beige silk almost the shade of her hair, and her sun-tanned legs, elegantly long and slender, ended in high-heeled sandals that exactly matched a green bag. As she put up her right hand to her chic hair, Lady Brace caught a glimpse of an immense green stone. Could it be an emerald, designedly worn on the right hand to avert suspicion as to the giver's intention?

Frederick Hollis, descending after Lydia, stopped to speak to the chauffeur and to extend to him an oblong white box. He plainly motioned towards the kitchen wing. Recalling her brother's remarks that morning, Lady Brace found herself wondering if Frederick Hollis, like Venerable Sir, allowed himself only certain kinds of food.

The pause for instructions to his chauffeur gave Lady Brace a chance to observe him in more detail. In another era, when youthful longevity was not taken quite so much for granted, Frederick Hollis would have been described as very well preserved. Now it seemed an inexact description, almost a travesty, for this was not an old man, it was a man without age. He had no paunch, no sag. His small close-clipped mustache was still brown, so was his crisp hair; nature or artifice, she could not tell at this distance. Even his clothes, the collegiate combination of gray flannel slacks and light-toned roughly woven linen jacket, seemed designed to throw one off the scent of any precise chronology of his years. But at least, she thought, recalling Stephen's unkind description, he was *not* wearing a tie painted with hula maidens, or an open-necked sports shirt sprinkled with hibiscus in full bloom. Could this, perhaps, be his concession to a meeting with someone from the "older generation"?

Halfway up the front steps Lydia turned back to say something to Frederick, who stood directly behind her. As she turned, Lady Brace saw Frederick Hollis's right hand close itself around the small pert roundness of her daughter's buttock, grasping it as a connoisseur of fruit might test the degree of a pear's ripeness. Lady Brace lowered her eyelids quickly over her eyes.

A few seconds later she heard the bell ring and then the front door open. She emerged from the Trophy Room.

"Lydia, darling."

"Mummy! Oh, how good to see you!"

Caroline Brace could not remember ever having received from her younger daughter an embrace as clinging and warm. She even had a moment's deep look into lovely gray-blue eyes with flecks of gold, before Lydia, turning, and still clasping her mother's left hand—almost as though determined to lead her forward should there be any hesitation in her greeting—said, "Mummy, you remember Frederick Hollis, don't you?"

"Of course." Lady Brace extended her free hand. "It has been a long time. You are looking extremely well, Frederick."

"And you, Caroline. What a pleasure to meet again."

"And how is Belle?" Lady Brace asked immediately. "I hear she has not been at all well."

"Her condition does not change." His face expressed no emotion. He added, "It is, I'm afraid, quite hopeless and has been for some time."

"I'm very sorry to hear it."

He inclined his head as though there was nothing more to say on the subject.

"Where is everyone?" Lydia asked. She had maintained perfect composure during the brief, stiff exchange about Belle Hollis.

"Everyone's away for the day. They've gone to the beach."

"Even Uncle Stephen? Oh, I *am* disappointed."

"No, Stephen is here. He refuses to lunch with us, but he has promised to join us for coffee."

"I find him perfectly fascinating," Lydia said, stopping at the drawing-room door and waiting for her mother to precede her. "So does Frederick. Why have I never known how fascinating he is? Everyone's been so silent about him, I somehow got the idea that he was the family's black sheep."

Passing a small table as she spoke, she stopped again—this time to pick up and examine, with a half-critical air, an old Meissen dish laid out for use as an ash tray. She replaced it without comment, and Lady Brace saw that it had a fresh nick on its rim.

Lydia continued about Stephen, "Aunt Bertha always closed her mouth like a trap whenever his name came up. Now I find he's an authentic charmer—though rather naughty at times—what he says, anyway."

Her younger daughter's deliberate survey of the drawing room was an act of inspection, and Lady Brace felt relieved, this time for Rosemary's sake, that it had been put in order.

"Stephen's a very sharp fellow," Frederick Hollis remarked, crossing behind Lydia like a man with a definite objective in mind. "Entertaining talker, I'll say that. Never a dull moment when he's around."

His tone of approval conveyed the impression that lightening life's tedium was, to him, an important, if not a major, endeavor.

"You've seen Stephen's friend, Venerable Sir, of course," Lady Brace said, seating herself. For some reason it seemed necessary to know at once what the attitude of these two people would be towards the singular little visitor from Ceylon.

Lydia replied, "Oh, yes, indeed." She sounded faintly amused and proceeded to ask her mother the very question Lady Brace had intended to put to her. "What do you think of him, Mummy?"

"I've hardly spoken to him at all," she evaded. "What do you think of him?"

"I'm afraid I find him insufferably smug."

Caroline Brace expressed surprise. "You do? I didn't feel any smugness in him. Of course, we only spoke briefly."

"Well, maybe smug isn't quite the word," Lydia amended. "What I mean is, I find people who go around looking so—so serene and bland all the time, *quite* unbearable." She addressed Frederick Hollis, "Do you know what I mean, Frederick?"

"Yes, I think I do."

Frederick Hollis was standing before the empty fireplace with a purposeful air, as though by established habit he chose a position from which any room could best be dominated. He began to teeter up and down on his toes in his beautiful white buckskin shoes. Lady Brace thought of Rosemary's exercises for her transverse arches the night before in her bedroom. Was Frederick Hollis also making physical profit from each golden moment of repose?

A little tray had been left in readiness with tomato juice, a bottle of vodka, a decanter of sherry.

"How thoughtful of Rosie," Lydia said, "remembering your Bloody Marys, Frederick."

Lady Brace decided she could not have heard correctly. She was also inclined to doubt her senses as Frederick Hollis, saying, "May I?" approached the little table, put ice, vodka and tomato juice in a small shaker, stirred it, poured it generously. He then extracted from one of his pockets a small flat silver shaker and dusted into the glass something that appeared to be coarsely ground dirty salt.

"I've never been able to like Bloody Marys," Lydia said, pouring sherry for herself and her mother. "That's vodka and tomato juice, in case you don't know, Lady B. A very sly drink. It *looks* so innocent."

Lydia's light, superficial manner did not seem to suit her in the least. Perhaps after all she is somewhat ill at ease under that composed exterior, Lady Brace thought.

"One hears," Lydia was going on, "of quite a few eminent ladies in the fashion world of New York who say to their pet headwaiter, 'The usual,' and get what purports to be tomato juice. But it's actually only protective coloration." She laughed and looked over at Frederick. "Soon their eyes begin to shine, and their voices rise wittily, and, alas, very soon, bags appear under their eyes and they're mispronouncing words. None of this description applies to Frederick, Mummy, so don't be alarmed. Actually, I think it's only ladies who look shattered by noonday drinking. Anyway, that's why I stick to luncheon sherry."

"Entirely notional," Frederick Hollis said, downing his first glass of vodka and tomato juice in a single gulp and immediately pouring another. "Whether you choose to drink at breakfast or at midnight doesn't really matter. It's what's already in your system when you *do* drink that counts."

Lady Brace settled herself, not without interest, to a discussion of body chemistry. She was surprised when Frederick Hollis chose to return to the subject of Venerable Sir.

"Of course those Eastern chaps sometimes know a lot," he remarked. "About the body and all that sort of thing. They can do practically anything with their bodies, some of those chaps. I've seen it, stomachs as flat as boards, that sort of thing. Lift enormous weights, absolutely control the pulse, heart, so forth. Never sick a day; look half their age—no age at all, actually."

"I think they look perfectly repellent," Lydia interposed. "That man you took me to see at the Pierre, Frederick, wrapping his ankles around his neck two or three times. I just don't see what there is in it, really, except some form of exhibitionism I don't understand at all."

"Remind me to give you that little book I spoke about," Frederick Hollis said, "written by that chap I met in Bali."

Lydia made no reply. Instead, she got up and poured herself another sherry, then started to reach for a cigarette, closed the box, sat down again and began lightly to swing her right foot up and down.

Lady Brace caught Frederick Hollis glancing furtively at her daughter's long elegant suntanned legs.

"I don't believe," she began, a little flurried, "that Stephen's friend is a—is that *sort* of yogi, do you?"

"Oh, heavens, no!" Lydia exclaimed. "I'm sure he's all the sweetness-and-light school; with no body in it at all."

This last phrase sounded so much like Stephen that Caroline Brace looked up, startled.

To her relief, the red-wigged maid, her apron still awry, entered at this moment to say the luncheon trays were on the terrace and would they please just help themselves and ring if something was missing. She recited this speech as though she had spent the morning memorizing it. Lydia and her mother exchanged a wry amused glance. Why do I feel that I would always understand Lydia so much better than Rosemary? Lady Brace wondered, as they moved towards the terrace.

Luncheon passed quietly. Frederick Hollis explained to Lady Brace in some detail about the importance of vitamin B^1 for people who drank hard liquor. Liquor, he informed her, used up the body's natural B content. He attempted also to outline the restorative and vital properties of something called thiamine, now to be purchased in pellet form. But he did not pontificate to any degree, and Lady Brace secretly felt relieved to have the conversation confined to the safe realm of health regimes. Lydia spoke very little. Only once or twice she made a faintly ironic remark that again reminded Lady Brace of her brother.

T W O

After lunch Stephen joined them for coffee, as he had promised. At his request, they moved into the cool drawing room, for he said he could no longer take the midday sun. Then, leaving the two men alone together for a few moments, Lady Brace and her daughter went upstairs.

When Caroline Brace emerged from the bathroom she found Lydia standing in the wide bay window looking out at the sunburned lawn and walled garden. She turned and put out a slim hand as her mother approached.

"Lady B, you are so lovely looking. I'd forgotten."

Touched by this unexpected compliment from her child, Caroline responded, "You're the lovely one, darling. You do look so smart, and your figure . . ."

But Lydia appeared not to be listening. "Tell me, Lady B," she began with sudden insistence, "how have we really lost all our money—or most of it—and why must Fox Meadows be sold?"

Caroline Brace looked at her, shocked. "But surely you were told, darling."

"Well, some things, of course. I seem to remember hearing about part of it being Uncle Edgar's fault. How, when we came to live with Aunt Bertha and go to school here, he was given charge of our money. He invested it very foolishly. Is that the story?"

Where Lydia could have heard this Lady Brace had no idea, for she had always scrupulously avoided placing blame on fumbling, inept and over-bullied Edgar Reed. She replied to Lydia in a voice that had, in spite of herself, a mournful intonation. "Yes, that is part of the story—as you put it."

"And what about you, Mummy? Have you enough to live on? I mean, how have you been affected—now particularly, with Humpy gone? Braceledge isn't yours, is it?"

Lady Brace, unprepared for such direct questions, replied with difficulty. She had always found it painful to discuss money, possessions, legal arrangements. "Oh, I'm quite all right, thank you, dear," she said, hesitant. She forced herself to add further details, "Yes, Braceledge is entailed, but Humphrey's nephew, who inherits it, has asked me to stay on, to the end of my life, if I wish to. He has his own country place elsewhere. And no children left either." She was thinking of Rupert, to whom, had he lived, Braceledge would have gone.

"You'd never consider coming back here? To New York, I mean?"

At Lydia's question, though it was in no way an unnatural one, a chill of apprehensiveness again passed lightly over Lady Brace. Yes, what would she do? What was the next step? And why had she found it impossible to make any plans about the remainder of her life? Could her habit of drifting along, day after day, be laid at the door of Humphrey's invalidism—or did it go deeper, much deeper?

She replied quite calmly, with no hint of inner disturbance, "Oh, I think not. I've been so thoroughly transplanted."

When Lydia continued to look at her with a cool inquiring gaze she again felt forced to explain. "I had to give up my American citizenship some time ago in order to keep anything at all. Double taxation—here and in England—was so terrible. But even what I kept turned out to be rather little in the end." Her voice, so low now it was almost inaudible, went on, "There was the fall of the pound, of course, and then before that, some stipulations in your grandfather's will about taking money out of the country."

"That was to trap Uncle Stephen, I suppose."

Lady Brace managed not to stare. Her daughter's acuteness amazed her. How had Lydia learned of her grandfather's stipulation that Stephen was to be kept from inheriting the bulk of his money until he reached sixty? She made no reply, and Lydia went on calmly but tenaciously pursuing her line of questioning, almost as if discharging an unpleasant, long overdue duty.

"But didn't Daddy have anything?"

"Not very much in his own name, darling. You see, we always lived on an allowance from his father—plus what I had. A very generous allowance, but it stopped with your father's death. At the time I never thought there would be any need to press for—well, a settlement for you girls, so I didn't. Then"—she could feel her breath coming faster—"you went to live with Aunt Bertha and . . . and she and Uncle Edgar took over your affairs." She stopped. "Probably very foolish and short-sighted of me—all of it."

She sighed as she finished speaking and Lydia, as if in echo, sighed too, long and deep.

"Do you terribly mind it, darling?" Lady Brace asked after a moment, now unable to hide her anxiety.

"Of course!" Lydia replied promptly. "I'd adore to have pots of money. Who wouldn't?"

"Oh, dear!" Lady Brace murmured. A feeling of complete inadequacy, unlike anything she had felt for years, began to creep like a miasma over her spirit. Had she been unforgivably remiss in not attending more closely to her daughters' financial futures? Was this because she was herself quite well enough off for all her relatively modest needs? Must she even accept indirect blame for Lydia's choice of Frederick Hollis for a second husband? The very idea gave her acute inner discomfort. She turned and looked out the window, sighing, "I *am* so sorry, darling."

Lydia, who had also been looking away over the lawn, now turned and faced her mother. "But don't be silly, Mummy!" she cried. She stretched out a hand to give Lady Brace's elbow a little impulsive squeeze. "It's not your fault at all." Immediately, she dropped her hand and gave a dispirited shrug. "And anyway—fate's fate! *That's* something I certainly believe!"

Her tone seemed almost angry, as if she resented the necessity of this admission. Lady Brace found it impossible to rise to this, though she would have liked to deny the truth of her daughter's resigned and secretly bitter observation.

After a moment, in quite a normal voice, Lydia said, "Did you know that Frederick hopes to buy the little walled garden—in toto? That is, if the lawyers decide to break up the place in chunks. He's paying for the care of it, until it can be moved."

"Really?" Lady Brace was surprised. "I'd noticed it seemed rather well kept up."

Why should Frederick Hollis, at his age, want to buy and move entire garden plots: walls, shrubs, trees, plants, statuary? Did he plan a new family with Lydia?

She asked, "Has Frederick children? I can't remember."

"One daughter. Married and living in Italy." Lydia's somewhat laconic reply might perhaps, her mother thought, indicate strained relations. Frederick's only child must be about Lydia's age. Would she ever learn any of these intimate details short of asking questions as awkward and direct as Lydia's to her?

Lydia was continuing, "I'm only sorry that Frederick didn't get Para and Dox, too."

Lady Brace smiled. "How strange! Everyone else calls them Pooh and Bah. Para and Dox was Stephen's second name for them."

"I know." Lydia tapped lightly on the window screening with her long pale nails, covered so carefully with opalescent lacquer. "I always loved the idea of it: Para and Dox from the Land of Paradox." Her voice had become soft, dreamy, without tension. This swift alteration of mood—did it indicate a nature at war with itself? Once again Lady Brace was reminded of Stephen.

A vision of the entrance to the inner courtyard without the lovable guardian monsters from China rose before her. She had her first sharp unmistakable pang of relinquishment. "What is to become of Para and Dox?" she inquired.

"Didn't you know?" Lydia seemed surprised now in her turn. "Lorenzo Lorenzetti, who bought all the gates, bought them too.

It was done one year when we needed extra money. He—Lorenzo—is old Tony's son, you know. He's just leaving them here until all the Langdons have departed. Very polite of him! Lorenzo's done very well as a local contractor." She smiled. "He even outbid Frederick's agent for Para and Dox." She laughed. "It *was* rather funny. Frederick was so furious. He never thinks anyone can outwit him, or outbid him, or out-anything him. Certainly not the son of an ex-gardener."

"Do you mean that Frederick is—" Caroline Brace groped for a word "—arrogant?" she finished lamely.

"Oh, I don't know if I'd say that exactly," Lydia replied without any defensiveness. "Let's just say he's self-assured—to say the least!"

Now, Lady Brace told herself, now is the moment for speaking up. She forced herself to begin. "Are you—?" She hesitated, changed her tack. "What is this, Lydia darling, I hear about you and Frederick Hollis?"

Lydia replied, quite composed. "I don't know, Mummy dear, since I don't know what you've been hearing."

"Well, I've heard—*Stephen* implied," she added quickly, to take any possible onus off Rosemary, who had been so anxious not to be involved, "that you plan to marry as soon—as soon as Frederick is free." How crass! she thought. I am speaking of the death of a woman I once knew well, of Belle Stewart, Frederick Hollis's wife, at whose wedding I was a bridesmaid forty-five years ago.

"Yes," Lydia said simply. "Does it shock you?"

Lady Brace decided to be direct. "Rather."

"Why, Mummy?"

She was silent a moment. "I don't know that I can entirely explain why. Not in a few words, anyway."

"Because he's so much older probably." Lydia still spoke with perfect composure. Then, before her mother could comment, she added, "I do want a good long talk with you, Lady B." She turned away from the window. "Whenever you can spare the time."

"But, of course, darling. My time is yours."

"Is—this week possible?"

"Any time. I've made no engagements at all."

"Then how about the day after tomorrow? I'll ask Frederick to have his man pick you up here. He goes into the city every day with fresh flowers for Belle. She's in a hospital, you know."

"Oh, please don't bother." Lady Brace spoke in haste. "I can quite easily go in with Todd, or even Uncle Stephen. I believe he goes in on that day, for his treatment."

"Todd? Todd has to leave at the crack of dawn because of traffic. And Uncle Stephen's Boy Friday drives him. So that is out!" Lydia was firm. "I mean, if he drives like most Orientals, he's a menace to life and limb, Mummy. Please don't go with them. Anyway, there's not enough room for three."

Lydia's note of urgent concern made Caroline feel absurdly frail and valuable. "Very well, darling, if you insist." She did not speak her thought, which was, "Though I'd prefer not to be indebted to Frederick Hollis in even the smallest way." She found this quick unspoken antipathy irrational, and wished she could explain it to herself.

She decided to inquire about Frederick's dying wife. "What is really wrong with Belle Hollis?" To her own ears her voice sounded cautious.

Lydia replied with cool poise. "Something to do with the blood cells. Something new—and complicated. I don't understand exactly, but she's been in bed over three years now—getting no better and no worse. As Frederick says, it's *quite* hopeless. He's consulted every specialist in the world, of course."

Lydia's tone definitely closed this subject. She walked across to her mother's dressing table, stood before the mirror, touched up her lipstick and ran her right hand, with its flashing emerald, expertly over her smooth pale hair. She then bent her head to examine, just as Rosemary had the day before, the six photographs in the leather folder. It was, Lady Brace thought, observing Lydia's suddenly focused attention, almost as though both she and Rosemary displayed by this acute interest an otherwise unexpressed curiosity about their mother and the past.

Lydia's first comment was, "Oh, I'd forgotten that snapshot of Rosie and me. Taken at Newport—at Grandpa Parton's, wasn't it? What cunning little girls we were!"

"Yes, very," Lady Brace agreed.

Then, lifting the folder to the light, Lydia continued, "And here's Uncle Stephen—with some heathen god, I suppose," and she laughed gently.

"No," Lady Brace said. "That's a very old statue of the Buddha."

"But isn't the Buddha a heathen god?" Lydia said, not eliciting information, more with an air of quiet correction.

To her own surprise Lady Brace contradicted her at once, "Oh, I don't believe so. That is—well, I'm sure your Uncle Stephen would never allow you to call him that. I believe the Buddha's not supposed to have been a god at all, or even divine. Just a very great teacher."

"Of course, I'm afraid I think that's all Jesus was," Lydia now astonished her mother by remarking. "Which, I suppose, makes me the heathen."

The thought crossed Lady Brace's mind, *Though I feel I understand Lydia better than Rosemary, she is, I'm sure, the child who is always going to amaze me.*

Lydia, after a moment, replaced the folder. "Sometime, Lady B," she said, "I do wish you'd tell me about Uncle Stephen in Ceylon. The whole idea of his going there to live always fascinated me. And your trip out to visit him. I'd love sometime to hear all about that, too. I remember so much from the letters you sent on to us."

"Oh, do you, dear?" Lady Brace was pleased. "Rosemary says she remembers them too." On impulse she asked, "What do you remember best?"

"About a migration of butterflies," Lydia replied promptly. "An annual migration to a mountain called Adam's Peak. No one could explain why they went, what drew them there, or what happened when they arrived, but all the valleys on a certain day, or days, of the year were filled with clouds of colored butterflies moving together to their mountain. Isn't that right?"

Caroline Brace nodded and murmured. For some reason she felt close to tears.

"It was my very favorite adolescent fantasy," Lydia concluded. "I still dream about them sometimes. I must ask Uncle Stephen if the butterflies still do it."

"Oh, I'm sure they do," Lady Brace said, softly. "Those things don't change, do they? It's one of the comforting thoughts about life—as Humphrey used to say—how the birds and flowers and stars and so on just continue repeating their pattern . . . But we must go downstairs, dear. We're being impolite."

"I wish I'd known Humpy better," Lydia remarked as they reached the door. She gave her mother's arm another, almost shy, squeeze. "I sometimes remember what stinkers Rosie and I were to him."

They passed into the hall. Lady Brace found it impossible to reply to Lydia. She wanted to say, "Yes, it did rather hurt Humpy —your attitude"—for it had, badly! But what was the good now of dwelling on any of that part of the past?—Humphrey in his grave; the girls grown, and with problems of their own. Did full consciousness of one's actions come only—if ever—well past the time of their occurrence? This thought seemed so unpalatable, indeed so gloomy, that she shook it from her with a little impatient movement of her head. She returned Lydia's shy squeeze. "How sweet of you to say that, dear."

10

When Lady Brace and Lydia reentered the drawing room Stephen, who was talking, paused to lift his cane in front of him and wave it once, half-irritably—an apology for remaining seated at their entrance. Frederick, again standing before the empty fireplace, was plucking grapes one by one from an imposing cluster held in his long, wrinkled left hand. As he extended the fruit to Lady Brace she thought to herself, noting the thickened veins and the liver spots, Not much to be done about aging hands! Before she could decline the grapes, Lydia spoke.

"They're from Frederick's place, Mummy. He's been experimenting with grape culture." Lydia's tone indicated that she was supposed to show interest.

"Ah," Lady Brace said, accepting the small clump that Frederick, with a precise deadly snip of highly polished nails, secured for her. "They do look very special." The grapes must have been the contents of the white box she had seen Frederick hand to his chauffeur, and they were, no doubt, the source of some newly discovered vital chemical element.

She sat down and looked at her brother, slumped low in his chair. She could tell from the arrested glower on his face that their entrance had interrupted something he had been interested in talking about. Plainly, she thought, he is pursuing one of his conversational wild hares, for his eyes held the curious angry excitement certain ideas aroused in him.

"We interrupted you," she said. "I'm so sorry. Do go on with what you were saying."

At her gentle apology Stephen visibly made an attempt to alter his expression and check his rising tension. She almost had the feeling that he counted to ten before replying, with forced calm, "We were speaking about how the only possible way to interpret modern life is in terms of myth."

Lydia, who had paused to study the unusual arrangement of the branches of pine and rhododendron in the old crackleware vases, turned around at once. "How fascinating!" She spoke in a tone of genuine interest.

Frederick, teetering up and down in his white shoes and still snapping at the grapes, said in a hearty voice, taking his cue from Lydia, "Right! Fascinating! All those modern types, you know, those fellows they made gods of—Lenin" (grape), "Mussolini" (grape), "Stalin" (grape), "and so on."

"What were you saying, Uncle Stephen?" Lydia asked, not quite concealing a slight impatience with Frederick.

"I was saying that they'll deify Hitler yet. We've not heard the last of all this pagan regression by a long shot."

An immediate feeling of unease took hold of Lady Brace. She recalled her brother's designation only that morning of Frederick Hollis: "pure power-elite type." Had Stephen deliberately chosen this after-luncheon topic, and, if so, from what motives?

Lydia had dropped into a low chair in a careless posture that would have been awkward in one less slim and graceful. She made the now familiar related movements of reaching for a cigarette, checking the impulse, starting the light steady swinging of her sandaled foot. Her attention, however, remained focused on her uncle.

"You mean our children or grandchildren may live to see all those Nazi monsters reproduced in marble in some new Hall of Fame?"

"Quite likely." Stephen shot his niece a glance not easy to interpret. Perhaps it was surprise at her interest in a subject of this kind. Yes, Lady Brace said to herself, my second daughter undoubtedly has many hidden layers.

Still with an air of genuine interest, Lydia inquired, "What about Goebbels, the cripple? Will he be included in that future pantheon?"

Before Stephen could reply, Frederick exclaimed with sudden fervor, "Yes, what about Goebbels? Odd thing, that! With all their worship of physical fitness, those Nazis, that they'd give a cripple so much power."

"Oh, sure thing!" Stephen replied—exactly, thought Lady Brace, as Alice Ford or the Carozzi boy might have spoken; like the freshly informed young to the doddering old, still caught in past forms of thought and theory. "That would follow! It's the opposite side of their particular coin, that's all!"

Lydia's foot stopped its swinging; Frederick's grapes rested in space. Caroline saw her brother check himself. Ah, she thought, he foresees that he may lose his audience if he gets into any tenuous maundering—and she was a little amused at her analysis of the way her brother's mind worked. But with familiar perversity, as though he did not care at all whether he succeeded in holding their interest, he remarked in a throw-it-away voice, "But probably I'm being boring. No one takes the interest in this subject that I do."

Lydia denied quickly, "No one's bored. At least I'm not. I love to hear you talk, Uncle Stephen. No one I know—any more, seems to talk about anything remotely interesting and I get so sick of endless pla-tra chatter."

Frederick returned to his grapes with a somewhat peevish expression.

"Which one of the lot of them—those famous Nazis—interests you the most?" Lydia persisted.

"Goering," Stephen said at once.

"Why Goering?"

"Because I find him more a subject for eventual myth than Hitler."

"I thought he was just a sort of funny fat man," Lydia said. "Wasn't there a joke that he had a set of rubber medals to wear in his bath?"

"Ha!" Frederick gave a small barking laugh. "That's a good one!"

"Goering wasn't just a clown," Stephen said. Warming to the subject, he embarked on a brilliant descriptive passage about Goering. He is really putting Frederick Hollis to the test, Lady Brace thought, as there rolled from her brother's lips some very literary phrases . . . "Pagan in the grand style . . . the reborn Etruscan, glutton and art patron . . . war hero who became a dope addict . . . the middle-aged Falstaff who was once, however, the dashing lover, and later the husband, of one of the most beautiful women of modern times, a Swedish Helen of Troy . . . Long before that, the boy who wouldn't be disciplined, who ran away from school, and gave away all his books to gypsies. . . ."

"Wait! Wait!" Lydia cried, her eyes alight with excitement. "Don't go whizzing on like that, Uncle Stephen!"

"Gypsies! I'll be damned!" said Frederick.

Now he has them! With relief Lady Brace took a sip of her cold coffee, discovered it was Sanka. Rosemary being thoughtful again?

"I want to know about that fateful Swedish lady, Uncle Stephen?" Lydia said. "How was she like a modern Helen?"

Stephen grinned at her. "I thought you'd find that enticing."

Those two are establishing a bond, Lady Brace said to herself. Will it prove fortunate or unfortunate, she wondered, as Stephen went on unfolding the tale of Goering's meeting with Karin von Fock . . . "on the stairs of her family's castle in Sweden, after a forced landing in a private plane on a frozen northern lake. How Wagnerian can you be? Love at first sight. She left her husband for Hermann—but remember he was handsome then, a war hero; flying ace from World War I, dashing, brilliant. It was Karin von Fock who taught Goering the first steps in the mystical hocus-pocus of nationalism. Her own family had a deep belief in that theme of Norse supremacy that was to become a part of the

Nazi *mythos*. Karin's mother, a baroness—can't remember her Swedish name, but she was born a plain Miss Beamish out of the British Isles—had indoctrinated the whole family—so there's nothing exclusively Germanic about the creed! For that matter, who—back as far as the Bible—started all this "chosen people" nonsense? Goering was apparently never the same after he attended services in Karin's family's private chapel; called, I might add, the Edelweiss Chapel—another nice romantic touch! However, that's beside the point. It was Karin who first believed in Adolf Hitler's destiny, from the moment she first saw him—after she and Hermann went to Germany to live—even though Hitler, then, was just a minor political fanatic with a silly mustache, a wild eye, one dirty raincoat. What's more, Karin never lost her faith in the Nazi cause or allowed Hermann to give up, not even during the gloomy time after that first abortive Munich *Putsch* when Goering almost died of wounds, lost his sexual potency, became a dope addict to relieve his constant pain. Yes, there's no doubt about it, Karin loved Hermann and believed in his great future—and Hitler's, too—but she was dead of tuberculosis long before her adored husband and his pal reached their great heights of power and pomp."

Stephen paused for breath, his color high. How could he get so involved in remote impersonal subjects, in pieces of forgotten history? Caroline asked herself, as she had many times in the past. But perhaps to him the subject was not impersonal; nor to Lydia, either.

Lydia's face appeared more animated than her mother had yet seen it. She cried, "What a marvelous story! Sheer drama. Nobody could invent anything half as fascinating!"

Frederick asked, raising his voice a little to dominate Lydia's, "What about Goering's beginnings? Where did he spring from? Not out of the gutter, I take it?"

"Far from it. Solid enough background—though not much money. And that's a part of the dark side of the fable, too. Hermann, in later years, liked to dwell on all the baroque trimmings of his childhood, his life in a castle and so on. But who do you think made it possible for the Goering family to live beyond their modest means? Who but Hermann's own Jewish godfather, a rich and generous gentleman who'd got a *von* added to his name somewhere along the line. And there's another unsavory ironical bit about Goering's subsequent record in relation to Jews. Long before the crimes at Dachau, long before even any open talk of purges, after that first *Putsch* had so disastrously failed and Hermann lay dying in the streets of Munich, who do you think rescued him—risked their lives to save his? Two little middle-aged Jewish sisters—total strangers. Put that together with the incinerators at Belsen and all the rest of the horrors, if you can!"

"Well, I'm damned!" Frederick exclaimed. "What a grisly joke! Hah!" He gave one of his short guarded laughs.

"I don't see anything funny about it," Lydia remarked in a voice that surprised her mother by its coldness.

"You don't? Well, I do—damned funny, *historically*," and he plunged into his grapes again, pleased, it appeared, to have had Lydia's attention drawn to him even in disapproval.

Lydia turned back to her uncle. "I do see why you call it a modern legend, Uncle Stephen." She added, "A very dark modern legend."

Stephen struck his stick on the carpet. "Round and round we go—forever! Nothing new! Nothing better! Nothing diminished, either. Increased, rather. For now the whole world, not just a piece of it, is sick—sick with what we choose to think of as a modern disease. Modern? Bah! It's as old as time, the disease of the ego, the will to power. But since we don't know how to read history in the round, only in chopped-up bits, we can't clearly see the fateful pattern."

He was glowering as though he felt there rested on someone in the room, perhaps on all of them, responsibility for this sorry state of affairs.

Frederick Hollis had become visibly uneasy. He had not bargained, so Caroline said to herself, for quite so much emotional fervor from Stephen. Probably he fears and dreads all "intellectuals"—and she recalled some terms of American slang she had recently heard on a B.B.C. broadcast: "egg heads," "long hairs." How, she wondered, did their status compare, in the present social scene, with her father's and grandfather's "pundits and panjandrums"? Would Frederick Hollis hold an "egg head" in any more esteem than, say, sloppy Clara, the television addict, whom she could now see hovering in the hall, uncertain about the coffee tray?

Awkwardness settled on them all. Frederick had at last laid aside his grapes. The bunch he had been working on was, indeed, picked quite clean, and, like a migrating bird who has stripped a bush of every berry, he appeared eager now to get on with his flight. He attempted to catch Lydia's eye but she avoided him. She was staring at her uncle, plainly puzzled by his abrupt outburst.

Lady Brace glanced at Stephen and perceived at once that he was not yet through talking. Some shapeless annoyance with Frederick Hollis led her to move to her brother's aid.

"What was Goering's end? Didn't he commit suicide in prison?" she asked. She did not mind sounding fatuous if it would save Stephen from a feeling, later, of intense frustration, of suffering at having begun something he had not concluded simply because now, due to his infirmity, he lacked the energy, the sheer physical strength, to dominate his audience until he had finished.

That she had been right in this hasty analysis she now felt quite sure, for Stephen flung her the grateful look of a drowning man catching a rope as he answered, "Hermann's end! Ah, there's legend for you; legend not only classical in its correctness, but *satanic* in its terrible, disgusting justice."

In the warm room Lady Brace shivered.

Stephen, quite calm again, but a little pale, continued, "I don't mean at the trial. No, for the truth is that Goering even managed to dominate his particular moments at the trial scene. Actually, he was the only one of the whole lot who made any kind of showing at Nuremberg, for himself or for the regime he represented. No, not the trial; not the fact he was sentenced to death for his crimes—which he never seemed to realize *were* crimes—but I mean the very last of him: the cremation, the disposal of the bones and ashes."

Lady Brace shivered again. "Bones and ashes"—"gloomy and nameless weeds." What was the quality of fateful suggestion that her brother could always interject so disturbingly into the simplest words? She had the strong feeling that Lydia shivered also, but

Frederick Hollis, though he looked uneasy, had had his interest captured once more.

Stephen was driving on. "After Hermann took that pill, that mysteriously secreted pill that killed him, where did they ship his body? Where but to Dachau, of course. Yes, the last act of this singular spectacle—what I call the *classically correct* denouement —took place in one of the very incinerators designed by his SS bully boys to burn the innocent Jews!"

In spite of his calm tone he began to breathe a little quickly. Perspiration broke out on his forehead, and Lady Brace longed to rise and wipe it off. She sensed that he, too, aware of the damp film on his face, was distressed by it, yet could not bear the prolonged and awkward effort involved in extracting a handkerchief from his breast pocket.

She felt a stab of anguish at this reminder of his physical disability, a feeling followed immediately by one of impatience. Or was it only malaise? What are we doing, how did we come to be sitting here on a summer's mid-afternoon in an old Long Island house discussing the fate of a Nazi murderer? Stephen's choice of an after-luncheon topic, the presence of Frederick Hollis, of her daughter Lydia—all these elements seemed, when put together, quite as fantastic and inexplicable as any of the mythical elements in the life and death of a political fanatic. Life seems to be growing increasingly unreal to me, she thought.

She observed Frederick's covert signal to Lydia, his impatience to depart. Lydia did not appear to receive the signal, but her voice, when next she spoke, assumed the tone of one about to rise and murmur polite goodbyes. "You know so much about the Nazis. How did you become so interested in them, Uncle Stephen?"

Stephen's reply was harsh. "Because we're all Nazis—somewhere! That's why. And we'd better try to understand ourselves before it's too late!"

Lady Brace winced. Oh, why must he always be so exaggerated, so violent? She saw Lydia's eyes widen. The force in her uncle's grating voice plainly amazed her; it seemed to threaten, to imply some buried personal rage, even fear.

Stephen made a brittle impatient gesture. "Forget it! It's too late anyway. I saw it coming years ago. I told you, Caro, that time you were in Ceylon, what was going to spring on us out of the bushes. Remember?"

Speechless, Lady Brace could only nod. Something about her silent gesture appeared to check Stephen. He gave a dour half laugh before adding, with greatly lessened pitch, "Probably I exaggerate. I *identify*—isn't that the new term? The truth is, I've always been drawn to sick and morbid subjects, Lydia. Ask your mother. She can tell you plenty. Get her to tell you sometime about her one visit to me in Ceylon." He gave another mirthless laugh. "I was working at the time on a Compendium of Evil—a collection of all the evil deeds of man." He appeared to be ridiculing himself.

Lydia turned her grave eyes from her uncle to her mother in a long, questioning look. The glance seemed to ask: "What is there, what has there always been, between the two of you that I find so strange—so mysterious and tantalizing?"

Stephen again waved his stick in the air. It might now have been a wand designed to break a spell. "Yes, Lydia, your mother gave me up—long ago in Ceylon. She decided once and for all that I was a thoroughly hopeless case."

"How absurd!" Lady Brace managed to smile. She added, in an attempt to match Stephen's satiric tone, "I'd given you up as hopeless long before that, darling."

Frederick Hollis got to his feet. He looked uncomfortable, anxious to escape, but Lydia, with unbroken calm, crossed to where her uncle sat.

"You have a wonderful gift, Uncle Stephen," she said, standing beside him. "You can make all life sound very exciting—and different—not dull as it really is so much of the time."

"Dull!" Stephen hooted with scorn, twisting in his chair. "Only to the deaf and blind!"

With a sudden surprising gesture of intimacy Lydia bent over and took the tip of his left ear between her middle finger and thumb. The great green stone in her ring flashed as she gave his ear lobe a gentle squeeze.

"You're a very rare person." Her voice was quite tender. "Sometime I *would* really like to have you—or Mummy—tell me about

Ceylon, and what your life out there was like. You know, I long to go to the Far East myself someday."

"Why?" Stephen asked in a curt voice, not stirring under her touch.

She hesitated a moment. "Because the whole idea of Asia fascinates me—and always has."

"It never fascinated your mother," Stephen said. "It upset her and—revolted her."

"Now, dear, that's hardly fair," Lady Brace began. "At least that's not the whole of it."

"I'll come someday and pump you, Uncle Stephen," Lydia said, smiling. She crossed over to give her mother a kiss.

Lady Brace accompanied Frederick Hollis and her daughter as far as the front door. On the steps, just before entering the green Rolls-Royce, Lydia turned to call over her shoulder with special emphasis, "Don't forget our date. Day after tomorrow, Mummy. In town. I'll be counting on it."

Lady Brace nodded and waved her hand—and they were gone. She closed the front door slowly and thoughtfully.

Glancing back into the room she had left a moment before, she saw the light falling on the remains of Frederick's mammoth grapes. They looked more unreal than the fruit in the Dutch painting on the wall.

Stephen sat staring straight ahead, past the grapes, to a single pine bough that rose in one direct thrust from a narrow-necked vase. Caroline Brace had the sensation that he was engaged in some definite mental exercise, some concentrated and quieting therapy. The fanciful thought occurred to her: Perhaps he is trying to see the pine not as a whirling, fierce, many-spiked green scorpion, but only as a gentle dance of harmless needles around a central point of fusion. For she was sure now that Stephen struggled every day, perhaps every hour, to change his attitude towards things and people, towards life itself; to "care" still, but in a different way, with less fervor in his dismissals and attachments. Was it really possible, after all these years, and at his age, to exchange one kind of personality for another? His performance this afternoon scarcely indicated a greatly altered Stephen, and yet the thought persisted that he was, somehow, a changed, or at least changing, man.

She tiptoed away from the doorway, signaling frowsy Clara—coming again for the coffee tray—warning her with a finger to her lips, a shake of her head, not to disturb her brother.

11

As she lay on her bed later that same afternoon, forcing herself to rest, Lady Brace tried to prepare herself for Lydia's possible questions about her long-ago trip to Ceylon and Stephen's life in that disturbing magical place. She found it difficult to put together, into a consistent whole, Lydia's candid admission to Stephen that she was fascinated by Asia, and always had been, with her amused and almost scornful dismissal of Venerable Sir and the practice of yoga. What was it, then, that Lydia found so fascinating about the Far East? What pictures did it present to her imagination: fragments from that fast-disappearing scenario of the lives of maharajas? Frosted minarets in the moonlight? Elephants with rubies embedded in their foreheads? Tiger hunts and secret chambers piled to the ceiling with uncut gems? "Be fair!" she chided herself, remembering suddenly the expression on Lydia's face as she spoke about the annual migration of butterflies to Adam's Peak.

Stephen had asserted that she, Caroline, had been revolted by the Far East. This summary seemed to her unnecessarily extreme. The truth was, her Ceylon memories, and Stephen's way of life there, retained the quality of dream experiences, intense but unreal—something unfulfilled, incomplete, a sense of perplexing questions unanswered. How, then, could she convey to her daughter any true impression of her visit to that haunted, and haunting, island?

Her first opportunity to speak to Stephen of the unsavory

newspaper piece that Bertha Reed had so carefully sent all the way to Somerset—the piece that had prompted her journey to Ceylon—had not come about until three weeks after her arrival at Stephen's remote bungalow in its exotic tropical setting.

She and Stephen had, at last, been alone together, for John van der Wadel had gone off to Colombo with one of the servants; "to get some supplies," he said.

The first evening after John's departure Stephen appeared to be in a particularly mellow mood. Following their pleasant supper of hot fish curry and cool native fruits he had asked her to play the piano.

"Some of those old classical pieces you used to murder," he teased.

"Since I play so badly," she protested, "I can't imagine why you want to hear me."

"Don't take me seriously," he said. "I love to hear you play, Lady B. And it will be like old times." Then quickly, as though almost afraid to speak of their common memories, he added, "Music is something I really miss out here. The Sinhalese seem to have none of it in their souls—strangely enough. Drums are about all they can manage."

She selected a few easy pieces from his stack of music kept on a bamboo stand beside the piano—for he, too, played, somewhat inaccurately but with feeling, and had gone to considerable pains to keep the piano in shape for his own desultory use. In spite of his efforts, however, several keys stuck with the tropical damp, and the persistent blurred tone from the others suggested mold on the felt.

Yet, to humor him, Caroline limped her way through a few sonatas. Then, uncovering a dog-eared book of *Easy Operatic Pieces*, she launched into "Home to Our Mountains," from *Il Trovatore*—singing as she played. She was both pleased and touched when her brother joined in with his high clear tenor.

"How nostalgic!" he cried at the end of their impromptu duet. "Makes me think of Mademoiselle Fleury. The way, when we made mistakes, she'd rap our knuckles with the end of that long string of carved ivory beads she always wore. Remember?"

"Of course," Caroline said. "And that adenoidal Peke of hers snoring right under the pedals."

Stephen grinned. "Oh, Lord, that filthy brute! How I hated him!"

It seemed the opportune time to bring out the newspaper clipping. If she hesitated too long Stephen might begin to reminisce about their childhood, and then she could not bear the risk of upsetting him. Making an excuse, Caroline went to her room and got the folded tabloid from a locked suitcase.

"What's this?" Stephen demanded, when she thrust it at him. He was lying now on one of the many couches in the spacious living room, his white Chinese-style cotton shirt open to the navel; his tanned legs in linen shorts high in the air, the back of one resting on the knee of the other.

"Something for you to read," she said, and dropped it on his bare chest.

He did not stir. "You read it to me," he suggested.

"No," she said, almost sharp.

At her brusque tone he shot her a startled glance, then took the newspaper off his chest without further remark.

The moment he glanced at it she sensed his shocked surprise. Almost at once, however, he laughed with what seemed to her genuine amusement. "That clever bastard! He really fooled me."

Pushing himself up on a pillow to see better, he read the article through, interrupting himself at intervals with short bursts of laughter. He flung down the paper and—still amused—exclaimed again, "That clever bastard! I really thought he was just an old pal of Ferdy Drake's."

He did not seem in the least concerned. In a teasing voice he went on, turning on his side to look at the sheet where it lay spread on the floor, "I wouldn't say that was your most becoming gown, Caro—that little item from Worth in which you were presented at court."

She sat fanning herself in the damp heat, trying to keep the strokes of her wrist slow and rhythmic, anxious not to reveal any nervous tension. "Do be serious, Stephen."

"Serious? What is there to be serious about?"

"That article," she said. "After all, it makes you sound like a—like some kind of decadent. It upset me very much."

"Well, maybe that's what I am—a decadent." He did not look in her direction as he spoke. He flipped off one of his loose sandals, brought it down hard on something invisible crawling along the floor, then returned the sandal to his bare foot and continued in a perfunctory voice, "What is it you really want to know about me?"

At once she was sure she didn't want to know anything at all, that she preferred ignorance. She wondered at her exaggerated concern, her temerity in making this invasion of her brother's privacy. But it was too late to retreat now. The time for that had been weeks back, on the terrace at Braceledge, when Humphrey had tried his best to convince her of her foolishness in worrying so much about Stephen.

She made an attempt to speak in a calm and judicious tone. "I'd like to know what you are really doing out here in this remote spot."

"Oh, is that all? Well, I'm doing just exactly what this paper says." He was, she felt, being deliberately supercilious. "Growing obscene orchids for amusement, and working seriously on research in the fertile field of Evil. *Human* Evil," he added, as though aware of innumerable kinds.

She could not keep from sounding impatient. "Can't you be a little more specific?"

Stephen still remained quite composed. "I'll try," he replied cheerfully. Although he had an unexpected air of wishing to humor her, she felt a faint brush of alarm. Was she about to be led, through her own foolhardy intrusion, into some invisible emotional trap; the kind Stephen knew so well how to set for her?

He sat on the edge of the couch now, looking down at the matting on the floor, his hands loosely clasped between his slender bare knees. The light fell full on the top of his blond head, and she recalled the many times she had seen him sitting like this—thoughtfully, yet carelessly—on garden benches, boat docks, arms of chairs, sides of beds.

"I've embarked on collecting a vast compendium of all the

authentic cases of pure Evil in the world," he said, speaking like a man dictating a formal legal statement. "This is not only a lifetime's job, it's more than a lifetime's job. That's why I have Van der Wadel to assist me. He'll carry on when I'm gone—or so I hope."

He rose from the couch slowly. "He'll be my literary heir," he said, opening a box that contained the pale native cigars which he only infrequently smoked. "And a fitting heir—combining as he does a mixture of East and West—though this is just a happenstance, just a piece of good luck."

He clipped the cigar, lit it in short quiet puffs, tossed away the match with a careless gesture. "That is, I didn't deliberately set out to find someone in whose veins both kinds of blood were flowing—European and Asian. No, I took on Van der Wadel largely because he could read and talk the old languages of this part of the world. That's invaluable to me."

He began to walk up and down the long dimly lit room. As he paced the floor in his quiet sandals, Caroline had the distinct impression that he struggled with an impulse to disburden himself to her in some more personal way. But when he spoke again, he only said, "Also, Van der Wadel is very much interested in the subject." He grinned suddenly. "In Evil." he added, and paused for a moment in his pacing to cast her an inquiring, teasing glance.

She felt she was expected to question him further, that he wished it, and she managed a feeble, "What drew you to such a morbid subject? I mean—why a compendium of *evil?*"

"Morbid?" he queried, raising his eyebrows in mock astonishment. She had done just what he desired; asked a question which permitted him to become airily daring. "Not morbid, Lady B. Quite the opposite. A compendium of evil could act as a tremendous psychological purge—a great universal catharsis. At least that's the way I see it."

She resigned herself to acting as audience for one of his monologues, wishing only that it were earlier in the evening, and that she did not feel quite so languid and thick-witted in the hot tropic stillness.

But Stephen did not immediately begin. He had stopped, in

his pacing, at the extreme edge of the screened veranda which adjoined the large living room. Here he stood looking out into the black night with the air of a man seeing and hearing something that no one else could.

In spite of the heat, Lady Brace suddenly felt chilled. Into her lap she dropped the fan she had been passing before her face and sat waiting, listening intently, as Stephen now was. But she heard only the familiar tumultuous orchestration that rose nightly from the flooded paddy fields and the gardens; a rolling swelling diapason of frogs and toads, blending with the singing rhythmic monotone of thousands of cicadas, a very wall of sound, so thick and dense that it seemed to her less the noise of earth creatures than the voice of the atmosphere itself. What was Stephen hearing? Had he caught, far off across the valley, or in the not-far-distant jungle, some higher sound, more individualized—jackals on the hunt, perhaps, or the trumpeting of an elephant? She strained forward but caught nothing—nothing that could account for her brother's air of tense and guarded expectancy.

But if he heard anything special, he made no mention of it. After several long moments, while she stared at his back and saw the moths striking the screens beside him with compulsive monotony, he began again to talk.

Without turning around he said, "One big thing wrong with Western man—he no longer believes in Evil. He's got a whole new vocabulary, a whole new set of theories, to account for the natural inborn cussedness and depravity of the human animal." His voice darkened. "But this optimism—if that's what it is—is entirely false. Unreal, dangerously unreal, Caro, for Evil *does* exist, and, if we refuse to admit its existence, it breaks out when least expected, and wreaks havoc on a grand scale."

Scraps of conversation—overheard, half listened to, between Humphrey and the local curate back in Somerset—intruded themselves into Lady Brace's mind. She was grateful to recall them, for they seemed now to possess for her some sustaining power— a defense of sorts against a complex, unsympathetic, even hostile viewpoint which she felt her brother preparing to advance.

Suddenly, with more heat than Humphrey, but with the phrases he had used to the Reverend Cyril Smith-Moxley, she exclaimed,

"But I think it's time we *did* forget the notion of Evil. All those dreadful, gloomy, paralyzing theories about Original Sin. It's high time we chucked all that medieval nonsense overboard!"

Stephen appeared delighted at her unexpected defiance.

"Ah, no, you're quite wrong, Caro," he said with his exasperating air of self-assurance. "It really amounts almost to a universal psychosis in our time—this refusal to believe in Evil. You may not see its dangers, but I do."

"Dangers?" she repeated, her voice tinged with both disbelief and impatience.

He remained unruffled. "Yes, dangers. Dangers because this kind of attitude towards Evil is, as I just said, unreal. And in unreality there is always extreme danger, for unreality in thinking, and in experience, produces fear; and fear, in its turn, is what often prompts violence—that kind of irrational violence no one can explain, seemingly *unmotivated* violence—as people say."

He was getting "wound up," as old Annie used to remark of him when, in summer holidays at the Adirondacks camp—and always in their father's absence—they would eat their breakfasts together in the forbidden kitchen, consuming stacks of flapjacks while Stephen, tossing out the wildest notions and theories about religion, would rouse not only Annie but the cook to delighted shrieks of Irish protest: "Holy Mother of God! You're a limb of the old Nick, that's what you are!" Crossing themselves as they poured milk into their endless cups of tea, ecstatically muttering, "*Save* us!" they waited for more. . . .

"Western man is afraid," Stephen said now. He was still standing with his back turned, still staring out into the vibrant tropical blackness beyond the veranda.

At that moment there descended one of those abrupt vast silences which Lady Brace had already experienced on this exotic island. As if at a given signal, all the manifold separate sounds of frog, toad, cicada, rustle of leaf, of palm, of moth, of gekko, stopped short. The very air seemed to wait, suspended, while something unseen, something menacing, passed by.

These sudden silences had wakened her from deep sleep upon several occasions. She had lain, with the rest of nature, tense and unbreathing as the night. Now she caught herself thinking of the natives' belief in the presence of universal malevolent spirits, in the Evil Eye, in subtle emanations from powers visible and invisible, and she remembered the bleached skull of a water buffalo Stephen had pointed out to her, placed near the valued betel vine in a small garden patch to protect the plant from possible harm.

Was it this silence for which Stephen had been waiting; had he sensed that it was about to descend? If so, he turned it now to dramatic use. "Yes," he said softly, clearly, with careful emphasis. "We are all desperately afraid."

A tremor passed swiftly over Caroline. I shan't be able to sleep again tonight, she thought in despair.

Stephen, still gazing away from her into the blind night that lay beyond the lighted room, was continuing in the heavy quiet.

"Yes, he's more afraid—the educated Western man—than he was even in the so-called Dark Ages. And there's a reason, Caro! Western man's afraid because of all the bogies and beasties he's got locked up in his basement under a lot of deceptive safe-sounding labels like Environmental Factors, Maladjustment, Split Personalities, Economic Insecurity, et cetera, et cetera. Western man goes around reading off these labels on the animal cages, chanting to himself a whole new lingo of 'It's *only*—,' 'It's *because*' —little, tight, safe Excelsior phrases, onward and upward, ever upward and onward, while in his guts he's scared stiff because he damned well *knows* it's going to break out one day from sheer pressure, and when it does all hell is going to break loose. You'll see! We'll all live to see it! Human bestiality may sleep for a while, but it always wakes up."

He was doing to her what he had always been able to do: filling her with shapeless apprehension, a sense of creeping decay, inevitable decline, malignant invisible forces to be found in the very spores of moss on the timbers of a rotting barn on Long Island, or in obscene orchids feeding on perfumed air here in Ceylon—ugliness in beauty, and beauty in ugliness. . . .

She made an effort to speak in a calm and casual tone. "If it's Western man you're so concerned with, Stephen, why are you living and doing your research out here in the East?"

He turned to face her. "A valid question," he approved.

Her heart sank. She was encouraging him to be expansive. It was long past her usual hour to retire; she felt unutterably weary but dared not say so.

"The answer is quite simple. I'm in Ceylon because here it's much easier to begin accumulating the material I need. In the East, life isn't so cluttered. Not so many interferences and outside drives and pressures as in the West—Europe, America. Here it is perfectly normal—if that's the word—to set off on some kind of highly personal search. You can be a little odd, or even *very* odd, without arousing community suspicion—community censure."

A note of bitterness had entered his voice, but it was not sustained as he went on more lightly, "Also, I find it easier to keep my mind on my subject in an environment where mechanical and gadget values haven't yet taken over. I never did find any reassurance in carburetors, dynamos and push buttons, and I still don't think a better garbage-disposal unit will dispose of all the garbage, either."

He walked back to the couch and stretched out full length. She had asked him a question, and obviously he intended to answer it fully.

"I thought first of making India my base, but then I decided India was too vast, too complex. Also, the general problem of Good and Evil is further complicated in India. There madness and saintliness frequently appear in a similar guise. If you're really insane enough in India, you get treated as a holy man. You'd never be locked up for smearing your body with the ash of cow dung, or sticking needles through your skin, or lying down on a mattress of spikes in order to get closer to some obscure ecstasy. Of course, this makes it fascinating to me. I'll get back there in time. But for the present it's the old island of Lanka for me. You see, Caro, in Ceylon, the very beauty of the natural setting points up the problem nicely, heightens the dramatic contrasts—don't you think?

. His voice had taken on mockery again. Was he reminding her how she had confessed to finding the beauty of Ceylon deeply disturbing? The dreadful thought crossed her mind that her brother might be slowly going mad. Immediately she rejected the idea, for, as she furtively studied him where he lay at ease on the couch,

103

she could not deny what she had already stated in her letters to Humphrey: Stephen had never seemed more healthy, balanced, serene and sure of himself, than here on this tropical island at the world's end. As for his bizarre talk—actually, when had he not been riding some wild and fanciful theory?

She made up her mind to be bold, to pursue at all costs the final purpose of Stephen's quest in the field of Evil. She must, she told herself, at least be able to answer Humphrey's questions when she got back to England.

In a determined voice she said, "Give me some examples of what you research, Stephen."

He turned his head to look at her. She avoided his gaze as, after a significant pause, he asked, "You're quite sure you want to know?"

His way of speaking told her at once that she had taken a dangerous tack. She temporized, "Of course. Why not? Isn't what you do going to be published eventually—for everyone to read?"

He laughed, then—scornful, derisive. "*Everyone!* My God! Hardly, you booby. A Compendium of Evil—it'll only be bought by a few psychiatrists, one or two neurotic millionaires, maybe some scholarly priests. I'd seriously doubt its appearing in any average library, short of maybe the basement shelves of the Carnegie Publics."

He shrugged. "Still, maybe you're right. It won't be long, certainly, before people everywhere are going to get so frightened they'll be *desperate* for any clues on why human beasts behave the way they do."

He spat out the two words "human beasts" like one getting rid of a bad taste, then fell silent for so long that Caroline began to hope he had been sidetracked and was pursuing some private line of thought he had no wish, or intention, to share.

But finally, almost as if an invisible current returned him to the abandoned track, he spoke, shifting his head on the flat cushion but not looking in her direction.

"Ceylon—why I'm in Ceylon?—Ah, yes! Well, one reason I chose this remote island is because of its history. Here, in a microcosm, you can study the rise and fall of powers and principalities and individual humans—noble and base. Also, I knew nothing at all about Ceylon and its history before I came. This kind of freshness is valuable. Has a real impact. For one thing, you get your own history a little better in perspective when you come face to face with a fabulous civilization of which you've never even *heard!*"

He turned, then, to look at her, his voice vibrant, his face shining with intensity. "Before you go back to England, Caro, I'll take you to see the so-called Lost Cities of Ceylon. They make all the antique wonders of the world, except perhaps those of the Egyptians, look like the work of pigmies!"

She murmured that she would love to see the ruins, that she had been reading something about them in a book found in her bedroom. She looked openly at her wrist watch. He ignored the hint.

"And they *had* wisdom," he cried, "those old Sinhalese—real wisdom—but what became of it? It went underground for centuries and popped up somewhere on the other side of the world."

"Wisdom," she repeated in a guilty voice, for she had not been able to stifle a yawn and he had frowned as if about to accuse her of mental laziness—a charge he had often leveled at her in the past.

"Yes—wisdom. You don't want an example, but I'm going to give you one anyway."

What complex and subtle forms cruelty could take! He seemed determined to ignore her obvious fatigue. He was sitting up now, fresher than ever, his posture alive, dynamic. "A rare type," Humphrey had once said of him, "the kind of human being on whom certain ideas can act like a shot of adrenalin." It's my fault, she thought. I should never have got him started. No use to resist now. I might as well listen. Humphrey will be interested.

He began to speak of a "globe-trotting Chinese—one of those world travelers of the early centuries A.D. who make today's tourists seem like weaklings—came to Lanka in the sixth century. He's left some descriptions of what he saw, Caro. Utterly fascinating. There's an account of a vast sacred road, along which could be seen five hundred different statues of the different bodily forms of their Supreme Being—that is, the Buddha. Just think of it! Miles of reproductions of all the *forms* the Buddha had passed through—animal and human—before he became the En-lightened One. Now, I ask you, what's that but the theory of evolution expressed in sculpture instead of expounded in words, as the West eventually did it?"

His expression of intense excitement almost resembled joy, yet why did it make her feel like weeping?

He rushed on. "Just consider for a moment, Lady B, the mysterious wisdom those sculptures expressed: the wisdom of accepting as present—invisibly present—in even the most en-lightened of human creatures, in a great World Teacher like the Buddha, all the varied forms of his—of man's—evolutionary past!"

Overhead Lady Brace saw one of the gekkos capture the moth it had been stalking. The gekko took the moth in his small jaws and proceeded to dash its head against a beam. She fancied she could hear, above the whir of the ceiling fan, the sound of the death assault and even the cries of the doomed insect, for there was, so John van der Wadel had told her the very day of her arrival, a species of moth in Ceylon that screamed in dying.

The whole world seemed to her suddenly hideous, meaningless, an endless vile chain of the attacker and the preyed-upon. I must get out of this terrible place, she thought, back to a more familiar Nature: the perky Somerset thrush under the bright holly tree with the string of red worm in his beak, the ugly naked mouths of the nestlings agape to receive the worm—*could* that be what she meant?—for these pictures, too, seemed equally re-pellent at the moment. Still, she argued with herself, there *is* less of the death-struggle in the temperate zone; at least it's not so overwhelming, so *open*. Almost in panic she thought, Surely this particular atmosphere, this fantastic over-active environment, can-not be good for Stephen, sensitive and suggestible as he is. Should she try to persuade him to leave?

Her brother was proceeding with maddening equanimity.

"Yes, it's the fashion now in certain circles—among the young 'liberal intellectuals,' I think they're called—to blame Europe for Asia's obvious sickness. But I can tell you, Caro, I've found a very real affinity on the level of *extreme bestiality* between the Portuguese invaders of several hundred years back and the people of this Pearl of the Orient. All 'demented,' we say now, 'psychotic'—whatever those inexact terms signify. The point is, since I'm concerned with exposing Evil at the heart of the world, and thus in the heart of man—every man—I'm naturally interested in being able to show an evenly balanced East-West account."

He was mocking again, but who, what, was the butt of his mockery? She could no more determine it now than she had ever been able to.

"Shall I tell you about the Portuguese coming to this island of surpassing beauty, this last paradise?" he inquired. Again the question was purely rhetorical. He swept on, not waiting for her acquiescence.

"They came not only to steal the cinnamon trade but, incidentally, to bring the message of brotherly love 'to the heathen in his blindness bowing down to wood and stone.' Well, the Portuguese—they had some very novel ways of spreading Christianity. One evangelist, for instance, took out his zeal by forcing native women, just before beheading them, to hold their own babies while millstones ground them to mush."

"Oh, Stephen, *please!*"

Her shocked response appeared to afford him only intense satisfaction.

"There are even more horrendous examples," he assured her. "But don't jump to conclusions about the depravity of the European! Before you join the throng of those now so popular critics of Christianity who enjoy recounting the bloody deeds of pioneering Westerners in Asia, let me cite a few examples of native, home-grown, Eastern Evil. Not just on the part of power-ridden psychotic kings and generals, either. The so-called simple people exhibited surprising talents in this direction."

He took from the ashtray the cigar, which by now had gone out, and relit it. "Do you remember that bird that frightened you so badly the first week you were here?"

"I'll never forget it."

Indeed, she had been so terrified that, in spite of her timidity at invading her brother's privacy, she had gone at once to summon him, for she had been wakened from a deep sleep by a succession of gruesome sounds which seemed to be issuing from a human throat. The noises, beginning with strangling, gurgling protests, had risen to razor-sharp screams, diminishing at last into the bubblings of some shapeless agony.

"You told me it was only an owl."

"That's what the natives claim. However, it's a *haunted* owl. Into this bird, according to folk legend, the soul of a terribly tortured woman entered at her death. In revenge for some misdeed—which it's rather significant that the natives can't name— a Sinhalese husband forced his wife to eat her own child."

"Oh, Stephen, stop!" She no longer cared about showing revulsion. She had had all she could take. "Do be reasonable! After all," she cried, her voice filled with resistance, "that's only a legend."

He pounced at once. "*Only* a legend? *Aha!* Where do you think legends come from if not out of man's consciousness?"

"Stephen! Really!" She spoke with scorn, determined not to permit him to trap her again into some futile argument. "You sound absolutely insane!"

The effect of this remark was instantaneous and entirely unexpected. Stephen grew very quiet and stared off into space, his face masked, icy. What have I done? she wondered, feeling her heart sink, reacting to her brother's abrupt change of mood with immediate apprehension and dread.

An ominous reserve lay under his voice when he finally said, "You told me that once before in my life."

She replied, nervous but quite truthful, "I did? When?"

He looked at her, his expression one of complete incredulity; no playing at dramatics now. "You don't remember?"

She shook her head, swallowed hard. "No, honestly, Stephen, I don't." She sounded like a frightened schoolgirl and hated herself for it.

He continued to stare at her, at first unbelieving; then his expression slowly changed; became vindictive. Some interior struggle seemed to pinch his features and pale his skin. At last, in his most acid voice, he said, "Well, if it ever comes back to you— the occasion on which you called me insane—I hope you'll be able to admit that what I told you then was right—whether I was out of my mind or not!"

"But you're—often right," she stammered, oppressed with the

conviction that she must somehow make amends, though she could not imagine for what. She could feel his pain, hidden behind his bitterness. "I'm—terribly stupid," she went on stammering, "and—I know it, I always—have known it, but you're you're . . ."

"Yes," he said cruelly, "grope around and find a good safe word!"

Tears sprang into her eyes. "I didn't mean—" She was floundering hopelessly now. Long-buried sensations and memories assailed her. How was it that Stephen could still do this to her; be entirely in the wrong, senselessly unjust, and yet somehow manage to make her feel to blame?

"Please, Stephen," she begged. It was a formula phrase, one she had employed in the past not only to her brother but with equal ineffectiveness to Ralph Parton at the first terrifying intimation of one of his rages. "Please, Stephen," she repeated.

After several moments, to her deep relief, Stephen spoke in a tone still unforgiving but controlled. "Oh, all right. Forget it. It's late. Let's get to bed."

She knew better than to beg him then to recount the obviously upsetting circumstances under which she had called him an idiot; no, not idiot, *insane*—that was it.

She left the room hurriedly with only a timid good night. Afterwards, lying troubled and wakeful in the tropic heat, she prayed only that she not hear again, this night of all nights, the agonized scream of the haunted owl.

12

Frederick Hollis's man, not the glamorous figure in bottle-green livery but a less conspicuous and older servant in more familiar dark whipcord, opened the door of the car for Lady Brace at the little house near Gracie Square where Lydia was living.

"At what time shall I return, Madam?"

Caroline Brace, still aware that she did not much wish to accept favors from Frederick Hollis, said quickly, "Oh, but you're not to bother with picking me up."

"Mr. Hollis gave orders, Madam. I was to give a number for you to call in case your plans were uncertain when I left you. Would you care to do that, Madam?"

"Oh, yes, thank you, perhaps that would be the best idea," Lady Brace agreed. I'll consult Lydia, she thought.

Lydia, who must have been watching, opened the door for her mother. They touched cheeks; not at all the sort of tender enveloping embrace of their first meeting.

As she entered the small drawing room Caroline Brace exclaimed, "How charming!" for the room had an immediate effect of gaiety, of a lively and imaginative use of color.

"It's a poky little place but rather fun," Lydia said in her offhand way. "It was so absurd to begin with, I just decided to make it completely ridiculous, so I went Victorian throughout."

"But it's Victorian *plus*."

"That's because of all those silly Easter-egg colors."

"It's charming," Lady Brace repeated.

"I'm glad you approve, Mummy. *Town and Country* ran some pictures of it. I intended to send the piece on to you, but I forgot—as usual. I'll look it up, if you'd really like to see it."

"I would, of course. You have a real decorating flair, Lydia. This kind of thing—delightful!" She was looking at a large framed montage of old-fashioned greeting cards: Valentine elaborations of paper lace, pierced hearts, mortuary hands holding prim bouquets; Christmas snow-scenes dusted with glitter, fat little girls in ermine tippets and muffs waiting passively under sprigs of mistletoe. "My childhood," Lady Brace said, smiling. She turned away and once more circling the room with her glance repeated, "Yes, you have a real flair, darling. Have you never thought of using your talent seriously; professionally, I mean?"

Lydia shrugged. "You don't remember how lazy I am, Mummy."

"Really lazy, dear? I don't quite believe it."

"Can't you remember how bad I was in school? Rosie always got the marks. I often think that may be why I got married so young. I didn't want to go on humiliating myself by barely squeaking through my courses. And Aunt Bertha was very strong on female education, if you remember."

"Oh, I know," Lady Brace murmured. "She quite despised my total lack of brains."

"Poor Aunt Bertha," Lydia said slowly. "How she hated to die!"

Lady Brace did not in the least wish to talk about her former sister-in-law. To discourage the topic she began walking about the room picking up and looking at the small amusing objects Lydia had placed on her tables.

Lydia continued, "But then I suppose it *is* hideous—old age, all the rest of it. Cancer, particularly."

I will not be drawn into a discussion of old age and death before lunch, Lady Brace said to herself. Nor after lunch, if I can avoid it. I do hope I shan't find Lydia one of those women who dwell morbidly on disease and demise, details of operations, that sort of thing. Perhaps it is uppermost in her mind because of Belle Hollis's dying with such aggravating slowness.

She said, "You've got so many absurd little boots." She was looking at a collection of tiny Victorian boots, long-toed, narrow, some of light wood, some of black papier-mâché with insets of mother-of-pearl.

"I know," Lydia replied. "I've been told I have a shoe fetish."

Caroline Brace ignored this remark also. She had come to a stop before a small oil near the fireplace, precise and elegant, showing figures in *fin de siècle* bathing costumes standing on a beach. She said, "Oh, I like this. Who did it?"

Lydia laughed. "Mummy, you're really the perfect guest. I did it."

"But darling! Why did I never know? You're very like your Uncle Stephen!" she cried in astonishment.

"I take that as a real compliment." Lydia seated herself near a small tray holding a carafe and some Waterford glasses. She poured each of them a sherry. "As I told you, Uncle Stephen fascinates me. I'd forgotten he once wanted to paint. I'd love to see something he did when he was young. What were his paintings like?"

"Well, there were different kinds." Caroline tried to recall Stephen's canvases. They refused to come into accurate focus. "I think you'd call them expressionistic," she said. "But he was capable of doing exquisite things too—like that," and she nodded again at the little oil. "And he loved subjects that just faintly caricatured the immediate past—also like that canvas of yours."

"Oh, I must see some!"

"Perhaps I'll uncover a cache in the attic." Lady Brace held back a sigh at thought of the attic. "Unless he destroyed them all sometime in the past—which would be quite like him."

"What made him give up painting?"

"He said he wasn't good enough."

"That sounds like me too." Again Lydia's voice held the down-beat her mother had caught in it when she spoke of having married young because her school work was unsatisfactory; a seemingly casual remark that had led directly to mention of disease and death.

As they drank their sherry, making only the most trivial talk, Lady Brace thought of the difference between her two daughters. There was about Lydia a neatness, a precision, apparent even in her house, in spite of its air of playful fantasy, that hinted of unexpected disciplines. Lady Brace had again yesterday's awareness of indefinable contradictory elements in her younger child. She sensed in Lydia a surprising untapped energy, greater than that of Rosemary, who evinced by contrast so much speed and dash. What held these forces underground in Lydia?

When a prim Negro maid announced lunch, Lydia slipped her arm through her mother's and gave it one of her little shy squeezes. "So lovely to have you here," she said.

In the dining room Lady Brace exclaimed again about the use of color. "You should do something with your talents, darling," she said once more, this time with added emphasis and conviction.

"Why?" Lydia's question was not antagonistic, merely curious.

Lady Brace hesitated a moment before answering. "You'd—well, you'd—give people pleasure with it."

"Would I? I wonder." Lydia sounded both amused and skeptical. She paused. Her voice changed. "I don't think I'm particularly noted for giving people pleasure."

This was, Lady Brace feared, the opening note of warning, the first fateful phrase, as forthright and formal as a passage in an opera's prelude announcing what is to come. *Tristan and Isolde*—was it not?—where a downward leap of a seventh prepares one for the lovers' death; and she saw Mademoiselle Fleury, their old governess, in the box at the Met with the open score on her lap and her little gold pencil tapping it lightly to capture the wandering attention of her young charges.

Recollections of Mademoiselle Fleury, of matinées at the Met, had interfered with a prompt rejection of Lydia's oblique self-denunciation. Lady Brace managed a belated murmur as the maid set before her a crystal bowl of soup: cream of chicken, ice cold, tasting subtly of lemon and curry. Yes, she thought, Lydia is a natural hostess, but she feared to remark on this discovery lest it prompt her child to further self-deprecation. Not that I can possibly avoid the moments ahead, she thought—for I do not believe what Lydia has to say to me today can be anything simple. Why did the fateful theme of *Tristan and Isolde* recur once more? But, of course, Rosemary's hints of passion, tragedy. . . . Now the maid had taken away the soup and brought on a cheese soufflé, properly brown outside, yellow as buttercups inside, moist, yet light as air. "What a wonderful cook you have!" exclaimed Lady Brace.

"Emma does it all," Lydia said. "She's an artist," and, although she did not look at the maid putting before her a field salad to be tossed, Lady Brace saw the smile the compliment called forth and sensed in Lydia the combination of firm hand and kind heart which alone can create a climate of efficient service.

I owe it to my child, Lady Brace told herself, to help her tell me what she has to say—no matter what the effort may cost. She began, "You made a remark in the drawing room a few moments ago, darling, about—about being married too young. Do you think you were?"

"Yes, Mummy, I'm afraid I do." There was no stress or undue emphasis in Lydia's reply and Lady Brace felt emboldened to press on.

"Can you tell me why?"

Lydia looked thoughtful. She cast her eyes onto her plate—

she had eaten very little—reached for a cigarette, checked the impulse. Returning the cigarette to its antique silver box, "It's hard to give up smoking," she remarked. "I find I reach for one automatically every time I'm asked a question—or whenever I start to think."

"Why are you giving it up?"

"Frederick wants me to." The flat statement had nothing in or around it which made possible the expression of Lady Brace's curiosity as to why Frederick Hollis should have authority in such matters.

"About being married young," Lydia continued, "I suppose I think that was partly why it didn't work out with Jack. We were both so ignorant—not suited to one another in any way. So, of course, it caught up with us in time—with me at least."

The answer was quite unsatisfactory. Yet because she did not get the feeling that Lydia was deliberately evasive, Caroline Brace, after taking a long sip of the hot tea she had requested to relax her dry, contracted throat, asked, "What do you mean—it caught up with you?"

"Just that."

Then, as though realizing her mother's questions might be costing an effort, Lydia gazed directly across the table. Her finely arched, pale brown eyebrows were lifted in the questioning wings that had given her face, in childhood, such an appealing air; touching, too, for it was an expression then far older than her years. Lady Brace had the distinct sensation of being measured; her daughter was asking herself just how real her mother's interest was, how far she dared go.

"I mean, Mummy, that I finally fell in love. I couldn't help it. It just happened—and it tore my life in half." She looked away as she spoke the last words.

"Oh, my darling." Caroline Brace imagined her own voice reflected the instantaneous panic that sprang up at utterance of the sad dead phrase, "it tore my life in half." Why have I let this happen—this moment of soul-baring? I might have avoided it—and should have—for it is all quite useless, "after the fact."

But since there was now no possible retreat, she faltered, "In love! You don't mean Frederick, do you?"

"No." The single word of denial came without emphasis of any kind. Lydia appeared almost to consider her mother's question irrelevant. Without further hesitation she explained in a voice that remained controlled and cool.

"It was a man called Alex White. I thought surely Rosie must have told you about him—it. It was fairly common gossip at the time. You must have heard rumors." She was again gazing at her mother as though wondering if she would catch her in some polite insincerity.

Caroline Brace managed to put down her sense of panic, to reply with at least half honesty, "Yes, I do remember something."

She did not say that she had debated at the time, when first she had heard the stories, about coming to New York to see Lydia; but Humphrey's condition had suddenly worsened and—she saw it clearly now—cowardice too had weighed against the decision. For what can I possibly say to my daughter on the subject of overwhelming, irresistible, illicit love? she had asked herself in extenuation. "Fate's fate," Lydia herself had said only a few days before, staring out at the neglected lawn of Fox Meadows. It was a thought she, too, had often had, though she would have not given it quite this flip phrasing. Around the notion of the fatefulness of fate there clustered, on her part, a whole vague accretion of evasions, fears and guilts, an emotional tangle she had never managed to sort out, had, in fact, never tried to sort out.

"You probably remember, you wrote and invited me to come to Braceledge for a visit," Lydia went on, "so I somehow felt you must have been told about what was happening."

Lady Brace's murmur expressed neither affirmation nor denial.

"I didn't come to Braceledge then, because I couldn't tear myself away from Alex. That's the truth of it. When I did come to England, a little later, you may remember, I stayed in London. What I was trying to do then, Mummy, to be quite honest, was to get Alex White back again. I didn't care how! I'd have crawled down Piccadilly on my hands and knees just—just to go to bed with him again."

I must, Lady Brace warned herself, no matter what comes out of my child, reveal no shock, no distaste or censure. I must try to keep my face from appearing stricken.

She raised what she hoped was a calm receptive glance. Lydia's face showed no special emotion after her startling remark, except a certain tightening around the mouth and jawline, a drained look in her eyes.

"Let's go into the other room, Mummy, out of earshot," she said. "Are you sure you won't have a little coffee—or more tea?"

When her mother said "No," Lydia took the small tray Emma had placed before her and carried it into the drawing room. They seated themselves on either side of the fireplace with its Victorian paraphernalia, its pleated white paper fan occupying the empty grate.

Here a distinct change came over Lydia. Her voice had a new intensity, a mounting pressure as she said, "I never talk about any of this, Mummy. Not to anyone—at least I haven't for ages. But lately—I don't know why—it's been crowding back. I keep remembering. I've had the feeling I had to talk—*must*—and to you. I'd hoped we'd find a chance to be alone while you were here." She added, "If you can stand it. I *loathe* hearing other people's troubles myself."

"But this isn't other people's troubles," Caroline Brace said gently. She wanted to say, "After all, I'm your mother, darling," but this statement seemed banal, theatrical, proper only to a drawing-room comedy. Instead she added, in lowered voice, "I only wish I felt I could be of some help."

"No one can help! It's too late for that." The desperate words were spoken with utter impassivity. Lydia swallowed the contents of her coffee cup in two gulps. She poured another cupful. "Have you ever been terribly in love, Mummy?"

How strange, how very strange, Caroline Brace thought—twice in as many days I've had this question put to me! It was less easy to reply to her daughter than to her brother. She answered with a certain hesitation, "Yes—I think so."

"Humpy, I suppose," Lydia assumed in a calm tone. "I somehow never thought you'd loved Daddy—not in a big way."

This last remark startled Lady Brace so much that her heart began to flutter. How difficult the truth is! What if I were to reply: "No, it was not Humpy I loved, it was your father"—but this was only partial truth; it all depended on the interpretation of love, for she had also hated and feared Ralph Parton and never Humphrey Brace—and how did one ever sort out these complexities within the bounds of formal speech—if, indeed, with speech at all?

She became aware of her old dislike and resentment of her dead sister-in-law, Bertha. "Did you get that idea from your Aunt Bertha —about your father, I mean?"

Lydia looked a little surprised. "No, I don't think so. Not that I remember, anyway. I think it's just a feeling I always had, as long as I can remember."

There was a short silence. Again Caroline Brace forced herself. "Why did you ask me just that question—if I'd ever been in love?"

"Because, Mummy, unless you've felt the way I did about Alex, *with* Alex—and I don't honestly think most people ever have— then the story will make no sense to you, ever. It never made any sense to my husband, or my sister—I can tell you that! They thought I was crazy. The truth is, I was in love, the whole of me, head over heels, immersed, half-conscious. . . ." She broke off. "No—that's not true. Not half-conscious, super-conscious: a sort of intensification of—of everything, including *me* . . . Well, I can't describe it, but if you've had it you know. It's what most people spend a lifetime wishing they could have—a completely terrific sexual experience."

She had spoken quietly, but each statement came with such calm, sure force that it seemed lifted out of her deepest being by an almost physical effort. Lady Brace, looking down at her own hands folded tensely in her lap, waited for her daughter to continue. When Lydia said nothing for several long moments, she knew she must once more help her to speak, to unburden herself.

"But then—what happened? Wasn't he free to marry you?"

"Yes!" Lydia said. "That's the really ghastly part of it, he was." There was another silence. "Bill was to blame."

Lady Brace asked dully, "You mean—Little Bill?"

Lydia nodded. "Yes, my son." She gave a laugh that had no humor in it. "Bill got terribly upset. Violently. I don't know how he knew what was going on—he was so young and we were very careful—but he did. One day when Alex came to the house to take me out somewhere (this was before Jack and I were separated) Bill came in from playing and began to scream and kick Alex and tell him to get out and leave me alone and I don't know what all. It was really simply frightful. The cook heard—everybody in the house heard. Bill had such a crying fit no one could stop him. Hysterics. Convulsions. We had to call a doctor."

Lydia got up, walked to the end of the room, walked back, sat down again and continued in the same flat, calm voice. "The effect on Alex was really grim. He'd had a broken home himself. He'd never spoken much about it, but—it all came back. He just couldn't take it—doing it to Bill, I mean. We talked it over for days. It was hideous. We were *desperate!* I'd already told Jack I wanted a divorce, but then, well, after all of that—we even had to put Bill under a psychiatrist for a while—then after weeks of it Jack and I finally decided we'd better try again—for the children's sake. As for Alex and me, we thought we could wait—wait until maybe the children were older, until Bill was steadier. Alex got an assignment in London, thinking—we both thought so—it would make it easier, not to be within reach of one another."

She broke off again. This time she was silent so long that Caroline, still not able to look at her, forced herself to ask, "And then?"

There was a pause. "Well, Mummy," Lydia's voice commanded Caroline's glance. She lifted it to see her daughter's jaw still firm, her eyes still expressionless. "My going back to Jack didn't work, that's all. It didn't work worth a damn—not for either of us. For one thing, something between us was dead, really dead. Dead in every way—including sexually. Mostly that. And it hadn't ever been much good. It had never been remotely, not within a hundred million light years, like my experience with Alex."

After another long silence Caroline asked, "Why?"

The most futile of all questions, she reminded herself when Lydia answered, impatient, "Oh, *why!* Who knows why? I don't!"

She appeared, however, driven to attempt an analysis. "Jack was—well—what? Repressed? Maybe that's not the word. Puritanical?" She shrugged. "I don't know. Terribly limited, anyway. No imagination in bed. Just routine procedures. It had always been like that—only I hadn't known the difference, that's all."

As she spoke Lydia's voice grew harder, anger crept into it. She is beginning to feel too much, her mother realized. Talking has revived the dammed emotions. She is holding back a flood that is about to sweep her away. . . . Lady Brace asked herself once more, Am I meant to help the dam to burst? Or should I try to prop it up? She knew her questions were not valid, for Lydia had said she wished to talk, and her need was apparent.

Speaking in a low tone—sounding, she felt certain, cringing, tentative, and quite undesirous of receiving a direct answer—Lady Brace inquired, "And with Alex it was . . .?"

She was in no way prepared for the explosive candor with which her daughter filled in the blank space.

"The works!" Lydia flung out the flippant, vulgar phrase like a child throwing a stone.

Lady Brace shrank back a little in her chair. But if Lydia observed this, it did not influence her. She went on, without trying to spare her mother's sensibilities, in the same unfeeling, flippant manner.

"I'm told it's the way the French make love. I don't know, never having been made love to by a Frenchman. I only know once you've had it, nothing else is ever any good."

Caroline Brace sat with her eyes fixed on the pattern of old-fashioned roses in the Victorian carpet. Please spare me, she begged silently. I am not at all sure I can endure this.

After a while she heard Lydia saying, as if from a long distance, "I suppose I'm shocking you terribly, Mummy. You probably think I'm perfectly disgusting—if you even understand what I'm talking about. I should have known better than to try to talk to *anyone* about it. We are all such moles—ostriches. . . ."

Caroline Brace rallied her tremulous forces. She tore her eyes away from the Victorian roses, raised them as far as her daughter's hands; saw her slim fingers twisting the big square emerald back and forth, back and forth, below a rigid joint. "No, of course not— not shocking—or disgusting," she was able to say. But she could not bring herself to look into Lydia's face, for she knew if she did that she would learn at once whether Lydia believed her faltering assurances, or thought her only a polite liar.

A silence enveloped them both; a clock on the mantel chimed two precise strokes. If the silence lasts long enough, Lady Brace found herself thinking, I shall utter something I may come to regret. I shall hear myself saying: "Your own father made love to me in very special ways, and the truth is, my child, that in the end it did not compensate for all the other terrible lacks and strains in our relationship; lacks and strains which would someday quite surely have forced me to leave him, a decision that death prevented my having to make" . . . But wait!—there was argument here: *Had* Ralph's love-making not, perhaps, compensated for the blows with the riding crop, the breakfast coffee cups hurled across the floor, the broken mirrors—so many mirrors! . . . Had she not said, only two days before to Stephen, that of the three people she had truly loved, Ralph Parton was one? The clear separation of A from B, right from left, black from white, began to waver and shift; the pattern shattered into elements she could neither equate nor reconcile.

To her relief Lydia began once more to speak, her voice again controlled, coldly purposeful, as though she had determined to get to the end, to scrape the bottom of the vessel, to empty it once and for all.

"The worst of it was, the children didn't seem much better—in spite of the sacrifices we had all made for them—Jack too. For it wasn't easy what Jack did—taking me back. I know that. Actually, Pam had never been very much upset, except as she reflected Bill's state. But Bill certainly didn't improve very much. Of course, he didn't have such terrible crying fits any more, but he was still very nervous. Sometimes it seemed to me he was even more so, as though when he'd had something tangible to—to *fight*—he'd been relieved." She broke off; cried after a moment, "Oh, it's all so tangled!"

"I know," Lady Brace whispered. "I know." She longed to be able to speak fully and wisely to Lydia's need, to express her passionate understanding of her child's unhappiness and confusion, but she could not find any words except her whispered affirmation.

After a moment, "We tried!" Lydia said, and for the first time her voice hinted at breaking. "God knows we tried! We did our best—all three of us—Alex, Jack, me. Oh, I've thought so much about it, Mummy, and I can't get it to make any sense."

"Oh, my darling," Lady Brace said softly, and clenched her hands to hold back the tears.

"The nearest I can ever come to the truth of it, is that our heads, even our hearts, wanted it to be right again. But our bodies—they just couldn't be fooled. Couldn't change. Jack and I were through. We were through because it had never been, that's all."

Confused questions, admonitions, rose and faded in Caroline Brace's consciousness. Heads, hearts, bodies—how separate them, how distinguish? "Were your hearts really as anxious to make it work as your heads were?"—she was tempted to ask. "Was what you had had with Alex, and not with Jack, so important after all—so really vital?" She saw, with a rush of happy memory, an image of Humphrey in his wheel-chair with his field glasses, watching a skylark rocket up, singing, from the meadow—the peace of it all—even the wheel-chair a part of it. But at once she rejected this. You are in your sixties, your reactions are those of a life on the down-slope. Could you have resisted Ralph Parton, in that first summer long ago, when the very sound of his canoe touching the boat slip outside your windows sent an electric charge through your whole being? Didn't people try to counsel you then—warn, even? Particularly Stephen.

A disturbing memory began to form, hovered, seemed close to emergence. Something about bats and lakes, Stephen and Ralph. What could it be?

But Lydia routed the shadowy image by continuing, "To put it perfectly bluntly, Mummy"—and again Caroline Brace instinctively stiffened against further intimate revelations—"Jack became impotent. I don't blame him, of course. How could I? I was probably responsible for it. His sexual feelings, his pride, had had such a blow—that's what the psychiatrist said. We both went to psychiatrists—little Bill, too. Oh, it was quite a jolly household!"

Lydia laughed then, very much as Stephen laughed when he wanted instead to sob or curse. There is something Oriental in them both, Caroline Brace thought; for isn't it true—or is it merely hearsay—that the Oriental who must tell you of personal tragedy laughs to lighten the load his suffering places on you?

"Then for the second time, we—Jack and I—called it quits. By then, as I told you, Alex had gone abroad for his magazine. The very day I was going to cable him about—about our new decision, that *very* day—I got a cable from London, from Alex, saying he was going to be married." Her voice grew rigid. "I cabled back, Wait! He cabled back to me, I can't. Impossible. Writing."

She spoke the last four words as though reading them aloud from the fatal slip of paper.

"I took a plane that same night. I told people I was going to visit you. In London I threw my pride to the winds. I did everything in my power to get Alex back. I said I'd even give up the children, simply live there, near him, just to see him, be with him once in a while. I even told him he didn't need to marry me. He could go ahead and marry the other girl. I'd settle for the crumbs, the leavings. . . . But he wouldn't listen. It was just over, as far as he was concerned."

Over? Impossible! Lady Brace thought, but did not say. There was a pause.

"I simply couldn't believe it," Lydia said heavily.

Caroline looked at her child. She was sitting with her hands folded in her lap, the green jewel quiet, her face masked, the lids down—were they hiding tears? What shall I do if she breaks? What can I say to comfort her, what explanations have I to offer, what ready phrase other than the ones she herself has used: "It is too late; it is all over"?

It was Lydia who broke the prolonged silence. She raised her eyes—they were quite dry, still expressionless—and remarked in a matter-of-fact, conversational tone, "Well, Mummy, that's the whole of the sad and sordid love story of Lydia Parton Frazier."

Perhaps it's wise to keep it on this level, Lady Brace thought, and, in a not-dissimilar voice, she inquired, "Who was the other girl?"

Lydia looked at her mother, wryly amused, faintly scornful. "Do you mean what was the girl?" (Again, how like Stephen!) "That's fiction, Lady B, I'm afraid, not life. She wasn't a who—I mean nobody you'd ever hear of, and she certainly wasn't a what. She was just a nice bright girl, half-Belgian, half-English, who was working for Reuters in London. I don't know what she had that I didn't —I never found out, for I never saw her. If I had, I might have killed her."

She means that! her mother thought in horror. Only by an enormous exercise of will did she manage to control a gasp.

"I'm going to have a tiny brandy," Lydia was saying now, rising, walking over to a painted cabinet and lifting a carafe from a lower shelf. "Join me, Mummy?"

"No thank you, darling."

"Not a little white mint, or anything?"

"I don't believe so."

"Quite sure?" Lydia poured a pony of brandy and put it beside her chair. "I'm glad you don't feel the need for support. I was horribly afraid I'd upset you really badly."

So I have revealed nothing! Caroline Brace had an immediate sense of reprieve, watching Lydia walk in her poised assured way back to her chair, after returning the carafe to its place. It is over now, she thought. Soon I can escape.

But then she heard herself saying in a stiff voice that seemed not at all her own, "You've left out one very important thing, Lydia."

Lydia raised her brows, waiting.

"The place of Frederick Hollis in all this. I mean in—as you call it—the story of Lydia Parton Frazier."

Lydia took a calm sip of her brandy. Her brows were still raised. "Frederick's place in all this? He hasn't any. Frederick came later."

"But you are—you do plan to marry him?"

"Yes, when he is free."

"But what does he mean to you, what *can* he mean—*represent*—to you?"

Lydia opened her gray eyes even wider and looked at her mother in genuine amazement. "But surely that's quite plain, Mummy."

Caroline felt a constriction the length of her spine; her hands began to tremble. With an effort she spoke firmly. "I'm afraid it isn't." She made herself look steadily at her child. A long, candid and challenging look—the first Lady Brace ever remembered exchanging with any of her children—passed between them. Lydia frowned finally and turned away.

When she replied, she gave each word its distinct enunciation, as though defying her mother to underestimate the values she was stating. "Frederick Hollis represents money, position, luxury."

"Haven't you always had enough of all that?"

"Not comparable to what Frederick has, and certainly never power, real power. No one in this family, since Grandfather, has had that. Power, Mummy, is a very big thing in the world today—just about the biggest thing there is. It means much more than just money—for lots of people have money and they don't matter a bit."

Memory of Stephen's talk about Goering, the shivery phrases he had used—"power and pomp," "bones and ashes"—flashed into Lady Brace's mind. She spoke with abrupt sharpness, just one word. "Don't!"

"Don't what?" There was now open resistance in Lydia's voice, yet under its hard surface, her mother caught a hint of something else: a tremulousness like that of a guilty child whose defiance invites, even desires, correction.

"Don't talk in that unfeeling way!"

The sternness in her own voice astounded Caroline Brace. An impulse she could neither resist nor explain pushed her on.

"It's not like you at all—any of this sort of talk, or attitude. You do yourself harm when you act this way. It's—it's against your nature."

The words began to tumble from her lips. "You're a very delicate, sensitive creature, Lydia. You always were as a child—brooding and troubled, so easily hurt. Oh, my darling, I can't bear it. I really can't. I feel so—so *responsible* for you, for your suffering. I'm to blame somehow. I know I am. Oh, it is almost unbearable to me, it really is!"

She buried her face in her shaking hands and began to weep, without in the least meaning or wishing to.

Lydia jumped up in awkward haste, almost overturning the table beside her. "Don't!" she cried in her turn, her voice brittle with fear. "Please don't! I *beg* you. I'm terribly sorry I spoke of it, Mummy, *any* of it. I should have known better. Oh, please, please don't cry!"

Caroline fought to regain control. Holding her handkerchief clutched between her palms over her face, she heard Lydia move in little staccato steps to the fireplace, heard the click of a cigarette lighter. After several moments of struggle Caroline dropped her hands from her face, dried her eyes, said in a muffled voice, "I'm so sorry. Do forgive me."

There followed a long tense silence. When she finally raised her head, Lydia was standing before the fireplace, her chin unnaturally high. It seemed to her mother that she was waiting with her back to a bare wall, facing an invisible enemy. Caroline remembered this particular rebellious stance, this look of secret, unadmitted fear, from Lydia's childhood. Again the stabbing sense of personal failure, of incompletion, of neglect, swept over her. She wanted to cry out again, "Forgive me! Not for upsetting you by weeping but for failing you all these years; for not *loving* you enough—ever."

But she could not get the words out and it was Lydia who spoke first. She had herself under control again. Her voice was strained but steady.

"It's probably a pretty boring subject from first to last—like a thousand others of its kind—my life and times!" Then in a quick contradictory burst, "Oh, I'm so heartily sick of myself—and all my mistakes and problems." There was a sudden apparent tremble of her lips.

In one swift impulsive movement Caroline Brace rose from her chair and crossed the room to her daughter. She managed, in spite of an immediate instinct of recoil from Lydia's rigid surprise, to clasp her arms around her, and keep them there. She heard herself using the words she might have used to a frightened child, "Don't be scared, darling!"

Lydia repeated the homely word. "Scared?" She stood stiff and unyielding in her mother's embrace, not responding in any way. But when for the second time she repeated the word "Scared?" something thin and young had crept into her voice.

Lady Brace began with a tentative, tremulous hand to stroke Lydia's hair. "Yes, darling," she said, half-whispering, "you're trying to be very brave and strong, and impersonal, and independent, because you're really so—so afraid." She paused, swallowed hard, forced herself to add, "I know because I'm afraid too—I've always been afraid—of so many things. . . ." Don't ask me what! she begged silently. Not now, anyway!

Lydia did not move or relax in any way, but she did not question her mother either, as Rosemary certainly would have done. Still without any physical response to her mother's embrace she said finally, "Yes, I'm afraid." In a voice harsh with restraint she added, "But I don't know what it is I'm afraid of."

Caroline said softly, "Oh, how well I know that feeling."

"What is it, then?" Lydia's demand was almost angry.

Where she found the next words, Lady Brace had no notion. It was as though they offered themselves for her use. "You're afraid of not being able to stand it at all—*to endure it*—whatever *it* is. You're afraid you'll just collapse—altogether."

"Oh, Mummy!" It was a cry.

Lydia's stiffened body began to give. She clutched suddenly at her mother. "Oh, Mummy, help me! I'm so terribly *sick*." She turned and put the full, limp weight of her head and arms on Lady Brace and began to sob in heavy broken gasps.

Her child's use of the word "sick" struck Caroline Brace like a physical blow. The familiar inner withdrawal from extremes of emotion quivered for a moment in her. But only for a moment. It was washed away in a wave of pity and love and personal anguish as she tightened her arms around her daughter's convulsed body and bent her lips to the soft head, pressing now against her like a nuzzling colt. Guilty! she was thinking. *I'm* guilty! I've neglected my child. Was it from fear? Yes, fear; fear of not knowing how to understand or help her, how to deal with her problems; fearing her father in her; fearing all feeling because feeling, emotion, were things identified with the surging, blind, intoxicating passion and subsequent terrible disillusionment of my life with Ralph Parton. Her tears began to fall again, and the two women stood clasped together, silent and weeping in the little, gay Victorian drawing room.

After a time Caroline, still with her arms around her child, pulled Lydia down to a sofa and placed the pale blond head on her shoulder. She took a handkerchief from her pocket and wiped the swollen and discolored face as she had wiped Stephen's bleached gaunt cheeks a few days before. She did not speak and it was finally Lydia who, with her head still on her mother's shoulder, and one hand clasped in Caroline's, said brokenly, "Oh, Mummy, tell me, what *is* the answer?"

"I don't know," Lady Brace said simply. She did not add, although she thought it, "For I do not know—have never known— what the question is."

"Does *anyone* know?" Lydia sounded quite desperate.

"Someone must. I'm sure of it." As Caroline spoke, she caught a vision of Venerable Sir coming from the garden in the dawn. "Someone like Uncle Stephen's friend, maybe. The little monk."

"Him?" Lydia's tone was frankly skeptical.

Caroline recalled again her disparaging remarks about Venerable Sir the day she was at Fox Meadows.

"Well, perhaps your Uncle Stephen knows—not *the* answer, but *an* answer. I sometimes think, in spite of all his odd, unpredictable ways, that he is a very wise man."

"Yes, he knows a lot—Uncle Stephen," Lydia agreed, "But he's sick too, somewhere. I'm sure of that, or I wouldn't feel I understand him the way I do. I'd trust what he'd say to me—but I wonder if he could really help me. Maybe nobody can, since I don't really know what's wrong." She sounded once more bitter and resigned.

A sense of total inadequacy led Lady Brace to remark, "Your Uncle Stephen considers Venerable Sir a wise and pure soul." But why am I urging the little monk on my child? After all, I know nothing about him. I have only Stephen's word for his wisdom and goodness.

"Pure because he's never been tempted." Lydia's tone effectively dismissed her uncle's guru. "That's the trouble with most priests and clergymen, all the so-called spiritual guides. They live outside life. They don't understand the pressures ordinary people are subjected to. Don't you agree?"

"I'm not sure." Caroline felt it necessary to add, "Humpy's great-uncle was a canon. I talked to him several times—after Rupert's death. He—I do believe he helped me." She feared she did not sound very convincing.

"With death maybe," Lydia said calmly. How easily they dismiss death, Caroline thought—those who have never experienced it. "Death is different. Alex's death would have seemed easy to me. At least easier than knowing he was in the world, and that I couldn't be with him." After a moment she asked, "What did the Canon say to you?"

"Let me see if I can remember." Lady Brace closed her eyes.

For a moment nothing came. Then she saw herself on her knees in the little chapel near Rupert's hospital. They had brought her word that his other leg must be amputated; septicemia was rising fast. "Oh, God," she had promised, kneeling on the cold stone floor, "if only You will let him live—mutilated as he is—I offer . . . I give . . . I pledge . . ." But Rupert had lost his battle for life, and when Humphrey's cousin, the Canon, had said to comfort them, "The Lord giveth and the Lord taketh away; blessed be the name of the Lord," she had voiced immediate protest, for these words in no way took care of her anguished question as to why she had borne a son in the first place only to have him die this terrible death. The Canon had admonished her then in gentle sadness, "Faith, my child! Faith! Many suffering people have been sustained all their lives by an abiding faith in the mysterious mercy and love of God. . . ."

She answered Lydia's question by saying, "Canon Brace lent me a book. A book about a woman mystic, someone who lived in the thirteenth century." The name surprised her by presenting itself. "Lady Julian of Norwich."

"A book!" Lydia gave a disdainful nod. "Not the Bible? Not that there's any help *there!* I looked."

Lady Brace protested, "Oh, darling, I don't think I'd say that. There are many beautiful passages in the Bible—soothing ones. Humpy used sometimes to read it aloud to me." Perhaps I can even think of something apropos to quote, she thought.

But Lydia was not interested. "Yes," she said, "beautiful prose, I agree. That's the whole of it, though. You might as well read Shakespeare." After a moment, "What was the book on the woman mystic about?" she asked.

"Love," replied Lady Brace. "As I remember it." The answer seemed rather feeble. She added, "The mysterious love of God for his creatures."

"Yes, I know." Lydia spoke with increased bitterness. She sat up on the couch. "Words!" she said. "Words certainly didn't help *me.* I started going to church in those terrible black days, when I was trying to—get over Alex. I even tried to talk to the young assistant rector at St. Jude's. He'd been overseas with the troops. He was a little younger than I. I thought he must surely have seen something of life in the raw—as it really is. He was terribly sweet, sympathetic, but he gave me simply nothing. I had a feeling he was an unconscious fag, and that he put me down as a nymphomaniac, outside the pale of the decent women of his congregation. I finally told him he'd do better to study more psychiatry and less theology."

"What about your psychiatrist?" Caroline Brace asked. "Couldn't he help you?"

"Some—yes. He made me see things about myself I'd never seen before, and he helped me to understand a lot about my past life—you, and Rosie, and Daddy's death, and your remarrying, and the birth of Rupert, and all of that—even why I got married so young. But I don't know, it was more like being given a flat map of a country, when what I needed was a contour map—something like that. I can't explain. I just came to feel that even if I did understand who I was, or why I did what I did, I'd still not know how to go on living any more happily, or—fully. I might be better adjusted, but not any wiser—if you see what I mean."

"Yes, I think I do," Caroline said. After a moment she added, tentative, "Perhaps what you must say to yourself, Lydia—the *only* thing you can say—is: I know more about life from these experiences; I am capable of deeper understanding."

"What good is that?" Lydia demanded. Her voice rose once more, in scorn now as well as despair.

Caroline had the feeling that they had come full circle; full circle to Stephen's original sharp comment about Lydia having failed in one field—love—and settling for fulfillment in another—money and power.

"The real mystery is, why it happened in the first place," Lydia cried. "Why did I feel this way for Alex White? And why never for anyone before or since, for I know—I'm *sure*—I could never feel like this about anyone ever again!"

"You're still young, Lydia," her mother said. "It might be—repeated."

But Lydia, emphatic, voiced her own inner doubt. "No, Mummy, it's no use pretending. I know! Something in me just came into full, sudden bloom and—and dried up and died, that's all." Her voice trembled again but did not break. She shifted away from her mother's arm. Their talk was over.

I have failed, thought Lady Brace. What should I have said—or done?

"Did you have to be back at any particular time?" Lydia was

asking, reaching with her so frequently checked automatic gesture towards a cigarette; a movement which this time she completed, taking one, lighting it as she rose from the sofa.

"No, dear," Lady Brace said. "But I am probably keeping you." She felt both shocked and relieved at the easy way in which, once more, automatic polite phrases rose to both their lips.

"Of course not, Mummy. It's simply wonderful to have you to myself this way—I was only wondering if you had any errands you wanted to do, or if you'd rather go right back to the country. I'll call Frederick's man and let him know."

Lydia, taking lipstick and powder from a little painted chest on a side table, began now to fix her make-up before a gilt mirror with sexless cherubs holding hands around its rim.

Caroline Brace caught herself wondering if her daughter kept make-up caches in handy places all over her house. The thought was vaguely distressing.

"I think I'll go back to the country, darling, if it's no bother." On impulse she added, "Come back with me, dearie, why don't you? Come down for supper and stay the night. I know the children are going off to a birthday party and a private movie. They'll be back late and straight to bed. It will be quiet. Oh, do!"

Lydia hesitated for just a moment.

"All right, Mummy. Maybe this would be as good a time as any to go over the china and decide how it's to be divided."

Lady Brace's heart sank. "Yes, we might do that," she murmured, "but I'd just rather leave all of that entirely up to you and Rosemary. I don't want any of it myself."

"Whatever Rosie takes will be in fragments in a year, unless she keeps it locked up." Lydia spoke in a cool critical tone. How my two daughters dislike one another, Lady Brace thought with regret. Lydia was going on, sounding aggrieved. "You know they had a frightful crash at Thanksgiving because of a table with a wobbly leg. All the rest of the Waterford and those beautiful French brandy glasses that were Grandmother's."

"But I thought all that glass was put away."

"It was, but Rosie called me and asked if I'd agree to letting her use it for a party, if the lawyers consented. What could I do? After all, Todd's firm represents the estate." Then, with abruptness, Lydia altered her tone. "But how silly," she said in light dismissal of her remarks. "It really doesn't matter a damn, except I do so hate to see old beautiful things disappearing for good. They'll never be made again."

"I know," Lady Brace agreed. "I can't help but feel that way sometimes, too." Then she added, with gentle emphasis, "Yet, during the war, I often said to myself, I'll never become attached to any *thing* again."

13

To Lady Brace's relief Rosemary seemed genuinely glad to see Lydia. The two girls, leaving their mother at the door of her room, went off to make up Lydia's bed for the night.

Lady Brace was changing her frock when Rosemary tapped and entered. "Do you mind, Mummy?"

Rosemary closed the door as though playing a spy scene in a film. She advanced a little way into the room and, in a voice tentative for her, said, "I just wondered if you had a chance to talk to Lydia."

An irrational and ill-mannered desire to cry out, "Oh, *do* leave me alone!" took hold of Lady Brace. She countered evasively, "Talk with Lydia about what?" Her tone expressed annoyance.

"You know—about—about Frederick Hollis, and—perhaps going back to Jack." Rosemary seemed to sense her mother's mood, for she added, in explanation of her intrusion, "The fact is—and it's really such a coincidence—Jack Frazier called me from New York this afternoon. He's down here from Maine on business. He was so thrilled to know you were here, and *so* anxious to see you."

"Oh, no!" Lady Brace exclaimed. She had begun to struggle with the zipper at the back of her frock. Rosemary crossed the room and deftly pulled it up to the neckline, then gave her mother two little pats on either shoulder. This is the way she handles Todd when he comes home hot and annoyed from driving through traffic. Ashamed of her momentary irritation, smoothing her brow, Lady Brace said, "It's not that I don't like Jack, it's just —what on earth is there to say to him—to talk about?"

"Well, after all, he *was* your son-in-law," Rosemary reminded her.

"But I never found anything much in common with him," Lady Brace remarked tartly.

"Do be fair, Mummy darling. You never knew him very well, did you?"

Did she imagine it, or was there under Rosemary's words a hint of censure, faint but definite; a suggestion that she had seen precious little of her daughters after early childhood, and almost nothing of their adult households?

"No, I didn't know him very well," Lady Brace admitted, "and that's precisely why I can't see myself trying now to give him advice, to suggest procedures for him or, for that matter, Lydia. I'm no judge of the circumstances of their lives, and it would be presumptuous of me to act as though I were."

Rosemary showed no signs of being put off. "I know, darling, but if Jack wants to come out sometime this week, while he's in New York, we can't very well say no, can we?"

"I suppose not." Lady Brace knew she sounded ungracious and was sorry. "Have you told Lydia? I hope she may be staying on for a day or two." She did not mention the impending division of the china.

"No, I haven't told her—but she won't mind. She and Jack often meet. They're very sensible about all that side of it. They consult *regularly* on the children. That's why I keep thinking it *could* be patched up. It isn't as though they were full of anger and resentment."

At that moment, to Lady Brace's relief, the outrageous clanging of the dinner bell sounded through the house.

"I must fly," Rosemary said, and with no further words she dashed from the room.

T W O

Although dinner passed uneventfully, Lady Brace felt her fatigue mounting instead of diminishing, and was grateful for the absence of Jennifer and Elliot and the strain their lively presences imposed. She had planned to go immediately to her room once dinner was over, but, at table, she had caught Lydia's guarded and concerned glances—for she was too weary to make small talk and her silence was noticeable. Since she did not wish Lydia to feel responsible for her depression—or to give Rosemary fuel for further probing questions—she roused herself to accompany them all onto the terrace for coffee.

As soon as she lay back in one of the long chairs next to Stephen, Lydia came over and dropped a cushion on the bricks between them. Without looking directly at either of them she reached out, almost furtively, with her fingertips and touched her mother's arm, extended along the side of the wicker chaise. The gesture seemed to say, "Forgive me. I'm afraid I did upset you after all."

Lady Brace did not trust herself to respond to this small intimacy. She felt her personal breaking-point dangerously near. (I am growing old; too old for such crises of emotion as I passed through this afternoon.) But she did manage to catch Lydia's eye and smile back at her. She found herself looking for some reflection of the anguish that had clouded those same lovely eyes only a few hours before. There was, as far as she could see, not the slightest appearance now of any emotional stress. How does she manage so quickly to hide all the pain?

Still, where have I hidden all of mine for a whole lifetime? Do all my past sufferings, my disillusionments, my unanswered questions show only somewhere in the depths of my eyes when I am very tired, or off guard? And who, after all, dares peer into the depths of another's eyes—even in the act of love? Perhaps the truth is, Lydia and I do not have the kinds of faces that reveal inner turmoil. Our strains never make themselves known by lines on the forehead or withered mouths. Is it merely a piece of good genetic luck—some quality for which we have to thank a nameless ancestor? Or *is* it good luck, after all—this ability to appear physically unmarked by experience?

She looked off towards the walled garden where the fireflies were flashing and saw the figure of the little monk passing quietly in the shadows.

Todd had also seen him. "There's . . ." he began.

Stephen cut in hastily, "Don't call him. He probably doesn't want to be disturbed."

But almost as though Venerable Sir had heard them, he turned at once and walked towards the terrace, calling out in his thin treble, "Good evening, all." Beaming around the half circle of recumbent figures as he stepped onto the terrace, he trilled, "What a beautiful black night! I never saw the fireflies so active. How much I enjoy them! They remind me of home."

If I were not so utterly tired, Lady Brace thought, I would now tell him that when I visited his island the fireflies there made me think of my home. This was just the sort of ordinary remark, she had observed, that always seemed to fill Venerable Sir with exuberance, as if in the commonplace he was forever finding the marvelous.

In spite of Stephen's assumption that he would prefer his solitude, the little monk, without hesitation, accepted Rosemary's invitation to join them; a further example of his unfailing tact. He took the chair Todd drew forward with an air of receiving some special boon: "Oh, thank you so much! How very kind you are!"

His voice and manner made Lady Brace smile. Dear little man, she thought. But when the usual desultory after-dinner talk began around her she deftly closed her ears, as she had done on similar occasions for half a lifetime.

T H R E E

Her mind began to skirt the afternoon's memories. How can I help my child? How can I rid myself of the gnawing conviction that I am somehow to blame for her unhappiness? She caught, again, the flicker and dart of more distant memories; images that seemed connected, by not yet discernible threads, with Lydia's confession: Ralph, Stephen . . . melting together . . . separating. Had she taken that second glass of wine at dinner? She must have. To be sure, Dr. Perry had said she should, at the end of the day, take a cocktail, drink wine, that they were very relaxing. Perhaps, here at Fox Meadows, they induced, however, quite the opposite effect.

But what if the opposite effect was just what she needed: to sharpen her faculties, not blunt them? Whether she chose it or not, an unaccustomed alertness seemed forced on her here, as it had been long ago in Ceylon when her brother and John van der Wadel, between them, had so shaken the roots of her orthodox faith.

Shaken? She questioned the word as much as she questioned faith—for could she be said to possess a "religious faith," or to have ever possessed one? Something had always stood in the way of a total commitment to this mysterious word, "faith," so meaningful, she knew, to many people. She had been confirmed, had attended on Sundays the fashionable church wherever she lived—if convenient to do so. But even before the death of her only son she had made little personal use of the religious forms in which she had been raised, though she had never openly questioned Christian beliefs as Stephen had in his stormy adolescence—indeed, throughout all his life.

Her eyes fell on her brother's cane with the circular snake lying on the ground between them. At once she saw herself in a tropical dawn in Ceylon with Stephen and John van der Wadel. They were standing before an immense stone cobra, its erect crest furled protectively above a serene human figure, seated cross-legged, back erect, hands folded quietly, gaze directed not out but seemingly *in*.

"The Great Teacher of Asia," John van der Wadel had murmured, "deep in meditation."

"And the snake?" she had forced herself to ask, seeing in her mind's eye the tabloid photograph of her brother with his hand on a stone serpent's head.

"What about the snake?"

"What is it doing?"

"Protecting Buddha in his hour of trial," Stephen had answered for John. He had added then, as though aware of his sister's mystification, "The Serpent isn't evil in Buddhism, Caro, as it is in Christianity."

And this had sent him off at once on the subject of his "research." Turning from her, he had said to John van der Wadel that they must "dig deeper into these opposites . . . For why should a serpent symbolize a Good Protector on one side of the earth and an Evil Tempter on the other?"

"I suppose," John van der Wadel had replied, gazing off into the blue distance with his annoying superior smile, and speaking in his soft native tinkle with its incongruous British overlay, "I suppose since the Serpent represents earth-wisdom—secret, invisible, instinctive wisdom—it's bound rather to frighten Westerners with their unholy worship of facts—*always* facts."

And later, strolling in the courtyard of a monastery, through which also walked a group of pilgrim monks in yellow robes, Stephen and John van der Wadel had gathered for the pious houseboys, back at the bungalow, pockets of fallen leaves from "the oldest tree on earth"; said to be a shoot from the very one under which the Great Teacher attained enlightenment.

"Which brings us to the myths again," Stephen had cried, half-scornful, half-troubled. "For after all, the Buddha's Enlightenment only preceded Christ's Crucifixion by some five hundred years—and certainly the California sequoia trees go much farther back in *time!* So what have we here, John, but the living symbol of the mythical World Tree!"

He had launched, then, into a perplexing, and, to her, disturbing monologue about the Tree of Life: how a Serpent in some legends gnaws forever at its roots; how the ancient Vedas of India sang of a mythological Carpenter who cut down this World Tree; how Jesus, the carpenter of Nazareth, had thus, by the laws of the Great Myth, to be crucified on this World Tree turned into a wooden cross. . . .

"Myths!" Stephen had concluded in his familiar impassioned voice of bewilderment and anger. "What do they *really* signify? Do you suppose they're the only truths there are?"

Then they were climbing up thousands of steps to a mountain ledge whose name, after all these years, still rang in her head like an eerie bell: Mahinda's Couch. At the end of their long climb they had stood for many minutes without words, gazing out over the vast jungle that here concealed miles of forest-buried ruins quite as stupendous, John said, as those they had been wandering among for many days. On these fabled remains, however, no human eye had fallen for many centuries.

Stephen, shading his eyes, looked down and muttered, "The Romans were only toymakers."

He spoke as if he could see through the thick green canopy

spread far below them; was, indeed, actually gazing at dry beds of artificial lakes, at miles of cracked, vine-wound pillars; at crumbled doorways with Lanka's delicately carved half-moon lintels showing sacred ganders, elephants, lotus; at chiseled chronicles of forgotten deeds and heroes; and, of course, at the Great Being himself, standing erect here, she imagined, the body vertical in the green gloom, the feet firmly planted on the earth—as always—the eyes staring unseeing into the dark thicket.

The image of the jungle-buried cities lost to view, with all their many beauties and wonders, had seemed to her then not so much awesome as inexpressibly mournful. Stephen had spoken aloud her own inner protest. "Oh, God! How meaningless life is!" She had shivered when he added, in a stony mutter, "Really almost unbearable." An old acute fear had again brushed her. Would Stephen find life truly unbearable some day, and take his own?

Perhaps that danger has passed, she thought, looking now at his stricken form in the dim light of the terrace at Fox Meadows. After all, he has survived the despair of his crippled body. And it was, she presumed, the little monk whom she had to thank for this reassurance. She looked across with a feeling of gratitude at the gentle dark face.

FOUR

As she returned from her reflections Lady Brace heard Rosemary's voice, faintly defensive, with the undertone of sharpness that sometimes marred its full warm volume.

"But I suppose I *do* believe in the importance of all those old forms and conventions," she was saying. "You know *perfectly* well what I mean, Uncle Stephen, what ladies and gentlemen 'do' or 'don't do.'"

"There were never any rules like that," Lydia put in before Stephen could reply.

Lady Brace got the immediate impression that during her reverie some argument had arisen; sides had been taken; Rosemary here, Stephen and Lydia there. Oh, dear!

"Ladies and gentlemen always did as they pleased," Lydia insisted. "They may have paid an enormous amount of attention to little matters, like how much lace frill could show at the cuff.

Or how properly to pinch snuff—that sort of thing. But as far as the rest of it went—morals, *sins*, if you like—well, just read a few memoirs of so-called ladies and gentlemen of the past."

How had a subject so pertinent got under way on this particular evening?

"I *have* read them," Rosemary replied, with impatience.

"Lydia has a point," Stephen said. Of course those two would be on the same side, Lady Brace thought. I must try to give Rosemary some support, as soon as I get my bearings. "The sewage was just better hidden in some periods than in others," he added.

Rosemary cried in a voice of accusation, "But, Uncle Stephen, you said you *believed* in Good and Evil—in capital letters—always *had* believed in them!"

Venerable Sir's tinkling laugh rang out. He seemed to find these last words of Rosemary's highly entertaining.

"You bet your sweet life I do!" Stephen shifted his position to address the little monk. "How about it, Venerable Sir? Do they or do they not exist—Good and Evil?"

Lady Brace turned her head also towards the visitor from Ceylon. He sat where the light from the dining room fell on him, his legs folded under and his yellow robes arranged so that his figure had the look of a full-petaled golden flower, out of which his dark face rose beaming.

Though he continued to smile, Venerable Sir did not reply immediately. He appeared to be considering Stephen's question with special care. There were several moments of complete silence before—soft yet distinct—Venerable Sir made his reply.

"I once knew a very good and wise Hindu monk," he began. "This monk tried, as best he could, even in this complex modern world, to keep his mind on Reality. *Brahman alone is real and the rest of the world is illusory*, he would say to himself many times a day. Now this is a very hard thing to realize. It is harder still to keep constantly in mind." He looked around, nodding in corroboration of his statement. "And so—in order to help himself to remember about Reality and Illusion, or Brahman and Maya— this wise Hindu always carried about with him a small prism from a crystal chandelier." He paused a moment. "For, as you know, although you can see many different colors through a prism, there is, in truth, no such thing as color." He came to a full stop.

After a long wait for more, Rosemary demanded, "Is that all?" Her tone was so blankly bewildered that everyone, including again Venerable Sir, had to laugh.

"You do not find that enough?" he asked in a teasing voice.

Stephen gave his short unmirthful hoot. "Venerable Sir has indeed uttered a mouthful!"

"It's a riddle, I suppose?" Todd had taken off his glasses and was rubbing his eyes like a man who hopes thus to improve his vision.

To her mother's surprise Lydia spoke once more in a positive voice. "No. I don't think it's a riddle at all. I just think it's saying that—well, there *is* neither Good nor Evil, it's all an illusion, like light which has no color but is lent color by what it passes through. What a lovely comforting thought!"

Venerable Sir nodded and smiled in Lydia's direction.

But Rosemary did not approve of her sister's interpretation. "I find it a very *dangerous* thought!" She could not keep from sounding sententious.

Venerable Sir looked from one to the other of the two sisters, his face alight with enjoyment.

"Oh, *do* say more!" Rosemary cried. "You're just leaving us dangling in space, Venerable Sir."

"With a prism from a broken chandelier in our hands," Todd concluded.

Venerable Sir laughed again at Todd's rueful voice and Stephen suggested, "Maybe we'd all just better go away and ponder on that prism." But he made no move to leave, nor did anyone else.

"Can't you add something—give us some *clues?*" Rosemary persisted. She continued to speak as though a guessing game was being played.

Venerable Sir gazed at her over his glasses. "Clues to what?" he inquired, his voice underlined with its persistent gentle amusement.

"Well, clues to wrong and right, Good and Evil. Are there, or *aren't* there, any such things? Is wrong-doing just an illusion? Is there *never* any *sin?*"

"But you are Christians! Surely your own priests and clergymen can tell you about sin?" The little monk looked around with a half smile that was not perhaps entirely innocent.

"It depends on what part of the Bible they decide to quote from," Todd said. Rosemary looked surprised at the skeptical candor of this remark. But Todd went right on, as if it was a subject on which he had done a little private thinking. "The plain truth is, though technically we are Christians, most of us are quite ignorant. We've learned the accepted forms—the creeds and prayers and hymns and that sort of thing—but, I don't know, they just somehow remain forms, if you know what I mean. Somehow we don't get them related to our everyday life."

"Mmm, yes." The little monk wagged his head gently up and down several times. He seemed to be trying to remember something. "I believe I can quote a quite comforting verse from your own scriptures—on the subject of Christian sin," he announced after a moment. "It's in the revised version of your Bible. In one of the Books of John. Yes, I believe I can speak it," and very precisely and sweetly he recited, *"Whoever is begotten of God doeth no sin because His seed abideth in him, and he cannot sin because he is begotten of God."*

"I certainly don't ever remember reading *that* verse," Rosemary remarked. She added, somewhat unnecessarily her mother thought, "You know, I took a course in The Bible As Literature at college."

Todd replied to Rosemary, almost sharp. "Just because you've never read that particular verse, Rosie, is no sign it isn't in print." He appeared to feel she was not being quite polite to their visitor.

"No, of course not," Rosemary agreed with easy good humor. "I just meant . . ." She didn't finish the sentence and Stephen took up the conversation where it had suddenly dropped.

"Todd has a point."

He is speaking like the arbiter of a debate, Caroline Brace thought. It seemed a new side to Stephen, usually to be found in the thick of any argument, advancing his own theories as though wielding weapons of defense.

"What I mean is," Stephen went on, "there are just about as many ways to interpret the Bible as there are people to read it. That's where the great Mother Church at Rome shows her shrewd wisdom—by not permitting the lay mind to upset itself by any private speculations on its own. But you're holding back, Venerable Sir—if I may say so. Get on with your *own* notions about sin!"

Venerable Sir cast a benign glance over his glasses at Stephen. He shook his head once, though whether in friendly reproof or at some unexpressed thoughts of his own was not clear.

"Sin," he said, repeating the word gravely. "Let me see now!" He placed his hands lightly together, the fingertips touching, and bowed his head. He seemed to be considering how to produce an answer acceptable to them all.

In the silence the fireflies went on with their compulsive signaling and, far overhead, red taillights on a plane winked on and off, moving across the dark sky.

"Perhaps it is merely a stage of development—sin," Venerable Sir suggested at last, lifting his head. "Evil. Is this something learned in a mythical garden by eating of forbidden fruit—the mysterious taint of Adam for which all you Christians are asked to pay so heavily—or is it rather something out of the world of animal instincts, not yet left behind?"

He paused to glance around at the little group stretched out on the wicker chairs. "Not yet left behind," he repeated, "in spite of all the millennia man has been climbing from the state of a wandering man-ape to these handsome and complex human organisms whom I now see before me." He bowed around the circle.

"*A-hah!*" Stephen cried. "Now we're getting somewhere!" He poked the point of his snake-headed stick into the bricks and began to recite, "*I teach you the Superman. Man is a thing to be surmounted. What have you done to surmount him?* That's the next step, eh—*surmounting?*"

"What an apt pupil!" Venerable Sir replied. He had playfully remarked this to her brother the first day in the garden, Lady Brace remembered.

"Nietzsche," Rosemary sniffed, identifying Stephen's lines.

"Don't despise Nietzsche," Stephen rapped, "just because the Germans debased some of his notions," and he took up his recitation: "How does the rest of it go? Haven't thought of it in years: *Ye have trod the way from worm to man, and much in you is yet worm. Once were ye apes, and even yet man is more ape than any ape. But he that is wisest among you is yet but a discord, a hybrid of plant and ghost* . . . so forth, so forth and so forth . . . The rest of it's gone. Anyway, the idea seems to be: Get on with that superman effort, why don't you?"

"Words, words, words," Lydia murmured, half under her breath, but audible to her mother.

Hybrid of plant and ghost. What an extraordinary phrase! Caroline Brace said to herself. . . . She was in Ceylon once more, wandering among the fabled ruins of the Lost Cities, seeing again the Great Being whose image had so captured her imagination. She glimpsed Him seated cross-legged, still intact, though veiled with creepers, deep in a ruined niche. Down a vista of crumbling pillars she approached his upright, headless body. She came upon Him suddenly, lying on his side, carved from the living rock of a lonely hillside. And whatever His pose—in the lotus posture of meditation, standing summoning the earth as witness to his claims of Supreme Wisdom, resting under the protection of the canopy of the cobra, lying asleep in the Great Demise—always the reiterated countenance seemed to speak of some mystery solved, some answer reached. . . . "But you must not capitalize the pronoun," John van der Wadel had softly informed her. "For he—the Buddha —did not wish to be considered divine. He was only a great man, not a Savior. 'Look within, *thou* art the Buddha,' he told his disciples near the end."

A similar tinkling voice, from quite other lips, was speaking now in her presence. Venerable Sir, unfolding his bare legs, adjusting his yellow garments, preparing to rise, "Each individual must know his own nature."

He spoke not at all like an instructor but more like one who muses among friends on a subject admitted to be of vital general interest.

"As for your sins—from which your great Western Savior has promised to save you all—has he not?—" and he gave a penetrating glance over his spectacles "—does not a sense of sin imply a sense of guilt? We Buddhists ask, How can guilt have meaning unless you hold each man wholly and *personally* responsible for his sin—*in one life or another?* But if a man is ignorant of *why* he sins, or the true nature of his sins, how then can he be held responsible?"

"In one life or another?" Lady Brace heard Lydia murmur.

But it was Todd's stronger voice that caught the little monk's ear. "I don't get it," Todd said. "That way it seems to me you would relieve individuals of all responsibility for what they do or don't do."

"Ah, no," Venerable Sir denied. "Not at all! Quite the opposite!" He made a darting gesture in Todd's direction. "*You* have choice!" One arm swept the fold of his robe in a half circle, including them all. "There is—for man—always choice. For you are not like coconuts that must fall from the tree with no power to avoid the pull down. No, no! You are like birds which may choose the boughs on which they light." He gave a little burst of laughter before adding on a soberer note, "Ah, yes, the whole burden of responsibility is placed on you! You alone are the masters of your destiny."

"Through one life after another," Stephen put in. Perhaps he had overheard Lydia's low murmur, or was merely sharpening their attention by mention of the always alluring theory of more lives than one. At the same time he seemed, by his interruption, to be questioning, even challenging, Venerable Sir on a point not new in their discussions.

But the little monk, making no direct answer to Stephen (though he smiled with a smile that appeared to promise, "More on this later, just the two of us"), continued, "Yes, *you* make your own fate; no one else. And this is because your happiness and un-happiness—indeed, all details and circumstances of your life—are determined solely by your *point of view*. There are great laws in the universe"—and with one of his singularly graceful gestures, he pointed towards the sky, lifting his face to the dark overhang where the Pleiades winked and the Big Dipper sprawled. "There are also laws for human conduct. Once you know the right ones it simply means you live—in adjustment."

"Nirvana?" Stephen inquired.

"Nibbana," the little monk corrected him, smiling. "You are forgetting your Pali, Stephen."

Stephen's reply held an edge of irritation, "Well, let's not get into the Pali-Sanscrit row! Nirvana is the way the West knows the term. That's why I used it."

The little monk appeared quite unruffled by Stephen's near rudeness. "Very well," he said, "Nirvana or Nibbana—that is merely a term, as you very well know, and a term is never quite an adequate description for a state of being: blissful, at rest. . . ." He drew the folds of his yellow robe about him once more and stood up.

But Lydia had something to add. "It all sounds to me like a rather highfalutin form of psychoanalysis," she remarked. In spite of the way she drawled her words, she did not, her mother noticed, appear indifferent or uninterested.

Venerable Sir turned in Lydia's direction.

"Quite right. But up to a point only." He added, "I have read a good deal in the psychoanalytic field. Very impressive achievements! But perhaps there is something beyond psychoanalysis after all?"

Though he made this remark a question, he had no intention, it was now quite clear, of remaining to discuss the point. What that "beyond" might be he would leave for another occasion.

With his most benign expression, moving his glance around the half circle of relaxed figures, nodding formally to each in turn, he spoke five separate good nights. Then pressing his palms together he bowed his head over them, his eyes closed while he chimed something in his own tongue. He followed immediately in English with, "May all beings be well and happy."

"Including gods, demons and mosquitoes," Stephen whispered.

Will he never be able to resist mockery? Lady Brace asked herself.

But Stephen's mocking whisper was lost to the rest of them in the sound of the children's arrival at the front of the house. Their voices, pitched high, rang out above the dogs' excited greetings. Alice Ford's clear, slightly nasal admonition came from the hall, "Only a moment now, mind! Both of you! You're very late for bed already."

Jennifer and Elliot appeared in the doorway in a noisy rush.

On the top step they hesitated, their small bodies poised in clear outline against the light at their backs, as if some mysterious emanation from the adult world held them in check.

"Hi!" Jennifer said finally, her voice a thin squeak.

Venerable Sir was quicker than any of them, even than Rosemary, to make the transition in mood imposed by this sudden shattering intrusion. He seemed altogether delighted at Jennifer's and Elliot's appearance. "Ah, dear children!" he cried, extending one hand towards them, the palm down. It was a gesture that seemed both an invitation and a blessing.

Jennifer went directly to the little monk. She held in her hand a long spray of wilted goldenrod which she tapped playfully on his sleeve.

"I picked this for you this afternoon," she said. "I kept it because it just matches your dress."

"I do thank you, my little friend." Venerable Sir took the spray from her. He made one of his lowest bows.

Elliot had gone to lean against Stephen's chair, and one dog had jumped, with complete assurance of his welcome, onto Todd's lap.

In her fatigued state the picture they made, this cozy family group, with the exotic addition of the little barefooted monk in his yellow robes holding Jennifer's wilted flower, seemed to Lady Brace to take on the quality of pure fantasy. She saw in this accidental composition the same fanciful proximity of unrelated objects on which surrealist painters relied for their startling effects. Her own presence here seemed more strange, more inexplicable, than any other.

Jennifer was looking slowly around the circle: her mother, her father, her aunt, her great-uncle, her grandmother—"What were you all talking about?" she asked. There was a hint of apprehension in her voice, reflecting a sense of exclusion from the incomprehensible world of grownups.

It was Venerable Sir who answered. Holding the drooping spray of goldenrod in one hand and Jennifer's small grubby paw in the other, he looked down at the anxious upturned face and replied, "I was just going to recite a poem, and now I'll teach it to you." His voice was merry.

Beating out the rhythm with the yellow plume of the flower, he recited in half-playful solemnity:

> "No one saves us but ourselves;
> No one can and no one may,
> We ourselves must walk the Path,
> Teachers merely show the way.

"How do you like it, my little one?" he asked Jennifer.

"I like it," Jennifer said. She was quite at ease again. "I like Robert Louis Stevenson, too. Do you know A *Child's Garden of Verses*? I got it for my birthday. I'll lend it to you."

"Oh, Jennifer," Lady Brace said tenderly. "What a dear creature you are! Come and give your old tired Gran a big hug."

14

On the stair landing Rosemary paused to talk about plans for the next day. She had already spoken, at dinner, about going to look at houses, saying a real estate woman was coming past early in the morning to take her to view two possibilities. "Perhaps you'd like to come along, Mummy," she had suggested, doling out spaghetti and meatballs with a flourish. "It will give you a chance to see some of the changes around Lynnbury."

"That would be nice," Lady Brace had said. But why should I wish to look at any changes? she thought. I am seeing quite enough changes as it is.

Now, however, when again the subject of the morning expedition came up, Lady Brace felt obliged to make a special effort, for she regretted having been short with Rosemary in her room before dinner. She saw, too, that Lydia was being amiable and cooperative, agreeing to go along, since her sister so plainly wished it.

"You've got such a good eye for *wrong* things, Lyd," Rosemary said. "I'm *terribly* slow at seeing when living-room doors aren't in the right place—that sort of thing. And how *about* you, Mummy? *Wouldn't* you really like to come?" She turned to her mother appealingly, but before Lady Brace could accept, as she now planned to do, Rosemary interposed, "No, Lady B. I can see you're absolutely pooped. *Don't* you *bother!*"

Lydia flashed an anxious glance in her mother's direction. "You do look tired, Mummy."

"Oh, no, I'm not really," Lady Brace denied quickly. "That is— I may just be feeling the heat a little. Of course I'm coming with you. I'd love to!"

Her daughters still looked uncertain and Lydia suggested, "Why not wait and decide in the morning, Mummy? If you feel like it then, come on down around ten. If you don't appear we'll understand."

They walked on up the stairs, Lady Brace between the two girls, her arms linked through theirs. At her door, as they kissed good night, Lydia repeated, "Don't plan on coming with us, Mummy." She appealed to her sister. "I don't really think she should, do you, Rosie?"

"Not if she's tired," Rosemary said. "Probably only a waste of time anyway. I've looked at *so* many houses these last few months!" Her voice sounded suddenly exasperated and a little depressed.

Again Lady Brace felt a twinge of concern to think of Rosemary and Todd being forcibly ejected from Fox Meadows. If, in the past, she had paid more attention to practical matters . . . Or should she comfort herself with the thought that the Jordans' casual and carefree way of life scarcely suited this formal mansion of another era?

"I hope you won't settle for a ranch-house, Rosie," Lydia was saying, as they moved on down the hall. "I do think they're *so* horrid."

"Well, I'm not sure," she heard Rosemary reply—that faint defensive note hovering again in her voice, "They're *terribly* convenient."

Lady Brace imagined Lydia presiding as mistress over the several elegant establishments of Frederick Hollis, saw Rosemary, in a

147

dusty station wagon crammed with dogs and children, coming to call. Would Rosemary be filled with resentment and envy of the easy luxury of her sister's life? Lady Brace caught herself up short. Have I settled in my own mind on Lydia's marriage; already accepted it as inevitable?

As she waited now to say good night to her brother, coming slowly and painfully towards her, she felt tempted to confide in him about her afternoon scene with Lydia. It was clear that Lydia needed guidance and help from someone, in spite of her outward poise and calm.

With a stab of pain Lady Brace heard again the cry of desperation bursting from her child. The memory filled her once more with a paralyzing sense of her own inadequacy. Perhaps Stephen would give her some advice, if she put it to him in just the right way; perhaps his new sincerity, the almost kindly tolerance, of which she had caught glimpses these last days, would show itself. Of course, he might also suggest that his niece be passed along to the ministrations of Venerable Sir, and that would never work, she thought, remembering the afternoon, and Lydia's cool rejection of the little monk. Still, this was before the talk on the terrace, where Lydia's interest had been so apparently caught by Venerable Sir's manner, his way of putting things.

As Lady Brace leaned forward to kiss her brother lightly on his left temple, she saw, then felt against her lips, the pulse in the distended veins. His unaided nightly climb up the stairs cost, quite plainly, more of an effort than he would admit. But before she could remonstrate about it he said, as if reading her mind, "Yes, I know!" He smiled his habitual mocking smile. "*You are old, Father William, and stiff in the knees.*"

"Old." She sighed. "We're both old, darling. I never felt older than I do this very minute."

Stephen looked at her with surprise, and at once she knew why. It was quite unlike her to comment on her physical condition. Fatigue, pain, alarm—these were states-of-being always to be kept private; a self-discipline going back so far she could not have told its origin.

"Your talk with Lydia?" Stephen asked.

She hesitated; lowered her voice. "I'm so troubled about her,

Stephen—really troubled—though I'm sure there's nothing I can do."

"No, I'm sure not." What did his brusque voice convey? "It's quite some responsibility being a mother! Glad I avoided it this time around," and he moved past her, only to turn a few steps further on, to say over his shoulder, "Dream well, Caro darling."

Perplexed, she stood looking after his awkward progress down the dim-lit hall. The labored and erratic gait reminded her of ants pushing ahead of themselves, in the rough terrain of an insect landscape, loads twice their size. She had a swift vision of young Stephen's graceful jackknife from a high diving board. How could it possibly be the same body?

She went into her room, closed the door, and began to prepare for bed. Stephen's strange words—or was it only his way of speaking?—had seemed to imply criticism, a suggestion that he, too, felt no particular sympathy towards her at the moment; and—as it had for over half a lifetime—this hint of censure from her brother made her tremulous. Yet so weary was she that the moment her light snapped off she fell into a heavy sleep.

T W O

Hours later she awoke from a dream about Stephen—a dream so real it extended itself at once, without any marked transition, into the recollection of an actual happening, as though the dream itself had pushed open a long-closed door in her memory, releasing it by some hidden spring.

She was in their Adirondacks camp turning up the wick of an oil lamp in the little dressing room off her bedroom. A pitcher of hot water, with a linen towel over its top, left by faithful Annie when she went to bed, stood on the table.

Caroline saw herself placing her hand on the pitcher's side to test the temperature. Still faintly warm. This somehow gave her a moment's reassurance about the lateness of the hour of her return.

When Ralph slid the canoe onto the boat slip with the quiet of an expert, her first quick guilty glance had been in the direction of her brother's windows. To her relief Stephen's lights were already out, but she felt nervous anyway and would not allow Ralph to, prolong their last embrace. She did not even wait for him to glide off into the thick darkness before hurrying with stealthy footfall up the pine-needled path, the beam of her hooded flashlight falling on the startling glitter of a doe's eyes near the water's edge, and on the comic posterior of Lionel, Stephen's pet raccoon, sliding from sight under the veranda.

She had reached her room and closed the door with a sigh of relief, immediately felt the water pitcher for reassurance, and then hastily undressed. She was putting her arms into the sleeves of her warm bathrobe when she noticed with a little prick of puzzlement that an extra towel, a rather large one, had been placed over the flowered china bowl in which she nightly washed her face and hands. What did that mean? What was in Annie's mind? she wondered as she went to remove it.

The moment she lifted the towel she started back with a smothered shriek. Floating face up in the bowl, which was already filled with water, was a dead bat!

She had never seen a bat before at such close range. The moment after her outcry, she stood transfixed, gazing at the misshapen creature lying on its back, a hideous tiny form dwarfed by the naked membrane of its wings. Long clawlike fingers curled to grip the empty air. There were no eyes—none at least that she could see; no nose at the center of the nightmare face—only a series of leaf-like folds of flesh; its ears hung half the length of its body.

She could not move. All the spectral horrors of which she had ever heard found immediate and evil embodiment in this grotesque form in the flowered bowl. This secret night-living creature, hitherto no more than a soft swish of wings on a darkening lake, appeared in this moment like a thing born of delirium, the creation of some demented super-brain. In a wave of revulsion her mind receded from its naked ugliness. Yet she continued to stare, horrified, fascinated, unable to tear her eyes away. Into her memory flooded old Annie's fantastic and ignorant nursery tales— goblins, vampires, bats—all coming in the night to put their mouths to human flesh, to drain away their victim's life-blood silently, secretly, while one slept. . . .

She did not know how long she stood looking down into the

china bowl. But at last she began to retreat slowly backwards, away from the washstand. When she got to the doorway, between her dressing room and bedroom, she seized the jamb in one hand, and clung to it. "Annie!" she called, but her voice was only a thickened croak.

Until now her body had been rigid, but the moment she called, a convulsive trembling began. She clung harder to the side of the door. "Annie!" In the cold stillness, suddenly unfamiliar and threatening, she heard overhead the old woman's long-drawn heavy snores.

She wanted, then, to run into the hall and cry out for help. But underneath her immediate terror lay another fear—the fear that her late return with Ralph would be discovered.

She had a moment's wild impulse to escape into the night, into the deep woods, away from their camp, away from everything. Some equally confused notion held her back, some nightmare thought that the bat, during her absence, might turn itself over—its life not yet extinct—struggle up from the water and find a hiding place behind her curtains. Then perhaps the very next night, as she undressed, or as she slept—! Hazy scraps from half-remembered books of nature lore sprang next into her inflamed mind; something about the bat's inaudible cry, a cry too high for the human ear. Already the unheard shrieks of the drowning creature might have summoned its vampire mate, lurking even now in the room's shadows, ready to pounce.

Sounds of sheer terror began to form deep in her throat—and then she heard footsteps in the hall approaching her room. She waited, not moving or breathing, as slowly the door opened to reveal her brother's head, with its rumpled light hair and pale set face.

"Stephen!" Her rigid fingers slid from the door jamb. She dropped into the nearest chair, clasping her palms over her elbows and drawing her whole body together in a single convulsive movement of relief.

"Did you call?" he asked in a whisper.

She could not answer. She could only shake her head, stare, tremble.

"What's the matter? You look as though you'd seen a ghost."

"It's . . ." She gestured towards the alcove. "In my washbowl! A dead bat!" she said, her voice rising.

"Shh!" he warned, not looking towards the washbowl. "You'll wake everybody."

"Oh, but Stephen—" Another long shudder ran through her. "I never knew how hideous, how sickeningly ugly—" She broke off. Then, almost at once she began to speak again, anxious to avert his certain scorn of her hysteria. "I know it's silly, Stephen, but I—ugh! It really did give me a terrible turn. It was such a shock." She ended on a quaver.

Her brother still waited near the door he had carefully and quietly closed behind him. She looked over at him, and now there was something about the way he stood, the masked expression on his pale face, which made him, too, seem ominous and strange. She shivered once more. "Have you—ever seen a bat—close like that—dead?"

"Yes," Stephen replied with solemn emphasis. "I have. I've seen *that* bat!"

She stared at him. "What do you mean?"

"I mean—*I* put that bat in your washbowl."

She continued to stare, at first too bewildered to reply to this absurd confession. "You didn't," she said finally.

She expected him to deny it, but he only shrugged. The shrug said plainly, "Why should I lie to you?"

She was aware of bracing herself for some further shock. Every nerve in her body grew rigid as she demanded, "Why? Why should you do that?"

"For a very good reason." His voice had become cold and hostile.

She waited for his explanation, but he remained silent, only staring at her from across the room, a gaze of uncomfortable fixed intensity.

Then, with relief, she felt a sense of irritation rising; the annoyance of a superior confronting a naughty child who has just committed some stupid, utterly senseless act. Eighteen years old, and still playing schoolboy tricks! she thought. His dramatic silence, his equivocal answer! Preparing his usual fancy effects! She was aware of looking at him with a new and quite unexpected detachment, seeing him clearly, without emotion, as if he were a stranger. For the first time she noticed, almost with contempt, the effeminate delicacy of her brother's face.

Ralph Parton's face interposed itself between them: the flaring nostrils, full passionate mouth, sweep of dark hair from the forehead. But this image brought back in a rush their hours in the little cove below the camp—and with this memory her fear and apprehension returned. Did Stephen know about Ralph and her? Had he guessed?

Stephen had at last begun to speak—very softly. Even in a half whisper his voice came through, cold and measured. "I knew that bat would frighten you. I know how you hate ugly things. But I wanted you to take a good close look for once at something evil and ugly."

She stared at him, speechless, trying to comprehend the motives behind his behavior. Stephen returned her stare, his face betraying no feeling of any kind.

"Yes, I wanted to frighten you. It was my deliberate intention."

She began to tremble again. "I don't know what you're talking about!" she managed to stammer.

Stephen took another step into the room. She saw then that the hand holding his cigarette was shaking—though to conceal it he had hooked a thumb through the belt of his dressing-gown. His other hand remained carefully pocketed. "I'm going to tell you what I mean." The words slapped at her, flat and cold, like a threat. "You won't like it, Caro, but you're going to listen anyway." He paused to give his next statement added weight. "Ralph Parton gives me just the same feeling that bat gives you!"

He waited, as if expecting some immediate reaction.

Getting none, he went on. "How you don't see what he's really like I can't imagine! You think you *love* him, I suppose. And that he *loves* you." He stressed the word love with disdain, continued with mounting violence, "The truth is, it's nothing but animal attraction—blind, animal attraction! That's what he feels for you, and you for him—like two blind bats following their animal instincts! And you—my *sister*—might just as well plan to live with a bat—*become* a bat—a stinking, misshapen, night-living bat—as to take up with Ralph Parton!"

His cutting voice, and the extremity of his speech, served to steady her. Her fear turned to scorn, and as quickly to open anger. "You're crazy! Get out of my room! Get out right now."

This outburst had no apparent effect. Stephen remained standing where he was.

"I'll not leave until I really scare you." He moved another step towards her. "Caro, I'm going to take that bat out of the water and put it on your pillow, then maybe you'll never, never, *never* forget how I tried to warn you!"

In all her twenty years she had never defied her brother or in any way stood against him. But now the swift transition from terror to rage gave her a force she could not have imagined herself able to command. She jumped from her chair and stood facing him.

"Don't you dare! If you try anything like that, I'll shriek at the top of my lungs!"

"Who'll hear you?"

"Annie!"

He half-laughed. "That old windbag. What would she do if she did?"

"I'll yell so terribly she'll get Papa!" Their father's sleeping cabin was too far from the main camp for him to overhear their scene; they both knew that.

Stephen's still unbroken calm roused her to a higher pitch. "I *will!* I swear I will!"

"Oh, no, you won't!"

His assurance had not wavered in the least. He was, she saw, convinced that she would never betray him, any more than in the past, when he had made her the butt of many small sly tricks.

The fire went out of her, leaving her for a moment cold and hopeless. "I despise you." She spoke in a flat dead voice. "I really despise you. I mean it! I'm sick of your bullying—telling me what to do, what not to do! You've bullied me all my life. Always interfering. Ordering me around. I hate it—I've always hated it—and what's more I hate *you* for doing it. I hate, hate, *hate* you—with all my soul!"

She might as well not have spoken. In the chill, half-lit room she saw his set expression.

"Go ahead! Hate me. I'm prepared for that—but I'm going to save you. I've made up my mind to it." He took another step away from the door. He was going to get the bat from the wash-bowl!

A spasm of renewed terror seized her. "I'll show you!" she cried. She rushed across to the mantelpiece and snatched up a heavy brass candlestick. Poising it above her head she heard herself shouting, "I'll hit you with this, Stephen! I promise I will! I'll hit you with all my strength—if you don't get out of my room this minute and leave me alone!"

Then Stephen did change. She saw his eyes widen with shock, glaze over. For the first time in their lives she had passed beyond his control, completely given over to fury.

"Get out! Get out!" she went on repeating. "I mean it! Get out and don't *ever* come back!"

Suddenly, overhead, a bed gave a heavy creak. They heard Annie turn, cough. They could imagine her up on one elbow, listening, half-awake, wondering what had disturbed her.

"Ssh!" Stephen hissed. "Ssh! For God's *sake*, Caro!"

They both continued to stand, facing each other, rigidly listening, caught in their separate poses of violent threat and fear—like the childhood game of Statues. All at once she found herself remembering the many times they had stood this way, transfixed, waiting for Annie to return to sleep, smothering their laughter, Stephen trying to deceive the old woman by making the sound of a saw-whet owl.

The upraised candlestick dropped from Caroline's clenched hand onto the bed. She collapsed, face down, on her pillow, clutching it to her. After a long moment, a tearing sob forced its way up her throat, burst from her mouth. Then she did not seem really to be crying, water was simply falling, gushing, streaming out of her eyes, nose, mouth, onto the pillow. She could taste the tears, acid and burning, flowing into her mouth and throat, yet she seemed to be looking on—from an infinite icy distance—at someone else sobbing wildly on her bed.

After a while she heard her brother cross the room; felt him standing beside her.

"Ssh," he said again, with a nervous caution very unlike him.

And still whispering, "Caro, please don't. Please, for God's sake, *don't! Stop!* Can't you?"

He put out his hand to touch her. She flinched away and went on crying, though more quietly now. He sat down cautiously on the edge of the bed and waited.

When at last, after many minutes, her tears stopped, Stephen once more put out his hand. Again she shrank from him and in a choked, uncertain voice said, "Don't touch me! You make me sick!"

He did not answer or protest. She turned on her back and stared unseeing at the wooden rafters overhead. Presently she sat up again. Stephen pushed a handkerchief towards her over the blankets. She ignored it, reaching in her own pocket. "This is your moment!" an inner voice said to her. "You had better make the most of it! He's never been this way before—never silent, never afraid or cowed by you—and probably won't be ever again!"

She wanted to feel triumphant over this reversal of their familiar roles, but no sense of victory came to her. She felt again as cold and dead as the voice she now heard issuing from her lips. "You're insane, Stephen. You belong in an institution. I'm going to tell Papa tomorrow he'd better commit you."

She dared not look at him, but she could feel him stiffen. It was as though her words had an actual physical impact; were the blow with the candlestick she had not delivered.

Stephen still made no reply—not even to this terrible charge and threat. The minutes dragged on. The stillness in the cold room grew deeper, more menacing, with every pronounced tick of the old wooden clock on the mantel. Somewhere in the wall near her bed she heard the small dry scurrying of a mouse; and once, from far over the lake, the eerie, manic night-laughter of a loon.

She longed for the power to go on speaking, to be able to scoff at him, to threaten him even more strongly, now that she had the advantage. But somehow her will failed. What had she said? That she hated him? She did not hate him. She loved him—more than anyone, more even than Ralph—in all ways but one. She could say none of this to him now. She had already said too much, gone too far in another direction.

She lay on the bed, her face still averted. Neither of them spoke or moved. As the slow seconds ticked off and her confusion and guilt mounted, she felt the mysterious, invisible control which, for a brief space, she had exercised over her brother passing from her possession.

When at last Stephen spoke, she knew he was again in command, again the master, as he had been through all their childhood and adolescence.

"Now that you've tried to kill me, Caro," he began, his voice lightly jeering, "I think I've a right to ask you to listen for a moment." He paused, lit another cigarette slowly, and added, "Of course, if Annie hadn't coughed when she did, you might have been spared these few remarks. I'd be flat on the floor now—my head bashed in by your candlestick!"

She closed her eyes in a wave of nausea, seeing Stephen stretched on the matting in a pool of blood, the gory metal object beside him. Then she knew how real her impulse had been and she shuddered. Inside herself she pleaded, "Please go away, Stephen. Please, for once, have mercy on me! Don't tell me anything more. You can't change things between Ralph and me. Don't talk about it. I can't stand it!"

But Stephen, who sensed her silent pleading—for he knew her better than anyone in all the world—intended to finish what he had come to say. He leaned nearer, demanding that she look at him, and, as always, she obeyed.

"Maybe I *am* out of my mind. If I am, it's with worry. Please, I beg you, *please*, Caro—just once more, and for the last time—try to listen."

She saw his tormented expression; his eyes at once calm and anguished. "Don't resist me, or what I'm going to say. I promise I'll take the bat out of your room when I go. I promise I won't ever scare you any more about anything—not if I can help it— ever! Only please, *please*, listen to me about Ralph Parton!"

She wanted to put her hands over her ears and shut out his words, but now she lacked the strength even to make this simple movement.

Stephen was going on, more intensely. "Oh, God, if I could only make you see what you're doing! You're walking into a trap. A terrible vile trap. I know what this guy is like. I tell you I know, I *know!*"

His voice, half-whispering, rose and cracked audibly on the last "I know," and this slight sign of weakness and agitation made it possible for her to stammer in protest, "You *don't* know. You don't know anything really *about* Ralph Parton. You never talk to him when he comes here. You don't know him as well—no, not anywhere *near* as well—as I do."

Stephen forgot then to keep his voice low and controlled. "You're right! I certainly *don't* know him as well as you. How could I? I've never been lolling about in canoes with him—letting him paw me all over!"

She struck out at him with her left hand. But the blow, half-hearted, only brushed his cheek. "Shut up! Leave me alone!" she muttered, speaking like a peevish child.

He seized her hand and held it in a tight grip. "Maybe you do hate me." He thrust his face close and looked into her eyes. "But I don't hate *you*, Caro. I love you—more than anyone or anything. That's why I want so much to protect you—to save—!"

When his voice broke, she was tempted to throw herself into his arms, to sob out all her guilt, to promise never again to see Ralph Parton—a promise her very blood told her she could not keep. But her fear of surrendering to her brother's will rose and forced her—as the one way to save herself—to reply, "Oh, sure. I know. You're Galahad!" So great was her necessity to free herself of Stephen's power over her that she added, in a rush, the words that would be for him, she knew, the most scarifying ones she could utter: "The trouble with you is, you're just jealous!" She jerked her hand from his grasp as she spoke.

He made no further attempt to touch her. He ignored her accusation. But, like a man committed to a course of action from which there is no turning back, he went right on with what he had to say.

"There are things I could tell you about Ralph. There's plenty of talk about him around here—how he's been making love to one of the club waitresses, how Mimi St. John's father kicked him out of the house. Maybe those things are true and maybe they're not. I'm just asking you one thing! Please, for God's sake—for your own sake—*try* to believe me when I tell you there's something very wrong with this guy. I don't just feel it, Caro, I know it. I'll tell you again, he gives me the same feeling that bat gives you!"

He reached for her hand once more, and this time she limply allowed him to take it. After one tense squeeze, he dropped it and said, "I'm sorry about the bat. I really am, Caro. It was a low trick. But I couldn't think of any other way to make you listen—to make any impression on you. This was something I knew you'd never forget, couldn't forget. . . ."

THREE

. . . But she had forgotten—until now, more than forty years later.

In her bedroom at Fox Meadows, Lady Brace attempted to raise her head from the pillow. Immediately she became dizzy. The room began to move and whirl in circles. She lay back against the headboard, struggling for breath, trying to bring some clarity to wavering, shifting images. What is happening? Where am I?

The faces of the past and present swam around her—Stephen, Ralph, Lydia, Frederick Hollis—fading in and out of the shifting mists of memory and dream. But what were they attempting to convey? She had a muddled notion of something important she should be trying to grasp, of some scattered design lying around her in fragments she must reassemble into a whole.

Like one emerging from anesthesia she stared about with slow caution, seeking some familiar, reassuring object. Her glance fixed on a wide, pale-gray oblong opposite her. As she concentrated, the oblong grew slowly lighter until at last, to her relief, it became the window of her bedroom.

"It is morning, early morning," she whispered, and the dawn outside took on a firmer reality.

She felt suddenly suffocated in the canopied bed, and throwing off the single sheet, put her feet to the floor. After a moment's hesitation she stood up, then crossed, weak but purposeful, to the window, wrapping her dressing-gown around her as she went.

At the window the room spun again, and she caught at the heavy curtains to steady herself. It occurred to her, as she dimly considered her unreal and bodiless feeling, that she might be dying. Hadn't she better try to call some member of the family? She would not like to be found like this, dead in her dressing-gown without a word of farewell. But at the vision of frightened faces, agitated voices, running steps, bells, doctors—all the nervous flurry that would follow—she decided to summon no one. Better alone! she thought, with no trace of self-pity.

She continued to stand by the window, uncertain still as to her actual physical presence there. Her spirit, if that was what it was, seemed to diffuse itself into all the formless, imponderable elements of the morning: the growing light of dawn, the quiet stir in the air, the unclouded sweep of the sky. No sense of personality or time remained to her. If this, indeed, was death, it seemed an easy and natural event—more a widening of consciousness than a closing in.

How long it was before she recognized again the brightening daylight, or heard clearly the waking birds tripping over their own notes of morning ecstasy, she could not have said. But her dizziness had stopped, and she was no longer holding to the curtains.

She left the window and began to dress in tremulous haste. Without reflecting on, or in any way analyzing, this unfamiliar urgency, she hurried down the hall and out the sunroom door, to walk with quickening steps through the damp grass to the gateless gate of the little walled garden. Once inside she went straight to the corner where the white azalea and the Chinese goddess stood.

When she sat down on the stone bench she again noticed that her breath came short, her heart beating sharp and fast, her whole body cold and hot by turns, as if engaged in some intense inner conflict.

Above the wall, and through the tops of the lilac trees, she became aware of the looming shape of the house she had left. Part of the roof was visible, and by leaning forward she could see even a little of the wing with the old nursery rooms where now Venerable Sir kept his mysterious private quarters. She imagined herself taking up an immense cosmic eraser and, with one sure stroke, wiping from the morning sky the last image of Fox Meadows. Quite plainly there was an empty space now where the great house had stood a moment before. This is the end, she thought, none of it need concern me any more, and she recognized she was suffering no sense of loss. It is because I am too old to feel anything again, she told herself. Old, and fatigued. But, as this moment of hypnotic fantasy passed and the house reappeared on the sky, she knew, in truth, that all her feeling was not dead. In a swift attack all her gnawing worry returned, and with it the mounting dread that some very real demand was being subtly laid on her by her childhood home and its sleeping occupants—a demand she could neither deny nor escape.

She looked straight up into the sky and saw far overhead a plane passing. The rising light caught its wings and turned it into a glistening spot of moving gold. Her troubled spirit in that moment rose and seemed to soar with the soaring plane, and then again to melt and disappear into the infinite cloudless space. She became calm once more, closed her eyes and leaned back against the vine-covered wall. Perhaps I *shall* die, she thought again. Hadn't she always managed to escape, one way or another, the crises of her life?

She had escaped from Stephen's first dire warnings about her marriage straight into Ralph Parton's arms; and then from Ralph's violence into the safer and less exacting union with Humphrey Brace; she had relinquished her growing daughters when their demands became strenuous and tedious; she had retreated from Stephen a second time when she had encountered his disturbing life in Ceylon. When, indeed, had she truly faced anything, or seen through any stormy event from its beginnings to its final consequences? She had been, as long as she could remember, a "lady"—one living within the conventional bounds and forms of that word and all it implied—protected, and wanting to be protected. Sometimes, she now admitted, she had been hopelessly unconscious, and sometimes only bored or fearful. But more often she had been stupidly smug, even vain, of her ability to sidestep deftly every undue strain. On those few occasions when a crisis had seemed unavoidable, she had conducted herself with a cool outward demeanor, a protective and invincible social armor, equal, she had imagined, to every occasion. She had thought of herself as an onlooker—one able to see, judge, and endure without real participation or emotional involvement. For over sixty years she

161

had politely nodded, smiled, demurred, murmured her way through life, and now, without warning, she was being drawn into full participation.

Why did I come back to Fox Meadows? she asked herself in despair. Why did I open my mind to all my carefully buried memories, mistakes, evasions, responsibilities? Was she going to be asked to pay for a lifetime of failure? For it seemed to her now that she had failed. But how? She had been, in every material way, among the world's fortunate; her father's adored daughter; twice a wife; three times a mother; once a loved sister; four times a grandmother. Yet what had she truly had? What high moments of happiness or completion? There were the days in childhood when she and Stephen had known a state of pure, ineffable sharing and communion, and the years with Ralph when, in spite of his brutality, she had experienced sexual fulfillment; and the brief, instinctual joy she had discovered when her infant son lay at her breast. Yet, in summary, it seemed all too little. Of late, there had been only the lesser moments to sustain her—the sight of an early crocus, the sound of a thrush, moonlight on an old wall, apples on a plate, a few passages of music.

Life—she saw clearly, and for the first time admitted freely—life for her had been a vast, farcical, rather tedious blunder from whose lessening grasp she would now willingly slip away, without further question or protest. A wave of self-pity broke over her and she began to sob, her body convulsed and shaking uncontrollably as it had on that night so long ago—or was it only last night?—when she had wanted to kill her brother Stephen.

"Help me!" she cried aloud—a cry of formless need that always before she had been too proud to utter. She gave herself over to tears, bending her graying head and watching the salty water streak down her blue-veined hands.

FOUR

She looked up with a startled gasp. Venerable Sir stood before her, gazing down in quiet puzzlement and concern.

"My dear child. Dear Lady Brace. Has something terrible happened? Can I help you?"

She averted her face in one quick gesture of awkward shame.

What could be more distressing than the sight of an elderly woman weeping alone! She shook her head without answering.

"But dear Lady Brace . . . tell me!" He waited.

Behind her wet handkerchief she murmured, "Please don't bother. I'm all right. . . ." and silently she begged, "Go away. Go away at once and leave me alone!"

But Venerable Sir did not move and, although her head was still turned from him, she had the impression he had seated himself.

She tried to regain control, to shut off her tears and think only of the peace around her in the walled garden: the gently awakening day, the faint singing sound of the summer earth, the stir of invisible life where leaves and bushes stretched and unfolded in the warming sun.

At last she half-turned her face and saw the little monk seated cross-legged on the path, his hands in his lap, his brown velvet eyes blinking at her kindly through his glasses.

"You are better now?"

She nodded. "Yes. Thank you."

"Why are you suffering so?" he asked, with a gentle insistence devoid of any hint of personal curiosity.

"For my terrible failures," she answered, turning from him again.

"Ah, yes, failures." He half smiled, then as promptly was serious again. "Who has not failed? Where is he?"

"Yes, yes, I know," she said with an edge of impatience. "But that doesn't help. Please don't try to comfort me."

"Why not, please?" The way he put the question demanded an answer.

She hesitated. "Because I don't deserve it," she said, her voice breaking.

"Ah, my dear child! Dear Lady Brace!" he exclaimed again. He allowed another silence to fall. It lasted a long time.

"I want to die," she said finally, as if addressing herself. "I am through with—with effort." She paused and looked over at him. When he made no answer, "No, that's not it," she denied. "For I've never made any effort—not really. But now—I know how much I *don't* want to make one—and at the same time I feel—

I *know*—I'm being asked to." Her voice grew tense. "Yes, it's being demanded of me—some tremendous effort, something that will make up for things I've done or not done—some effort to *change*. I can't explain it . . . I'm only sure of one thing, I am too old."

"We are never too old," he said in the gentle lilting voice that had now become pleasant and familiar to her. (She saw him pulling up a stool for her brother's paralyzed legs that first afternoon on the terrace; heard him saying then, "Old age agrees with us all —if only we let it.")

"That's not just a pollyanna truism," he added, smiling across at her as if he enjoyed his use of the colloquial Americanism. "No, no, it's the plain truth. We are never too old *because*—because there is only the Now—and the Now allows for all miracles. In a moment anything can happen! Is that not true?"

Her voice rose, sounding faintly querulous. "I've never understood this idea about 'only the Now'—'the present moment'—and I fancy I never will. How can one *ever* escape the past?"

Venerable Sir replied without hesitation, and with an air of authority. "One cannot. It is unalterable. Nothing can change the past, for it has been. But the future—that is different. The future grows from the present, from the Now. Its form—the future's— is not fixed—only conditioned."

She did not answer or move. They both sat motionless for so long that a bird, roused from the azalea bush minutes before, darted back and regarded them both with a beady, surprised eye, then darted away again as the little monk spoke.

"Try thinking this," he began, then paused while his eye followed the bird's flight. "Try thinking this," he repeated. "When you live 'in the past,' as the saying goes, it is only memory. True? You are not *really* living it. When you live in the future—what is that? Only anticipation. For it is not yet in existence—may never be. Thus, Now—the present moment—is the *only* reality."

"All right," she said shortly, like someone worsted in an argument but not prepared to give in, "the point is, in this Now, as you call it, I feel I'm going to be asked to act in ways that are— are very difficult and unlike me."

"Good!" he said at once. "You can do it."

She repeated, "I am too old."

"Ah-ah!" He raised his finger in humorous admonition. "How you bind yourself with fixed notions, saying, *You can't teach an old dog new tricks*, et cetera—eh? But also you say—do you not?— it is a very fine optimistic Western expression, one I have often quoted to my colleagues at home—*It is never too late to learn.* And also you say—if I am not incorrect—*It is never too late to mend.* And, finally, you say, *You are only as old as you feel*," and he burst into his soft childlike laughter.

Then, in a single movement of unfolding, he lifted his body from the garden path. "Come," he said, "let us go back to the house, shall we? Everyone will soon be up. It's a new day."

He stood beside her quietly and without any show of insistence, but she knew he would not allow her to remain where she was.

"Whatever you have to do," he said, his voice low but still positive and reassuring, "I know you will do it—you can. And if ever you wish to talk with me, about any of it, well—I live in your old nursery, you know," and again he laughed.

Lady Brace rose stiffly from the stone bench. There was nothing she could do about her ravaged face, but she automatically smoothed her hair and dress as she walked with Venerable Sir towards the open lawn.

At the empty gate she paused, feeling once more the necessity to exclaim, "I'm still confused—and so very tired. I'm not sure I can endure any more of life without breaking." She faced him for the first time in direct appeal.

His expression grew solemn as he looked at her closely for a moment, and then away. He folded his hands together, placed them against his chest, lowered his chin on the tips of his fingers. "Let me see," he said softly. Again, as on the night before in the garden, he gave the impression of searching for the altogether acceptable fragment of truth.

Presently he lifted his head. "Yes!" he announced happily, as if he had surely found what he was looking for. He began to fumble inside his voluminous yellow robes until he brought forth, to her surprise, a small pad of paper and the most modern of ball-point pens. She had to smile, seeing, at the same time, an image of his sandaled foot on the pedal of Stephen's Thunderbird.

When he caught her smile, he smiled back. "I have quoted enough for one day. Quotations are such boring things—if over-indulged in. So I will write this out for you, if you please." He leaned the pad against the end of the brick wall, wrote a few words in his fine precise script, tore the page from the pad and handed it to her with a little bow.

Lady Brace held the page up and read aloud, " *'The Path itself will enlighten you, if you but trust yourself to it.'* " She looked over at him, puzzled. "What does it mean?"

He smiled again—more broadly now, as if in high good humor. "Just go on walking the everyday path of life," he replied, "looking around you as you walk. Awareness—constant awareness—that is what we are after!"

As they came through the empty gates they both heard the sound of a screen door slamming. The dogs erupted onto the lawn, followed by Jennifer, who at once saw her grandmother and Venerable Sir and waved. Running towards them across the grass she called out, "Why, Gran! Why're you up so early?"

"Oh, dear!" Lady Brace murmured. "My face—I look so dreadful! I'll frighten the child. What shall I say to her?"

"Tell her you have been crying. Tell her that grandmothers sometimes have to cry, too." His eyes looked merry again. "The truth never frightens children."

And now Jennifer was near enough to see them both clearly.

"It begins," Venerable Sir said softly. "Go right ahead!"

As Lady Brace went forward to greet her grandchild she had the sense that the little monk's words extended far beyond this immediate moment.

15

Jennifer, skipping over the sun-dried grass beside Venerable Sir, had gone off happily on her grandmother's "secret" mission. She returned alone to the corner of the terrace where Lady Brace waited, hidden behind a sun umbrella. Jennifer brought with her the make-up kit for which she had been sent.

"What a clever child—to find it just like that," Lady Brace said, opening the leather case and glancing in dismay at the reflection in its mirrored lid. "Gracious! I do look rather awful, don't I?"

Jennifer made no reply. She sat gravely watching her grandmother apply powder and the pale pink lipstick she habitually wore.

"Mummy never cries," she volunteered.

"Doesn't she? Maybe only the old and the young do the crying," Lady Brace suggested.

"Why were you crying, Gran? Did Venerable Sir make you cry?"

"Oh, indeed not! I had just been thinking about—some sad things."

"Then don't!" Jennifer suggested. She took a small green rubber ball from the pocket of her denim shorts and began to bounce it up and down on the bricks. Without looking at her grandmother she repeated, with an odd, grownup pursing of her lips, "Just don't, that's all!"

Lady Brace could not keep from smiling. "I'll try, darling," she promised. "How do I look now?"

Jennifer regarded her with a solemn expression. "Not bad," she conceded. She stood up with her grandmother and accompanied her thoughtfully to the sunroom door. How I wish, Lady Brace thought, I could just lift the top of that blond head and look in.

As they opened the screen door together, Rosemary, on her way upstairs, paused on the landing. "Why, Lady B! What are *you* doing up at this hour?"

Lady Brace's first feeling was one of relief. Caught this way, the light behind her, and at a little distance, she doubted that even Rosemary's sharp glance would detect the signs of recent tears. "I'm reforming my lazy morning habits," she replied lightly.

Rosemary waited, one foot on the stairs. "Let me get you your tea right away," she offered. Something in her tone indicated that her early-morning routine was being—indeed had already been—put off, and that her mother's unexpected appearance added another straw to a mounting burden.

"Please don't bother," Lady Brace protested. "Jennifer and I will get it together, won't we, Jennifer?"

Jennifer said, all eagerness, "I'll get it *for* you, Gran. Let me do it, alone."

"You're sure you can manage?" Rosemary seemed to be questioning her child less than her mother.

"Good gracious, Rosemary," Lady Brace answered a little testily, "what is there to manage?"

"I'll ask Clara for it," Jennifer cried, legging off towards the kitchen, bouncing her little ball.

Rosemary, half-apologetic, her left hand resting firmly on the rail as if to indicate imminent flight to invisible duties, explained, "I'm a bit off the beam this morning, Mummy. It's just one of those days. Funny, isn't it? Some days are like that. Makes you believe in the stars." She lowered her voice after glancing around with caution. "I've just been talking to Jack—Jack Frazier. He *is* coming down this afternoon, Mummy. He seemed delighted to know you were here—and that he'd have a chance to—*talk*."

Lady Brace chose to ignore Rosemary's special emphasis on the word "talk." She said only, "Will Lydia mind?"

"I'm *sure* not. Anyway, she may not even *be* here." Rosemary dropped her hand from the rail and came down one step, lowering her voice another notch. "At quarter of twelve last night Frederick Hollis called. I answered the telephone. Lydia was already in bed. He told me not to wake her but just to leave a note saying something important had come up, that he wished to see her early in the morning and would send a car to fetch her. She's *already* gone! What on earth do you suppose it can be?"

Lady Brace determined to show no concern. "I've no idea. Perhaps it's nothing important. Frederick Hollis may just be the compulsive type."

"Ho! Not him!" Rosemary cried. "He's always as cool as a cucumber. Everything's planned down to the very last little detail. No, I *distinctly* got the impression something unusual was up!"

"Rosemary, you should write mystery thrillers," her mother said. "You'd have just the right touch."

Rosemary smiled with a good humor which at once made Lady Brace ashamed of her mild annoyance. "Todd sometimes calls me

Agatha. Meaning Agatha Christie, of course," she explained. She turned towards the stairs, "Anyway, why *should* I worry the way I do about Lydia? It's *her* life, not mine—and I've got enough to tend to in my own! Today in particular." She paused again to ask over her shoulder, "Do you really want to go with me to look at that house, now that you're up so bright and early?"

"That's one reason I'm up," Lady Brace said, excusing her small fib on the grounds that it gave her a chance to be generous to her child. "I hope you told Jack I'd be happy to see him."

Rosemary's inquiring glance seemed to ask whether her mother was in earnest. "I really couldn't say anything else, Lady B," she answered, wary.

"Of course you couldn't."

"And anyway," Rosemary added, as if daring to speak more directly now that her mother seemed so amenable, "I'm still hoping *you* can do something about—you know."

Lady Brace was spared a reply by the reappearance of Jennifer, who advanced, making her way with infinite slow care through the dining-room door, carrying a tray with orange juice, toast and tea. Rosemary watched the entrance nervously, then hurried away to answer a ringing telephone.

Lady Brace was still drinking her tea when Rosemary came back.

"I *told* you!" she cried from the stair landing, with tragic intonation. "It's one of those days! Julia Corbett—that's the real estate woman—just phoned. She can't make it this morning. We'll have to do it early this afternoon."

"It doesn't matter in the least," Lady Brace said in a soothing voice. She was, in fact, relieved at the delay. It would give her a few hours to collect her shattered forces. That she could appear so calm in Rosemary's presence was merely the effect of long-established disciplines. Behind the serene façade she could feel the telltale trembling.

"But will you be able to do both?" Rosemary was demanding, "I mean look at a house and *then* see Jack?"

"I don't see why not," Lady Brace replied, aware as she spoke of a qualm of distaste at the prospect of an intimate prolonged talk with her former son-in-law.

Promptly at two o'clock Julia Corbett, a pretty woman about Rosemary's age with a professionally confident manner, hair the color of spun aluminum and a voice that matched it, came to pick them up. She said she had an errand to perform en route—if they didn't mind a slight detour—and so, once again, as on the day of her arrival, Lady Brace was driven through the streets of Lynnbury. She noted, as she had on her first glimpse after many years of absence, how every shop seemed swollen to the bursting point with excess goods; a veritable avalanche of "things.". . . Things to buy, wear, rent; things to see, eat, drink, pressed on her from every side. "The Land of Plenty," she murmured, half to herself, "sex, sensation and the stomach"—for this appeared a proper summary of the appeals that flashed and beckoned, invited and commanded, the pocketbooks and appetites of every passerby.

". . . one of those dreadful new developments," Mrs. Corbett was apologizing as she turned the car into a residential section where endless streets of houses stretched, built all to pattern as though produced by some gigantic cutting machine. Only the color of an occasional nonconformist's door or shutter, a singular shrub on the minuscule patches of lawn, set apart one dwelling from its neighbor. Conformity extended even to dozens of blackfaced metal urchins leaping from bushes holding lanterns aloft, rows of trim jockeys offering invisible bridles to nonexistent horses, and innumerable black iron setters guarding doormats that displayed, with a flourish, the owners' names.

When Rosemary, turning from the front seat, asked her mother what she thought of it all, Lady Brace confessed that it "frightened" her. She added, "It makes me glad to be as old as I am."

"You mean it's bound to get *worse?*" Rosemary questioned. "I wonder!" As she went on talking she seemed anxious to reject her mother's implied criticism. She spoke with admiration of the "philosophic" acceptance of mass living by "young people—younger than Todd and I are, Mummy." She suggested benefits from, advantages to, enforced community intimacy. She even quoted Alice Ford on the subject, and Julius Carozzi. When Mrs. Corbett returned from her errand Rosemary, warming to her subject, leapt to possible future residence for Earth Dwellers on other planets, then trailed off, as they dodged in and out of trucks on the teeming highway, to the more mundane topic of Planned Parenthood.

Behind the immediate scene and her daughter's remarks Lady Brace was aware of the hovering outlines of a nostalgic mirage, one that encompassed the old stone house in Somerset, the ragged straggle of cobbles leading through the village of Bishop's Overpass: the Widow Lavery's musty sweets shop where she also bought her yarns, the cosy drabness of the local *Unicorn and Crown,* and one-armed, ruddy Major Trench-Thwaites' collection of *Antiquities.* I am homesick, she admitted to herself and, leaning back, closed her eyes.

When they turned again into the quieter roads that still threaded the landscape of her Long Island childhood, Lady Brace looked out again, with mixed feelings, on the remaining great places, barely to be glimpsed by motorists, hidden up winding drives and behind screens of magnificent planting: laurel, rhododendron, gigantic elms, copper beeches, maples, conifers, silver birch.

She noticed, with amusement, two little gate-houses Stephen had once called the "Georgian privies" still standing beside a box-lined entrance where now an unfamiliar foreign name gleamed in gold on black. In the hidden courtyard at the end of this wide driveway she had often waited for the hunt to gather on frosty fall mornings. Her father, impeccable in his pink, had frowned at Stephen slumped glumly in his saddle, his white stock awry; she heard the ring of horses' hooves on the bricks, and the low whine of the hounds, eager to be off. How fast the change has come, she thought, too fast for me to assimilate.

Mrs. Corbett brought the car to a stop beside a high fence of closely woven wooden slats. When she turned off the ignition she remarked to Rosemary, "I do think we ought to prepare your mother with a little briefing, don't you?" Rosemary acquiesced and she launched into a blithe account of how this particular house happened to be up for sale "at such a sacrifice price."

The story, to which Lady Brace listened with feigned interest, had to do with the breakup through a series of divorces, and a realignment through new marriages, of a group of "close friends." As the account continued Mrs. Corbett appeared not to be discussing human beings but merely dealing with separately labeled integers, an aggregate of impersonal, movable parts in which the children also were included. "The offspring of the entire lot," she reported, in a neat summary, had been handily ensconced in one of the houses belonging to two of the recently severed members of the rearranged equations—this while the assorted parents were scattered to Reno, Mexico and the Virgin Islands getting their various divorces. "Susie Rhodes' old cook, Hilda, is coping with all six of the kids," she concluded. "It's really *something!*"

The sordid story confused Lady Brace. She found Mrs. Corbett's bland recital of tragedy more wearisome even than Rosemary's conversational italics. When she looked over at Rosemary and saw her studying her reactions, Lady Brace wondered what she had let herself in for by agreeing to house-hunt.

Now, however, there was nothing to do but see it through. As they entered the grounds, then the house, she supported herself with the reminder that only by paying close attention to Mrs. Corbett's various points of salesmanship would she be able later to give Rosemary any helpful advice. With spaced nods and murmurs she listened to the realtor's patter—to praise of the "clever way in which gravel was used instead of grass to keep down the grounds' budget—for it's two dollars and fifty cents an hour, you know, Lady Brace, *just* for raking leaves, around here." There was a tennis court out of sight behind a hedge of cedars. The "wading pool could be easily deepened." The flagstones in the wide front hall could not be "scuffed" by children. The living room was air-conditioned and possessed, besides, a "romantic" hooded fireplace at one end.

They came at last to the "charming library" and Mrs. Corbett flung open the door with an operatic gesture. A blast of stifling air rushed towards them. The room was in total darkness except for the white face of a television screen palely shining at the far end.

At sight of this ghostly object the little gnomelike servant who had admitted them to the house—her hair in curlers and carrying a dust mop—darted forward like an angry sparrow. She switched on all the lights and terminated the television program with one fierce movement.

In an agitated voice she cried, "*Dumm* kids! Shoo! Out! Outa here into *Gott's* sunlight! I'm tellin' you!"

A chorus of childish voices shrieked in protest. "Hilda! No!" There was a sudden scramble of legs and arms; heads shot up from sofas and off floor cushions. "You stinker!" cried two little girls in one voice.

"Somevun come to see the house," Hilda said, grim. "Stand up. Polite." No one stirred. "*Dumm* kids," she repeated. She turned to Lady Brace, seeking an ally. "Iss a shame, ain't? Like dope fiends, I say it. I tell 'em, get out in *Gott's* sunlight! But who listens vat I say? *Dummheit,* iss it!"

Lady Brace found herself speechless but Rosemary managed to address the blinking children with an air of cajolery. "It's a wonderful day," she said. "Just *perfect* for tennis!"

Mrs. Corbett seized on this suggestion with immediate experienced fervor. "Yes, why don't you get up a game?"

"The boys—they don't know how to play," said the elder of the two girls, sulky. She looked about twelve and her blond bang badly wanted cutting. Her remark obviously referred to two younger children who appeared to be twins.

"Well, why don't you *girls* play—and give the boys a lesson?" Rosemary demanded, quite prepared to resolve the dilemma.

"*Because,*" cried the second little girl, who must have chopped off her own hair with a rather uncertain hand, judging from its uneven lengths and general dishevelment, "I've busted my racket."

"You mean you've lost a shoe, *liar,*" cried the girl with the bang. She flopped back onto the couch and dangled her feet over one end. She was wearing long, knitted ski socks with leather soles. The room was so warm Lady Brace could only wonder how the child endured the wool.

"She means Bruno ran off with it," put in one of the little boys in a shrill voice. "He ran off and hid it!"

"Probably chewed it up by now," his brother remarked in a gloating tone. "No one gave him his supper last night and he was hungry."

"Vat am I tellin' you over and over?" cried Hilda, shaking the dust mop, wagging the gleaming curlers. "Them dogs here iss for you to tend. Not me. I didn't take on no job feedin' animals. You had orders, no? I heard 'em," she concluded darkly.

The children were silent.

Before Rosemary could again intercede Mrs. Corbett said, in a tone of dismissal, "Well, anyway, this is the library—so-called." Ignoring the children, she proceeded to call Rosemary's attention to several salient points of dimension and fenestration. Lady Brace remained near the door. Avoiding, in embarrassment, the stares of the silent sullen children, she dutifully looked about. Here, as in the library at Fox Meadows, she caught the same pervasive air of neglect—undusted furniture, undusted books, subtle indications that the rows of leather-bound "classics"—wedding presents, in all probability—had never been so much as opened. A litter of paper comics and the remains of lunches lay on the floor before the wide davenport facing the television.

The little gnome, her eyes on Lady Brace, now moved closer to mutter, "I tell 'em and tell 'em. Get out in *Gott's* sunlight, I say. But will they? *Nein.* Sits in here, look, look, all day long. *Bang! Bang! Bang!*" she cried suddenly, firing an imaginary pistol, making Lady Brace jump with surprise. "*Smack! Smack! Smack!*" She made an absurd sucking noise plainly intended to represent a kiss.

At once loud hoots of scornful laughter burst from the children. Their heads, arms and legs dived around violently among the cushions in spasms of derision.

"Nobody makes love on TV!" cried the little girl with the chopped-off hair. "Didn't you know *that*, Hilda?"

"Then why sit around all day and look? For vat?" the gnome demanded. "Waiting for nossin'? Bah!"

"Because!" the same little girl cried, her voice shrill and angry. She raised a pillow high above her and whacked it down hard on the couch. "There's nothing to *do* around here, and you know it!"

"Let's leave them to their addiction," Mrs. Corbett said, still cheery. Before the door had closed behind them Lady Brace heard the sound of running feet and an announcer's fruity voice saying, "And now for our matinée audience today . . ."

Rosemary paused beside her mother. "It's absolutely *tragic*," she whispered. Although her overemphasis was, as always, faintly irritating, Lady Brace found it easy this time to nod in agreement. I don't wonder Rosemary finds house-hunting painful, she thought, pressing her daughter's arm in sympathy.

She could hardly face continuing the tour but she made no protest as Mrs. Corbett led them towards the stairs. Absurd as the idea was, she began to find in the entire experience some element of expiation.

On the second floor the rooms seemed all alike; again regimented taste: chintzes, flower prints, pale wooden furniture—illustrations for a woman's magazine. Mrs. Corbett's main point of salesmanship centered on an enormous glassed-in needle shower occupying a space off the master bedroom. "Men just *adore* them!" she cried.

Outside the door of the last room, at the hall's end, Hilda, who had traipsed along behind them still carrying her dust mop, said in a whisper, "Kids iss sleepin' here. But you can easy take a look."

"Oh, no, please don't bother!" both Lady Brace and Rosemary protested, but Hilda already had the door ajar.

There was an immediate scrabbling movement in the nearest crib. A little boy of about three lurched to his feet and, clutching the railings in both hands, looked up with eager sleepy expectancy. "Daddy?" he asked.

"No, no, not daddy," Hilda said quickly but kindly. She went over to the crib and bent down. "Be quiet now, *liebchen*," she whispered, "you vake Johnny, no?"

But Johnny was already awake; he spoke up from a cot near the window. "I hear you," he said in a clear decisive voice.

"Naughty, not to sleep," Hilda admonished, crossing to him.

"I slept," Johnny said. "A long time." He stood up yawning, gouging his fists in his eyes. He was wearing only his underpants. "Who's that?" he inquired, staring at the women in the doorway.

"Daddy?" again questioned the three-year-old from the crib. "Daddy come?"

"Not yet," Hilda said. "Some day soon, huh! Get up now, if you vant it, Johnny. Yah, the clothes on yet."

"Too hot," cried the little boy, and, leaving his bed, shot out the door and down the steps. "I'm going to wade," he called back over his shoulder.

"Vatch yourself, vat you do!" Hilda cried after him, but he had already gone. She lifted the little blond boy then, and he put his arms around her neck and clung tightly. "Such a loving little vun," Hilda said, her tone tender. "Every time he iss askin' for his *vater*. Sad, ain't?" She whispered secretly, "Never for his *mutter*. Dat vun! But she gets him—*das Kind*: yah, a course, said the judge. The law! Hah! Vat good iss?"

As they started back downstairs, "I'm going outside, if you don't mind," Lady Brace said in a low tone to Rosemary. "It seems breathless in here."

"Do, Mummy," Rosemary said at once. "We'll not be much longer—just the dining room, kitchen and basement."

Lady Brace let herself out the front door and sat down weakly on the stone steps. She closed her eyes, trying to shake off the feeling of faintness that had assailed her for a moment in the upper hall. Then, in the distance, she heard a child's thin voice calling, "Hi!" When the bleak monosyllable was repeated for the third time, shrill yet tentative, she opened her eyes and looked towards the pool. The little boy called Johnny stood at the water's edge gazing in her direction. Between his legs he had placed an inflated rubber animal, a red and yellow legless pony. For a moment he looked to her like some mythological creature, a child-centaur.

When he saw her face turned towards him he called in a high voice that sounded desperate, "Wave at me!"

Lady Brace could not believe that he was addressing her, and she glanced behind her and across the graveled grounds. But since there was no one else in sight, she raised her right hand and waved it once.

"Go on!" he commanded. "Go on waving at me!" His own small right hand was flopping up and down in jerky rhythm.

Lady Brace continued to wave until abruptly the small figure plunged down the shallow steps into the pool and began to push the rubber steed fast ahead of him. When she lowered her arm he called out again, his eyes still fixed on her, "Watch me! Watch me now! Keep watching!" Holding his nose but without immersing his head, he rose and fell in the water. "I can dive, see?"

"Marvelous!" Lady Brace cried.

"Keep on watching!" he admonished.

"I will," she assured him. "Do it again."

At that moment Rosemary, Mrs. Corbett and Hilda, with the littlest boy still plastered against her chest like a plump blond limpet, opened the front door and appeared on the steps.

"We've finished, Mummy," Rosemary said, in a tone of relief.

Lady Brace rose. As she did so Johnny, up to his waist in the pond, paused transfixed.

"Do you have to go now?" he cried, shrill and desperate again.

"Yes, I'm afraid so," she said. "I'm sorry. I loved watching you. You dive beautifully. Goodbye, Johnny."

But he made no reply. He stood gazing after them in stricken silence; his terrible loneliness seemed to Lady Brace to move out from him in actual waves, in rings that eddied around her feet as she moved away, forming a very whirlpool, threatening to pull her down.

"Oh, *how* depressing!" she heard Rosemary saying, and then Mrs. Corbett's reply, "Yes, I know. But don't let the *human* situation blind you to the good points this place has."

Mrs. Corbett paused by the entrance gate to indicate a large square sign painted with a row of names. "The other people here are *terribly* nice." She read the list aloud: "Erwin, Jones, Meade, Tucker, Russell," giving each name a particular stress as though, without saying it, she was clearly establishing the racial background of the other occupants of this special plot of land.

"Have you time to look at one more house?" she asked as they got into the car.

"Mummy has an appointment," Rosemary said. "But we might take her back to our place and then go on, Julia—since you're free."

Yes, Lady Brace thought to herself, I have an appointment. I am going, with reluctance, to meet my former son-in-law, and if Rosemary had planned, in advance, to put before me some graphic examples of the lost and bewildered children of divorce she could hardly have done better.

16

As she came into the drawing room Jack Frazier rose from a chair and, stubbing out his cigarette, moved forward to greet her. He has put on weight around the middle, she thought, a thickening, a softening. She extended her hand and he took it warmly. "Lady B," he said, "—a long time!" He seemed completely at ease, though she had not seen him since before the divorce.

"Does it seem too dark or warm in here?" she asked, noting all the curtains half-drawn as she sat down opposite him.

"I like it," he said. "I'm one Texas resident who finds it a distinct pleasure not to have air-conditioning."

Lady Brace grasped at this trivia with relief. She needed time to adjust herself to an interview with a former son-in-law with whom she had never been on intimate terms. "I hardly know what air-conditioning feels like, I'm afraid. I suppose in all Texas there's not a house without it."

He gave her a half-smile, sardonic and, at the same time, shy. "I couldn't say as to that."

Lady Brace continued with somewhat forced animation, "I have the notion about Texas that it is all terribly modern and *avant-garde*. Isn't everyone fearfully rich? And don't they all live in glass houses and collect Picassos and fly about to barbecues of their own beef cattle in their own private planes?"

He grinned again and shook his head. "Purest fiction. Though I must admit I do find it all rather different from, well, let's say, Maine." He reached in a pocket and took out a wallet. "I brought some pictures of the children for you, taken at my family's place."

As he crossed towards her she said to herself, I'm going to be plunged into this before I'm quite ready.

When he gave her the snapshots she noticed his hands—large, moistly soft, with a sprinkle of freckles and a thick growth of red-blond hair on their backs. To her horror the image of these hands moving over Lydia's trim body rose before her, and when she repressed this picture, her imagination perversely substituted the withered claws of Frederick Hollis. She caught herself in a slight shudder.

"Little Bill and Pammy," she said quickly, glancing at the first of the several photos. "How they've grown!"

She put on her glasses to look more closely at a tall-for-his-age boy with an elongated melancholy face and a plump pretty little girl with short cropped hair. Two large fish dangled from Pamela's proudly raised right hand.

"How much Pammy looks like you!" Lady Brace could not keep from exclaiming. Where, she wondered, had Little Bill acquired that gaunt sad face?

"Yes, she does, rather," Jack admitted, obviously pleased, though he added, "She needs to lose some weight, like her old man. We've got her on thyroid now."

"And she's already a sportswoman, I see. Those are very impressive fish."

He smiled and shook his head. "Pam's not very good at sports, really, though she's very keen on fishing. As a matter of fact Bill caught those particular fish. He just let Pammy hold them for the picture."

"But how generous of him!" Lady Brace said. "He must have very good manners. And do you still call him Little Bill? He looks tall for his age."

"He is tall. Yes, it's funny—we've always called him Little Bill. Probably always will. He's the second William Dekoven Frazier, you know. Uncle Bill died in World War I, as you probably remember. At Vimy Ridge."

"Ah, yes." Lady Brace could think of nothing further to remark, half-caught again in a curious sense of time being not linear but spiral, an endless repetition of events with no end, no goal; no tidy or satisfactory terminations of any kind—ever.

Then, reminding herself of her firm resolve to get down at once to the matter most pressingly on her mind, she laid the photographs on her lap with an air of postponement and faced her former son-in-law.

"Jack," she began in a forced voice, trying to smooth away the

179

troubled expression she could feel forming on her face. "I hope you'll allow me to talk frankly about something that—worries me rather a lot."

He evinced no surprise. "Of course, Lady B," he replied with perfunctory politeness, reaching for his cigarettes. "You don't smoke? Do you mind if I do?"

"Not at all." She waited for him to light up before she continued, "It's not easy for me to speak about this, Jack. For one thing I do not know you very well, though you were once my son-in-law. For another, it may seem a little—late for me to concern myself, to presume to interfere. And that is the way it may appear to you, like interference in your private affairs."

She was becoming flurried and nervous. She paused to take a deliberate steadying breath. "I hope you will understand when I say that somehow, lately, very strongly since coming back here to my old home, indeed, more and more in the last few days, and even in the last hours, I've had such a growing sense of the— shakiness of the life I see all around me. In spite of all the comforts and all the many *things*, I mean the countless objects, the easy luxuries that everyone now has, somehow, I get a feeling— this may seem absurd to you—but I do get the very strong feeling that all of it is resting on a sort of *quicksand*."

Jack was looking attentive, politely puzzled. She did not wonder at his expression. She was being much too vague and general, yet now she could not immediately alter her course, for there flashed into her mind the deserted children in Mrs. Corbett's "sacrifice" house, and without the slightest intention of speaking about them, she found herself doing so.

"Just this afternoon I went with Rosemary to look at a house for sale. It was filled with children of several marriages, their families all away, getting divorces. It—upset me very much. One little boy in particular. He—I'm afraid he is going to haunt me." She broke off and added hurriedly, seeing that he was looking even more uneasy. "Not that I'm opposed to the idea of divorce. I know it is often necessary, the only possible solution. But I don't know, all those children today—they seemed so lost, so hurt and belligerent—lonely and bewildered . . ."

His face had, she noticed, stiffened perceptibly. She hurried on. "Forgive me, Jack, for saying all this, and so ineptly! I'll try to come straight to the point. I wonder if there isn't some way for you and Lydia to—start over again together?"

At this abrupt directness he seemed genuinely taken aback. She was certain from his startled glance that he had not been at all prepared for such a question from her.

She forced herself to continue in spite of his guarded silence. "I have surprised you. What did you think I was going to discuss?"

He hesitated a moment before replying, "The children."

"But it is the children I'm talking about," she said with deliberate emphasis.

He nodded. "I only thought you were going to question my taking them to Texas with me for all of next year."

As the significance of this remark sank in, there fell another silence, a rather awkward one. "I didn't know that you were taking them to Texas," she said finally.

He looked increasingly ill at ease. "I assumed Lydia would have told you. She hasn't?"

"No—not yet."

"Perhaps—" It was now his turn to hesitate. He broke off, cleared his throat. "You do know about Lydia's plans, of course?"

"You mean—?" She could not bring herself to phrase what she knew.

He came to her rescue. "Well, you must have heard something about Frederick Hollis." His voice remained dry and tight.

She nodded. "So you know too?" It was a tactless question and she regretted it the moment it had slipped from her tongue.

"It's hardly a secret."

She would have been relieved to detect in his manner, or intonation, a hint of pain, of resentment, irony even, anything but this flat, impersonal monotone. Was it, perhaps, a studied indifference, concealing deep feeling? She tried to keep Lydia's words about him from her mind, to judge him wholly, freshly, as she saw him in this moment. Hardly aware that she was staring, she looked fixedly across the space between them. He had slouched down a trifle in his chair, his mouth concealed by his freckled paw—she could only think of it as that; the paw of one of those stuffed, spotted-velvet leopards, well-formed, powerful, but with no spring in it, no strength, no menace, because no life. . . .

He began to talk in a low tone, as if her silence roused in him the necessity to assure her that he understood what had prompted her to speak as she had. "I believe I see what troubles you, Lady B. I know because it's the same thing that troubles my parents—particularly my mother—and I know it's perfectly natural. The children. Mother worries about them constantly. I try to tell her it's no use. The harm was done long ago. Done before Lydia and I ever separated the first time." There was a short pause. Then, still without any sign of emotion, he added, "We shouldn't have had them in the first place. The truth is we should never have been married!"

Lady Brace checked an impulse to clap her hands over her ears to shut out these sad, doomed words, almost the same ones that Lydia had uttered to her a few days before. Again she saw the derelict children in the library given over to television, the lonely little boy waving at her from the pool.

"Oh, I can't bear it!" she exclaimed aloud. "Those poor children!" Her voice trembled.

As if to hold back a threat of rising emotion Jack lifted towards her one of the spotted velvet paws. "No, wait a minute!" he said, turning on her his honest, if not very profound gaze. "Wait!" he repeated. "That's not saying I—both of us—don't love our kids. We do. We both do. We're devoted to them. It's just that we're pretty clear now about our mistake—in marrying, I mean. You know we both went to psychiatrists to get some light on the subject. A lot of their ideas are pretty silly, I'll admit, but there's some sense in 'em too. One thing we both learned beyond a shadow of a doubt—we didn't belong together. Never had."

His words seemed to Lady Brace like a gigantic wave towering over her, threatening to carry her out beyond her depth, beyond any possible rescue or return. She clung desperately to her original thought about the children. "But still—in spite of that—couldn't you—for the children's sake . . . ?" She did not speak these words aloud; she could only wait, cowering, under the threat of the curling wave about to roll down over her.

Jack Frazier rose, took a few steps towards the nearest window, turned back, sat down again as if in this brief space he had made up his mind to speak with even greater candor. "The truth is, Lady B, I don't think I'll marry again at all. I seem to manage pretty well without it." In a determinedly lighter tone he added, giving her a faint smile, "Maybe bachelorhood runs in our family. My Uncle Bill never married, you know—and he was already in his middle thirties when he was killed."

The threatening image of the wave was gone, its place taken by the snapshot picture of Little Bill, the dead uncle's namesake. Her grandson seemed to Lady Brace to be carrying, like an invisible pack on his back, a valued family trait—bachelorhood. Jack had, indeed, spoken of it as though it was some rare Frazier tradition which should not be allowed to die out.

A strong desire to terminate this profitless and disheartening exchange rose in Lady Brace. But she reminded herself how much initial effort it had cost her to agree to Rosemary's urging that she see Jack Frazier in the first place, and she was sure the moment he left she would only recriminate herself for cowardice, for too feeble an effort on behalf of her convictions. But what were her convictions? They seemed again unclear, and almost with longing she thought of the fixed and undeviating position of the Roman Catholic Church on the subject of divorce. How much easier, in all ways, the acceptance without question of priest-fixed "laws" on morals, ethics, right and wrong . . .

"I am an old woman," she began.

Jack turned on her a kindly glance. She imagined she saw in it some identification of her with his own mother, and to her surprise, she resented this. Not even for a moment did she wish him to think she would use her years as a way of softening his heart; to win him over through pity for her gray hairs.

In a stronger tone she repeated, "Yes, I am an old woman, and I have spent my life avoiding everything painful—including honesty—whenever possible." Then with a complete abandonment of her usual reticence she added, "I cannot tell you how I— *despise* myself for my many years of weakness and evasion and for my many cowardly mistakes."

The effect of these abrupt, unexpected remarks was reflected at once in Jack's pale eyes. He appeared discomfited and about to protest, but she made a peremptory gesture, silencing him.

"I am not saying this to hear it denied, Jack. I am saying it because I—must." She rallied herself for further confession. "I want you to know that it is with the deepest sense of my own failure, my own—" she hesitated, swallowed hard on the next word "—guilt—yes, *guilt*—because of my absence of responsibility towards Lydia when she was young, that I am now asking you, as I intend to ask Lydia even more forcibly, to return to your marriage and make a settled home for your children."

Her increasing vehemence seemed to daze him, but she hurried on before the impetus could slacken, "After all, you and Lydia are not enemies. You speak kindly of each other. It isn't as though you cherished hatred and anger . . ." I am sounding just like Rosemary, she thought, and at once broke off.

Jack remained silent for several moments while he lit a fresh cigarette from the butt of the one he was holding. He seemed to be waiting for her to continue, but when she did not, he asked, guardedly, "You haven't talked to Lydia about this?"

"No, but I intend to—today." She kept her voice firm.

"She would never agree," he said.

"Let's not make up Lydia's mind for her," Lady Brace suggested. "Could *your* position ever change? That's what I must know."

Another silence fell between them. As the clock in the drawing room ran no more, there was not even the tick of time passing to break the stillness. A leaf detached itself from the laurel branches on the mantelpiece and dropped softly.

Jack Frazier spoke at last with quiet finality. "I'm afraid, Lady B, the answer is still No."

At that moment, as if on cue, the door into the hallway, which Lady Brace had so carefully closed behind her, opened and in walked Lydia.

"Hello, Jack." Lydia spoke casually, crossing the room with her slow graceful walk to offer her hand. "Rosemary told me you were coming. How are the children?"

Jack had risen looking unsurprised, unruffled. "Fine, just fine!" He seemed, if anything, relieved at her arrival, as though it would spare him any further private exchange with Lady Brace. He and Lydia shook hands with easy informality. "I brought along some new pictures."

Lady Brace lifted the snapshots from her lap and extended them to her daughter in silence. Lydia dropped into one of the low chairs she seemed always to choose, and began to gaze calmly at the photos, one by one.

"Lots of sailing and fishing, I suppose. What fun for them!" Glancing at Lady Brace she remarked in explanation, "Jack's father has his own little lake. The children love visiting there. They both adore to sail and fish. Little Bill is already a very good sailor. I don't believe I told you, Mummy, he's simply wonderful at all games and sports. It never ceases to surprise me. He seems such an introvert. Perhaps he harks back to Daddy's side of the family."

"Oh, no!" Lady Brace exclaimed too quickly. When they both stared in surprise, she gave a little embarrassed laugh. "I just mean," she said, "that somehow I find it—upsetting to hear people saying he 'takes after so and so.' It seems always so fixed, so—forever *ordained*."

When they both continued to look at her as if further explanation was called for, Lady Brace made a gesture towards Jack.

"Jack was just saying that bachelorhood seemed to suit him and that maybe *he* took after his Uncle Bill. And Little Bill is named for that same uncle. And now, you, Lydia, come along and tell me that Little Bill takes after his grandfather, Ralph Parton, who was so very good at games . . . Oh, don't you see what I mean?"

"Yes, I think so," Lydia said, almost indifferently. "But I guess there's not much to do about genes, after all, is there, Mummy?"

At her daughter's quiet words, dropping so controlled and spaced in the strained silence, Lady Brace shrank back in her chair. I am defeated, she thought, for what answer *is* there to the mystery of the genes? What must I do now? Accept the verdict of these two people on their lives and their children's lives; resign myself to what I think of as their "fate"—my daughter's fate, the fate of my grandchildren? Why am I suddenly concerned—so late, as I have already admitted? "Too late" is perhaps more accurate. Isolated, a castaway on an uninhabited island in an uncharted sea; no hope of rescue since no one so much as knew she had embarked on her unscheduled journey. . . . How did I get here? What prompted my foolish bravado in undertaking this course?

She heard their voices, as bodiless as wind, weaving back and forth in the shadowy room, and at last she was able to raise herself from the chair in which she sat.

When she rose they stopped speaking. She could feel their eyes uneasily on her, and she wondered if her face revealed her inner turmoil. Jack got to his feet and she walked towards him, hand extended. She made one last attempt to speak of the subject that had been so burningly in her mind when she first entered the room.

"I'm so glad to have seen you, Jack—though our talk has ended, apparently, only in an impasse—and this saddens me very much." Perhaps Lydia will question him when I leave the room, she thought. Something may still come of my efforts. "Please give the children my dearest love. I hope so much to see them before I return to England."

"Of course!" he said with forced heartiness. "We'll see to that! You aren't leaving for a while, are you?"

"I am leaving," she said, amazing herself with her own words, "as soon as I possibly can. Much sooner than I expected."

"Why, *Mummy!*" Lydia began, her voice rising in surprise.

But Lady Brace did not look at her daughter. She continued to gaze instead into Jack Frazier's pale, shallow eyes as his moist hand once more closed around her thin cold one.

"I appreciate your—the effort you made, Lady B," he said, faltering only a little. "I think I understand about it—and I'm sorry it's the way it is. I really am."

"I know," she said. "I'm sure you are. Goodbye," and releasing her fingers she turned and left the drawing room.

17

Lady Brace managed to get to her bedroom without being seen. She had feared that Rosemary, back from her tour and anxious to know the possible outcome of the talk with Jack, might be loitering somewhere ready to pounce. She lay down prone on the bed, but only for a moment. So great was her inner restiveness she could not remain quiet. I must do something to pass the time! she thought in growing desperation. I cannot simply lie here and feel time passing!

At once the postponed task of opening the attic trunks came into her mind. She welcomed the reminder. It was something specific and concrete to occupy her, and she recalled how, after Rupert's death, she had feverishly torn up and replanted whole sections of the flower garden at Braceledge, doing much of it herself, to the dismay of the gardeners and even, at last, of Humphrey. Seeing her coming in from a morning's work exhausted and disheveled, her hair awry, her face streaked with perspiration and dirt, he had admonished her not to "overdo." The sudden painful awareness had struck her then that Humphrey, pinned to wheel chair and bed, had no possible chance for any physical release from his grief.

Now she thought, as she rose compulsively from the bed, Perhaps this is, in truth, the unvoiced dilemma of the old: how to resolve the interior tensions when there is no longer the possibility of active physical outlets. Or does Nature—said to be kindly, but surely only as a euphemism—take care of this problem by reducing in tempo all the bodily functioning from circulation to glands?

The idea of death as extinction was not in the least alarming, but the possibility of a helpless old age fell on her like a sudden dark shadow as she climbed the hot stairs to the third-floor attic. How did one accept the slow, inevitable slackening of the vital forces?

Where the hall forked towards the nursery wing she hesitated a moment, picturing Venerable Sir. Was he, perhaps, behind the closed door at the end of the corridor, sitting cross-legged in some ritual of meditation or dreaming calm? She dismissed a fleeting temptation to knock at his door.

T W O

In the large, crowded attic she found all the old trunks conveniently lined up, side by side, as Rosemary had told her they would be. Someone—Rosemary, or perhaps Todd—had already plugged two large electric fans into the baseboard so that she might have a little ventilation while performing her onerous task. How considerate they are! she thought, half-ashamed of her wish to get away from Fox Meadows as soon as possible.

With a faint sinking feeling—for she had no idea what disturbing relics of the past might be exposed—she took from her pocket a bulging miscellany of attached keys, brought all the way from Braceledge, where for years they had been kept in a safety box marked *Trunk Keys, Fox Meadows*.

Choosing one at random she approached the nearest trunk. To her amazement the key fitted, and she lifted with ease the lid to an old-fashioned steamer trunk with two compartments; the top one given over to papers and notebooks, the bottom containing— she knew immediately as a strong smell of camphor assailed her nostrils—clothes stored away some autumn day many years ago on the household's return from the Adirondacks.

She placed the top drawer back over the camphored clothes thinking she must help Rosemary make up some boxes for Korea, or wherever Americans were now sending boxes. She began to stir through the papers and notebooks. Surprisingly, they all seemed to belong to Stephen, who prided himself on never keeping anything. Perhaps, she thought, these books and papers went back to the long-ago summer when he had been tutored. Doubtless, in September, old Annie had collected these papers from his room, along with his mountain clothes, and tidily preserved them.

Lady Brace opened the composition book under her hand. Her eye fell on the words, *The Natural Death of a Snake*, the word "natural" heavily underlined, three times, with a red crayon.

She read: *We have all seen snakes stoned to death or beheaded, but how do snakes die when they grow old? This is a question not many people ever ask themselves, but it is a good question. Do snakes shed their skins once more, one last time, but this time underneath it there isn't another skin, only an exposed unprotected squirming length of red pulp? The snake . . .*

Here the writing broke off. The next sheet had been roughly torn from the book—and the other pages were empty.

Lady Brace stood holding the paper. How like Stephen, she thought, to choose a provocative, faintly repellent theme; a theme broken off and left to tantalize and mystify. The scene with the drowned bat came back to the fringes of her mind.

Now she did not want to be alone. Much as she wished to continue the self-imposed task of finding what remained in the old trunks, she could not do so. A sense of loneliness that was not really solitude swept over her—a loneliness enmeshed in invisible filaments of relationship with the dead as well as the living. She felt impelled to seek out Stephen's company. Her fatigued mind even went so far as to offer in extenuation the thought that the finding of this notebook, with its cryptic message about the shedding of a snake's skin, was a "sign," one that she could not safely ignore. Closing the lid of the trunk, detaching the electric fans from their sockets, she went back downstairs.

Again to her relief she encountered no one in the hallway or on the stairway. She paused for a moment listening for voices in the drawing room. She could not hear them but through the screen door at the front of the house she could see Jack Frazier's car still standing under the chestnut tree. So he had not left yet! She went quickly through the sunroom onto the terrace, where, at this hour of the day, her brother usually reclined in what she believed to be some sort of fixed and formal reverie.

She had, in her increasing agitation, passed beyond her normal timidity at arousing Stephen's irritation over intrusions. She made, indeed, no apology whatsoever as she approached him, notebook in hand.

"I've started to go through the attic trunks," she began. "The first thing I found was an old composition book of yours." Without awaiting any gesture of invitation or interest she sat down near him and read aloud the paragraph about snakes. "How do snakes die?" she asked when she had finished.

Stephen did not so much as open his eyes. He answered in a bored and weary voice. "I suppose they just stop when the time comes; like the rest of us—if we're lucky."

He wants me to go away, she thought; but so complete was her feeling of disorientation, so much was she now at the mercy of her troubled mind that she could not act on the old automatic responses to her brother's unspoken wishes. Without meaning to, she let out her breath in a long tremulous sigh.

189

The effect on Stephen was immediate. He opened his cold blue eyes and glanced at her. "What is it?"

"What is what?"

"You just sighed a very gusty sigh—and now I look at you and your face is tied in knots."

"Yes," she said. "I'm sure it is." She had a feeling of immediate relief. Perhaps it would be possible to rid herself of some of her formless oppression by laying it on him. "I've just seen Jack Frazier and—he won't consider returning to Lydia."

Stephen looked tiredly scornful. "Why should he, or Lydia either, consider such an idea?"

"For the children's sake," she said stubbornly.

He made a short sound of scorn. "You surprise me, Lady B. They don't love each other and never did! What's come over you suddenly, Caro? It's not like you in the least. You know it's not your problem and certainly none of your business."

She flared up. "How can you say such a thing?"

"I can say it because it's true."

His unfeeling tone nettled her further. She exclaimed, quivering, "That's very easy for you to say! You know nothing about the feelings of a mother, a parent—a grandparent. You've never had any kind of close, personal relationship—or responsibility." She heard her voice rising, almost hysterical. "You've managed to evade all the responsibilities and burdens of life very effectively, I'd say—so of course you can act superior about the problems and worries of others."

He remained maddeningly unruffled by her attack. "Your remarks would be more effective if you didn't sound so envious of my corrupt and selfish state," he drawled, derisive.

"It's very simple to assume this supercilious tone," she went on. "You've always remained outside the—*battle*, outside all the conventional, boring, difficult, hateful, painful, human bonds! But just don't treat me to your insufferable superiority today—because I simply can't stand it."

Her voice broke. She hated herself for it and, clenching her hands, she looked away across the garden with blurred vision. Why am I acting this way? It is quite irrational. If I tried to explain to him about the effect on me of those strange children, would he understand, or would he only call me sentimental, tell me I was tired, needed more rest; that I was not used to the frenzied pace of American life? He would end by accusing me of being too long "protected," secluded and "cut off." She could not bring herself to embark on any explanation of her outburst. She found it difficult enough to hold back her tears.

When Stephen spoke again his voice was kind. "Every life has its own special strains, Caro. You know that. My life may look, to most people, relatively uncomplicated and free. Actually I've had plenty of—trouble and suffering." His tone hardened. "And you for one should know that."

"Well, I don't!" she cried in answer. "I don't understand you, I never have, and I never will—not for one moment!"

He replied in a level voice, "That's not true. You've just pretended never to understand—because it was always—more comfortable, and a lot easier, not to."

She wanted to deny this charge, but somehow she lacked the spirit to put up a further defense. She could only wish in exhaustion that she had not come down from the attic. What had prompted her to stir him up? It was almost as if some inner perversity that she did not understand was forcing her into more and more entanglements.

In the distance, to her relief, she heard the children and the dogs. She prayed that they would burst around the corner of the house and break up this painful tête-à-tête before it went any further. But the noise of the children and the dogs faded again. She glanced at Stephen. His eyes were closed once more. There was a curious expression on his face. She had for a moment the fantastic thought that he had somehow *willed* the children not to appear.

He opened his eyes as though aware of her fixed gaze. She looked quickly away.

The question he asked next took her by surprise. "Did I ever tell you how John van der Wadel died?"

She faltered, "No—I didn't even know that he was dead—I've been meaning to ask you about him."

"He died," Stephen said in a still, very quiet voice, "from the bite of a poisonous serpent."

Lady Brace felt the weight of the notebook in her lap. The bite of a poisonous serpent! Then perhaps she truly had had a "sign"; a mysterious hint, in advance, of an occurrence not yet in view? The familiar feeling of apprehension began to form in her mind. Now I am going to hear more than I bargained for. I am going to be punished for my temerity in breaking in on his afternoon privacy.

Stephen was beginning to speak, precise, steady.

"We—John and I—had gone into the jungle alone—following a tip on some buried ruins. We didn't want anyone to know about our interest in these particular ruins until we'd had a look ourselves. We thought it might be a real archaeological find. We didn't even take a bearer." He paused a moment. "It was an insane idea. John was bitten the first day. On the leg. He couldn't walk. I'd had to cut his leg rather a lot to release the poison."

At this point Stephen's voice quickened, grew a little tense. "First I tried to carry him. It was too much for me. Then I tried to drag him out as far as our jeep. Finally, I had to leave him and run for help—and that was what I did, literally—for miles. When I got back he was already dead." He broke off again.

"Oh, darling!" Caroline breathed. She hoped the narrative would end here. How much can I take in a single day? But in a moment Stephen, without moving, continued, his voice dry now and more remote.

"It was the beginning of my illness. I'd overexerted myself, strained my heart, sustained a terrible shock. I very nearly died too! That's when I had my—stroke. For a while I couldn't use either leg, and only my left arm. Our old Tamil gardener—you probably remember him—told me that we—John and I—had stirred up an ancient curse that lay on those particular ruins. All the servants believed it too. Some of them were terrified; left me. I got to half-believing it myself. I even began to wonder if by working on the problem of evil I hadn't roused some sleeping force . . . I'm not sure yet that wasn't the truth."

He paused here but she could think of nothing to say. She lay with her lids down over her eyes, waiting, supine, for the rest of it.

After a brief pause he went on, now in a ruminative, equable manner. "I believe for a while I *was* really insane; right over the line, not just hovering on it, as I'd been most of my life." He gave a little half laugh. "Anyway, I was finally in such bad shape they took me down to Colombo to the hospital. To die, I guess . . . And it was there I came to know Venerable Sir. My native doctor brought him to see me. He saved my reason; even finally got me back onto my feet . . . When I asked him what I could do in return he said I could assist him to get to America, as he'd heard they badly needed help there!"

He laughed full out at this remark before he added, turning his head in her direction, speaking with the mocking derision so familiar a part of his ordinary speech, "And there you have a piece of my simple, uncomplicated life story, Lady B."

Her anger quite gone, she was filled only with pity and sadness; was able to ask, holding down her agitation, "Why did you never tell me any of this? Why did you never write me about it?" She did not ask the third question that hovered on her lips: "Why did you choose just this particular time to tell me, at last?"

He replied, quite matter-of-fact, "Why did you never ask?"

"You mean about John?"

"Yes."

There was only one honest answer, one she did not wish to make: "Because I did not want to hear anything about him."

When she made no reply Stephen finally said, "Part of my not writing was because somehow I felt you'd—blame yourself for my illness. And I didn't want you carrying any extra load—not with Humphrey ill, and you alone in that gloomy Somerset house."

She forced herself to inquire, "Why should I have blamed myself?" She made herself look at him then and caught the beginning of one of his bitter, mocking glances, saw him check it as he pulled his sun hat over his eyes.

For a moment he said nothing, then with unexpected moderation, "Because you were all tied up with me and my struggle. Always had been, from the beginning. I know that, Caro—always have known it." His voice still modulated, he added, "And you know it, too. You were just brought up to *pretend* not to understand anything difficult or—unpalatable."

Her heart was fluttering its signal of imminent danger, but she made herself inquire with false equanimity, "What is it I've always understood and pretended not to?"

Let him hurt me, she thought, if he must! Perhaps in his helplessness he needs the release of this stab; longs for it as I longed to tear up the old rose bushes at Braceledge in the pain of Rupert's loss.

"What a fraud you are!" He gave a little temperate laugh that did not sound in the least like him. "And always have been, Lady B."

"A fraud?" she whispered. Then, after a pause, "Yes," she admitted. "You're right, Stephen. I am a fraud—and always have been." She felt momentarily gratified by this surprising self-accusation.

They both stared out across the lawn in silence. Suddenly, before them a flock of dancing birds appeared on the pale sky. A troupe of gifted aerial entertainers, they began to perform an elaborate piece of spontaneous choreography. Or was it spontaneous?—for the routines were very defined. Surely the performers must have already rehearsed! Following a few preliminary circling movements they shot up like rockets for a fixed distance before descending in feathered dives, skimming, floating, pirouetting. Dipping on one wing-tip before rising again, they spread their feathered fans and floated saucily, then dreamily, alone or in pairs. Was this performance for their own pleasure or for the approbation of an invisible audience? The measures of the airy dance went on for some moments until, quickening to a pitch of jubilant intoxication, the ensemble at last appeared to overreach itself. It broke up, fell apart, degenerated into a series of careless solos, performed loosely, almost indifferently on the calm sky. They became, Lady Brace thought to herself, like so many bored and restless children playing hop-scotch.

When in a single swift rush the birds disappeared into the weedy jungle beyond the walled garden, Stephen again began to talk.

"All during my childhood and adolescence, Lady B, you seemed like another part of me. I know you must remember how close we were then. I've often thought it was like being caught in the— same enchantment. I loved you, as I told you the other day, more than anyone. The truth is"—his voice grew drier, drawled again a little—"if we had lived as royalty in ancient Egypt I could have had you in the way I wanted you—even if you were my sister."

At last it was out! There was less of shock than of relief—though I must keep from trembling *too* visibly, Lady Brace thought, forcing herself to an exact botanical observation of a small unfamiliar weed, with a yellow blossom, growing in a crack near her foot. Humphrey could surely have named it; one of the countless varieties of wort, no doubt.

Stephen seemed now to be speaking from a distance. Or was it only the sudden ringing in her ears that made him sound remote? She had to strain to hear his words, though he was speaking clearly and distinctly. "I can never remember being free of a feeling of subtle competition. With you for father's attention and love; with father for your attention and love. I know now, of course, how jealous I was of the hold you had on father. How inferior I always felt! I wasn't the kind of son he wanted, and I wasn't a beautiful little girl, either. I often wished I'd been born a girl, I can tell you. Actually, it would have made it much easier for—my kind of person."

His brief pause seemed deliberate, as if he wished her to fill in an unspoken gap.

"When I went out to Ceylon I was a hopeless mixture of warring feelings, all confusion and guilt and anger and repressed sex. Since I felt deeply, basically guilty—even evil, sinful—due to all my repressed emotions—I naturally set out to prove that Evil dominated the universe. Hence my Compendium of Evil. You remember?"

She looked up to catch a faint grin crossing his face, making it at once young and appealing.

"Of course I remember," she murmured.

Stephen went on, quite laconic now. "That's the psychological abc of it. Also, since I was—split myself, I naturally gravitated towards other split people. It was quite proper to my—" he hesitated "—*pattern* at this time to establish a relationship with a young man who was carrying a really heavy psychological load; much heavier than mine; in his own cells and blood, a mixture of East and West. What a fate!"

He stopped once more and this time for so long Lady Brace concluded he was through. She looked up and he met her questioning glance full on. With bland directness he remarked,

"You never liked John van der Wadel, Lady B. You acted suspicious of him from the start. Probably you guessed the nature of our bond and you disapproved."

She did not feel that he expected her either to deny this or agree, but, amazed, she heard herself say, as she looked off across the lawn to the walled garden, "Perhaps I was simply jealous—and didn't know it, or wouldn't admit it."

Now an equation has been balanced, she thought: my accusation long ago on the night of the bat, with this admission on my part more than forty years later.

Stephen made no reply and she did not glance again in his direction. The birds sailed into sight again, sailed out.

In a sudden access of self-reproach she continued, "I failed you, Stephen. You're right. So right! I always refused to *see*; to understand—anything. I always have—always did—with Ralph too . . ."

She broke off, carried away by unaccustomed thoughts of her long-dead husband. For the first time she saw his unpredictable temperament, his periodic dark rages as evidence of a hidden struggle. Some painful interior disturbance must surely have lain behind or beneath his wild lashings out at life, objects, people. But had she ever tried to discover the source of his unpredictable behavior? No, she had only run, hidden, waited, cowering, for the seizures to pass, or endured them in mute bewilderment, and, finally, in cold hatred. And yet all the time I *used* him, she thought. The discovery was, for a moment, stupefying. Yes, I, she insisted grimly, used him to satisfy my sexual needs, my never-admitted appetite for the sharp fierce pleasures of the flesh. Stephen is right; I am a fraud and always have been.

She heard herself saying aloud, contrite, regretful, "And where I failed you, Stephen—when I wouldn't understand—or ever give you a chance to say anything straight out"—for she felt, in this moment of humility, responsible for her brother's lifelong habits of devious indirection, his sideswipes, dark mutterings, unexpected darts—"John van der Wadel, I suppose, *saved* you?"

She ended on a note of question, a bit flustered by the verb she had used. She had almost said "John van der Wadel, I suppose, redeemed you."

Stephen replied at once, accepting the full implications of her question, not scoffing, "Yes, John began my liberation." With unshaken gravity he added, "He started me on what Venerable Sir would, I suppose, call the 'path'—though where the path really begins is pretty hard to say. Anyway, it was John, certainly, who first gave me the courage to live out what was—bottled up inside me."

He paused, apparently to allow her time to interpret this remark as she chose before continuing, "Then, by sharing my neurotic research on universal Evil"—and here the note of half-derisive humor crept again for a moment into his voice—"John dignified it, gave it a meaning that went beyond merely the sick and personal."

Lady Brace noticed how little of the lawn remained in sunlight. The smell of evening rose in melancholy sweetness from the grass.

"There isn't much more," Stephen said. Then in abrupt but calm contradiction, "What I mean is, of course, there's a great deal more, but it can be reduced to a few simple sentences. I've been practicing reducing my entire life to a few simple sentences ever since I got back here to Fox Meadows, saw you again—and all the rest of it. This return has helped me, just as Venerable Sir assured me it would."

Out of another extended silence there seemed only one further, related question she could ask. She put it to him with a hint of her familiar reticence. "And—what are your conclusions?"

The question appeared to amuse him. "Conclusions?" he echoed, smiling, looking ready to tease her for her earnestness.

But she would not retreat. "Yes," she insisted, "your conclusions. For that's what you are trying to arrive at, isn't it, as you sit here every afternoon alone?"

He gave her the smile she thought of as new, unlike the old Stephen—warm, open. "How well you know me!"

You are wrong, she thought. Never more so, for, in a way, you grow more mysterious to me every moment. The closed doors you have opened all look out into even more strange and incomprehensible vistas of your personality, and of mine too, and of all human relationships. . . .

Stephen had begun to answer her question about his possible

conclusions, speaking in a manner that reminded her of Venerable Sir: moderate, slow, careful, as if anxious to make no misstatement, to lead no listener astray.

"Everything has its place, fits into the pattern, or *a* pattern. At least so I now believe. From father to you to John van der Wadel to Venerable Sir. From that old composition book of mine in your lap"—and he nodded at it—"to stone serpents in the jungle and to John's death from snake bite. And, finally, from my researches in Evil to Venerable Sir's research in—Goodness."

He paused, appeared for a moment to ruminate, then continued. "I can't make all the links and connections yet, but I do, from time to time, get a distinct sense of their presence. For instance, if I hadn't known so much about Evil—or let's call it, non-Good —as I did when Venerable Sir first came to see me in the hospital in Colombo, I wouldn't have been able to get down with him quite so soon to the—fundamentals."

Here he broke off and gave his little hooting laugh, but not harshly this time. "So I suppose I could even say that Evil led me to Good. Perhaps a rather dangerous doctrine for public consumption," he ended.

Before she could question further—and a tumult of ideas, emotions, doubts, fears, suddenly flooded her mind—here was Lydia once again, standing at the screen door, chic and charming in her pale blue linen.

There is simply no chance at Fox Meadows for any continuity, any concentration, Lady Brace thought, unreasonably irritated by Lydia's sudden appearance. I should go quite out of my mind in this goldfish life in less than a year! Yet the face she turned to her child in no way revealed her inner agitation.

"Jack has just gone," Lydia said, with finality. "Mummy, may I speak to you a moment—inside?"

At once Lydia came out to the terrace steps. "No, don't bother getting up," she added quickly. "I don't know why I said that. I don't mind in the least your hearing, Uncle Stephen. It's just that —Mummy, Frederick would very much like to have a talk with you at your convenience, as soon as possible. Tomorrow, if you can. Could you possibly give him half an hour or so?"

"Yes, of course." Following the promptings of her new courage, she inquired, "Has something upsetting happened, Lydia?"

Lydia plainly put up her guard. "What do you mean, Mummy?"

"I don't quite know what I do mean," Lady Brace admitted, falling back a pace. "It's just that I got the feeling, when you came out, that—something might have gone wrong."

Lydia dropped into a chair. She opened a metal box and took out a rather crumpled cigarette. Regarding it with extreme distaste, she nonetheless lit it before remarking, "You're very intuitive, Lady B." She blew out the match and laid it with meticulous care in an ashtray. When in a moment she began soberly to speak she somehow gave the effect not so much of answering her mother's question as addressing her uncle.

"You remember I told you how they were giving Frederick's wife some special new treatment, some new wonder drug? Well, no one thought there was the slightest hope of her improving, but suddenly, very suddenly, not slowly at all, almost like a miracle, she has improved—enormously! The reaction has been so decided, and she's sustained it now so long that only yesterday the doctors told Frederick *definitely* she is not going to die at all. At least not for years. She has—their phrase for it—a new lease on life."

Lydia had recited it all in one key, quite composed, even tranquil.

"Oh, *no!*" Lady Brace breathed. She did not know whether to feel relief or an increased anxiety, and she cast a furtive glance at Stephen seeking a clue. She got the shocking impression that he was inwardly laughing—silently, terribly.

Without surprise she heard Lydia inquire, "It amuses you, Uncle Stephen?"

"Amuses me?"

"Yes, I thought you were laughing to yourself."

"If I was it was *not* in amusement," he retorted. "What a lesson!" His tone bordered on contempt. "Unbearably to the point!"

Lydia persisted, still evincing not the slightest discomposure, "I don't see quite what you are saying, Uncle Stephen. What do you mean?"

Stephen was silent for a moment. Then, "You really want to know?" he inquired, shooting his niece a speculative glance.

"Careful, Lydia!" Lady Brace warned in silence. "From your uncle this question is a danger signal."

But Lydia showed no dismay, no intention of withdrawal. "I do," she said.

Stephen took a long breath, pulled himself up a little on the chaise longue, began, in his well-you-asked-for-it voice, "It's the myth again—another modern myth. Here's a certain rich man, very rich and full of power, who has discovered certain secrets of longevity, and he wants, above everything on earth, to be rid of his old worn-out wife in order to marry a young and beautiful woman. But he's so rich and so full of feelings of guilt that he naturally has to hire the best medical talent in the world to work on his wife's supposedly *hopeless* case. So, of course, with the help of all that guilt-prompted money, the doctors come up with the miraculous cure that will keep him from getting his wish."

He paused, not looking at either of them. A sardonic grin on his face, he added, "No, on second thought, maybe it's not quite a big enough theme for a myth. Too commonplace, really. Let's just call it a modern type of farce-tragedy. Yes, it's a subject for a certain kind of laughter, for the point is, a *poor* man might have won out."

And now he did laugh out loud, but there was no joy in it. The laugh sounded, indeed, to his sister, like the distant yelp of an animal in distress.

Lydia had not so much as batted an eye during her uncle's remarks. "You don't mince words, Uncle Stephen, do you?" she observed when he had finished. Her intonation seemed almost to convey admiration. Then in her tranquil, poised way she stood up and faced her mother. "And so you will see Frederick tomorrow, Mummy? What time?"

"Any time in the afternoon." Lady Brace spoke with composure, but her sinking heart seemed to tell her in advance the substance of the dreaded interview.

"Then shall we say four? Frederick will come here—unless you'd like to drive down to Southampton for the day instead?"

"No, here—if you don't mind."

"Whatever you wish." Lydia, with no further words, turned a straight back to them and walked into the house.

Lady Brace could find nothing to say, and Stephen, his eyes closed, seemed also disposed to silence. She heard again the voices of the children and the dogs. This time she welcomed the intrusion as they came tearing around the side of the house in a rush of movement and sound.

"Gran, Gran," Jennifer cried at sight of her grandmother. "Look at the trick I've taught Bumpy! Watch him beg."

Without opening his eyes, with a quizzical smile on his lips, Stephen said, "You have won Jennifer from me. How did you do it?"

She had only time to reply, before Todd and Rosemary appeared on the scene, "She saw me crying in the garden."

18

Lady Brace sat waiting in the Trophy Room when Frederick Hollis drove up to the front door of Fox Meadows. This time he came alone, driving a gleaming low-slung car of a make not familiar to her. Once again she spied on him through the curtains, as on the first day when the green Rolls-Royce had deposited on the steps under the chestnut tree the smart chauffeur, then her chic daughter, and lastly Frederick Hollis himself with his box of fabulous grapes.

As soon as he stopped the car Frederick removed an impressive pair of gold-banded ovoid sunglasses of a design, it occurred to her, not unlike the front of the car he was driving. He adjusted the small rear-view mirror above the wheel in order to regard his reflection. She saw him bare his teeth and run his tongue across them, then take a small brush from a side compartment and brush his close-cropped hair; artfully tinted, she was now quite sure. When he got out she observed he was wearing one of the sports shirts Stephen had mentioned, though rather more on the conservative side than Stephen's description: black and yellow checks. No hula maidens; no hibiscus? She registered an absurd fleeting disappointment. She watched him, before he slammed the door, slip on a light linen jacket that lay over the back of the seat. Further concession to the "older generation"? she asked herself. When finally he stepped jauntily onto the porch, she caught a glimpse of his feet encased in black canvas mandarin slippers with thick white rope-soles.

She opened the front door to his ring, as she had the first day. He appeared a little startled to see her once again answering bells at Fox Meadows, but he made no comment. They shook hands and exchanged a conventional greeting.

"I'm going to take you in here, if you don't mind," Lady Brace said, turning back towards the Trophy Room, "where we'll be safe from interruptions."

When he set his noiseless mandarin feet inside the Trophy Room door, Frederick Hollis glanced at once towards the lighted vitrines with their glamorous collections of gold and silver trophies. "Remarkable!" he exclaimed. Lady Brace caught herself wondering if she had unconsciously chosen to receive her complacent visitor here in the hope of awing him with reminders of past Langdon glories.

"It must be a big undertaking—disposing of all this," he said, casting an appraising glance around the crowded interior, nodding, as if in personal recognition, at the photographs of eminent jockeys, politicians, actresses, social figures, that graced the tables and part of the wall space. "What will you do with it all?" His voice reflected a fleeting concern. Had the thought, Lady Brace wondered, suddenly presented itself even to Frederick Hollis that all things must, without exception, come to an end?

"I am not quite sure," she replied evenly. "I have washed my hands of it. Rosemary and Lydia will have to settle it between them."

"And does your brother want none of it?"

She answered, "My brother has stated that he is through with all possessions."

It had not been her intention to disconcert her visitor, but she sensed that this remark had, for a moment, almost done so. He moved at once to safer ground. With a glance that fell just short of patronage, he regarded the row of mounted animal heads, part of the motley loot of the Trophy Room. "Some fine specimens here," he commented. Did his keen eye detect moth damage? "I've been wanting to get back to Africa myself—before all those native uprisings make it impossible."

Lady Brace led the way down the long room to the far end, near the cases of *churinga*, at which she had been looking with mixed memories on the day of his first call. When she saw his eyes rest with apparent curiosity on the bizarre contents of the glass-fronted shelves she explained, "One of my grandfather's special collections. They're stones that primitive races put over their graves to hold down the dead."

She regretted this explanation the moment she had spoken, for the thought of Belle Hollis's long-awaited death and astonishing last-hour reprieve crossed her mind in an uneasy flash.

"Ah, yes," he replied, unruffled, and he added in a tone of amusement, "I've heard about another of your grandfather's collections—those animal headstones. Matter of fact, I took a look at that graveyard plot the other day with Lydia. Fantastic! But some real gems of sculpture there, too. Several by Ferragil, you know. Greatest animal sculptor of his period!"

She thought, how well apprised he is on all the unique objects at Fox Meadows: Para and Dox, the little walled garden with the dreaming Chinese goddess, the animal gravestones, even my younger daughter.

Lady Brace seated herself at one side of the empty grate with its enormous golden peacocks and andirons, the same design of proud birds that had once guarded the gates of the garden. Frederick remained standing near the glass cases. He was reading for the second time and, she concluded, from sheer disbelief, a card under a small collection of oddly shaped green stones: *Jade from the body apertures of Chinese corpses. (Chou Dynasty) Inserted after death to prevent entrance of wandering vampire spirits into ancestor.*

He perhaps felt her glance resting on him, for he turned away, seated himself and began to dab at his forehead with a large extravagantly monogrammed linen handkerchief.

"Would you like to turn on a fan?" Lady Brace gestured towards the large electric one on the table behind him.

"Oh, no, thank you," he said, emphatic. "Electric fans are a menace. Very bad for one's sinuses, you know."

"I'm sorry this house has no air-conditioning," Lady Brace continued, "but do feel quite free to remove your coat."

If he recognized this as a thrust, he showed no signs of being disconcerted. "Thank you, I'm quite comfortable."

He leaned back and picked up from a table a jeweled dagger that served as a paper knife. "Persian," he remarked replacing it. He formed a triangle with the fingers of his long, spotted hands and, after swinging this singular formation up and down in front of him three times, lifted it towards his face and tapped with his two index fingers—again three times—on the faint cleft in the center of his chin. He then pulled the two hands apart and dropped them into his lap as though dismissing them from his service. Lady Brace watched him in absorbed fascination. The movements possessed the exactness of a fixed ritual and she longed for an interpretation of their possible significance.

"It's good of you to give me this time," he began in a smooth casual voice. "I know how busy you must be with all that's going on here now."

Lady Brace murmured, noncommittal.

"You may perhaps have some notion of what I wish to speak to you about?" He glanced over at her inquiringly.

"Not the faintest, I'm afraid."

Her reply appeared to make him pause.

"I thought perhaps Lydia and you had talked together."

"Yes, of course."

"Then you do know that I had hoped—we had both hoped— that fate was going to be kind to us, was going to make possible our—" he hesitated and came up with a word so archaic Lady Brace was almost tempted to smile "—our union," he said unctuously.

"Now I know," he continued, unhurried, staring straight at her with no hint of embarrassment, "that you may well be thinking about the"—he reached into the air and lifted from it, as if helping himself to something from an invisible tray, the two words "bad taste"—"I mean the bad taste of my speaking this way, when my wife is lying seriously ill in a hospital. I understand this attitude very well," he assured her, nodding in encouragement, as if to relieve her of any possible, and naïve, self-distrust. "It is quite a natural one."

He is closing every avenue of counter-attack, Lady Brace warned herself, sensing again the cool calculation, the complacent single-pointedness of this man with whom her daughter's future was so intimately involved. I, too, she thought, must remain relaxed and aware, or I shall find myself caught in a place from which there is no possibility of a graceful exit, if, indeed, any exit at all.

With his next words she realized that he had decided on an abrupt alteration of manner. Perhaps some new fixity in her attitude had warned him. He was now going to treat her with the air of one worldly sophisticate to another, cosily philosophical.

"But as you well know"—and his tidy plucked eyebrows twitched in humorous resignation—"facts are very different from feelings, all too often in life." He invited her to share an equivocal smile. His invitation ignored, he next essayed a dash of manly straightforwardness, "I think it only fair for all our sakes— Belle's as well as mine, Lydia's above all, even yours, as Lydia's mother—to tell you quite frankly that Belle and I have been husband and wife *in name only* for many, many years."

Lady Brace, outraged, sat upright, very still, her eyes cast down, her hands folded in her lap. I will not give him one spark of help, she thought grimly. Not that he appears in the least to need it!

Frederick looked straight ahead, suave, even smug. "I have spent what might be called a small fortune on trying to cure my wife." He cleared his throat modestly. "And, apparently I have— succeeded. Her condition has, within just this last week, undergone such marked improvement that the doctors say she is going to recover. As a matter of fact, she can return to her home within a few days. She will still be a semi-invalid, of course, confined largely to her bed, but no worse off—indeed, some better—than she was fifteen years ago when the first signs of her—physical disability appeared."

He got up then and walked once more to the case of *churinga*, stared in at them again, appeared even to be rereading some of the small explanatory cards. Imagine my thinking the association of gravestones might be awkward for him, Lady Brace thought, watching him begin to teeter up and down in the black canvas slippers, up and down, rhythmically, softly, his back still turned to her.

"What am I to do?" he murmured.

It was quite plain the question was not being put to her, and again she had the vision of the invisible tray moving towards him through space. Soon he will lift from it the ready phrase. She believed she heard him murmur again, "What am I to do?"

His back still turned, his eyes on the primitive gravestones, he went on speaking softly in the shadowy crowded room.

"I could, of course, end the long travesty of my marriage by divorcing Belle—that is, if she would consent to it. I doubt her personally being strong enough to—embark on getting a divorce herself. But just now there's been so much publicity about her cure—these columnists, you know, always looking for copy about prominent people—just at this particular time, well, I can see quite clearly how it might look to outsiders. I'm thinking particularly of Lydia in this, believe me, though I do see also, perfectly plainly, how bad it might be for—Belle's state of mind. Not that it would kill her." Surely that happy solution has crossed his mind! thought Lady Brace. "But it would in all probability lead to—er—melancholia, depression, and so on, to which she has long been unfortunately subject."

He turned from the case and sat down again, still without looking at her. Again he repeated the ritual of the tent-shaped fingers, up and down three times, the three mysterious taps on the cleft of the chin, and the quick, almost contemptuous, toss into the discard.

"I'll get to the point of this call," he said with sudden cold decisiveness. This is the tone, thought Lady Brace, which he doubtless employs after looking at samples of bottled seaweed, lists of common stocks, the legs of a horse, or the label on a wine bottle: "I'll take it," or "Not interested."

"I want your help. I need it." There was, however, not the

slightest plea in his voice. He was simply stating a fact. "Lydia, too, wants it. And needs it," he added, still without any special emphasis, merely marshaling further obvious and incontrovertible facts in the situation. "It has been a great strain for her—and for all of us. Very awkward. Yes, indeed. Lydia very much needs to get away, quite far out of it for a while. This has been apparent to me for some time."

He let this last statement sink in for a few moments before continuing evenly, "Lydia, as you know, is very much interested in the Far East. She spoke of it the other day, you may remember. Yes, she seems to have been bitten with the same bug that bit your father, and your brother. In a different way from Stephen, of course," he added in a semi-jocose tone, quick to exonerate Lydia of any fantastic religious interests or social deviations. "As a matter of fact I, too, have been interested—for a long time—in the Mysterious East, as they call it. Lots of strange things out there, you know." He paused, weighing this pronouncement. "Frankly, it would give me the greatest pleasure to indulge Lydia's wish to see that part of the world. Not just a hurried tourist trip, you know, but, well, to stay as long as she liked, and—in absolute comfort. Also, quite honestly, I'd not want to lose the pleasure of showing some of it to Lydia myself—that is, seeing her enjoy it. So naturally, I would plan to be around."

Lady Brace had not shifted her position since she first sat down. There followed a silence that contained, for the first time, more than a hint of awkwardness.

It was Frederick Hollis who broke the silence with an unexpected note of candor. "I've not had many pleasures in my life," he said. "Though you may not find this easy to believe—it is all too true! I've had quite a few indulgences, but not many pleasures. Lydia can, for some reason, always give me pleasure."

It was the one bearable thing he had uttered so far. Lady Brace found herself at last able to speak.

"Am I to understand that you are asking my permission to send —or to take—my daughter to the Far East?" Without waiting for his answer, she added, "Lydia is a grown woman, Frederick. She has been making all her own decisions for many years now. I might conceivably use my influence to get her to follow a course that I thought—fitting—but I would certainly have no assurance I could affect a final decision of hers in any way."

Frederick Hollis shook his head, a firm denial. "No, my dear Caroline, that's not it at all. Not at all. Lydia has already made up her mind. She *intends* to go." He gave her a level penetrating glance. "Lydia, I may say, dwells on the possible *consequences* of such a move far less fearfully than I. Lydia has a real streak of the devil-may-care in her, you know." And then, as though anxious to use a more current phraseology, "She simply couldn't care less!" he concluded, and he gave a short, furtive laugh.

Oh, the dreadful old goat! Lady Brace thought. He is not vulpine, he is cacklingly senile. She looked at him as if he were someone she did not quite remember, or wish to recognize, but he seemed unaware of the quality of her survey.

Decisive again, "I'll get to the point," he said. "I want *you* to accompany Lydia." He spoke with a flat finality that assumed her agreement as a foregone conclusion; they had only to arrange details. He must, however, have sensed her stiffening, for he leaned towards her from his chair and, for the first time, spoke with open persuasiveness.

"I ask it for Lydia's sake, for her protection—and also for the sake of our eventual marriage. I want all of it to be quite aboveboard, you know. Safe from dirty talk, that is." He shifted, avoiding her veiled glance, added, still glib, "Oh, well, of course, that's probably not entirely possible. There's bound to be some gossip, I suppose. Unavoidable. But with you accompanying Lydia, standing by, so to speak . . ."

He hurried a little now, as though anxious to get it all out before she had a chance to indicate any possible recoil from his suggestion.

"I'd thought of Bangkok, as a base. There's that new luxury hotel out there. We could get some really decent living quarters, you know; not have to sacrifice our comfort in any way. We could settle in without much fuss, use Bangkok as a center and fly anywhere we liked. I would arrange all that, of course. As a matter of fact, it's already in the works. I'm laying on a private plane for Lydia's use, and so on. Lydia's set on seeing Cambodia, Java, getting to remote places like Angkor Wat, Borobudur. That kind of uncanny place seems to strike her fancy, for some reason. I'd come out and join her—join you both—once you got settled in. You get the picture?" He stopped at last.

Lady Brace plainly heard the ice in her voice as she replied, "Very clearly."

Frederick Hollis heard it too. "Don't answer me at once," he said, cleverly depriving her of the chance of an immediate rebuff. "I beg you not to! Please talk to Lydia first. I'm sure you will come to see how important it is to—" he hesitated "—to *protect* her," he finished deftly.

Lady Brace managed, with great effort, to retain her cold composure as she inquired, "Am I to understand that you've just told me Lydia intends to go to the East anyway—*will* go—and that, no matter what the possible consequences, you intend to accompany her, or join her out there?"

He was equally composed and cool. "I shall certainly join her at some point," he replied. "Yes! Definitely."

They were both on their feet now, for Lady Brace had risen. As they stood facing one another, she could feel her cheeks burning. She had, along with her anger, a novel sensation of being unprotected, wretchedly alone, stripped of all familiar support. How had she ever come to such a pass, where she, Lady Brace, born Caroline Langdon, could be approached in this way by Frederick Hollis? How, for that matter, could a man born into Frederick Hollis's world change as much as these past moments of conversation clearly indicated? So complete was his assurance, she could imagine no method, no words or course, to shake him. Even if she abandoned all pretense of good manners, ordered him out of the house, out of her daughter's life, it still would not affect him in the least. She thought of Stephen's early words about him: "pure power-elite type." He stood before her unabashed, sure of himself; the man who has never had the experience of being thwarted, one able always to make his own rules, from childhood on never required to deny a selfish personal wish.

He was looking now at his wrist watch, avoiding her eye but still very much in command of the situation. "It's time I was running along. I know what a lot of details you must have to tend to. I do appreciate so much your seeing me today. Very good of you, indeed. I'm sure Lydia will appreciate it, too, just as much as I."

Tremulous, enraged, feeling completely outmaneuvered, Lady Brace preceded him in silence around the teak table supported by its file of carved elephants, bearing the untidy pile of abandoned school books, the red typewriter. She had the impression Frederick Hollis took note of every detail of disorder or disorganization in this household, and that all of it gave added assurance to his own carefully ordered life. A man of foresight, of well-made plans and unspontaneous schemes, was he not bound in the end to get what he desired in a world full of the impulsive, the careless and maladroit?

At the door into the hall she paused. "Do you mind letting yourself out?"

"Not at all." He extended his hand.

Lady Brace ignored it. With an unexpected belated malice that pleased her, she heard herself saying, "I am delighted to hear the good news about Belle. I shall write her a little note and tell her I hope to see her before my return to England."

At last a thrust seemed to penetrate his invincible armor. Certainly, the surface appeared, for a moment, dented. She saw his eyes, now so near her own, waver somewhere in their depths.

"Do!" he said. "Do! Yes, do!"

The senseless repetition revealed, she hoped, the effect of her remark about seeing his wife. In this hope she struck again, deliberately. "I was always very fond of Belle—though we have quite lost track of one another. We took classes from Miss Hurley together many years ago, and I was, as you probably remember, one of the bridesmaids at your wedding."

It was inconceivable that he had forgotten—yet his manner of receiving this information almost indicated that, if he had not forgotten, then he had buried it very carefully. Somewhere in his basement mind it remained only as a trivial incident in the course of another life, one from which he had now passed; a transition made possible through hormone injections, electrical therapy, special vitamins and other assorted "wonder drugs," until at seventy he could tell himself he looked younger, felt better, than he had at forty.

"Ah, yes," he said. He succeeded in conveying the impression that he found her remarks quite out of key; a surprising piece of gaucherie on her part.

Before he had his hand on the front door Lady Brace was on her way upstairs, her back stiff, her head held high.

19

Once safely behind her locked door Lady Brace collapsed in a tremble of frustration and fury. That he could dare! It was unbearable! Indeed, the whole atmosphere at Fox Meadows was unendurable. And the environs too. She thought of the crass overabundance of the bulging stores of Lynnbury, the manic repetition of TV and radio commercials with their ceaseless injunctions to Buy, Try, Get, Use. They all seemed to relate in some confused but undeniable way to the abandoned children in the house "for sale at a sacrifice," and also to Frederick Hollis's unfeeling temerity. It's all of a piece, she told herself; a universal insistence on immediate satisfaction for every whim and appetite. Installment Plan Buying: It's Yours for the Wanting! After all, only Frederick's enormous wealth makes him more vulnerable to criticism for his smug assurance that he has a right to what he wants without delay; he only reflects a general point of view.

But after some minutes her old habit of calm appraisal reasserted itself. She told herself not to exaggerate, to be fair. How had Frederick succeeded in upsetting her so drastically? It was a question she must try to answer.

She found herself recalling her recent candid talk with Stephen. Had she not come away feeling that her brother's honesty, though startling and disturbing, was also exhilarating? Although it had laid a demand on her, had she not also found it challenging to be asked, in this direct fashion, to look at life free of certain masks and disguises? Why, then, should Frederick Hollis's candid approach seem only an outrageous affront? Was it because she could not tolerate his assumption that there could be no possible opposition? Was it his bland unawareness of the impression he was making, or, worse, his total unconcern about her possible response that made her tremble and clench her hands? No, surely so marked a physical reaction on her part could not be brought about merely by a perception of another's degree of unconsciousness. Perhaps the clue to her acute anger and shame lay in his slyly amused remark that her own daughter "couldn't care less," and this fact about Lydia—if fact it was—directly reflected on her personal status as a mother.

I cannot accept my own failure, she thought. I cannot bear to realize that my belated efforts to do something about Lydia, my breaking of that tacit rule of noninterference in the lives of others which I have so long practiced, has brought me only unhappiness, a sharpened sense of personal failure. I am not only defeated, I am somehow cheapened. It seemed the *mot juste*.

Her restless thoughts, whirling and bobbing like so many corks in a turbulent sea, turned first to Rosemary to fix the blame for the dilemma in which she found herself, then shifted at once to Venerable Sir. Was the little monk responsible? Was it his words in the garden—at the time seeming so clear a directive? Had he deliberately misled her?—for she remembered Stephen saying of him the very first day, "tough as nails." . . . "What will he teach in his mission when he founds it, Uncle Stephen?" she had once overheard Rosemary asking. "I don't think he'll *teach* much of anything." "I don't understand what you mean." "I mean—maybe he'll just be—like a plant." "Be *what?*" "Be what he is—a good human being." "Oh, Uncle Stephen, you and your riddles!"

Lady Brace had again the vision of the smooth dark face rising flower-like from the neck folds of the yellow robe; she thought of Venerable Sir meditating in the dawn, driving the Thunderbird, cooking his own meals, quoting learned scripture. "No hocus-pocus, extreme practicality"—Stephen's voice again. Could this baffling little man conceivably help Lydia? Would Lydia even permit him to talk to her? Perhaps—for hadn't she listened, very attentive, that night on the terrace?

Suddenly, it occurred to Lady Brace that Frederick Hollis might not, after all, have been telling her the truth. Why should she accept the Bangkok story until she had it confirmed by Lydia? Might not this simply be Frederick's clever, devious way of working out his own private plans?

This unexpected idea sent a surge of renewed vitality through her. Lydia might still be in her room. She would go to her at once and learn the truth from her own lips.

T W O

In response to her light tap on the door she heard Lydia speaking from a distance, "Who is it?"

"It's Mummy."

"Oh, just a moment." There was a slight pause before Lydia opened the door. She was wrapped in an oversize bath towel; her face above the towel appeared fresh and glowing. Lady Brace could only think how lovely she was, how untouched and young she looked.

"I'm so sorry, darling. Were you in the tub?"

"No, just out. I was giving myself a pedicure." She held the door wide. "Come in. Do you mind if I finish?"

"Not at all." '

Lady Brace entered, sat down and looked about her. Because she felt shy and ill at ease she began to make irrelevant conversation.

"I did over this room myself. How well I remember about it. I bought all this furniture in Provence on our wedding trip and sent it back to Fox Meadows for storing until your father and I could decide where we would live. But I came home to find my father unwell, and so insistent that we share this great place with him—he said he was rattling around in it like one lone pea in a big pod—that, well, we couldn't say no—or I couldn't—and so the furniture remained. We uncrated it and put it in these rooms; and here it still is!"

"I've always thought it was beautiful," Lydia said, not looking up from her pedicure. "I don't think I knew before that it represented *your* taste, Mummy. It should bring a good price at the auction. This sort of furniture is very hard to find these days."

At Lydia's remarks Lady Brace had an instantaneous picture

of hordes of strangers trooping through Fox Meadows, peering, prying, touching, looking, whispering, gossiping. . . . Gossiping about Lydia? She stiffened herself to begin her questions.

But Lydia was going on in her charming voice, stooping in one of her careless easy poses, so full of unconscious grace, "I should think you'd have hated coming back to your father's house with a new husband, Mummy."

Lady Brace said nothing. She watched her daughter fit flat metal pincers on her separate toes and begin to paint each nail carefully with pink lacquer. "Wasn't it hard?" Lydia persisted.

"There were many hard things about it," Lady Brace admitted. In a further nervous retreat, which she deplored but could not check, she reached out to the little table beside her chair. "What a beautiful necklace," she said, lifting a triple strand of pearls.

"Yes, aren't they lovely?" Lydia agreed. "I put them out to remind myself of something. They were Aunt Bertha's. She never took them off for years, you know. Even wore them when she rode, hidden under her stock—and even when she gardened, and, at the end, to bed at night. It was really queer. She had some kind of *fix* on them, I guess. Well, she left them to me when she died. It upset Rosie terribly at the time. I didn't understand it myself. I don't yet. Rosie always seemed her favorite. But anyway I got them and I put them there today because I wanted to tell you that I did have them and to be sure to leave yours to Rosie, not to me. I'll leave these to Pam, of course."

Her tone was very much that of someone disposing of possessions in the face of drastic changes of circumstance. This might indicate that the Bangkok plan was true. Fearful of having her hopes shattered, Lady Brace could not bring herself to advance directly on the subject.

"Your Aunt Bertha was a strange woman," she remarked. On impulse she asked, "Were you unhappy with her—you and Rosie?" Had there been a note of unexpected pathos in her voice?

Lydia continued to look calm and thoughtful. "Not really." After a moment she added, "Not that we were happy either, of course." She gave a faint smile, not raising her head. "We were rather troublesome, I'm afraid. Just as troublesome as we'd been to you and Humpy at Braceledge."

Lady Brace made no reply, for Lydia did not give her time to frame one.

"That's how I learned—" she was going on, her tone sharpening "—looking back, that is—that one daren't pay too much attention to children's notions—or wishes. Once kids get off the track—and who knows what causes *that?*—they just become impossible! They're going to continue to brood and complain and be tiresome and difficult no matter *what* one does to give in to them, to try to understand or placate them."

Is she justifying herself for what she is about to do to Pammy and Bill? Lady Brace wondered. Is she telling me that my marriage to Humphrey, though her own father was already dead, actually created as many problems as she has created by divorcing her children's father?

The pearls were still in her hand. As she laid them back on the table Lady Brace heard herself say, "You'll probably have more jewels before you die than you could possibly use—if you went to a coronation ball every night." She plunged in then, without further ado. "I've just been talking with Frederick."

Lydia's even strokes with the little nail brush did not falter. "Did he tell you about the Bangkok plan?"

"Yes." Lady Brace added with clear distaste, "He also talked about his wife—an old friend of mine."

If she had had the notion that this particular reference to Belle Hollis would disconcert Lydia, the thought was quickly dispelled. Neither Lydia's expression nor her posture altered in the slightest degree. Still not looking at her mother, and after only a moment's silence, she said, "And?"

Lady Brace took a deep breath. "I was—I am—inexpressibly shocked by the whole thing. And shocked most of all by you, Lydia."

Careful, deft, Lydia went right on moving the little brush over her elegant nails. "Why?"

At the single word uttered with such cool detachment Lady Brace could not keep exasperation from her voice. "Do you mean to say you don't know why?"

Her mother's brittle tone caused Lydia to raise grave eyes. But there was no hint of resentment in her manner as she answered,

"Well, I know what the *conventional* attitude would be, of course, Mummy. How could I not know that? But somehow I thought you'd passed beyond that sort of—reaction."

"What would give you an idea like that?"

Lydia drew up her bare shoulders in a little shrug that half-released the towel twisted around her torso. As it dropped for a moment below her breasts, Lady Brace saw how beautifully formed and delicate they were, still young, firm and round. Lydia hitched up the towel and twisted it again under one arm.

"I don't quite know," she replied, "just a feeling I've always had since I can remember, that you'd been through a lot and—and knew the score, even if you didn't talk about it."

"*Knew the score?*" Lady Brace repeated. Her voice took on a cutting edge. "What does that absurd phrase mean?"

Lydia made no answer, almost as if determined to be, at all costs, patient and tolerant with someone acting stubborn and obtuse. Lady Brace took another deep breath and tried to regain her customary composure. She must not let this situation pass from her control as she had in the interview with Frederick. The only thing to do was to keep straight on her course of inquiry, to give no quarter, to remain on the offensive.

After a brief pause she said with deliberate flatness, "Then you really intend to go out to the East to live with Frederick Hollis as his mistress while you—both of you—wait for his wife to die?"

Lydia had finished with her pedicure. She began to put away the little shining tools in a green leather case. "I *am* going to the Far East—yes, Mummy. I want to get just as far away from everything here—as soon as I can—and for as long as I can."

Her voice rose. "I'm sick to death of all of it! Every bit of it!"

Now she looked straight at her mother. "I don't want to hurt you, Mummy, I don't want to disgrace you, or my children, or my sister, or my former husband—believe me, I don't. So I hope you'll agree to come with me—with us. But if you feel you can't, then I'm going anyway. I'd made up my mind to it, weeks ago—even before Belle—improved. I'd talked with Jack about taking the children to Texas for a year. He said, yesterday, he'd told you. Naturally I didn't tell him—the whole plan." She broke off, said more quietly, in an almost pleading voice, "It's just—you must believe me, Mummy—it's just that I can't bear the life I'm living one more minute!"

Lady Brace heard the unmistakable note of despair, but she refused to be softened by it. "Then why not lead another kind of life?" she inquired, resolute.

Lydia was ready for this question. "What kind?" she demanded, with her first show of truculence.

"I can't answer that," Lady Brace replied, then continued in unshaken firmness, "I can only ask you if you really think you can solve your problem—your life—by running off to the remote ends of the world!"

Lydia said, softly sly, "Uncle Stephen did, didn't he?"

This question stopped Lady Brace, but only for a moment. "Do you find your Uncle Stephen an example of a fulfilled and happy life?" she countered.

Lydia appeared to consider this before replying, "No, not necessarily. But I do think he's the most *real* person I've ever known. And"—speaking with renewed aggression—"I think he's real precisely because he's gone along for years following his own peculiar bent—and to hell with the rest of the world!"

"Oh, Lydia!" Lady Brace exclaimed. "How little you know!" She thought of her last talk with Stephen. In a smothered voice she added, "Your Uncle Stephen has been tossed about by all the winds and waves of repressed feeling—frustration, despair— quite as much as any of the rest of us. Perhaps even more." Her voice quavered. "And how terribly he has suffered!"

There was an uncomfortable pause broken finally by Lydia, hesitant now and more restrained. "I know that, Mummy. I'm sure he's suffered—a lot." Then swiftly passionate again, she exclaimed, "But who hasn't suffered? I'm prepared for that—for suffering, I mean. Anyway, it's all just a choice of suffering—the *kind* you settle for—isn't it?"

Lady Brace had an alarming intimation of some dark wildness in Lydia, a fatal force under her cool chic exterior that could not be brooked. Was it some impetus to self-destruction? Was Lydia, in her own particular way, like her father, who had heeded no warnings, refused all restraints?

The silence that fell between them had a special quality, as if fate had entered the room, an invisible presence lending its added weight to this encounter between a mother and daughter who were also strangers. How alone we both are! We face each other across a burial ground of secret memories: unspoken resentments, painful failures, unconscious intrusions, cowardly evasions. . . .

Lydia said at last, her voice soft again, almost inaudible, "Then you won't do this for me, Mummy—go out to Bangkok with me?"

Lady Brace shook her head. "I can't," she whispered.

Looking off into space, Lydia murmured, "That's very hard to accept, Mummy. It's the only direct thing I've ever asked of you —do you realize that?"

I will not receive this stab, Lady Brace said to herself. I refuse! On the defensive, she answered, "It wasn't you who asked me in the first place. It was Frederick."

Lydia raised her brows. "But it was I who asked Frederick to speak to you."

Now we are beginning to circle one another warily, Lady Brace thought, despairful; we are proceeding guardedly, going nowhere! I must reassemble my convictions. I must speak out with renewed force and candor—for this will be my last chance.

In a tone of decision she managed to say, "I'm sorry but—no, I cannot go with you to the East, Lydia. That is, I won't—if you wish to interpret it that way.

When Lydia neither moved nor spoke, she forced herself to continue. "As a mother I have probably always failed you. I said as much the other day. And I meant it. And it saddens me— terribly. Yet, because I am your mother, because I—brought you into the world, I feel I must warn you, in the strongest terms, that I see you about to make a grave mistake, even perhaps a tragic one. And I want also to tell you that I would understand what you are planning to do, I might even feel able to—exonerate it, if you were being carried away by a great irresistible physical passion."

Lydia looked at her mother with an enigmatic half-formed smile. "How very Somerset Maugham of you, Lady B." She spoke almost with humor. Then more strongly, in genuine curiosity "Do you honestly think it's more—excusable to yield to a big physical passion than just to give in to the need to run, to— escape?"

"Yes, of course," Lady Brace replied with conviction.

"Why?"

That recurrent cool monosyllable of Lydia's! She refused to be put off by it. "Because," she said, faltering only a little, "one is positive and the other is—negative."

"I wonder." Lydia did not sound in the least convinced. "Maybe the negative is equal to the positive—like in electricity," she suggested.

Lady Brace evaded this trap by pursuing with fervor her own point. "Anyway, why must you run? What are you escaping from? If it's yourself, you know that's useless. You can never escape from yourself."

Lydia said, aggressive again, scornful, "Myself! I've not the foggiest notion who or what *that* is, and I doubt if anyone else has either. Maybe if I go a long way off into a different kind of environment, another world, I'll find out who I am—or whether I'm really anybody at all—or just what Uncle Stephen says one is —a series of events in time; nothing fixed, or separate—what he calls a psycho-physical *process*."

She said this last as though speaking to herself, and it was again so like some of her brother's baffling ruminations that Lady Brace felt she was losing the thread of argument altogether.

Lydia now leaned forward in the low chair and, clasping her hands in the lap of the bath towel, gazed down solemnly at her slender feet. She went back to her mother's question about running away, as though she had not spoken in between.

"I *must* run, Mummy! I must! And I'll tell you this—and you can tell Rosemary and anyone else who's interested—it will be wiser for all of you to settle for my . . . taking this way out. In the end, no matter what you think, it will be better for everyone concerned. You probably keep thinking of the gossip, Mummy. So does Rosemary. But you know perfectly well, people forget. They forget very soon."

"I am not thinking of the gossip," Lady Brace denied with heat. "At least only as it affects your children. I am thinking of the—of the values," she finished, with conviction.

Lydia looked up. "I'm thinking of just the same thing. Believe me, Mummy, I don't want to turn into a local tramp, trying to find again what I had with Alex, jumping in and out of different beds." Although her voice was hard, yet to her mother it sounded also piteous. "I'd like to keep *that* the way it is, if I can. I mean—keep it at least in my memory. So—I'm running."

"You're running out on your children," Lady Brace forced herself to say, sternly passionate. "Why can't you make up your mind to stay and make up to them for—for what has already happened to them?"

"Oh, Mummy darling." Lydia spoke with soft impatience, again as though dealing with some form of stubborn obtuseness.

After a moment she added, slow and clear, "I can't fool my children, Mummy. I don't know how to. Maybe nobody can fool children. That's what I really believe. Even if I'd *resisted* Alex it would have been the same in the end. That's what I think now, anyway. The children—Little Bill, at least—would have guessed the truth: that I didn't love their father. Children are all intuition, Mummy. You must know that. And utterly self-centered. And irrational."

Her voice rose a little. "Why, it's a well-known fact that children whose parents die—particularly their mothers—think the mothers have run out on them. It seems to them like a *deliberate* desertion . . . so why on earth is everyone always talking about not upsetting children? It simply can't be avoided, can it?"

Darkness is closing in, thought Lady Brace. Her head was whirling, her heart thudding. She saw from Lydia's concerned glance that her interior distress must have become apparent . . . But I cannot, will not, repeat the futile emotionalism of our scene on Gracie Square! By an enormous effort of will she rose from her chair. What she said to Lydia in conclusion she did not know, for as she moved toward the door she was thinking: It has all become like an interminable piece of theatre—a play with a series of similar scenes, endless entrances and exits, no final curtain. And I am taking part in it as both performer and audience.

20

As she climbed the third flight of stairs to the old nursery Lady Brace knew that her steps lagged. Committed as she was to this visit with Venerable Sir, she felt ill at ease and sorry that, out of the troubled night following her painful interviews with Frederick Hollis and Lydia, she had asked the little monk to spare an hour of his time.

To make the appointment she had risen early in order to catch him on his way back to the house from his garden meditations. She disliked breaking in on him at just this moment. In fact she considered it not only a graceless intrusion, but even a presumptuous infringement on the calm space he had, in his hour of morning solitude, collected around him. But she wanted none of the household to overhear her request, and, besides, during the day, Venerable Sir was seldom to be seen. So she had set her mental alarm for five o'clock, and was pleased to have it nudge her awake right on the hour.

She had waited for him inside the sunroom door. As she watched him approach across the lawn, wrapped cocoon-like in extra saffron robes—for the morning had an autumnal sharpness—she experienced again her earlier amazement at the sight of this odd figure walking familiarly behind her father's Long Island house.

The moment Venerable Sir saw her, his face broke into a wide smile of pleasure.

"Good morning!" he cried. "Are you up early to see the cobwebs?"

"Cobwebs?"

"All over the garden. Everywhere," he cried. "Marvelous constructions. Quite breath-taking. Do go and look while they are still strung with little beads that the sun will soon be melting. Promise?"

She had to smile. "I promise." Then she added quickly, before her resolves could desert her, "But I didn't get up early to look at cobwebs. I got up to—waylay you. I—do you think we might have a little private talk, sometime soon, at your convenience?"

"Delighted!" he exclaimed. "Delightful anticipation. I look forward to it. Would this afternoon be suitable?"

They fixed on four o'clock. She murmured words of apology for claiming any of his "precious time."

He appeared to consider her concern comic. "Time? What is that?" he asked. "You mean that funny thing people insist on carrying around in their pockets, or even on their wrists—where they'll be sure not to forget it?" He ducked his closely shaved head into the folds of his robe in merriment. "I assure you, dear Lady Brace, time—I have an enormous supply of that particular commodity. More than I can ever use, so you must feel quite free to help yourself to my store of it whenever you like." . . .

Now he must have heard her footsteps, for the nursery door opened suddenly and he stood beaming at her over his spectacles. "'Will you walk into my parlor, said the spider to the fly,'" he recited with a little chortle of pleasure at his quotation.

When Lady Brace laughed at this bit of childish doggerel coming so unexpectedly from him, Venerable Sir laughed with her. "Is not that how you are feeling?" he demanded, but he did not make it a direct question that she must answer. With a formal bow, ushering her in, "And did you look at the cobwebs in the garden?" he inquired.

She said she had.

"I made very careful observations of the several varieties," he told her, "for I intend to ask your learned brother to name for me the geometric forms these little creatures conceive. Out of their own spittle, I believe. What a true marvel!"

As Lady Brace paused for a moment on the threshold, Venerable Sir made a second bow, turning his head, moving his flexible hands in an inclusive gesture which seemed to say: "Though I am welcoming you here to my living quarters as if I were the host, I well know that it is I who am the guest in this house."

At first glance, the nursery appeared to Lady Brace essentially unchanged. She realized that she had expected to find it stripped of furniture, like a monk's cell. The fact that no alterations had been made in a room designed for the active, scattered life of children struck her as remarkable. Did it indicate that Venerable Sir was able to put his body down anywhere; that he did not require, demand, or perhaps even need, special surroundings or an atmosphere peculiarly suited to meditative moods? The room did, however, smell faintly, though not unpleasantly, of incense. She noticed, too, a very fine small bronze Buddha in the pose of meditation on a table near the daybed where Venerable Sir slept, and, on the opposite wall, a painted hanging showing the Great Teacher seated on a garishly rendered lotus with a multicolored halo around his head. Lady Brace, struck by this unlikely juxtaposition, remembered again how often in the Far East she had been amazed to see an object of beauty and distinction displayed side by side with one of cheap banality. She had wondered then, as she did now, whether this implied that the objects possessed to their owner equal value—or was it no value?

She seated herself in the wing chair near the empty grate. Aware that her quick survey of the room must certainly have been noted by the little monk, she commented hurriedly on her choice of chair, explaining how all during childhood neither she nor her brother had ever dared sit in the wing chair. By the strictest of unwritten rules it had been always reserved for their governess.

While she spoke Venerable Sir gave the full concentrated attention he consistently bent on trivial comment, as if expecting it to reveal facets of rare significance.

"Then you have grown up," he said, nodding, bubbling, "for are you not sitting in teacher's chair?"

Although again he made her laugh, her face became solemn immediately. "Alas, I'm afraid I am no teacher," she sighed. "I doubt that I am even a very bright pupil."

"No?" Venerable Sir gazed at her inquiringly, his head a little on one side. She was reminded of an alert bird listening for faint underground noises on a lawn. He appeared to wish her to amplify. She stumbled on.

"I feel I've spent my life learning nothing, or learning too late— that my whole life has been quite without direction . . ." She broke off. (For I simply mustn't let it all pour out of me in a torrent. I have no right to impose on him, just because he seems so generous and willing to listen.)

After a moment's pause Venerable Sir picked out one word from her inconclusive remarks. "Life," he repeated. "Ah, yes, life." He gave the word a half-serious, half-amused emphasis. "How to live in this predicament!"

Predicament! Once again his use of a particular word fell with freshness on Lady Brace's ear. Something beyond the everyday interpretation seemed indicated.

Venerable Sir had gone over to a bureau at the end of the room and, taking from a top drawer two flat palm-leaf fans, he placed one near her and, retaining the other, seated himself in one of the low chairs covered in faded Mother Goose chintz. Curling his legs under him, he began to move the fan before his face.

The sight of the softly moving object was soothing and a little hypnotic in the warm room. It might put me straight to sleep, she thought, and, almost fearful of the fan's power in Venerable Sir's grasp, she took up the one beside her and began to wave it back and forth while she listened to his lilting voice, with the undertone of joy, of childlike satisfaction—whatever it was, she could not truly say—that bubbled up through it like a hidden spring.

"Let us add to that word 'predicament' the word 'present,' " Venerable Sir was suggesting. "Let us rather say, the 'present predicament.' How to live in this present predicament! For that is where the emphasis must fall—on the Now, as we agreed the other morning in the garden, did we not? There lies the great secret, the mystery—so we said, did we not? Only by living this moment free of memory, free of anticipation, can one be truly alive. For that is, in final truth, all there is: the present! Let us catch it if we can!" He looked across the space between them, smiling blandly and nodding his round, shaved head.

"Free of memory?" Lady Brace repeated uncertainly. For had not Stephen told her how he had had to "remember" in order to be able finally to "forget"?

"Ah, yes, very hard at first," Venerable Sir agreed. He did not labor the point. He sat waiting, without impatience or insistence, for whatever she might care to say to him. She became aware again of the space he created around his person, so that he seemed at once completely related to his surroundings, yet distinct and separate from them.

After some moments of silence it was he who put a question. "Perhaps you feel you would not want to live free of memory?"

"I was wondering about that," Lady Brace admitted.

"Then all your memories are so sweet? How fortunate!" His voice was not in the least ironic, only delighted at the idea of such a possibility.

She shook her head in immediate denial. "Very few of them, I'm afraid."

"Then perhaps you say to yourself, If I do not remember, and also if I do not make myself—forget, the very universe itself will surely fall to bits around me. For do I not hold the world, my world, together with my personal remembering and my forgetting —or my *repressing*, to use a modern word? Is that how it seems?"

He spoke very gently, and the words seemed to her, though she could certainly not have explained them, or even quoted them accurately, to touch on a deep vital truth, deceptively simple, undeniable.

She said in a surprised voice, "I believe it is something like that. I suppose, somehow, I have always felt that I must keep things in order with my own will. Though on the surface, at least, I seem to have been more acted upon by life than ever able to act on it." She could not keep the tone of regret from filtering through her words.

The fan across the room continued to stir the empty air in a steady soothing rhythm.

"But you did not come to me today to talk in abstract terms," Venerable Sir suggested finally. "You have something specific to speak to me about."

Lady Brace, as if forced by some inner compulsion she feared to delay any longer, replied at once in a swift rush of words, "Yes, you are right. I want help with my daughter. With Lydia. I feel she is about to make a disastrous mistake. I want to save her from it, if I can. And please don't tell me that no one can possibly save another, for I know that you have saved my brother."

He denied quickly, "Oh, no, he saved himself."

"But you helped him. This at least you can't deny. Certainly he believes so."

Venerable Sir extended his fan towards her in a gesture that implied: "Have it your way. We will not argue the point." He asked, "You wish to save your daughter? From what do you wish to save her?"

Lady Brace considered a moment before answering. "From unnecessary suffering."

"And you think this is possible?" He was now abruptly still; not even his fan moved.

Lady Brace reacted to this question as though she had been offered a challenge. In a firmer tone, she replied, "Not entirely. But at least she needn't suffer—too late—the pangs of hopeless regret. For, if she doesn't make this—this particular tragic mistake, she may decrease, at least a little—or so I believe—the suffering of her children, my grandchildren. And so she may not come to the place, as an old woman, where she must condemn herself, without mercy, for all her thoughtless errors—as I do now for mine."

The fan still did not move. "And you feel so responsible for your daughter's destiny?"

"Recently—*now*—yes, I do." She sounded faintly defiant, as if, in her turn, she was preparing to challenge him.

"Explain, please." It was a request, not a command.

Her answer came without delay, like something long waiting to be uttered.

"Because without me my daughter would never have been. There's no escaping that fact. I gave her life. And . . ." She stopped, her own fan quiet now as she added in a voice low but very distinct, "And I feel she was born under a dark shadow, for I did not love my husband when she was conceived. I—hated and feared him."

She was struggling once more with a wish to abandon all restraint, to break down completely and talk, talk, talk, about her new awareness of how she had "used" Ralph Parton, about her guilt, about her whole selfish life. Words like lust, greed, sensuality, swam darkly on the surface of her mind.

"My dear child." The little monk spoke softly. "Dear Lady

Brace." His tone held deep compassion, as though she had, indeed, revealed to him a fact of enormous, and tragic, significance.

With the utmost difficulty Lady Brace managed to restrain herself. I will not break into tears again, she told herself. I will not have him think me an emotional, uncontrolled old woman. She held her hands rigidly clasped in her lap, fingers curved tensely on the handle of the palm-leaf fan.

A long silence followed. She began to feel—almost like some subtle emanation from the little man across the room—a sense of renewed calm. Perhaps he does have unusual powers, she thought, some curious and healing tranquillity. It seems to be even in the very movement of his fan as it passes slowly through the air.

When Venerable Sir finally spoke, he did what she had noticed the night he talked to the family on the terrace: he approached the point by a circuitous route.

"We have, in the East, a word with which I believe many Westerners are also familiar. It is the word Kamma—or Karma, as Stephen insists I must call it here. You are familiar with the term?"

Lady Brace nodded. "Yes."

"How do you understand it?" he inquired.

"As fate, destiny."

He nodded. "That is near enough for our purpose at the moment."

He arranged his robes across his knees, gave the effect of one preparing to utter a formal discourse.

"This law of Karma—it is really very much misunderstood, not only in the East where it is believed, but in the West where it is rejected. In the East, people frequently make an excuse for themselves from the idea of having more lives than one to lead—many behind, many ahead. They find in this law of periodic return to life an excuse to do nothing at all in the present, or to make little effort. In the West, on the other hand, people dislike the idea of inheriting their personal destiny from past existences. This seems to them so fatalistic, so fixed, that therefore they view Karma as a negative concept, and finally they reject it as dangerous altogether."

He peered at her over his glasses with sudden eagerness. "As a matter of fact—if a learned Anglican friend of mine has not misinformed me—the belief in reincarnation was once a part of Christian dogma. But it was deleted from the body of the approved doctrine at one of the great Church Councils. Was it the Council at Constantinople? I cannot seem to remember."

He appealed to her, as if hoping she would be able to supply a definite answer.

"I know almost nothing of Christian theological history. Or of any other, for that matter," she added.

"It is of no consequence," he quickly assured her, with a wave of his fan. "Only a minor historical fact. I bring it up only because it is perhaps important to realize that this ancient theory is much more widespread than many might believe. And I speak of it now—of Karma, rebirth—because it is pertinent to what you have just been telling me."

He paused and again adjusted his robes over his knees.

"Karma, as *we* see it, is not a negative concept. We view it as a positive one. We see it not as blind destiny, but as opportunity. We believe it involves the use of that particular human trait the West values so highly—namely the *will*. For you see, we do not believe— people like me who have had a certain specific kind of training— philosophical, religious—that the will does not exist, that one's life is all blind fate, or the foreordained plan of some all-powerful Supreme Being. No. No, no!"

He tapped his fan almost sharply on the empty air, as if in reproof. Then, laying it on his lap and folding his hands over it, he continued in his usual bubbling voice, "Two thousand five hundred years ago our great Teacher was concerned with helping man to get control of his own life, that is, his individual Karma, at the only point where such a thing is possible—namely, in the present moment. This was because the Teacher saw what is so true, and so very hard to grasp, that there is, indeed, only the Now!"

Is this perhaps his teaching method, Lady Brace wondered: the use of repetition; over and over a theme reiterated until it becomes a very part of one's consciousness?

"Do you follow me?" he asked, bending his head to look at her over his glasses. "Am I quite clear?"

Lady Brace hesitated. "You are quite clear," she said, "It is I who am fuzzy."

This made him laugh. "Dear Lady Brace." He seemed to think she had said something exquisitely funny. "Do enlarge!" he begged.

She fumbled for an answer. "I mean—I hear every word, it even seems to make sense, yet I don't feel that I really grasp it, or ever could—the idea of only the Now."

"Then we must repeat our garden lesson," he said sweetly, "for repetition makes for knowing; something the old Chinese learned long ago. The mind!" he cried out in a suddenly exultant voice. "Think what it means to have a mind! How blessed we are, we humans, for we have not just the mind of the instincts, like the animals, but the mind that can learn and *know* it is learning—is that not something truly wonderful?"

He waited for her nod of agreement before continuing, "So now let me repeat our first lesson. When we live in the past, it is memory only. We are not truly living it. When we live in the future, it is anticipation. It is not yet in existence, may never be. Therefore this breath, this very fleeting moment, the Now—" and he held up thumb and forefinger to make a circle in the air; then a series of them, opening and closing in swift succession "—this is all there is or ever can be. Do I make myself clear?"

"You do," Lady Brace replied, "but I cannot see, if I struggle with this idea of the Now and even come to understand it, how it will help me to help my daughter. Can you tell me that?"

He answered at once, "Not definitely, for no one can tell you that who cannot read the future—and who can accurately do so? However, one does know this: The future grows from the Now and the Now changes with each breath of what we call time. The form of the future is not fixed. It is, to be sure, influenced by—and, to some extent, conditioned by—the past. But man is not just a mechanical assemblage of parts. He is a free organism—in that he makes his fate by *his attitude towards it*. And also he has *choice*, and choice is his chance to escape the automatic, hereditary, instinctive forces that do their best to make him their slave." He stopped. "Can you apply any of this to your problem?"

She thought a while. "You are telling me not to feel responsible for my child's future. Is that it? You are telling me it is her fate, not mine—and that at any moment her decision can change. But I resist all this because—at long last—I am now feeling responsibility for my child and I suppose I believe that, for me, this is growth."

"Ah!" He darted the fan at her. "*Your* growth," he said, "your pattern. No one else's. Your daughter's fate is cut after another style."

"Then I am not to feel responsible for the fact that I brought her into the world?"

He turned his head to one side. "If you must interpret it that way, I suppose you must," he said, slowly. "I view it differently. I consider that your daughter *chose* her physical vehicle to enter her present life, which is, in a sense, her destiny, her present opportunity."

"Chose it? When?"

He hesitated again. "Before birth—and thus all the choices of her life are her own and no one else's."

"Then we are quite separate—though she entered life through my body—as separate as if we were not related at all?"

"That is simplifying it too much," he said. "Give me a moment to think."

There was a long pause, at the end of which, unfolding his legs again and letting them hang straight to the floor, Venerable Sir said, "Every human being is the last inheritor, and the last result, of the Karma of a long series of past individuals—a series so long that its beginning is beyond the reach of calculation, and its end will coincide with the end of all human existence."

As the words fell distinctly, quietly, on her ear Lady Brace had a sudden feeling she was about to understand something never understood before; something very familiar yet, in the moment, new and startling; something akin to but larger, more mysterious, than Lydia's remark about genes: "I guess there's not much to do about genes after all, is there, Mummy?"

Lady Brace tried to capture the flickering images and intimations, to form them into some concept she could hold and remember later when alone. But the strain of her effort dissolved them as completely as if they had been a mirage. She was aware of a feeling of abrupt deflation, of emptiness, of utter bewilderment.

"But what am I to do?" she cried. "What should I think about—

how should I form my thoughts in the days ahead, in relation to my daughter, to both my daughters, to my grandchildren, my *descendants*—if their lives are their own—entirely, privately their own—and none of my concern?"

"But I did not say that," he said quietly. "All of life is our concern. V*enerate all life*, said the Great Teacher more than two thousand years ago—for *all life is one*."

A fleeting memory of the deserted children in the house she and Rosemary had visited crossed Lady Brace's mind once more.

"How does one learn to venerate all life?" she asked humbly.

The little monk again appeared to reflect on her question. "How to venerate life," he repeated. Then, soft but not tentative, he suggested, "Some of us practice *metta*—*metta*, meaning loving-kindness towards all mankind, all life. We specifically exercise ourselves in the difficult task of emanating this *metta*—morning and evening —until it is no longer a task, but as natural as breathing."

He leaned towards her. "To begin with, try just two things. First, the practicing of loving-kindness towards all life. Second, constant awareness. The two are, in truth, not two but one. Will you try?"

Lady Brace leaned back wearily in the chair of her old governess. After a long moment, "I'll try," she said. Without meaning to, she added, "But I can only wish I were much younger—or in my grave and through with effort."

He began to laugh. "Back to Lesson Number One." He raised his finger and shook it at her. "Garden Lesson Number One. Remember? 'You are only as old as you feel' and 'It is never too late to mend!' "

She said again, like a child, "I'll try."

"Good!" He rose and put his hands together. Bowing over them, he repeated as he had the night on the terrace, first in Pali, then in English, "May all beings be well and happy."

Lady Brace realized that the interview was terminated. She too rose, murmured vague words of thanks and left.

Halfway down the stairs she heard the nursery door open. Turning, she saw the little monk's round, shaved head thrust from it. He was smiling. "Beware of all ready-made manufactured defeatist ideas," he whispered.

Her face, strained again, and perplexed, seemed to lead him to a further suggestion; one of a different nature.

"Dear Lady B." He emerged further from the half-opened door. Was he intentionally, for the first time, using her childhood name? "Dear Lady B," he repeated, "try to rest a little if you can."

His stress on the word "rest" suggested that he meant more than merely putting her body on a bed, taking a nap. His next words confirmed the suggestion. He seemed now concerned about her personal welfare, her state of mind. His brown eyes held hers with a penetrating intensity.

"Try to think of yourself as a bubble on a river—inseparable from the river; or a cell in a great organism—inseparable from the organism. This should rest you. For at times the separate ego—" and he sighed, shaking his head "—is a truly heavy load. So, from time to time, one must make the effort to lay aside this distressing burden. Only thus can we lessen the grip of all the transient and unimportant things by which we are everywhere surrounded."

Again touching his two hands together, lowering his shaved head over them, he bowed slightly towards her before once more closing the nursery door.

Lady Brace continued on her way downstairs. She repeated to herself the words he had uttered on first reappearing: "Ready-made manufactured defeatist ideas." What did he mean? Was he saying, Beware of ideas born out of the life, or the atmosphere, around one—ideas springing only from one's milieu, not necessarily related to one's *inner* beliefs or feelings?

21

In the night Lady Brace awoke, aware that she was feeling feverish. She put a cold hand to her forehead. It felt burning to the touch. She thought of rising and searching for the little thermometer she carried in her drug kit, but an extreme lassitude made it impossible to lift her body from the bed. She lay back on the pillows and allowed her restless, unsorted thoughts to have their way with her.

The thick darkness seemed to be moving about her, moving her with it, swinging her gently in the wide bed so that she envisaged herself lying on a raft drifting over a vast and, at the moment, windless sea. She felt entirely cut off, eternally alone, and this all-enveloping sense of her unique solitariness returned her to the little medieval English chapel near the hospital where, for so many weeks, her son had lain dying.

It was the day before Rupert's death. He was failing rapidly, the doctors told her, yet now his right leg must also be removed. Kneeling rigid in the icy church until she was quite numb with cold, she had desperately continued to beg mercy, generosity, of some shapeless Power far removed from her above the worn gray rafters.

At one point in her private anguish a wrenching groan had escaped her parched lips; a groan so terrible it seemed to splinter the very air on which it broke. Even then, she remembered, in spite of her abject despair, so strong was her sense of the necessity for maintaining privacy that she instantly raised her glazed eyes to see if anyone had overheard. She had found herself staring into the face of a strange woman who had also come to kneel in the cold; a woman with a flabby countenance under a hat like a Punch drawing. The anguished groan had been heard; that was plain! Yet in the pale close-set eyes, so intimately near her own, Lady Brace had seen reflected not sympathy, not fellow-feeling, but only curiosity sharp and vulgar: "Who is *she* there on her knees with 'er pearls and furs! Precious little good *they*'ve done 'er!"

She had averted her gaze in haste and noticed then, for the first time, the sculptured wall of the old chapel where a row of contorted human figures struggled in the coils of a hideous dragon. St. George, their rescuer with lance and horse, was hidden from immediate view. All she could see at the moment were the hopeless human shapes, caught in the dragon's deadly grip; each of them vividly, eternally alone; not bound together—as one might have thought—by sharing a common peril and misery, but separated into individual, entirely personal agonies.

She remembered how she had longed then for some simple reassuring sight, even a bad stained-glass window of the late nineteenth century, showing Christ, the Good Shepherd, carrying one of the lost sheep; something familiar, stable, even trite—the theme of the parent and child, of the strong and the weak, the responsible and irresponsible.

And now she thought, turning on her father's bed at Fox Meadows, I understand why human beings, suffering from all their manifold secret doubts and misgivings, must turn with relief to formal Christianity. It is easier, much easier, for—one lays the burden down.

But at once the image of Venerable Sir's Great Teacher, as she had so often seen him in ancient sculptures in Ceylon, rose in her memory: the untroubled countenance, the meditative posture, the inward direction of the glance—an inaccessible serenity, it seemed now as it had seemed then. "*Metta*," Venerable Sir had suggested that afternoon, "loving-kindness towards all beings—the oneness of all life—bubbles on the one great river. . . ." And was the figure of this ancient Master, the Buddha, saying to mankind what the Christ, another and later Master, had also expressed with his broken body on the crucifix? If so, which way, then, was the truer, the greater, the right one? Who could tell, who could say— once the question was admitted as tenable?

The figure of the mutilated Christos hung now in the dark before her, bringing with it such acute memories of the gradual dismemberment of her own injured son that she could not permit it to remain. She forcibly erased it, putting in its place the image of the smiling Virgin with the Sacred Babe at her breast. For one clear wonderful moment she felt almost able to grasp the symbolic meaning of infinite, all embracing Mother Love; the meaning of the elevation once more in the spiritual hierarchy—at a time of world conflict and darkness among men—of Mary the Mother of God. "*Metta*," she murmured aloud once more, but as she voiced this alien word from the other side of the world, the figure of the Virgin Mother turned at once into the aging, sorrowing Mater Dolorosa mourning her dead Son, and once more the old buried pain of Rupert's loss flooded her heart.

How was it she had loved Rupert so much more than her

daughters? Was this a part of what Stephen would term "old links" —part of the unsolved mystery of human relationships, of affinities and antagonisms? Yet the difference in the quality of the love she had given seemed to her a grave fault, a serious wrong, even, she felt, a sin. How expiate this great deficiency—perhaps the greatest of all—unlovingness, or, more accurately, a difference in the *degree* of love one gave? How learn to practice, at her age, the difficult science—if science it was—or art, of constant loving awareness, of equal love and compassion towards all life; even towards the vulgar woman in the medieval chapel spying on her private grief?

She saw the child Johnny standing with his rubber pony in the wading pool—the little boy she would never forget. She thought of the snapshots showing Little Bill's melancholy elongated face, Pammy proudly holding aloft the fish she had not caught. She saw Jennifer tapping gently with her wilted goldenrod on the sleeve of Venerable Sir's yellow robe. Tears that she made no attempt to check fell from the sides of her eyes into her pillow. Perhaps I am seeing for the first time, clearly, one of the uses of children, one of the purposes they indirectly serve. For children can, in their vulnerability, their touching candor, melt and renew the world-weary heart. I must practice thinking of Rosemary and Lydia on the beach with their pails and shovels, as they are in the picture I always carry with me, in silent reminder.

Her thoughts were no clearer, she felt increasingly feverish, but the assembled faces of the children—past and present—somehow soothed her. She slept.

T W O

She awoke to the realization that she was seriously unwell. Her burning body was shaken by chills. She rang her bell with a trembling hand, and when Clara appeared with a breakfast she could not touch, she asked her to find Rosemary at once.

Rosemary came immediately. Calm, efficient, her cheery bounce somewhat subdued by the sight of her mother's drawn face, she took Lady Brace's temperature, refused to reveal its reading, but sent promptly for a doctor.

235

The doctor was a young man, impersonally kind. He informed Lady Brace that she had a "virus that's going around; nothing serious, but not to be taken lightly either." He arranged for a nurse to come and he ordered her not to rise from bed or see anyone "for a week at least."

"You've tired your mother out," he reproved Rosemary.

When Lady Brace weakly tried to protest that this was quite untrue he shook his finger in stern admonition. "No talking," he said. "Remember! Utter quiet—until I give the word!"

Lady Brace welcomed the reprieve. She gave way completely to inaction, mental as well as physical. She dozed, dreamed, slept, took without protest a variety of medicines at specific intervals—medicine which mercifully increased her inertia—submitted her body and will, without resistance, to the ministrations of Miss Foley, a strapping Irish nurse.

Slowly, gradually, after several days had passed, she again recognized the outlines of her familiar consciousness rising like an iceberg from the sea. And to her amazement, as though it had all been decided by someone, or something, operating mysteriously in the depths of her mind, during what she thought of as her "absence," the first strong unarguable thought she had on returning to normal was: "I must go to Bangkok with Lydia!" There was now not the slightest doubt that this was an offer she must make without delay.

She called Miss Foley and, over her voluble protests, insisted on sitting up in bed to pen a brief note. *Darling Lydia*, she wrote. *I want you to know that I will go to Bangkok with you. I want to. All my love always. Mummy.*

After she had written the note she lay back on the pillows and allowed her now calm mind to consider a little the source of her irrevocable decision.

Although Venerable Sir had, in effect, told her that Lydia's fate was her daughter's own private concern, Lady Brace felt—and this in spite of any seeming contradiction—her action to be the direct result of some understanding the little monk had conveyed to her about the "self." Venerable Sir had planted a seed which had sprouted, grown and borne fruit in the days while she lay abed feverish and half-conscious. To "give up the ego"—this he had said must from time to time be done, by the deliberate practice of disciplines and exercises if there was no other way to achieve it.

Looked at on the surface, her life, she realized, would appear singularly free of ego-pressures. But in her heart she knew this was not the case, for she had laid on her personal existence the most exacting of all demands: the demand of "peace at any price." Now, however, she was not going with Lydia to Bangkok in order to keep the peace—for Lydia would say no more, of that she was sure; and Rosemary, too, would not nag her further. The surest way of peace would indeed have lain in an immediate return to Braceledge. Why then was she going with Lydia? As far as she could see, it was simply because it had been asked of her.

Thought of the slow serene pace of the days at Braceledge brought Humphrey into her mind. She remembered how, though confined to a wheel chair, he had nonetheless been able to experience over and over again a rare, pure and unfailing joy. The sight of a bird pecking at the bark of a tree or feeding its young, the leap of a rabbit on the lawn, the first crocus piercing the dark winter earth—these were to Humphrey moments of complete release—so she now saw. In a total response to the flight of a bird, the unfolding of a flower, one flies with the bird, unfolds with the flower, and thus, for a breath of time, one is free of the crippling illusion of the ego. This was a truth about selfless joy that Humphrey had shown her on countless occasions, had even "taught" her, she might say, but without full consciousness until this moment. Now he was gone and she could never tell him of her belated discovery. But the memories he had left behind him at Braceledge were, she now knew, the reason for her growing longing to return. Still, she thought, without sadness or impatience, I can wait. Perhaps even the trip to the East will further expand what Venerable Sir calls "awareness."

She fell into a peaceful sleep from which she awoke so much refreshed that the doctor, coming by on his daily visit, found her well enough to permit her a single visitor at tea time.

"Make it your brother!" Miss Foley suggested with good-natured bossiness. "He's been worried sick about you. Never saw such devotion," she rattled on. "You don't often see a bond like that between a brother and sister."

But, if Stephen had been "worried sick" by her illness, he showed no signs of it as he came limping into her bedroom at four o'clock. Miss Foley had fixed Lady Brace on the chaise longue in the large bow window in her prettiest negligee, and as she watched her brother moving awkwardly across the space from the door she thought that his sunburned face looked unusually peaceful and serene. As he bent to kiss her, tenderly, without the old awkward restraint, he said, "What a relief to see you up again, Caro. You had us all terribly worried."

"It was purest escape," she confessed.

He grinned. "Of course. But how far were you prepared to push it? That was the question."

"It seems a long time—a very long time—this last week."

He remarked in a provocative voice, "Well, a lot has been going on."

The suggestion in this remark did not immediately register itself, she was too anxious to tell him of her decision. "I've written Lydia to say I'm going with her to Bangkok." She gave him the envelope containing the note. "Will you see that she gets this right away?" She added, with a rueful shake of the head, "I don't know why, before now, I felt I couldn't do this for my child. It's little enough, after all."

At the announcement of her intention to go with Lydia there flitted across her brother's face the expression of one receiving unexpected delightful news.

"That's wonderful of you, Lady B," he said, pocketing the letter. "Lydia's coming out this evening. I'll see she gets the note. But—I might as well tell you"—and he gave her a direct, ironic glance—"you probably won't have to go to Bangkok."

She raised her eyes in swift hope. "You mean Lydia has changed her mind?"

"Not exactly—but at least, temporarily, her plans. She's coming first to visit me in Ceylon. She'll stay there for a while and then go on—if she still wants to. Life being the way it is, she may never go to Bangkok. You'll probably be free to go home to Brace-ledge."

Lady Brace's eyes misted over. "Oh, how good of you, Stephen —so generous, unselfish . . ."

He hooted. "Rot! Utter selfishness on my part. I'm looking forward to it. We've agreed to start our painting again, and we'll go to Adam's Peak to see the butterflies and—well, a lot of other things I'll tell you about later when you're stronger."

"No," she said firmly, "tell me now. Most of all I want to understand how you could persuade Lydia to change her mind— or at least postpone Bangkok—where I failed so utterly."

He began to answer, lightly teasing, "I was just clever enough to observe something hidden in your daughter that you didn't quite catch." Then entirely serious, "The truth is, Lady B, in spite of what Lydia says about wanting to escape, she doesn't want to escape at all. Not a bit of it! Just the opposite, in fact. She wants involvement. She longs to be *engagé*, as the Existentialists say; not just *engagé* with her mind or her senses, but with the totality of her being."

With mild impatience he stabbed his snake-headed stick into the red carpet. "Oh, damn all the silly words anyway!" he exclaimed. "What I'm trying to say is—Lydia wants to be captured and— commanded by some experience, *any* experience, so long as it makes possible again what happened to her in the one big over- whelming love of her life."

He stopped at this point, and although Caroline felt that she understood, at least vaguely, his meaning, she could not resist asking, "And what was that? I mean—what did happen to Lydia in the one big love of her life that she wants so much to repeat?"

"What," he said very quietly, "but the loss of the sense of separateness? Freedom, temporary but blissful while it lasted; freedom from the terrible burden of the cut-off, separated self. Isn't that what love really is?"

There was in his voice a thread of longing, or regret—which, she could not say. Did he feel that this was something he had altogether missed; did he look back on something forever terminated; or did he look ahead in hope? His words served to recall the scene with Lydia at the little house on Gracie Square—Lydia saying how her love for Alex White had made her "not half-conscious" but "super-conscious"—a "sort of intensification," Lydia had said, "of every-thing—including me." And was this *enlargement* in Lydia's terms not incompatible with Stephen's phrase about *loss:* "loss of the sense of the separated, cut-off self"? It would seem so. A loss, then, without diminishment, with increase, rather—could that be it? Puzzling, tantalizing, yet somehow reassuring, her thoughts brought back the last admonition of Venerable Sir on the nursery stairs; his remarks about "rest."

She turned to her brother. "And you know how to—that is, you can provide this—this experience for Lydia?"

As if he feared he might have sounded a bit pompous, Stephen grinned, gave a half-deprecatory shrug. "Well, I think maybe I can—if she's interested, and I think she is—provide her with something almost as demanding, as stimulating—maybe even, in time, as delightful—as sexual love." He grinned again. "And something that needn't die when the glands stop functioning!"

He will never entirely change, Lady Brace thought, and I'm glad. She said, feigning a concern she did not feel, only to see what he would answer, "Now, Stephen, you aren't going to turn Lydia into some kind of religious fanatic!"

His laughter rang out, hearty, prolonged and reassuring.

"A temple call girl? Or a nun with a shaved head?"

Then suddenly sober, almost stern, "Look, get this straight, Lady B! I'm not going to do anything with Lydia or make anything of her either. I'm just going to put certain, well, let's say, opportuni-ties in her way—and see what comes of them.

"And don't get your hopes up either!" he ordered, thrusting the stick in her direction. "What I mean is, don't plan on any definite results—the kind *you* want, and think are right! Remem-ber, there's an old Eastern saying: *Many paths lead to the moun-tain but the mountain top is the same for all,* so Lydia may, in the end—it's quite conceivable—decide to go on to Bangkok and meet Frederick Hollis, after all. But if she does it won't, I feel, very much matter—then."

She complained, "Now you *are* bewildering me! Why won't it so much matter then?"

He was silent a moment. "It's just that I believe, from my own experience, that Lydia—once having seen even a short distance through the murk—will never be quite the same again. She might perhaps do the same kinds of things—old habits, behavior patterns, are hard to break—but it wouldn't be, couldn't be, the same person doing them, and thus the end result would be bound to be different."

Lady Brace was half-convinced, half-puzzled by Stephen's words. Again the memory of his young lean hand tracing the contradictory forms of the laughing, menacing chimera on guard at the inner gate presented itself as it had the day she returned. To herself in an undertone she murmured, "Para and Dox from the Land of Paradox."

But Stephen heard what she said. He grinned with pleasure. "Right! The whole show rests on paradox. Which reminds me—Para and Dox are not leaving Fox Meadows."

She stared at him in momentary disbelief. "Now I know you're quite mad," she said lightly. "Why aren't they leaving?"

In reply he asked with a solemn face, "Tell me, honestly, Caro, am I tiring you?"

"Quite the contrary. You're doing me good," she assured him.

"Then brace yourself for the big news. I've bought Fox Meadows."

She gazed at him in protracted stunned silence. At last she managed to stammer, "You? But how? With what? And what for?"

He gave another burst of unaccustomed hearty laughter. "I'm a rich man. Never knew how rich. All that loot Father so carefully kept from my clutches—well, it's been lying around all this time piling up like crazy. I think it's so funny I wake up in the night laughing about it. In fact I felt I had to make the point of the whole thing apparent by buying back Para and Dox—so I did—at a price!"

She was still bewildered.

"But what on earth do you want with this great place if you're returning to Ceylon?"

He hesitated a moment to give his answer its full dramatic weight. "I'm turning Fox Meadows over to Venerable Sir—for his mission. And he can have the money too."

Lady Brace was spared the necessity of an immediate reply, for Miss Foley rapped on the door and came in with the tea. While the tray was being placed on the table, the tea poured, Caroline looked from her windows over the lawn and saw once more, in the full sun of late afternoon, the little monk crossing to the walled garden. No longer a golden ghost glimmering in a pale twilight, no longer the incongruous figure he had appeared in that first dawn when she watched him from her father's windows walking in the sunrise with his yellow robes pulled up around his ankles, he had become, she realized, familiar to her and—though not less mysterious—no longer disturbingly alien. Once more, and strongly, the sense of time as a turning spiral suggested itself. But she did not need to speak these thoughts to her brother, or even direct his glance out the window at Venerable Sir.

She put a slice of lemon in her cup and remarked, pretending pique, "I should retire oftener from the scene. Things seem to get done—big things—more easily in my absence." Stephen, the guide and mentor of us all! she was thinking. It is really not to be believed!

Stephen answered, calm and grave. "But of course! That's a law of life you should know by now, Lady B. No one ever solved a problem by gnawing at it endlessly like a dog with a bone. Don't you remember how Father always told us we learned games and sports—tennis, diving, that sort of thing—in *rest* periods?" He stirred his tea slowly.

Kind words for Papa again, Lady Brace thought to herself. Is Papa also admitted to have been a "teacher"?

"As I see it," Stephen pursued, still grave and thoughtful, "living life is all a question of balance, of alternate rhythms of doing and not doing, of taking hold and letting go, of breathing out and breathing in—until you finally get to that alleged 'place between the opposites.'" He cast her one of his appealing, impish, young-old looks. "At which time, presumably, you're *through!*" He lifted his teacup in his good hand and holding it as if proposing a toast he smiled at her over its rim. "So—to departures and returns, Lady B," he concluded.

Again, as so frequently in the past weeks, ordinary words seemed to her to convey more than their surface meaning: white light reflected as color through a prism . . . bubbles on a great river . . . departures and returns. . . . She lifted her own cup and let her deep love for her brother look out of her eyes.

They drank their tea together in companionable silence.

ABOUT THE AUTHOR

NANCY WILSON ROSS was born in the Pacific Northwest. She has lived and traveled in many parts of her own country, Europe and the Far East—including the Asian island of Ceylon about which she has written in the present novel. Miss Ross's published works, both fiction and nonfiction, reflect a wide range of interests. Her novels include *The Left Hand Is the Dreamer, I, My Ancestor* and *Time's Corner.* She has written two historical and sociological studies: *Farthest Reach* and *Westward the Women,* and a number of essays on such subjects as Paul Klee, the mystic rites of the Oglalla Sioux, Zen and surrealism. She has also contributed poems, short stories and articles to the *Atlantic Monthly,* the *New Yorker, Harper's Bazaar, Holiday, Vogue, Perspectives.* Miss Ross, a student of the famous German *Bauhaus* in its last two years, is a collector of modern art. She has also long been interested in the arts and philosophies of Asia and is currently engaged in writing an introductory study of Buddhism for Western readers.

Miss Ross is married to Stanley Young, the publisher and playwright. They have made their home for some years in Old Westbury, Long Island.